Tor Books by John Farris

JOHN FARRIS

FIENDS

A TOM DOHERTY ASSOCIATES BOOK
NEW YORK

FIENDS

Copyright © 1990 by John Farris

A Tor Book
Published by Tom Doherty Associates, Inc.
49 West 24th Street
New York, N.Y. 10010

Cover art by Joe DeVito

ISBN: 0-812-51786-5

First edition: September 1990

Printed in the United States of America

0 9 8 7 6 5 4 3 2 1

For Robert Gleason

In sorrow thou shalt bring forth children.

—*The Book of Genesis*

The following is taken from an article by Katherine B. Singerline, arts editor of the *Nashville Tennessean*, which appeared in that newspaper's edition of August 2, 1970.

Perhaps the most striking talent in evidence at the inaugural Patients' Fair and Art Show belongs to Mr. Arne Horsfall, whose age is "about seventy" according to officials at Cumberland State. Mr. Horsfall is mute; he does not read or write, and thus is unable to provide information about himself. No one at the hospital is able to say for sure when he was admitted; all records of older patients were destroyed in the disastrous fire that claimed many lives in 1934. But psychiatric nurse Althea Tidball, who will retire this year after forty years' service at the hospital, says that Mr. Horsfall had already been in residence "several years" before she joined the staff in 1930. It seems reasonable to conclude that Mr. Horsfall has spent all of his adult life at Cumberland State. Where he came from, who his parents were, remains a mystery that may never be solved.

Nor do we have a clue as to the inspiration for his remarkable series of drawings, all of which, in an explosion of creativity, he has produced in the past two and a half years. He works exclusively with charcoal pencil and white shoe polish on pads of newsprint provided by the hospital. According to his art instructor, Vanderbilt graduate student Enid Waller, Mr. Horsfall's technique is largely "pure"; that is, he does not seem to

have been influenced by or even to be aware of
such modern masters as Klimt and Munch, some
of whose paintings come to mind when we study
the wintry compositions in dusky black and
shocking white, the not-quite-earthly faces that
haunt us long after we have left the exhibition.
Mr. Horsfall paints only portraits—one in particular, the hairless woman or wraith who may dom-
inate his dreams. Who is she? Did she ever exist?
If only Arne Horsfall could speak, what a tale he
might have to tell!

AUGUST, 1906:

The Road to Dante's Mill

1

The boy awoke to familiar sounds: the morning songs of hooded warblers and ovenbirds, the crackle of new dry wood on the fire, the daily sharpening of the ax, the skinning knife. And the unfamiliar: his father, weeping.

Arne flinched beneath his blanket, wishing he could go back to sleep, no matter how bad his dream had been, how uncomfortable the ground he slept on. But the pointer dog lying heavy against his side raised his head and yawned; warm, stenchy breath, also familiar, and preferable to the reek of hot tar that stung Arne's nostrils and brought tears to his eyes before he could focus on his surroundings.

He was thinking what had been, until now, unpardonable to think: *crazy*. His father must be crazy. But Arne's point of reference was questionable, and he knew it: the only son of Luke and Elvira Slater ("Son" but full-grown, gray-haired in fact, hugely fat and slovenly in his overalls) sat with bare feet dangling from the tailgate of the Slaters' wagon on town days, swigging Coca-Cola and crying out moon-eyed and rapturously when the mood was upon him, unable to speak intelligibly. "Born without brains," an older friend of Arne's had said, contemptuously, as if this were "Son" Slater's own fault. *Crazy.* Without a doubt, Arne's father was behaving more and more oddly—but unlike "Son" Slater he had brains, so how could he have suddenly gone crazy?

Yet there was no accounting for why they were here, with chores to do at home, a cow that needed milking. Maybe, Arne thought, some of the corn could still be saved, along with the apples and pears in their orchard. Instead of laboring at this salvage they roamed almost aimlessly by day, staying to the woods, and hid at night . . . no, that was wrong, his father didn't hide. He frequently left Arne and went off alone, never saying where or troubling to explain what was on his mind. He didn't answer questions. Often he seemed not to hear Arne because he was listening so keenly to something else—in his head, in the distance. Unenlightened, Arne felt smaller than he knew himself to be, not worthy of trust. Or love. How their relationship had changed, in so few days.

Propping himself on an elbow, Arne wiped his eyes. Hawkshaw rose and stretched. Arne's father was sitting with his back to a windfall on the other side of the fire, holding down the whetstone with one foot. Honing the handax blade. Through the heat waves and wood smoke Arne looked at his oblivious father and saw him in tears. *Men didn't cry.* Fear crowded the boy's heart—like crowding a small frog, throbbing and cold, in his cupped hands. His father was crying because he was in terrible pain.

Tears on one cheek, the other a ruin. Three greenish bruises there, like putrescent fingerprints. Arne's eyes went to his father's left hand. All he could see of it was

a big lump of bandages stiff from ichor. Arne didn't
want to think of what the hand must look like by now.

(It froze)

That was all his father had been willing to explain,
when Arne questioned him. *It froze.* In high summer,
in baking heat, the hand had frozen.

Will it get better?

No.

How did you do it?

I don't know!

Crazy . . .

Arne got up clutching his blanket around him Indian-
fashion and without another glance at his father walked
to the edge of their campsite. The sun wasn't yet above
the tree line, but most of the frost had vanished, although the bright night had glittered from it. A hard
white frost, in the middle of August. But it wasn't
everywhere. It seemed to follow them, from camp to
camp in the remote hollows where they had been living
since they left their farm—*no* (Arne corrected himself
severely), they'd *run away,* with the clothes on their
backs and not much else . . . Arne was shivering and
fumbling, and he nearly started peeing in his pants before he managed to get them unbuttoned.

He wet down the furze which the mysterious frost
had blighted or killed. The leaves of a nearby redbud
were brown at the edges, and many had fallen. He heard
his father muttering, then a loud sob. Arne shut his eyes
tightly, trying to stop his own tears. He'd lost two sus-
pender buttons, and his denim pants were low on his
hips. His bare arms and ankles were covered with the
festering bites of deerfly and chigger. Full-faced tow-
headed boy, small eyes, like a blond hedgehog. He was
dirtier than he'd ever been in his life, and hungrier. Last
night, when his father returned well after dark to their
camp, he had no food with him, not even a red squirrel
to fry in the last of their cornmeal. He was in such a
daze, so pale, nearly stumbling into the fire as he

dragged more wood to it, that the boy was afraid to complain.

Hawkshaw, who must be hungry too, was already foraging among the shrubs and understory trees that grew in the moist creek bottom. But Hawkshaw was trained to silently hunt and retrieve, not kill; he had to be fed or he would die.

His mother missing, his father hurt, his dog dying— it was too much for Arne. Trembling from anxiety and anger, the boy approached his father, who had slumped, mouth open, the ax gripped loosely in his right hand. He was far gone from fatigue. He had stood watch the remainder of the night while the fog clung to the trees like spider shrouding and the chill deepened, the moon a weak gazer, stone giant's eye.

"We're hungry!" the boy protested, and almost started to cry again. His face itched from shame, but he was scared. Scared of lies, scared of truth—whatever the truth might be. He glanced at the liquid tar in the iron pot over the fire. A bubble swelled fatly on the surface. He seemed puzzled; what was it for?

"Where did you come by that pitch?"

His father opened and closed his mouth, momentarily unable to speak. He was a young man, not yet thirty, strongly built. Only his youthful strength had carried him this far. He hadn't shaved for more than a week. Nor changed his clothes.

"Dante's Mill," said his father.

"Is that where you went last night?"

"Yes."

Arne felt a surge of excitement; now he was going to find out something, for sure.

"Who all did you see?"

"Nobody."

"You didn't?"

"Wasn't . . . nobody there." His father looked down at his left hand. His lips tightened. He looked at his son, ignoring the disappointment, the disbelief in Arne's eyes.

"You can go. It's safe for you now. You'll find food. You know what to pick, what to dig."

"Can I take the rifle?"

"No. Almost out of . . . ca'tridges." Arne's father shook his head slightly, annoyed by his forgetfulness. "Don't know why I didn't remember that last night. Could've helped myself to all I wanted. But bullets . . . ain't no good."

"They're good for shooting squirrel," Arne said, almost belligerently.

"Go do you some fishing. I need to . . . sleep now."

"When can we go home?" Arne fidgeted at his father's blank stare. There was the odor of wood smoke, and of tar. Corruption too, from the swollen, absurdly dying hand. "Don't you know you need a doctor?"

"I do know that. Promise you, boy, we'll go home soon. Tomorrow, when it's done."

"But what are you going to do? Can't we go home *now*? I want to see mother!"

Groaning, growling, his father stroked the blade of his ax against the whetstone again, as if unsatisfied with what was already the sharpest edge the steel could take. There was such a look of despair in his face that Arne had to dig his fingers into the bones of his chest to keep from screaming.

"Where *is* she? Where did mother go?"

His father lay back against the windfall, eyes closing. A log popped on the fire, showering sparks across the boy's bare feet. He danced wrathfully.

"Not so far that . . . God be willing . . . I can't bring her back."

The putrescent marks on his face shimmered as he turned his face into a shaft of sun. He looked at Arne. He was able to smile, for the first time in days. A strong man, who always made jokes, sang, was happy. At eighteen and still growing he had knocked down a frac-

tious stallion with his fist, earning him the nickname
Horsekiller.

"Green vine," he said softly. "Strangler fig." His
mind seemed to wander then; his eyes looked vague,
reddened by the wood smoke and glare of flames. Before he could say anything else he fell asleep. He was
so inert that for a few dreadful seconds the boy thought
he had died. Then the big chest shuddered, his father
snored. Arne covered him with his own blanket.

2

Arne took fishing line, two hooks, and a sinker from
their knapsack and left the campsite. He carried a gnarled
club of hornbeam, the hardest wood that grew in the Tennessee forests, for reassurance and protection—he was
almost nine years old now, largely on his own, although
Hawkshaw was somewhere around and would catch up to
him before long.

He worked his way up from the creek bottom to the
ridge line, chewing a handful of spearmint leaves to
give his stomach something to be grateful for. It was
cool where he walked through the oak and hickory forest, bathed in fuming mist that condensed in his hair,
on his forehead, while the dew on the ferns that grew,
luxuriantly, everywhere, soaked his pants as high as the
knees. Wood pewees and vireos flickered in sunspots
but it was dark, still, up in the rafters of the great trees.
He heard woodpeckers and saw more red squirrels than
he could count. His mouth watered when he thought of
plump, fried squirrel, almost his favorite meal next to
roasted tom turkey. As always, and without constantly

thinking of the necessity of it, he kept track of land-marks: two half-fallen trees sagging against each other and overgrown with clematis, forming a natural arch; an outcrop of limestone with a cave centered like a watchful eye. He would never lose himself in the woods, no matter how far removed he was from home.

From the summit he looked east. There was a golden haze in the valley where the Cumberland and Harpeth rivers joined; he could make out the copper spire of the new Baptist church in Sublimity, the town where he attended school and hung around the stores two Satur-day mornings a month. He felt heart-tugs, sadness. Closer, there was smoke from isolated cabin chimneys. Although he didn't reckon distance in terms of miles, Arne knew how far he could walk in a day, and most of the cabins as well as the town of Sublimity were within reach. But his father, obsessed by unnamed dangers, continually glanc-ing at the night sky while he fed wood to the fires, had warned him to stay away from everyone. To hide, even in daylight, from strangers, or those he knew as friends. Children his own age.

He couldn't think of a single boy near his age he had cause to be afraid of; he could lick them all. Girls he never paid attention to.

Crazy. Crazycrazycraz—

Arne swallowed the word like a stone, like bad med-icine, and was sullen, heartsore, trying not to think very hard about his—their—predicament as he walked a little way through an understory of redbud and dog-wood toward the sound of trickling water. He located the spring which fed the stream that coursed through their campsite below. There were deer tracks around it. The water flowed clear and inches deep over velvet-green slabs of limestone. Runners of purple violet and watercress drifted in small eddies. He went to his knees to drink, shivering as the water touched his face, his tongue quickly going numb.

He had not quite satisfied his thirst when he heard

something, larger than a rabbit or a woodchuck, moving down the leafy slope behind him.

Arne looked around, instinctively raising his club. But it was Hawkshaw, and he was okay. Arne hugged Hawkshaw, his hands on the liver-spotted dog's prominent rib cage. Hawkshaw had a wood tick feeding behind one ear, but before Arne could do anything about it the dog squirmed loose and began lapping water from the spring.

Arne opened his barlow knife and got down to business. He was soon fully absorbed in doing familiar and pleasurable things, so that all of the unpleasantness, the confounding and difficult events of the past week, while not fully forgotten, were put aside in his mind.

He cut a fishing pole, as his father had taught him, from a straight piece of rattan. Then, taking care not to disturb a couple of ground-level nests of yellow jackets, he dug around in a rotted stump until he came to a teeming mass of beetle grubs. There was life everywhere around him, buzzing, singing, pulsating, life that renewed his spirits. He began to sing a song his father loved.

"Life is like a mountain railway
with an engineer that's brave;
you must make the run successful
from the cradle to the grave."

Nearby, growing in the fertile, dark litter of the forest floor, were tempting mushrooms, and Arne licked his lips. He'd eaten succulent, white-capped mushrooms like those. But he was afraid to choose, to try his luck. If they were the mushrooms called Destroying Angels, they killed with the certainty of a bullet to the heart.

Arne carried the beetle grubs in his pocket down the stairsteps of the broadening stream until it tumbled six feet into a pool that lapped, in a sun-filled vale, around the old dark knees of river birches. He baited his hook with a grub and anchored the pole on the bank, wedging it upright in a vee of a young cottonwood's branches.

Not far away he located plum trees the birds hadn't stripped and gobbled handfuls of the ripe fruit, almost swallowing a couple of stones in his hunger. He washed the plum juice from his chin to keep the midges off and located a stand of white oak in a dry area not far from the creek. With his knife he cut numerous oak withes, then sat down cross-legged to fashion his baskets, one to fill with hickory nuts and spring beauty tubers and plums, the other with the fish he hoped to catch. There was not much good fruit to be had in this month: it was late for all but highbush berries, too early for bittersweet black cherries, persimmons, or the custard-flavored paw paw of which he was uncommonly fond.

When Arne returned to check his line he found it taut from the tip of the pole to the roiling water, and pulled out a good-sized carp. By late morning he'd added three more to the basket and was humming again. The day was fair, the deerflies had almost disappeared from the woods, and mosquitoes were few; he thought poignantly of home, of hilly cultivated fields and ripening corn, and almost made himself believe that if—when—they went there again, it would all have been miraculously restored. The healthy ears of corn; his mother's smile. But the power of his faith was not equal to what he knew was lost, unrecoverable. The killing frost had come ten days ago, riming the windows of their house, shriveling what had been a lush acre of vegetables, turning the newly tasseled corn tobacco-brown as far as the eye could see.

On the morning of the frost, his mother was gone. His father was frightened, and the strange marks that would slowly deepen in putrefaction were on his cheeks. But nothing had happened to his hand yet. That was later—Arne didn't know for sure just when he had frozen his hand.

He must know where she is, Arne thought.

The humming stopped, and his mood took a sudden turn; he felt even worse than he had on awakening.

Why won't he tell me?

The truth chewed in his breast like a fox to be let out. Stoically he denied it, and walked back to the campsite with Hawkshaw leading the way. He carried the baskets at each end of the pole across his shoulders. As he started down from the ridge line he heard his father scream, scary as dynamite.

3

Hawkshaw stopped and bristled, whining.

Arne, throbbing from terror, dropped his baskets and went skidding downhill on his tough naked heels with the barlow knife open in his hand.

He found his father stretched out on his back next to the dwindling fire. He was twitching but breathless, as if he'd fallen out of a tree. The tar pot had overturned, there was an odor of seared flesh in the air. His father was still holding the handax. Bright blood spotted the blade. Even so, Arne was slow to comprehend what had happened until he saw that his father's left arm now ended at the wrist in a clot of smoking tar. The hand he had crudely amputated, partially wrapped in dirty streamers of bandage, lay palm up a few feet away.

Then Arne understood the tone of the nerved-up scream he'd heard, could visualize his father with his left arm laid just so across the windfall, and—raising up, reaching high with the ax and bringing it down as he screamed, the hand flying away (long squirts of blood glistened on the smooth weather-bleached wood of the windfall and on the ground). His father must have had just enough courage left to plunge his pumping wrist into the tar pot. His face was sweaty suet, veins had popped, the decaying flesh of his cheek coruscated like dragonfly wings.

"Had to," his father groaned. "Gangrene. Wouldn't last an hour if that poison . . . reached my heart."

Arne sobbed helplessly. His father let go of the ax and grasped him weakly by the shoulder.

"I know . . . where they are. Know what to do. But I need two hands. You'll have to help me . . . put them all to sleep."

The boy nodded, not understanding him. Tears fell on his father's tremoring hand.

"Cut you some strangler fig. Twist it into loops. We need . . . thirty, maybe forty pieces of that green vine. God, there's aplenty more of them than I thought I'd find. Huh? Must be . . . every last soul in Dante's Mill. The son of a bitch . . . turned the whole town."

"Turned? What? Who?"

"Theron."

The boy shook his head, slowly at first, then with a motoring agitation until his father stopped it.

"The Dark . . . Man. That's his name. Theron."

The damp hairs on the back of Arne's neck stirred, then fear bolted up to electrify the base of his skull. "The Dark Man . . . *woke up*?"

His father nodded.

"How?" But Arne remembered his mother telling him what could happen, should the dried vine clutching his neck be loosened. The legend was specific, the consequences—and he knew. *"Mother?"*

"She could have done it. That's been my suspicion right along. She cut the fig."

"Why? Why would she do that?"

"I don't know."

"Did the Dark Man make her go with him?"

"I—I'm not sure. I ain't seen Birka since—"

"You must have seen her! *Don't tell me a lie!*"

"No . . . no, Arne. I wouldn't lie to you." He found
the strength to tighten his grip on the boy's shoulder.
"Get busy. Huh? Bring me that vine. But remember
. . . the sun. After the sun sets, look up. Always be
a-looking up, because they don't make no sound when
they come."

His last words were nearly lost in a sigh. And he was
out again, slumped heavily across Arne's thighs.

"Look up for what?" the boy asked futilely.

He tried to make his father more comfortable on the
ground, covering him with his own blanket because his
father felt so deathly cold despite the noonday heat. He
thought, *Vines* . . . no, strangler fig. He knew what to
look for, his father had pointed it out to him growing
in the trees not far from their farm. Wrapped around
and around the trunks, taking a mean choking grip from
which the name derived. Crushing the life from the
trees.

The sun was overhead, he had hours yet. He added
wood to the fire, cleaned and fried his fish, and made
a soup, pungent with thyme and wild onion. He
pounded slippery elm, blackberry leaves, and chamo-
mile flowers to pulp and mixed the pulp with water.
His father was in and out of consciousness during the
early afternoon, his coldness yielding to a rattling fever.
In his wakeful moments Arne made him drink. Only
after his father had taken some nourishment did Arne
eat, choking down part of the fish. The rest, with a
couple of hush puppies, he gave to Hawkshaw.

He had been trying not to look at the cut-off hand,
the moldered fingers. His father was a cripple now. How
would he be able to handle Ol' Vol the plowhorse, flat-
break their fields come next spring? Finally Arne nerved
himself to pick up the severed hand between two pieces
of charred firewood. He carried the hand to the edge of
the campsite, batted the inquisitive Hawkshaw away,
dug a hole deep and buried the hand, then set a large

rock on top of the filled hole. He wondered if he should
say something, like at a funeral, but couldn't think of
any words from the Bible that would do. Funeral for a
hand. But his father was still alive, praise God for that.

He was ready then to search for the strangler fig he'd
been told he must find.

4

Arne scrubbed the handax with creek sand and moss
and took it with him. Now it was mid-afternoon, hot
and still in the woods along the looping streambed he
followed. The air was humid, and felt thick as paint in
the shadowed hollows where no breezes stirred—only
the frying hum of insects mimicked the sound of wind.
Hawkshaw growled at a six-foot black racer twined
around a bare limb on a windfall. It was swollen and
sluggish from feeding on voles or frogs.

The anthracite sheen of the snake, its lofty, sinister
eye, reminded Arne of the figure lying on its side in a
deep bed of excelsior, hands clasped between the
drawn-up knees, sleeping the Black Sleep of the legend.
The boy's stomach tightened into a fiery knot. What
was true, and what was a story? How could something
that looked like a statue of hardened tar be up and walking around now; and if he—*it*—was, what had become
of Birka, Arne's mother? Was she dead? He felt a little
dizzy from apprehension and stooped to splash cool
water on his face. The dizziness went away, but the
heated, almost panicked churning of his brain continued.

Dead? *Dead?* Was that what his father knew but couldn't bring himself to tell?

Panting, Arne sat down to rest, the ax in his lap, its edge (he reminded himself, flicking it carefully with the ball of his thumb) more than equal to the tarry strength of the Dark Man if they should meet . . . He couldn't make himself believe in what he had not seen with his own eyes although, while he rested, he was looking, searching the hidden places of the wood.

He didn't know how far he had come, but he wasn't concerned about finding his way back before sunset. And he had Hawkshaw—but the bird dog had disappeared. Arne couldn't recall when he'd last seen him. As for hearing him, Hawkshaw was trained not to bark.

Arne forced himself to get up. He crossed the creek where it was divided by small sedgy sandbars. Some tiger swallowtails were playing in the sun; one of the butterflies alighted on the back of his hand and he carried it, gravely, a little way up the bank to a stand of shagbark hickory and mixed oaks. For some reason the butterfly made him uneasy. It was beautiful and harmless, but he had dreamed of butterflies recently . . .

No, moths . . . lunas, prometheas. And they had been huge, with the eyes, or eyespots, of human beings.

Arne surveyed the trees, which had been invaded by wild grape, Virginia creeper, and the tenacious vine he was hunting. He blew on the butterfly, which vanished, and set to work, chopping, sizing, his hands becoming sticky and the ax dulling from the sap that oozed with each slashing. He stopped when he had two large bundles of shoots.

With his work finished, despair returned. If there was only one Dark Man, why did they need so many vines? Hawkshaw was still missing. Arne slung the bundles of strangler fig across his shoulders and began to call as he worked his way down to the creek. The day was nearly sunless now, in the deep hollow where he'd spent so much of the afternoon.

"Hawwwkshawww!"

His dog gone, all he needed with his other worries. Standing in midstream, watering down sore feet, Arne had an attack of the shudders. His father must be awake by now, and agonized. How could he live through another night of the numbing frost? They needed to move on before it was too late, establish another camp. But Arne was already tired; his right arm and shoulder ached from the effort of hacking the tough vine.

Out of the corner of his eye he saw something, and stiffened. But it was Hawkshaw, moving downstream, more at home in open fields than woodland but graceful nonetheless as he slipped through a thicket of hydrangea and spice bush at the water's edge. He was carrying something in his mouth—a bird or small animal, Arne thought, but when the dog took to the middle of the creek and came splashing closer the boy made out a childlike shape; dangling arms and legs dressed in blue calico, a square sewn-together face with button eyes and a yellow mop of yarn curls.

"Where did you find that?" Arne said crossly. "C'mon, we have to go."

Hawkshaw stopped a few feet away from him, not letting go of the cornshuck doll, not making any sound, just watching Arne as if he were in the mood for teasing. The boy had a good whiff of his dog, who, in spite of his partial bath, smelled awful, worse than pigshit mixed with buzzard vomit, how could he stand himself?

The dog turned as if put off by Arne's expression and lunged, high-headed, upstream.

"Not that way! Come with me."

Hawkshaw continued to the far bank before turning to give Arne a solemn look. But the boy was impatient with dog habits and dog wiles.

"Hey you, dog! Come back here to me right now!"

Arne had a premonition then, inspired by the doll in Hawkshaw's mouth and the rotten stench of him, that he didn't want to know any more about. But Hawkshaw appeared anxious for Arne to follow him. No, he couldn't waste time, there was too much to do . . . the bird dog waited remorselessly for him, hindquarters dappled by a volley of sun motes through overhanging leaves.

"This better not take long," Arne muttered, and splashed his way up the creek behind Hawkshaw, the bundles of vines rubbing against his back and shoulders, ax swinging free in his right hand.

They had to cross the ridge line and descend into a valley with few open spaces. Arne, unhappy, fighting brambles, lopped a few branches and kept an eye on his landmarks. A deer path wandered through a ravine overgrown with huckleberry and then sumac, almost as hard to get through as a tangle of fence wire; abruptly the undergrowth gave way to red cedar and a lone Judas tree growing beside the road to Dante's Mill.

From the position of the sun over the empty road, Arne calculated that it was past five in the afternoon. His forehead smarted where a branch had lashed it; he was running a good sweat.

"Now what?" he asked Hawkshaw, but the bird dog already was off at a fast pace up the road, going in the direction of Sublimity and not Dante's Mill: toward home. Arne chewed his lower lip and followed.

They had covered a couple of hundred yards when Arne became aware of two things: a slow float of buzzards close to the treetops and a frost-bitten patch of woods, and a clouding of the air, dreadful odor, dead things but not newly dead.

An unplaned log bridge crossed the branch that ran beside the road, then a track entered a cover where a decrepit wagon was standing, the wagon sheet almost in tatters on the wooden hoops that supported it. Arne had seen relics like this wagon in the courthouse square on market days. Hill people, those who lived so far back in forested crannies there was almost nothing that could be called a road, still used them for transportation on those rare occasions when they went anywhere.

Except for the low notes of a mourning dove, it was very quiet.

Arne saw a chestnut horse down in the trace chains of the wagon, not moving. Flies circled around the bloated corpse and a beaky scavenger was jerking at something tough and unyielding, pinkly purple as new sausage in the hazy drift of sunlight through the trees surrounding the cove. A part of the horse's intestines burst with a fetid popping sound, but the odor already concentrated in the cove was nearly enough to knock Arne over. The grass was cold-burned, and nearly all of the leaves to the highest tree limbs hung lifelessly, grayish-green, a touch of bleak horror. Except for the heat and humidity, it might have been a winter's day: like "Old Christmas," when horses talked at midnight, and cows walked on their knees. And ghosts just walked.

Arne went slowly to the cookpot, suspended over the blackened heap of a fire, staying as far from the horse as he could. Last night's—last week's?—stew had congealed in the pot; not even the bluebottle flies were interested in that grease with more attractive meat strewn on the ground behind and to one side of the wagon. Two, no, he could make out three bodies: a man, for sure, the dark full beard lively with red ants was unmistakable even though he was bald from the eyebrows up, or: (scalped?   My Jesus!) . . . and two women

            (they had the shapes of women but blunter, fantastical, without all the skin),

                        one of whom had the sunshine-blond hair of his mother. Arne was strangling, hand pressed against his nostrils to smell dirt, *anything,* dirt and sweat weren't strong enough to block that other odor but he had to go closer to see, to make sure it wasn't her.

Flies roared up from the nude, skinless torso except for one, pulsating, embedded like a jewel in the navel pit where a scarce patch of skin (there, on the ears, around the eyebrows) remained. The woman's open eyes were as cold as stars, her bared teeth thickly lacquered with her own blood. The corpse appeared bitten in places, perhaps by wild animals or Hawkshaw the dog. No, it wasn't, couldn't be, his mother! A fly squeezed out of her mouth through a space where a tooth had been and walked across her lip. Arne turned with a bawl of distress and ran, throwing up on the dead run, past other flayed corpses: little ones, all in a heap. By the road the air was better and, bless the mercy of the Lord, someone was coming, help was on the way.

5

He saw through tears but heard nothing of the running horse because of the pressure of blood in his ears. From his knees Arne watched as the horse and shay came nearer. The woman with the reins wore a short-sleeved white dress, like a wedding dress, that glowed in the shade of the hood, a white Sunday hat with a heavy, glossy veil, and white gloves past the elbows.

Sick and trembling, Arne got slowly to his feet, conscious of the weight of the bundles of strangler fig on his back. The horse, a gray mare not too well cared for, slowed to a walk and the shay, one wheel squeaking, drew alongside him.

There was something bulky knotted in a red and white checkered tablecloth on the small seat beside the woman. The horse snorted and pawed at the dirt road, made nervous by the smell from the cove, the presence of buzzards. There were raw whip slashes on the mare's lathered flanks.

The woman slowly, cautiously lifted her veil and peered out as if from a secluded parlor, her colorless mouth pursed in astonishment.

"Mother!"

"Arne, what are you doing here?" Birka said, and smiled fondly.

He turned toward the cove, trying to frame an explanation, but his knees were buckling. He turned back to her and lifted his arms, still winded, wanting at the moment only to be held and comforted.

"Yes," she said, socketing the butt of the whip into the holder. "You come, too."

Arne took a step toward the shay. His mother frowned, drawing back on the seat.

"But get rid of those awful things."

He didn't know what she meant. Birka gestured toward the bundles of strangler fig still oozing their clean sap, then quickly withdrew her hand. But not before Arne saw that something had popped through the kid glove where her little finger should have been.

It looked like a long black thorn.

The bundle on the seat next to his mother bulged, and Arne heard a terrified squeal. He thought it must be an animal, a baby pig, but then the bundle spoke.

"Help! *Help* meeee!"

A girl's voice. His thoughts flashed to the cornshuck doll in Hawkshaw's mouth. Horrified, he looked into his mother's eyes, just before she dropped the veil. The next thing he knew she had lifted him from the road by one arm, nearly wrenching it out of the shoulder cuff. She was a tall woman, but he had never known her to have this kind of strength. One of the bundles of strangler fig slipped from his shoulder and fell into the road.

"Never mind," his mother said grimly, and she hit the tablecloth with her other hand, hard enough to pro-

voke more squeals. "She's mine. You just come along
and do what I say."

Even through the glove leather he felt the shocking
coldness of her fingers. Her breath was like a blue
norther on his cheek and there was no familiar odor
about her, of sachet, of clean and well-brushed hair.

He swung wildly with his free hand, knocking away
the wide-brimmed hat and veil.

His mother's head was perfectly bald.

Before she could pull Arne into her lap, Hawkshaw
came snarling up from the road between them, going
straight for her throat. The mare reared and his mother
let go of Arne to fight off Hawkshaw. The carriage tee-
tered on one wheel and Arne fell hard, the breath
knocked out of him. Then Hawkshaw dropped beside
him, thrashing, his wide-open throat spraying blood,
and the shay, settling down on both wheels, lurched
ahead, the big right wheel spinning in the dust past
Arne's head, just inches away. He saw his mother, whip
in hand, standing precariously, lashing the mare down
the road to Dante's Mill.

"Noooo!"

She turned her head momentarily, that frightening
head with no hair, eyes big and furious, features like
clever painting on an Easter goose egg in the window
of Bauman's Mercantile.

"I'm going to Theron!" she called. "Tell Enoch to
stay away this time, or it'll be the end for him!"

Arne was stumbling after the shay, not thinking about
what he was doing, certain that what he thought he'd
seen was not real but some kind of elaborate, awful
joke (*his mother had hair!*). But he couldn't make her
out any more because she had settled back in the seat
next to the child bound up in the checkered tablecloth
(had she been acting bad, was that why she—but his
mother would never punish anyone that way, so it had
to be a joke too, part of the joke on him like his father
pretending to cut off his hand) and there was a length-

ening rooster tail of dust between Arne and the shay.
He was really busting his gut to catch up so the joke
could finally be over, and laughing: he screamed with
laughter until he fell headlong and the cut ends of the
remaining bundle of strangler fig jabbed at the back of
his head. He breathed dust until his tongue was caked
with it. His chest heaved as he still tried to laugh. Then
he sat up, looking expectantly down the road; but the
shay was gone, and so was the dust, the sun was lower.
She hadn't come back to explain the complicated joke,
to take off her hat and veil and shake down her abundant
hair, to unknot the tablecloth. (*Wait until you see who's
inside, Arne/I know I know it's Mary Louise Petrie.*)
And that's who it was! (*HA HA Arne Horsfall didn't we
fool you!*)

When he looked back the other way, toward Sublimity, he saw Hawkshaw down and motionless in the road,
as if he were taking a nap.

(Ha ha, get up, Hawk—)

But he couldn't laugh any more. The laughter was all
used up and he felt extremely tired; the only sounds he
made were pathetic moans of grief in his parched throat.

6

When next he was aware of anything, the shadows of
trees across the road had lengthened and the leaves were
flooding with the breeze that accompanied the setting
of the sun. Arne struggled up feebly but Hawkshaw
continued to lie there, and a buzzard had come down
to the road a few feet from the dog's head. That revived
Arne. Yelling, he picked up rocks to throw at the scav-

enger, which took flight. Arne continued to walk up the road until he could see clearly that Hawkshaw was dead, his throat had been cut. The handax lay in the road nearby. Had somebody used—but the ax blade had no blood on it.

"Who killed my dog?" Arne muttered, stupefied.

The last he remembered of Hawkshaw, alive, was down by the creek where he'd been cutting strangler fig. Hawkshaw had appeared with a doll in his mouth. No sign of the doll now. Where had they been since the creek, what was he doing here on this road with the day almost gone?

When Arne tried to squeeze something out, like a thorn embedded under his skin, all he got for his efforts was a searing headache, the worst headache of his life. It was accompanied by a bright light, bright as the flare from a photographer's flashpan. But steadier, a small sun in his brain. It illuminated peripheral images of his mother—hoeing in their garden at home, taking a pie from the black iron stove in the kitchen. His mouth watered. Was that today? No, he didn't think so . . . yet he could taste her apple pie, the crust shot through with dark amber juice and sugar and lots of cinnamon, as plainly as if he'd just cut a big slice for himself. Arne shuddered and shuddered. While he was savoring the goodness of apple pie the sun in his head wasn't so painfully hot, but he couldn't make out his mother any more—oh, there she was, they were in the barn by lantern light, he and Birka with crowbars prying up the lid of the packing crate they'd found on the bank of the Cumberland River after the big June rains. *Scree, scree,* as the nails pulled out one by one . . . and Arne suddenly shouting:

"Don't open it! Don't open it!"

But it was now that he was shouting; two months ago he'd been the most curious to see what was in the coffin-size crate constructed of rowan wood—*It has magical properties*, his mother had said.

"That'll be the end of us, pa."

He was talking to himself, sure enough, while the flies swarmed briskly around Hawkshaw's slit throat, the tacky blood that had spilled into the road. Arne lifted his head abruptly, as if he'd heard something—

A shay?—

—And for an instant Arne thought he saw a gray mare and a buggy far up the road, his mother holding the reins with one hand and waving to him—but the sun blazed again in his brain, staggering him. He clutched his head with both hands and fell back, began awkwardly to run, his right foot clumsy and dragging, as if it were not a part of him any more. He left the ax and the bird dog and the other bundle of strangler fig behind.

As he ran he thought: *I'm running straight to hell.*

A chill overcame him and he faltered, then saw a lone Judas tree in a stand of red cedar and made for it.

The ravine he entered seemed familiar. He knew without having to think that the ravine would run uphill a fair distance. Then, over the ridge line, he would come to a wide creek, and later on to a nice fishing hole. From there it wasn't much farther to the campsite where he'd left his father . . .

Looking up through tangles of sumac and dogwood branches, he saw the pale yellow moon rising as the light of the sun began to fade. It was a three-quarters moon. He could make it back, he was sure, before dark, before the frost, before the beautiful white moonflyers who came with the frost and watched them, hovering well out into the dark and away from the fire that Arne and his father did not dare let go out.

7

In Arne's absence his father had been active, collecting new wood for the fire, a roaring beacon Arne had no trouble homing in on.

As soon as he reached their sanctuary Arne slumped down and shrugged off the bundle of stranger fig, saying nothing. When he looked at his father Arne's mind permitted him to see his father whole, just as his mind would not permit him to remember the encounter with his mother.

His father looked at Arne's eyes, and looked away.

"Where's the ax?"

"I lost it."

"Where's Hawkshaw?"

"Well, he's—"

Arne tried to cram both fists into his mouth then, but too late; he had sensed that once he started to scream he wouldn't be able to stop, for as long as he went on living.

His father realized it, too; he hitched around with a grunting effort and hit Arne hard across the face in mid-scream. Arne chomped down on his tongue, his eyes going wide and blank.

His father hit him again but not as hard this time and Arne, who had been rigid as a fence post and white to the tips of his ears, folded up against him.

"Don't go off like that. I need you. Get hold of yourself, Arne."

A little later Arne crawled away from his father and sat up, arms wrapped around his knees. He rocked a while and stared at the fire. He was shaking. There was blood in his throat and on his lips from having bitten his tongue so savagely.

"I love you," his father whispered.

Arne nodded.

"Are you afraid to die, Arne?"

"Yes," the boy said.

Certainly he was afraid of death—but at the same time he wished for a mouthful of mushroom, the Destroying Angel, and a quick end to his torment. But that was crazy. Now he was going crazy too, he thought, and he was more afraid of that than dying.

Gradually his shaking stopped. His gaze was steady and sad.

"Tell me what happened," his father said.

Arne secretly bit his tongue again and again, betraying no emotion, no hint of pain, bit hard and deep so he would not be obliged to speak his thoughts, to share what he had seen and knew to be true.

AUGUST, 1970:

The Sunday Dinner Guest

1

Marjory Waller drove down to Nashville to pick up her sister Enid, who was, as usual, late in meeting her. Marjory passed by the main gate of Cumberland State Hospital, didn't see Enid waiting there or on the grounds where she often conducted her art classes on sultry summer days, and swung around into the visitors' parking lot. She drove the wrong way down a lane and, with a finely developed intuition for knowing what she could get away with, grabbed a slot in the deep shade of a pin oak, ignoring another driver, who honked at her.

"I was fixing to park there myself, little lady!" he yelled as Marjory got out. Because of the angle of her approach she hadn't parked well, but at least she had got there first and possession, when it came to parking places, was everything in Marjory's book of rules.

"I'm sorry, sir, can't you see my car's burning up?"

Some white vapor was coming from beneath the hood, which didn't close all the way any more because of a crumpled left fender. The '62 baby-blue-with-rust

Plymouth had been overheating for a month. Ought not to be driving it, Marjory thought, until she coerced Buddy or Lyle at the Esso to pull the radiator and do a little soldering for free, but Enid's Corvair was in the shop again and they were making do.

Marjory untied and yanked up the hood without blistering her hands and stood looking at the Plymouth's innards as if she were a consulting surgeon on a rare and tricky heart case. The other driver didn't go away; was he being a sore loser? He opened the door of his car and stood up, looking at her.

"Use a little help?"

She didn't like his know-it-all grin. He looked to be a lot older than Marjory, thirty at least, and pure-d country. Worked in town, maybe a sessions picker to judge from the length of his hair and his appaloosa vest (but musicians drove better cars than the unwashed 88 he'd stepped out of). He was the type to have a wife and kids stashed in the sticks, while he fucked everything that didn't fly or have webbed feet.

Marjory tugged the red bill of her St. Louis Cardinals cap a little lower, so he couldn't see her eyes, and said, "Know anything about the modulator fimbus?"

"Reckon I could locate your fimbus if I look for it long enough."

"No, thanks," Marjory said. He went on grinning and staring at her. She held up her driver's license. "I'm sixteen and a half," Marjory said. "Does that tell you anything?"

"Well," he said, "I could've swore you was older, hefty as you are."

Marjory shook her head wearily and gave him the peace sign, went over and slumped down under the pin oak, elbows on her knees, chin on her fists. After a few seconds he drove away and found another parking place.

Marjory took off her baseball cap, wiped her steaming brow with a frayed handkerchief, and stared at the logo on the front of the cap: a bird with a big yellow

beak and a crimson tail, perched on a bat. The Cards
were not having a good year. Even Harry Caray, the
St. Louis broadcaster, had sounded a little exasperated
when the team blew a three-run lead in the bottom of
the ninth in San Francisco. But that was nothing com-
pared to Marjory's reaction as the ball sailed over the
wall above the centerfielder's glove. *Everybody* knew
you pitched McCovey inside, jammed him, then showed
him the low-breaking curve. She hadn't been able to get
to sleep for two hours after listening to the game.
Prickly heat was only part of her problem, although
she'd suffered from it since she was a baby. Some fudge
ripple ice cream would have calmed her down, but when
she went downstairs in her babydolls at two in the
morning there was no fudge ripple in the freezer, only
some rainbow sherbet that had ice whiskers on it and
looked unpalatable. Enid and her boy friend must have
sat on the front porch until after midnight eating all of
the ice cream and most of the sour-cream cake, satis-
fying one appetite and working up another before
sneaking upstairs to Enid's room (but Marjory was alert
to that, even though she was hanging on every pitch of
the ballgame and the old oscillating fan on the window
seat of her room was making its usual racket). She wondered what time Ted had gone home. She didn't mind
Ted as much as she pretended, but was scared Enid was
going to slip—if she was on the pill then she must be
keeping them in her purse, the one place Marjory
wouldn't snoop—and wind up having to marry him. Ted
Lufford was not what Marjory had in mind for Enid.
Not with her looks, talent, and brains.

There was no breeze where she sat on the parking-
lot island. They hadn't had much rain for a couple of
months, only a few brief thundershowers that didn't
provide long-lasting relief from the torrid days and humid nights of middle Tennessee. Marjory went through
the pockets of her shorts looking for a box of fruit-
flavored Chiclets she hadn't finished, and popped two

into her mouth. She looked at the high gates of the mental institution and the dozen buildings on the landscaped grounds. Two big sprinklers near the gate were at work on parched lawns. There were flowerbeds, magnolia and mimosa trees among the larger oaks, wide walkways—from her perspective it might have been a college campus. Inside, Marjory thought, it was like a morgue where they let the corpses walk around. Enid had given her an abbreviated tour. Once was going to last Marjory forever. She had such a horror of the asylum her knees locked before she had gone very far; listening to the inmates, cries and babble echoing, her underarms boiled with sweat and a tight, terrible grin stayed on her face so that she thought she must look like one of *them*—any second the people who ran the place were going to make a bad mistake and lock Marjory up. *Night of the Living Dead,* which she had been persuaded to see at the drive-in a couple of months ago, hadn't bothered her nearly as much as fifteen minutes inside Cumberland State.

How Enid had the stomach for it, she just couldn't imagine.

Since Marjory, two years ago, had taken over trying to manage certain important aspects of her sister's life, she had not (might as well admit it) met with much success. Enid had breezed through the finals of Vandy's Maid of Cotton contest when she was a junior; then she balked at entering the preliminaries of the Miss Tennessee Pageant, although Marjory argued with her until she was just about blue in the face. "Balked" wasn't quite the right word: Enid didn't argue back. She seldom felt the need to defend herself or a cherished viewpoint. She would not enter another beauty contest, period. Not because she had doubts about her looks (Enid was serenely aware that God had been generous with her). She simply had no desire, as she put it, "to compete in frivolous areas."

Frivolous? Okay, forget about the full-length mink

coat, the scholarship, the wardrobe, the pretty good diamond jewelry—it was the opportunity for travel that mattered so much, to Marjory if not to Enid, and the high-type men, unmarried men, she'd be introduced to. Entertainers, advertising executives, Wall Streeters, even men who didn't have to work because they had so much money but were still serious about their lives, financed expeditions or invented things or got appointed ambassador to Greece. The kind of man Enid deserved, someone Marjory could take pride in as a brother-in-law, knowing in her heart, although she was only sixteen, that she didn't stand a cut dog's chance of ever landing anybody decent herself. Uh-uh, rule that out: not with her superstructure and big thighs.

So Enid wouldn't enter the Miss Tennessee Pageant, which of course led straight to Atlantic City and even more prestige, as Miss America (it was no secret that the judges up there doted on Southern women). Marjory was just able to bear this frustration, but she hadn't given up yet on another crucial promotion. Their house in Sublimity was free and clear, except for some piddling taxes they were only a year behind on. But the house was worth twenty thousand dollars, according to a local real estate agent Marjory had consulted. Nashville was booming; Sublimity was practically a suburb now, and they were putting up tract houses not two miles down the road. Marjory had calculated that they could live for *two years* in Paris, France, on twenty thousand dollars, where Enid, by virtue of her proven talent, would be admitted to whichever of several art schools she chose to attend and study with the finest portrait painters in Europe. Rich people were lining up over there to be immortalized in oils. The president of Vanderbilt University was having his portrait done now, by an artist from New York whose fee was three thousand dollars. Three thousand dollars! If Enid only painted one portrait a month, that came out to be—

Enid wouldn't hear of selling the house. She thought

it would be foolish to move to Paris and live off their capital when she already had an offer to go to work for $125 a week, plus benefits, in the art department of Curtis Sewell and Wainwright, Nashville's heavyweight ad agency. With that much security, then she could afford to paint portraits in her spare time, a potentially profitable hobby that appealed to her.

"Marjory," Enid had explained patiently, the last few times Marjory had hurled *Paris* in her face, "it sounds perfectly lovely and of course I've always dreamed of someday visiting the Louvre and the Arc de Triomphe, what girl hasn't? I know you mean well, hon, but don't you see? It's all 'pie in the sky.' " Sighing deeply, which Enid did so well it could bring tears to a creditor's eyes, she went on. "Mama and daddy would revolve in their graves, Marjory, if I let go of the house, unless of course it was a life-or-death situation—"

"Well, it *is* your life we're talking about, and I wish you'd try to understand that. You can be a big shot or a little shot, Enid. It's the *big* shots who study art in Paris."

"Now, how many times did we hear daddy say that the worst thing you can do is trade your birthright for 'pie in the sky'? Speaking of big shots, Half-uncle Averill mortgaged his home and cashed all of his savings bonds just to get hold of that fried-chicken franchise, and do you know what?"

"Yeh, I know. It's terrible fried chicken, and the sheriff's at his door."

Enid looked well satisfied; all would-be entrepreneurs were on trial, and she had just forced a confession from her guilty sister.

"That will never happen to *us*. Because we have a paid-up roof over our heads, which is our most valuable material asset. Our Rock of Gibraltar. See, I'm thinking about you, Marjory, and not just myself. I want to guarantee you the opportunity to finish college, like I did, so that you'll always have a vocation. I'm responsible for you, hon, and I take my responsibilities *very* seriously.''

Well, at least according to law Enid was her guardian, and responsible for Marjory: Enid had just turned eighteen when their mother and father died, crushed and burned beyond recognition at the most notorious unguarded railroad crossing in Caskey County. A terrible accident which Enid, who was on the church bus not far behind the Wallers' station wagon, unfortunately had witnessed.

Enid had been so devastated by the death of her parents that, withdrawn and vulnerable, she was reluctant to take any sort of risk in her own life. It was an understandable void which Marjory, who also grieved but perhaps had a hardier outlook, instinctively tried to fill with her well-meant schemes. Enid was such a good person, and so talented, that Marjory was loath to see her settle for a well-worn rut, when fame and prosperity could be hers for the asking. This was particularly galling because Marjory (assessing her own prospects) knew that she would never earn a red cent, or receive more than local accolades, for her one great talent, which was whacking the hell out of a grapefruit-sized ball with a skinny bat.

Marjory drew a couple of heavy breaths and glanced at the gates of Cumberland State—no Enid yet—and chewed her gum and examined a wart at the base of her right thumb, trying to decide how big it was going to get and if she should try castor oil or just have it burned off like the others. Marjory had a lovely complexion that other girls her age envied, but as if to make up for a pimpleless puberty Mother Nature had decreed that she must be a wart-grower.

Then, with nothing much doing, Marjory turned her attention to composing a letter in her mind to her reigning idol and the love of her life, although she had prudently refrained from hinting at her passion for him in the three letters she had actually mailed to date.

Dear Tim:

Although I'm sure I'll remain a "true-blue"
Redbirds fan until the day I die, I still haven't for-
given them for trading you and Curt Flood to Phil-
adelphia this season. I don't think Simmons's arm
is that much better than yours! It wasn't just luck
that the Cards won three pennants in five years
with *Tim McCarver* behind the plate. That's some
loyalty!

Anyway, I hope your broken hand is healing
okay and you'll be ready for the stretch drive. By
the way, it seems to me that before you went on the
DL you were getting the best results with the
thirty-two-ounce bat you were swinging when you
hit that three-run homer in Cincinnati, a game I
was lucky enough to catch on TV. That's just a
suggestion from one of your biggest supporters who
~~adores would die~~ wishes you the best in your new
"baseball home." I know that in spite of their ~~mis-
erable~~ slow start the Phils will be near the top of
the NL East by the end of

2

"Marjory?"
Enid was walking across the parking lot toward her,
carrying a folded easel, her pencil box, and some large
sketchpads. Marjory got up, a half-smile on her face,
still in the afterglow of her devotional. Of course she
was well aware that Tim McCarver was married and
had two darling little girls. His wife's name was Anne.

But Marjory wasn't envious, she didn't feel the least ill will toward Tim's wife. As far as Marjory was concerned, she and Anne were sharing Tim.

"There you are; I thought I was going to have to break in and rescue you."

"It's not a bad place, Marj. You have to get over thinking it's a bad place."

"It's a *bad* place, Enid. They're all crazy in there."

"You have to get over thinking that too, because it isn't true. There's a big difference between needing help to cope with your life and being, well, you know—totally defective."

Uh-oh, Marjory thought. Enid was leading up to something; this wasn't the usual Christian charity and goodwill toward fellow human beings you expected from her.

But Enid didn't pursue her theories of mental illness; she was looking at the car, which was no longer smoking. But the hood remained up.

"Is anything wrong, Marjory?"

"No, it's just overheating. The thermostat may be stuck, or—"

"What's that?"

"Some gizmo we don't have the money to replace. But when it sticks, the radiator heats up and starts leaking. I've got half a gallon of coolant in the trunk, that'll get us home okay. When will the Corvair be ready? Did you remember to call today?"

"Yes. They still aren't sure what the problem is. They think it's electrical."

"They think? They've had the car for five days, they damn well ought to *know* by now."

"Marjory—"

"You don't have a clue how to talk to mechanics, Enid. Why don't you let me handle Cutter Brothers?"

"I'm sure they're doing everything humanly possible. And you can be so obnoxious when you get worked up."

"Enid, would you like to know what my philosophy of life is, in a nutshell?"

Enid smiled tolerantly. "The squeaky wheel gets the grease."

"Right!"

"Marjory, could we go now? I've had a full day of classes, and I'm tired, and I have to go to work tonight."

"Yeah, okay, just let me pop the top on the radiator and pour the coolant in."

Marjory took a piece of bath towel, a funnel, and the jug of coolant from the trunk while Enid loaded her art supplies into the backseat. She kept one of the big newsprint pads and looked through it while Marjory filled the radiator, then tied the hood down.

"At least it's under warranty."

"What, Marjory?"

"The Corvair. They ought to give us a new one, all the trouble we've had."

Enid didn't say anything. She was studying a charcoal drawing in the pad. Marjory looked over her shoulder.

"Good God, what's that supposed to be?"

"It's a portrait, Marjory."

"No hair?"

"I think it's wonderful."

"Which one of your artistically inclined loonies did that one?"

"Arne Horsfall."

"Come on, let's go. I made potato salad for supper. Snapbean casserole. Green tomato pie with walnuts."

"I'd starve to death if it wasn't for you, Marjory."

"No you wouldn't. You'd eat three gallons of maple-nut and fudge ripple ice cream a week, but you wouldn't gain a pound. No zits, either."

"I get them on my derriere, Marj."

"Those are more like boils, that's different. At least you don't get warts. I am *so* sick of warts on my thumbs and under my arms, like little titties."

"They're probably caused by a virus."

"No, I'd say it's a curse."

Enid laughed. "Who would put a curse on you, child?"

Marjory said darkly, "I could name a lot of people."

Enid looked down at the pad in her lap as Marjory pulled out of the parking lot. Marjory glanced at the portrait again, with a crimping of her thin-lipped mouth.

"Is that supposed to be a man or a woman or a ghost or what?"

"I don't know."

"Didn't he tell you?"

"Mr. Horsfall's mute."

"Oh. What are you going to do with that thing?"

"Frame it. Hang it in my room. It's a gift from Mr. Horsfall."

"I don't think we should have that in the house, Enid."

"Why not?"

"It's spooky-looking. It was drawn by a mental patient. It'll be bad luck. I'm telling you, I can feel it in my bones. We don't need any more curses or bad luck."

Enid sighed, and closed the cover of the pad. "I want to stop at that new Zayre's store before we get on the Interstate."

"We're going to bump into the rush-hour traffic before long, and I've got a game at six-thirty."

"I won't be but a minute, hon. I just need to pick up a few things."

"Is Zayre's having a sale? I could use a bigger bra."

"Already?"

"Enid, I don't take that too kindly."

"Marjory, I didn't *mean* anything!"

"I know," Marjory said, forgiving her immediately. There wasn't a mean bone in Enid's body. Couldn't be. Rita Sue Marcum had them all. She was the franchise holder for middle Tennessee. You took one look at Rita Sue and you thought, *mean bones.*

"Rita Sue's pitching for the Presbyterians tonight."

"Is she good?"

"She'll try to smoke a couple across, even if it is slow-pitch, everybody does that to me. But I'll fool her. I'm going to drag a bunt down the first-base line, then when Rita Sue comes over to make the play, I'll tromp all over her behind."

"Are you two feuding again?"

"It's just our ongoing adversarial relationship."

"I don't know what it is about you girls. I could never baby-sit the two of you together, you'd all the time be putting peanut butter or dead beetles in each other's hair."

"Now she curses me, and I get warts."

"Marjory, I can't fathom how your mind works sometimes—don't forget about Zayre's."

Marjory made a hasty turn into the shopping center and glanced at the temperature gauge of the Plymouth. So far so good.

"Coming in with me?" Enid asked, while Marjory cruised for a parking space.

"Might as well, it's a regular bake oven in here. Am I all sweaty to you?"

"Not bad. I'll buy you a cherry Coke to cool you off."

"Thanks, Enid."

"After I pick up a pair of pants and a short-sleeved shirt for Mr. Horsfall."

Marjory braked a little late and bumped the car in the slot opposite them.

"Say . . . *what*?"

"Also I was wondering, could you fix something special for Sunday dinner, like paprika chicken and eggplant Italiano?"

"In this heat?"

"Well, maybe a nice cucumber salad to go with it, and lemonade."

"Why?"

"Mr. Horsfall's coming to dinner."

"A *mental patient*?"

"I don't want you to get the wrong impression of Mr. Horsfall, just because he's been—"

"Coming to *our house*?"

"Yes," Enid said, with a certain smoky stubbornness in her usually placid brandy-brown eyes. "I invited him to dinner at our house. It's part of—"

"Enid, you didn't ask me and it's my house too and I—"

"Will you please let me finish? They're starting a new program at Cumberland State that allows some of the patients to visit sponsoring families' homes for up to a week—"

"A week!"

"Mr. Horsfall is coming for dinner around noon, and if he's comfortable—we are going to try to make him feel *very* comfortable, Marjory—he might spend the night. I hate that look. Remember what daddy used to say? 'Are you catching flies, Marjory?' He used to say that when you'd sit on the porch with your mouth open. I know it's going to take a little time to get used to the idea, so that's why I brought it up now. To give you—"

"Time to get used to the idea. I'm not going to get used to the idea, Enid."

"Sure you will," Enid said cheerfully. "Once you understand that Mr. Horsfall is really a very sweet and docile human being. So grateful for any attention he's given."

"What's he in for? He probably took an ax to his wife."

"Why don't we talk about Mr. Horsfall inside where it's cool, and I can be picking out a shirt for him."

"Doesn't he own a shirt?"

"Just a charity rag. All of his clothes are donations. Come on."

3

Marjory was of a mind to sit in the car and sulk, but a big drop of sweat ran down the side of her nose, so she got out, unnecessarily slammed the car door, and followed Enid into the department store.

"Okay," she said to her sister as they walked down an aisle stocked with men's wear. "He's a sweet and docile human being. That's because they've got him on a bunch of stuff, right? What happens when he doesn't get his stuff? Come on, Enid, tell me the honest truth. Did he kill somebody? Is he a rapist?"

"This is nice-looking," Enid mused, holding up a blue Arrow shirt with a wide stripe.

"How do you know his size?"

"Oh, he has to be a large."

"Big guy, huh?"

"I'll take this one, and, let's see—"

"We're really going through with this?"

"Yes."

"Why don't you invite Ted, while you're at it?"

"I already did." Enid turned and gave her sister a smile. "Feel better?"

"Nuh," Marjory said noncommittally, and rummaged through another bin. "What about underwear? Should you buy him some underwear? He probably doesn't have any. I don't like the thought of sitting down to the table Sunday knowing Mr. Horsfall doesn't have underwear on. That totally kills my appetite. What's large for a man?"

"Thirty-six or thirty-eight," Enid said promptly.

"Is that what Ted wears?"

"No, he—" Enid paused, then smiled again, a shade thinly. Marjory shut up. Enid did have a bad side, and the penalty for getting on Enid's bad side was about a week in Coventry. It was very difficult for Marjory to live a week in the house without having Enid to talk to. So they were having a guest for Sunday dinner, and she'd lay out a delicious spread and try not to spoil Enid's good-works project.

Enid selected a pair of dark blue Dacron trousers, and held them up. "I can hem these."

"We'd better get going."

"He'll need a belt."

Marjory followed her to the belt rack. "Does he have a family?"

"Not that anyone knows of."

"How long has he been at Cumberland State?"

"Maybe sixty years. There aren't any records."

Marjory was stunned. "Sixty years? How old is he?"

"He might be seventy. But—"

"There aren't any records." Marjory shook her head. "That's unbelievable! If he's not any trouble, then why have they kept him so long?"

"Well, it's just one of those things. They kind of lost track of Mr. Horsfall." Enid chose a fabric belt. "This goes good with the blue. Okay, that's all. Unless you want to shop for a bra?"

"I'll do it Saturday. What if he tries to hang himself with that belt?"

"Will you stop? You are so *morbid*. Mr. Horsfall is not suicidal. Probably he shouldn't be in Cumberland State at all. But after so much time, they just don't know what to do with him. And they can't release him. He's not capable of supporting himself. What we need badly in Nashville is a halfway house for people like Mr. Horsfall. But try to get the politicians to realize that."

They each had a cherry Coke from the pizza place

next to Zayre's, and Marjory took the Interstate around downtown Nashville.

"Did they find out what caused the fire at the KA house?" she asked her sister.

"Probably it was somebody careless with a cigarette. There was a lot more smoke than fire, actually."

"It was on the news last night. All those Greeks lying around on the lawn in their formals and tuxes, it looked as if they died from overdressing."

"They just moved the party outdoors, that's all."

"I heard Pete Dunleavy jumped out of a third-story window."

"He does that when it's not on fire."

"Hey, Enid, does he still call you?"

"Oh, sure."

"His daddy's the third-largest poultry processor in the Southeast."

"That's a lot of feathers."

"That's a lot of chickenshit, but who cares? They're rolling in it."

"Chicken do-do?"

"No, money."

"Marjory, I don't know where your avid interest in money comes from, I swear I don't."

"It comes from never having any."

"Tell the truth, now, wouldn't you be just a little disappointed in me if I went out with somebody like Pete Dunleavy?"

"No."

"Well, I don't think I could be comfortable socializing with a boy who had his whatzit tattooed."

"You mean his ding-dong? His tallywhacker? Merciful heavens! Just call it a dick."

"I don't enjoy being vulgar."

"Do you suppose he really did? Have it tattooed?"

"I'm sure *I* can't verify the truth of that. But I know someone who probably can."

"The Swedish girl who always has a gorgeous tan, even in the middle of winter?"

"I forgot about her," Enid said thoughtfully.

"Lord, can she wear clothes! Or not wear them, as the case may be."

"You are being *catty*. How did this get started, anyway?"

"We were sort of on the subject of being impoverished, and what a few plucked chickens can do for the checkbook."

Enid shook her head slightly as if she needed to clear it and leaned forward to fiddle with the buttons on the radio, which buzzed a lot while occasionally providing soothing moments of music.

Marjory glanced at Enid, but held her tongue about favorite subjects—the frustrated lawsuits, the poor advice they'd received from lawyers following the death of their parents. They hadn't been paid a red cent in compensation by the railroad or the county for this tragedy; only a meager Social Security check each month had sustained them, along with what Enid earned as a part-time supermarket checker and the cash from Marjory's two jobs. She worked three days a week as a mother's helper, and on Tuesdays and Thursdays she fixed lunch for a group of shut-ins at the Sublimity Trailer Park, then read to them for an hour. Relatives had always been generous with the bounty from their summer gardens, hen houses, and fishing trips, so it wasn't as if they'd ever starve to death; but an injustice had been done to them.

As far as Marjory was concerned, there was only Right or Wrong: she did not recognize gray areas, such as the vast earthly limbo created by bureaucrats. She hadn't made up her mind yet whether she would become a lawyer for the downtrodden, someone with real guts like William Kunstler, or a crusading journalist, but the day would dawn when no one would *dare* to give Marjory Waller the runaround.

They were across the river and in Caskey County, a few minutes from home, when Marjory looked up and saw a flashing red light in the rearview mirror.

"Hey, Enid, it's Deputy Dawg."

The sheriff's car pulled even with them and Ted Lufford honked.

"Make it short, Enid, okay?" Marjory said, and she pulled off the road.

Ted Lufford got out of his patrol car and walked back to Enid's side of the Plymouth. He was tall and almost hipless and sauntered beautifully, not cocky but cool, like John Wayne before he got older and put on a paunch. Ted was going to get one, eventually: he liked his beer too much. He was a 180 bowler and went bird shooting a lot. Other than that there wasn't much to say about Ted Lufford, except that he owned the distinction of being the only deputy sheriff in Caskey County who didn't have a relative doing time somewhere.

He leaned on the Plymouth and looked in at them. "What d'you say, Marjory? Hi, Nuggins."

Marjory didn't know where the pet name had come from and was reluctant to ask Enid. Bad enough they were at the pet-name stage, but then by Marjory's reckoning they'd been sleeping together for at least a month. Not Enid's first affair, Marjory was sure, but probably no more than her third since mama and Daddy Lee had died. Before that Enid wouldn't even kiss a boy at a High Creek Baptist Church weekend retreat. In the midst of her chaste life a minor demon had popped up, like a pimple on the chin of the Madonna.

"Hi, Ted."

Marjory said, "The body's in the trunk, Awfuhsur. I don't know what come over me. I just couldn't rightly stand it, night after night for thutty-seven years, settin' across the table from the Mister while he gummed his pork chops and dribbled them crumbs all over my nice clean oilcloth."

"Don't mind her," Enid said with a grin, "she's morbid today."

"I think the old ladies are getting to you, Marj."

"They have some *very* interesting stories to tell."

"Going to the Peace March this weekend?"

"My ride fell through."

"What she means is," Enid said, "I put my foot down."

Ted Lufford turned his attention to Enid, who was waiting wide-eyed for a quick kiss. Marjory tapped her fingers on the steering wheel and tuned them out while they negotiated conflicts in their schedules for the next week or so. Then Ted straightened and popped his chewing gum, which Marjory always found endearing. The radio in the patrol car was squawking something urgent.

"See you Sunday, Marj. 'Bye, Nuggins." He jogged back to the patrol car with one hand on his holster and screeched away in a gravel-spitting U-turn, siren pitched high.

Marjory said, "The cops must think all the bad guys are stone-deaf."

"Probably just a traffic accident, it's that time of day."

"Yeh, let's go home, I'm starving."

But when they pulled up beside the frame house on Old Forge Road, Enid rubbed her forehead and said, "I need to lie down until about five-thirty, Marjory. Can we eat then?"

"Are you okay?"

"I think I'm getting my friend."

"Your *what*? It's not a *friend*. Why don't you call it what it is? It's cramps and gas pains and sore breasts and bleeding like a faucet and raunchy, yucky tampons and every boy in school smirking because they just *know* when you've got it, like male dogs know about bitches. What did we ever do to God that he has to put us through *that* once a month?"

"Don't blame God. It was Eve. I think."

"I wonder how many other mistakes she made that we're supposed to pay for?"

"I don't know," Enid said wanly. "They never taught us much about Eve in Sunday school, did they? Well, I'm going upstairs and put a cold cloth on my head for half an hour."

"I'll call you when supper's on the table."

"Thanks, Marjory."

4

The phone was ringing; Marjory grabbed it in the kitchen. The caller was her great-aunt Willie Lloyd, who lived a few miles away in McHenry's Ford. Aunt Willie Lloyd telephoned frequently to assure herself that the girls hadn't been murdered in their beds by "tramps from the highway," as she put it. A widow, she was alone in her own eight-room house, and had often urged the girls to move in with her. Marjory had never cottoned to the idea, because Aunt Willie Lloyd was a nonstop talker and not much of a housekeeper: chickens wandered in and out of her house through gaps in the screen doors.

Marjory patiently refused an offer of two pecks of tomatoes, allowed that they could use a couple of jars of blackberry preserves, promised to run up to McHenry's Ford before Saturday, and extricated herself from the telephone after nearly ten minutes of "uh-huhs" and "yes, ma'am's". She went out on the back porch for a breath of air, but there wasn't a breeze yet. The trees in the deep backyard were motionless. She fed two of the cats, Zombie and Tom-Tom, emptied the laundry hamper and started a wash. The old wringer Maytag was sounding worse than ever; another month and they would need a replacement. But they had forty-five dollars in their joint savings account.

She wandered outside, uncomfortable from the prickly heat that had popped out on her behind during the drive from Nashville. Ted Lufford had kept the grass mowed all summer, but the rest of the property, three and a half acres, looked shabby. Her mother's garden plot had been overgrown for four years, and so had the scuppernong arbor. The padlock on her father's shop had not been disturbed since shortly after his death; it was thick with rust. Daddy Lee had been the neighborhood fix-it man, one of those jackleg geniuses who could repair any kind of machinery. So he'd always had plenty of work (it was amazing how many people would pay three or four dollars once in a while to keep a ten-dollar toaster alive); enough money for his family and for his abiding passion, the swapping, training, and showing of Tennessee walking horses. Daddy Lee's stable was empty now, so forbiddingly empty Marjory couldn't bring herself to walk inside. Even while he was alive Marjory had avoided his horses; they were dumber than dirt, in her opinion, with bad dispositions to boot. But she was always so proud of her daddy when he was showing the three-gaited animals: Lord, he was a handsome man in the saddle!

She'd loved him most, however, because he understood her own passion, for baseball, applauded her skills, and never said a discouraging word about her body. Standing still, Marjory was tall but with big shoulders; she looked top-heavy, awkward, physically incompetent. Babe Ruth hadn't looked like much, either. Marjory could throw hard with either hand. She had kept four balls in the air the first time she attempted juggling, had hit her first golf ball 150 yards, straight and true. She was a self-taught swimmer with phenomenal endurance. When she ran (one step, and she was at top speed), Marjory achieved a fluidity and grace that seemed aerodynamically impossible, given the contours of her body.

Marjory picked up an old baseball with unraveling seams that had been kicked aside by Ted's Toro and threw it high, then turned and caught it deftly behind her back. This small amount of exertion caused her to break out in a sweat again; her blouse was sticking to the small of her back. She sought relief by stretching out in the macramé hammock in the eight-sided gazebo, but there was no position that was comfortable because of her prickly heat. She heard a diesel horn on the L and N line three quarters of a mile away, and today for no good reason the sound of a train gave her a run of the shudders.

She still found it difficult to believe that the fix-it man, the master of machines, had stalled his car in front of an oncoming freight train. Most of their friends and relatives agreed that it must have been a heart attack or stroke, freezing Daddy Lee to the steering wheel for those ten crucial seconds. But there was no comfort for Marjory in this assumption. Her parents were gone, a wrenching lesson in the black ironies, the implacable treachery of life. Maybe, after all, Enid was the smart one for craving safety and security. Maybe she ought to marry Ted, who would move in with them and slowly fix up the place until it was the way it used to be, and Enid would have babies and Marjory would take care of them for her while Enid worked for that steady paycheck at Curtis Sewell and Wainwright, and they wouldn't have anything to be afraid of, ever.

But there was a potential irony in this scheme, like a worm in an apparently healthy apple, that disturbed Marjory: she and Ted got along okay now, but once he was married to Enid he could well have a change of heart, suddenly not like Marjory and find fault and want to get rid of her. Would Enid stick up for her? Marjory

wondered. She really got on her sister's nerves sometimes, and she knew it.

The thought of a disloyal Enid, along with the prickly
heat, was more than Marjory could stand. She barreled
into the house and upstairs to the bathroom, pulled
down her shorts and panties and liberally applied med-
icated baby powder to the affected areas. The shower
head was dripping, there were stockings draped over
the shower rod, blue toothpaste in the cracked porcelain
sink, a half-empty disposable douche bottle on the
floor—they were both indifferent housekeepers, hadn't
the time for it, really, but company was coming on Sunday, and Marjory knew who was going to be stuck with
most of the chores when it wasn't her idea at all . . .
she went down the hall, knocked rudely on Enid's door,
and was sulking at the kitchen table when Enid came
downstairs looking refreshed.

"This looks delicious, hon."

"Does it?"

"Is that all you're having? A glass of milk?"

"Yeh."

"Oh. I thought you might be on a—"

"If you think I need to lose a few pounds, just come
out and *say* it, Enid!"

"Well, that's not what I—awfully touchy, Marj."

"Is it my fault I got daddy's build, and you—you got
all the best genes in the family?"

"I wouldn't say that. You're so beautifully coordi-
nated, and I can't play croquet without hitting myself
in the ankle with the mallet."

"Who cares about that? Do you think Ted cares because you can't play croquet? That is not what turns
him on."

Enid helped herself to green tomato pie, and sprinkled grated Parmesan cheese on top.

"Everybody agrees that you have the most beautiful
eyes in the family, going all the way back to Great-
grandmother Emmie Jones Clawson, and your com-

plexion—look at me, I just get all sort of muddy-looking around my eyes this time of the month. But I put up with it, Marjory. We all have to put up with things we don't like about ourselves.''

''Why are you trying to make me feel better when I don't want to feel better?''

Enid reached for the snapbean casserole, and smiled. ''Because I love you.''

Marjory sat with lowered head, picking at a wart. ''If I walked out of the house tonight and never came back . . . would you miss me?''

''Miss you? Marjory, I would die. Literally die.''

''Oh,'' Marjory said, and wiped her nose on a napkin.

''Now tell me, what's got you this way?''

''I don't know. I forgot to mention, Aunt Willie Lloyd called.''

''Poor old soul. How is she?''

''Well, she sent twenty dollars to that radio preacher in Del Rio, Texas, for a prayer shawl. She was supposed to wear the shawl and place both hands on the radio while he was sending out his healing message over the air. But she must have been allergic to the dye in the prayer shawl, because her eyes swelled shut for two days. She still has water on the knees. Why don't you pass me the casserole, maybe I'll have a couple of bites after all.''

5

Enid dropped Marjory at the Baptist church before going on to work at Kroger's on the Falling Spring Pike.

There was a Youth League game in progress on the diamond behind the Sunday school building. Some of her own teammates and a few of the Presbyterian girls, in orange and white jerseys, were there already, pitching softballs around while waiting for their game to start.

Marjory, carrying her glove and a favorite bat, walked toward a group that centered around Rita Sue Marcum. Wherever she went, Rita Sue had a natural attractive power. She sweetly sparkled and teased without much substance, like ice-cold Seven-Up. But when her effervescence failed, her personality could become sticky and cloying. Thanks to sturdy Norwegian genes on her mother's side, Rita Sue was bona fide platinum. She had begun to make up her Nordic blue eyes too extravagantly, Marjory thought, since her father had come into a substantial inheritance and the family, upgrading everything including their religion, broke with the Baptists to join the Presbyterian church. In Caskey County this defection caused as much shocked comment as if the Pope had suddenly renounced Rome to become a Talmudic scholar.

Rita Sue's latest acquisition, other than a new tomatored Fairlane convertible, was Boyce Bledsoe, whom Marjory had mooned over briefly in seventh grade before settling down to her long-lasting crush on the unobtainable Tim McCarver. Boyce was a thoroughly freckled boy with hair the color of a plaster flamingo. He played quarterback on the high school football team, grinned a lot, and had little to say, which made him a good match for Rita Sue, who had everything to say.

Marjory stabbed smoothly at a softball rolling toward her and pegged it back to Boyce, who was half turned away from her and only managed, because his reflexes were as good as hers, to keep from being nailed in the ribs. But he dropped the ball.

"Uh-oh, bad hands!" Marjory called.

Rita Sue turned and shaded her eyes: the sun was

low behind Marjory's back. She smiled. She had an intensely white smile.

"Is that you, Marjory? I thought somebody put a T-shirt on Boyce's Volkswagen."

"Hi, Rita Suuuue! Remember when I turned your bedroom into an ant farm? Wait'll you see what it looks like when you get back from majorette camp."

Rita Sue indicated the weakness of this riposte with a little swish of her hand past her left ear and a wide, indifferent smile. Marjory dug in and swung a little harder. "How come you've got all that gooey makeup on? We're playing ball tonight, not doing *Titus Andronicus.*"

Missed again. Over her head, actually: Rita Sue probably thought *Andronicus* was a bad chest cold. The three of them unconsciously closed ranks against the hangers-on. Rita Sue perched a slim tanned hand on Marjory's shoulder. As usual her frosted-pink nails looked flawless. Marjory chewed her own nails, to the quick.

"Honeybunch, you know I'm on the teen fashion board at Creekmuir's; we had our Fall Preview show today."

"Darn, I went and missed it."

"They just have so many cute new things in the store! You ought to drop by tomorrow—" Rita Sue frowned delicately, veiled in thought. In the late solar glow her bouffant hairdo looked incandescent. "I believe I did see *something* in your size."

"I don't look good in cute," Marjory said, wished she hadn't as she recognized the gleam of a comeback in Rita Sue's eyes, and was saved when Boyce nudged her.

"What are you doing Sunday, Marjory?" Rita Sue punched him lightly on one of his marvelous biceps for interrupting.

"Sweet of you to ask, Boyce. Sunday? Well, I—"

"My cousin Duane's coming up from Franklin to

stay with us while his folks are in New Orleans for the Shriners' convention.''

"Duane who?''

"Eggleston. He said he wanted to get together with you, so—''

"Get together?'' Rita Sue rocked back and chortled at her expression, which only added to Marjory's confusion. "Does he know me?'' She was studying Rita Sue's face closely, aware that this might be the start of something elaborate, and nasty, on her part. "Do I know *him* from somewhere?''

"Two years ago, at Retreat,'' Rita Sue said. "He was the kid who was so busy collecting butterflies.''

"The lepidopterist?'' Marjory said, horrified.

"No, *butterflies*.''

"Oh, hold it, Rita Sue,'' Marjory said, and looked at Boyce. "*Him?* He's only about four and a half feet tall! How old is he, twelve?''

"Duane just turned sixteen. He's grown a lot. You wouldn't recognize him. Anyway—''

"Boyce, really, I'm sorry, but Sunday—we're having company. Some—ah—friend of my sister's, and Ted Lufford's coming, too. I have to make dinner.''

"Oh. That's okay. Duane's gonna be here for two weeks, until school starts again.''

"Fine. We'll all get together. Hey, it looks like the Little Leaguers are through, what d'you say we go warm up.''

Rita Sue stepped in next to Boyce, urgently linking pinky fingers and, worshipfully, wagging her tail a little. She'd always been a tease-toucher, coming on, then backing away with the grace of a fencing master. Marjory figured she must have poor Boyce half nuts by now. His Barney Rubble haircut seemed to be standing up a little stiffer, and that probably wasn't the only stiffness he was experiencing.

Rita Sue scampered to fall in beside Marjory on the way to the diamond.

"Could I talk to you seriously about something, Marjory?"

Marjory staggered back a step, a hand clasped over her heart. But the apparent ruthlessness of their vendetta disguised a telemagical empathy. The girls had grown up very near each other on Old Forge Road, until Rita Sue's father removed the family to a gentleman's farm a few miles from Sublimity. This change in Rita Sue's status hadn't altered or done in the relationship: an ongoing cutting contest suited their competitive natures.

"Mama pitched one of her *fits* and said I better bring this up to you personally," Rita Sue said in a low voice, looking around for eavesdroppers.

"Algebra or Biology?"

"Both. Because you know what'll happen if I don't—"

"Say no more. I'll tutor you."

Rita Sue glanced at her with a hint of suspicion. She'd been prepared for some wheeling and dealing, but Marjory shrugged guilelessly; no, there was nothing she wanted in return. Somebody needed to pitch in and help the long-suffering girl, otherwise Rita Sue was not going to make it out of high school with anything better than an equivalency diploma. Which would spell the end of her ambition to pledge Tri-Delt at the University of Tennessee.

"Well—I do appreciate it, Marjory."

Bursting with good feeling, Marjory took a deep breath, let it out, straightened her face, and said, "How about if I hold your hand when you go pottie, too?"

Rita Sue paused, kneeling in the dust along the partly obliterated third-base line and retied a sneaker with such vehemence she popped the lace. She was smiling her wide, dazzling, vacant smile.

"Honestly," she said, "there are days when I'd just like to feed you to the polecats."

6

Sunday after church Enid Waller drove down to Cumberland State Hospital while Marjory stayed behind to prepare dinner.

With the chicken in the oven and the salad in a covered bowl in the refrigerator, she made a tour of the house, giving a lick here and there with the featherduster, straightening the sturdy old mahogany furniture and repinning the yellowed lace antimacassars on the chairs in the parlor. She had the nervous flits, as her mother used to say. The guest towels, taken from the cedar closet in the hall, looked odd in the newly scrubbed bathroom (Enid had been up until three in the morning cleaning). They used them so seldom the towels seemed to belong to someone else's house. Back in the kitchen to baste the roasting hen, Marjory heard a car on the gravel at the side of the house. She took off her apron, gave a few tugs to her tight-fitting white piqué dress (it felt glued to her hips), and went outside by way of the back porch.

It was Ted in his Firebird. Marjory waved to him from the steps, simultaneously made a misstep, and caught the heel of her only pair of summer dress shoes in a crack. The heel broke before her ankle did but she went sprawling, with a yelp of indignation.

Marjory got up, red in the face, as Ted hastened from the Firebird to help her.

"Hurt yourself?"

"*No.* " She kicked off the shoe with the broken heel and balanced on one foot so as not to list. Some high clouds blocked the sun but the day was still a humid dazzler, and she already felt as if she had been spritzed with a garden hose.

Enid picked that moment to arrive with their other dinner guest.

"What happened?"

"Oh, I caught my heel and it snapped off."

"Looks like you've got a little grass smudge on your dress."

"I'll bleach it out."

"I've probably got a pair of shoes you can squeeze into; poke around in my closet."

Marjory took the other shoe off, and looked into the eyes of Arne Horsfall, who was standing a couple of feet behind Enid with a sketchbook under one arm.

He was a lot bigger than she'd assumed he would be. Even with a pronounced stoop he was half a head taller than Ted, who went six one and a half. There was more tangly white hair growing out of Arne's ears than he had on his skull. His features had retreated to the bone; where there was flesh it was deeply scored. He was thin, nearly gaunt. He did not give the impression of being frail but he had a strange, hung-together look, as if he had been composed from the ill-matched bones of others. The new clothes Enid had bought him fitted okay, but they didn't suit him. He might have looked better dressed all in black. He was so quiet and somber he seemed barely alive.

Marjory had become accustomed, in her brief tour of Cumberland State, to inmates who were quenched and passionless, and others with clownish, synthetic personalities, all side effects of psychoactive drugs as powerful as rocket fuel. Arne Horsfall was a different case. He looked like a migraine felt, but he had the power to hold her attention. She had a sensation of excitement, of discovery—someone lived there, all right, behind the small, dark eyes. He was distant, but not subdued in some dire, brainwashed manner. It was as if he had learned long ago to turn most people away with the rigid cast of his face, a bloodless indifference. The better to study them, as he now studied her.

"Marjory, Ted—I'd like for you to meet Mr. Horsfall, one of my very talented students."

Ted reached around Enid with his right hand. Arne Horsfall looked at it noncommittally for several seconds, as if no one had offered to shake his hand before. Then he took it, gingerly, with a glance at Ted but no change of expression. Marjory kept her distance and smiled, with a little flickering wave of welcome; she just couldn't bring herself to touch him, that long yellow hand with brown spots like motor-oil stains, and gruesome black veins.

After eyeing Ted, Arne Horsfall looked, long and searchingly, at the house. The sun came out and his eyes narrowed, he hunched his shoulders as if he found so much light punishing.

"Well, why don't we all go inside?" Enid suggested. "It was a long drive, and I'm sure Mr. Horsfall is perishing for a drink of something sweet and cold—"

Marjory observed that whenever Enid spoke, Arne Horsfall gave her his full attention, listening as if to an oracle, a saint of his realm—Marjory could have died, but, abruptly, she had a change of heart and thought, *What of it?* He was a man, after all, and any man no matter how aged who didn't fall in love with Enid after spending a little time with her was, well, out of his mind. Reassured by that revelation of humanness, she began to feel a little better about Arne Horsfall, not so unhappy to have him around.

Enid slipped an arm gracefully inside Mr. Horsfall's and Ted smiled as if he were really looking forward to an afternoon of talking hunting and fishing with their guest. They all went into the house by the front door.

In the kitchen Marjory looked again at the golden hen in the oven, then set out a pitcher of lemonade and glasses on the heirloom silver tray they had been tempted to sell when funds were critically low. But selling the few handed-down treasures her mother had loved seemed a betrayal. Ada May Waller had never been one to put on airs, but she was a genealogy buff who knew intimately every sprig of a family tree that included persons of quality in Scotland and England. Enid had her mother's inbred sense of style and propriety. Marjory sometimes joked about herself that she looked like the family cleric who had been fond of charbroiling heretics; but the joke could be painful.

She carried the tray with the lemonade into the parlor, where daylong light filtered through the oak tree that, like a big green cumulus cloud, sheltered nearly the full front of their clapboard house.

Arne Horsfall, still clutching his sketchbook under one arm, was touring the walls of the parlor, where many portraits and photographs of forebears—men and women anciently composed in too much clothing and with their hair parted down the middle—had been hanging since before Enid was born. He seemed momentarily fascinated by a stuffed red squirrel, up on its hind legs and with forepaws spread in a menacing way, as if it had grizzly genes. Marjory reckoned that it might become tedious talking to a man who couldn't respond, although Enid didn't seem fazed. She could talk on and on about things that would bore most people to tears, yet Enid was never boring because her voice, her natural cadences, were so pleasing that words didn't matter. Ted watched her as if he truly appreciated how lucky he was.

Marjory placed the tray on a table in front of one of the rigorously uncomfortable horsehair sofas and poured lemonade.

"Anything interesting happening in your life?"

Ted replied in a low voice, "Well, I was shot at last night."

"What? You're kidding!" Thrilled and apprehensive,

Marjory inspected him quickly for damage. Ted shrugged. "They missed, huh? What happened?"

"Oh, it was about nine o'clock over on Deacon's Mill Road. A car was in the ditch and the wrecker was there. Traffic was moving okay. I never heard the shot, but it busted one of my reds to smithereens. I was standing a couple of feet away. Couldn't identify where the shot came from, or who fired it. Probably some yahoo in a pickup who got a speeding ticket last week, and wanted to take it out on me."

"That must have given you the runs."

Ted shrugged again, a little proud of his grit under fire. "Nah. Those things happen. Listen, maybe you better not say anything to Enid—you know how she is."

"Hey, *Enid,* have I got news for you!"

Enid turned, smiling. "What?"

Ted said quickly, "Thought you all might like to catch Bob Dylan at the Parthenon next weekend."

"Wonderful."

Marjory handed up two glasses of lemonade. Ted sat back on the sofa, looking painfully amused. "Anything else I can do, Marjory?"

Marjory, wide-eyed, shook her head. "Oh, no, Ted. Bob Dylan sounds terrific. And it's so thoughtful to invite *me.* I just never seem to go anywhere lately."

Arne Horsfall sat on the edge of a Queen Anne chair with his sketchbook in his lap. He sipped lemonade and, for the most part, looked at Enid. The ceiling fan shuddered annoyingly but kept them cool. Ted commented, as he usually did, "I need to fix that thing the next time I'm over." Enid talked about the art class she conducted at Cumberland State, and the surprising number of her students who were doing original and interesting work. Presently Arne Horsfall's eyes closed and he appeared to fall asleep sitting up in the chair.

"Poor man," Enid murmured. She got up to gently remove the lemonade glass from his hand. His nearly

lashless eyelids fluttered, then his head tilted forward
another inch and they heard him snore. "But I think
he's doing real well. You know, he hasn't been *anywhere* in donkey's years. I could just tell he was terrified in the car, all those huge trucks thundering past on
the Interstate. He never shut his eyes once, though; he
was so busy taking everything in. That tires out your
brain if you're not accustomed to it."

"Enid, I think the chicken's about done. Should we
wake him up?"

Arne Horsfall woke himself up, with a rasping snore
that caused his eyes to open and his head to jerk sideways. Ted started off the sofa to keep their guest from
toppling out of his chair. But Arne righted himself, then
looked around uncomprehendingly, the wispy white hair
clinging to the back of his head stirred by the fan pad-
dles over them. He needed to clear his throat, which he
did but with great difficulty. Marjory tried to dig her
fingers into the hard, slick horsehair. Then, as if he
were attracted by the cooking odors, Arne rose in the
manner of stiff, old men—lurching half erect, then
pausing, suspensefully, before lurching all the way up—
and made his way back to the sunny kitchen. Enid, then
Marjory followed.

After looking around in his rapt, obsessive manner,
he moved circuitously to the screen door where he
stared out at the backyard and the heat haze over the
glum green surface of Crudup's pond, blinking, his
eyes watering. Finally he turned to Enid as Marjory
opened the oven door and brought out the roasted
chicken. He began, using his hands, to silently con-
verse with Enid, gesturing to the stove, tapping the
side of his head with a long finger, always in motion
like a symphony conductor hearing ghostly music, ca-
joling invisible instruments.

"Stove . . . this kitchen . . ." Arne nodded vigor-
ously, and Marjory wondered how his skinny neck could
stand the strain. "Reminds you . . . of where you used

to live, do I have that right?'' Arne nodded again, also tapping his foot in an excess of nervous release. "How long ago was that, Mr. Horsfall?'' He put his hand, palm down, near his waist. Enid frowned, trying to interpret the message. "Oh! When you were a boy? I see. Where? Do you remember?'' Arne shook his head this time, but gazed out again through the screen, extending a hand from the level of his brow. Marjory thought of Cochise in the movies, communicating sternly with the white-eyes. Maybe Arne Horsfall had seen the same westerns she had. It was almost funny; but the way his lips worked, and the small amount of drool he was producing in his efforts to get them to understand, didn't impress her as amusing at all—she was a little sick to her stomach.

"Were you raised on a farm?'' Enid hazarded, "like Crudup's farm over there?'' Arne now clasped his hands together, nodding, nodding, his sign language failing to keep pace with his thoughts, his memories. He made a steeple with his index fingers. "Church? Uh . . . your father was a preacher?'' Arne shook his head. He glanced at the pots and pans hanging on racks beside the stove, took one down, ran his fingers over the copper bottom, made the sign of the steeple again. "The church you attended had a copper steeple?'' Enid interpreted, her face pinked from excitement. Yes. She turned to Ted, who was standing behind her in the doorway idly swishing ice cubes in an inch of lemonade.

"Didn't our old sanctuary have a copper-covered spire?''

"Yeh . . . I think so. But it burned down, shoot, that was before I was a gleam in daddy's eye. Back about nineteen forty, forty-one.''

"You were born in Sublimity!'' Enid said to Arne Horsfall.

He shook off that conclusion, then spread his hands, turning toward the screen door as he did so.

"But *near* here. Across the river? The Cumberland

or the—Harpeth!—River . . . well! How about that?
And your father was a farmer. Your mother—''

Arne made a sudden move toward Marjory, who
looked up, startled, and shied away as he touched the
bob of her hair, blunt-cut like a paintbrush.

''Your mother had blond hair like Marjory's and she
was . . . tall, is that correct? We're getting to know
quite a bit about you now, aren't we? Did you have
brothers and sisters? Oh, you didn't. I wonder what else
you have to tell us, this is *so* interesting—''

''Enid, I think I'd better carve the chicken.''

''I'll do that for you, Marjory,'' Ted offered.

''Thanks. I just need to go up to my room for a
minute; be right back, why don't you put everything on
the table.''

Shoeless, Marjory hustled up the stairs in her stockings and closed the bathroom door. She splashed cold
water in her face (it came from their own deep artesian
well and was always bitingly cold, even at the height of
summer), which got rid of the nausea that had suddenly
come over her, but she was still a little shocked and
chilled at the heart because of the way Arne Horsfall
had lunged at her. Maybe Enid thought he was okay
because he could draw, a harmless old cuckoo at worst;
but Marjory had her own opinion: solid instinct told her
something was dangerously not right—more than memories were dammed up in Arne Horsfall, there was some
dreadful passion that might come bursting forth at any
time. She didn't want to be around when it happened.

Marjory decided to take off her panty girdle because
she knew how uncomfortable she was going to be while
sitting down and trying to eat, although at this point
she had no appetite—smelling the plump roaster sim-
mering with onions, carrots, and celery in fatty juices
had contributed, along with tension and the heat of the
kitchen, to her nausea. She needed to remove her dress
to get shed of the onerous girdle. When she put the
dress back on it was damp in several places, and so

tight it was a good bet to tear if she didn't carefully
consider every move she made. Tears filled the corners
of her eyes and dribbled hotly down beside her nose;
her chin trembled as she heard Enid calling from the
foot of the stairs. With a washcloth she mopped her
face (in the bleary scheme of the bathroom mirror such
a ringer for her father's broad, likable, slightly fishy
face, eyes an almost incandescent, illimitable blue) until her chin was steadier. Then she went slowly down
to the dining room, still without shoes, and, with wide
bars of shadow from the stair railing across her white
dress, looking like a canceled bride.

Arne Horsfall had calmed down and was contem-
plating the slices of steaming chicken breast Enid loaded
on his plate. But he glanced at Marjory as she took her
place at the table and she felt the turmoil beginning
again, like a bad gas pain below her heart. It was as if
he sensed her fear and dislike of him, which somehow
focused everything that was dark and unsettled in his
personality on her. Ted had had experiences with all
kinds of weirdos (of which Caskey County could claim
more than its share); why couldn't he see that all of
Arne's dogs weren't barking? But Ted was heaping
squash with sweet peppers and au gratin potatoes on
his own plate and chatting amiably about the good fishing to be found up around Paris Landing. Marjory settled into a dismal silence and, during the blessing that
Enid asked, prayed contrapuntally that the day would
come to an end without incident; she prayed Arne Horsfall would be returned to Cumberland State before the
sun set on him. The silence she enforced on herself
soon made her giddy, and she had fits of laughter about
nothing much while trying desperately to avoid everyone's eyes. Enid studied her with a rocky forbearance
and redoubled her efforts to make Arne Horsfall feel
like one of their little family.

7

"Are you coming down with something, Marjory?" Enid asked her in the kitchen while they were doing the dishes. Ted had taken fishing tackle from the trunk of his car and gone down to the torpid green pond with Arne to see if any bream were biting in the afternoon heat.

"Now that you mention it, I guess not."

"You outdid yourself at the table. I mean, you haven't carried on like that since you were four years old. I was embarrassed for you."

"I'm sorry," Marjory said grimly, and mishandled a plate Enid gave to her dripping from the rinse water. She caught it before it hit the floor.

"Careful."

Marjory sucked a breath and said, as if she'd been accused of going to the devil, "It was your fault; I never have broken a piece of mama's best china, and I never will!"

"Oh, Marjory, *hush*, what is it with you today?"

"Him," Marjory said, doing a quick, overly frenzied impression of Arne Horsfall's sign language.

"I cannot *believe* you. Don't you have compassion for anyone but your own selfish person?"

"That's not fair!"

"Of course he acted nervous—to begin with. Don't you understand what a day like this means to him? To be accepted in our home, treated with kindness, afforded his dignity? That's the first thing they take away from you in an institution, Marjory, your dignity. And without it—do you see what I'm saying?''

''Yeh,'' Marjory mumbled. ''When's he going back?''

''Tomorrow.''

''Oh, Enid, you don't mean—''

''Yes, I do mean, he's staying the night, I've already arranged with—''

''Enidddd,'' Marjory moaned, ''that's the dumbest—''

''Marjory Waller, shut up!'' Enid said, in a tone of voice that Marjory hadn't heard for nearly two years. Marjory stared at her for several taut seconds, then turned and put the plate she'd been drying on the table, turned again and stalked out of the kitchen.

''You'd better,'' Enid called after her, a little shrill from temper, ''just stay in your room until you get ready to act right again! And while you're at it''—She had reached the kitchen door, the better to make herself heard as Marjory hit the top of the stairs with a resounding thump and went down the hall so fast she was getting nylon burns from the carpet runner—''you might open your Bible and read—'' Marjory slammed the door on this suggestion hard enough to loosen a little more of the plaster next to the jamb and jumped on her bed, not thinking about how careful she needed to be in her piqué dress. It opened at the seams like a dropped sack of flour.

Marjory clubbed her fists into a pillow, expelling a few feathers that floated lazily in the hot slant of sun through open windows. Then she lay, rigidly, for a few minutes in a deepening bath of perspiration, studying the cracks in her ceiling, the shadowy shapes of expired insects in the milk glass of the lighting fixture. She heard Ted's voice from the pond. She felt awful, too wretched to cry. Not wrong, exactly, but guilty because she knew she ought to be outgrowing tantrums by now. After a while she got up and stripped soggily, blotted her breasts and shoulders with a corner of the nubby chenille bedspread, then pulled on shorts and a Grateful Dead T-shirt of a faded blue still dark enough to disguise the absence of a bra. She switched on the fan, which began swiveling its ugly old black head like a creature in a Godzilla movie, and fiddled with the antenna of the black-and-white TV set on the shelf of her armoire. There wasn't much to see this time of the afternoon but a gospel quartet—all of them wearing baggy silk suits and pompadours with bushy sideburns, none whom she would call cute—and *The American Sportsman,* with Curt Gowdy. Stalking bighorn sheep in Alaska was low on the list of things she hoped to do someday, ranking just ahead of communal farming in British Honduras, and autopsies.

Marjory returned her attention to the backyard. Enid had (unselfishly) finished doing the dishes and was strolling to the gazebo, accompanied by several cats, theirs and the neighbors'. She had a sketchpad and a box of colored pencils with her. Marjory yawned. A nap began to seem like a good idea. Then she could stay up all night with the lights on and her door locked, and she didn't care what Enid might think. The guest room where Arne Horsfall would be laying his head was right next to hers, while Enid was safely down the hall. Marjory tried to find enough nail on the pinkie of her left hand to nibble. Over by the pond Ted was teaching Arne Horsfall the technique of fly casting. She turned away from the glare of the windows, crept facedown onto her bed, and took a pillow soothingly into her arms.

8

Marjory heard the train like a ghost in a well and saw, as she sat up in the back of their station wagon, the big, blunt yellow and blue diesel engine coming into view through the trees. The tailgate of the wagon was down, blurry asphalt unwinding behind them. She was apprehensive but not scared; Daddy Lee must have seen the train too, and he wasn't going to let anything happen to them: nothing bad ever happened to a Waller, they all just got very old and died of natural causes. Wizened fruit falling from the eternal family tree. But the wagon was getting closer to the intersection with the shining rails and the oncoming behemoth, its headlight flashing in broad daylight. *Daddy,* Marjory said, calmly and deliberately, *stop*. Then he turned his head and grinned back at her and she saw that it wasn't her daddy; Arne Horsfall was driving. *No brakes,* he said. Marjory began crawling toward the tailgate of the wagon. Behind them on the road Enid and Ted were bicycling, and they didn't seem to realize anything was wrong. They smiled and waved to Marjory. She tried to call to them, but couldn't utter a sound. Of course not, she'd forgotten she had been born dumb. Trouble and woe. Why had she let Arne Horsfall borrow the family wagon? Mama and daddy would never forgive her. *He* wasn't one of them. He didn't belong. But here he was, causing a peck of trouble after they'd gone out of their way to be nice. All Marjory wanted to do was to roll over the edge of the tailgate before the train hit them. But now, in addition to being voiceless, she couldn't move. Marjory lay on her back staring at the green woods flashing by, and she heard the train again, wild and dismal, she could smell the heat and oil and feel its power, but no thank you, she wasn't going to look—*God damn it—*

9

Marjory, lying on her back on her bed, heart pounding right through the mattress, heard the door of Ted's Firebird shutting and then, a few seconds later, the throaty engine turning over. She felt, for a few panicky moments, incapable of movement, as if she had willed a state of paralysis as a result of the nightmare.

No, I wasn't there.

She raised a hand lethargically to her damp face and swallowed several times as Ted backed around Enid's Corvair to the street. Probably he was working the six to two A.M. shift, Marjory thought. The sun had moved on, it was no longer shining directly into her room, and a whiff of breeze stirred the lace curtains framing the windows. Cicadas were loud in the locust tree that needed to be pruned back from the upper stories of the house; it dragged its branches across the roof and clapboards whenever the wind rose.

About four hours after the accident, with the house getting crowded, the kitchen table overloaded with all the food brought by the callers (Enid had been hospitalized for shock, but everybody apparently felt little Marj would be ravenous after hearing how mama and daddy had been snuffed out), she had sneaked away on her bike and gone over there to see for herself what it had been like. Carrying grief like weights around her wrists and ankles, a big lead collar enclosing her throat. Pedaling furiously down the narrow curving road, wind in her face redolent of summer woods and the muddy creek bottom, the light below her handlebars barely peeking into the dark. At the scene of the accident tall corn grew in a wedge-shaped plot hard by the railroad right-of-way, and only in late summer was the view of the tracks obscured on the north side of Doylestown Road. The road was blocked in both directions by the train. Red and yellow dome lights on official vehicles streaked the sides of well-traveled boxcars. Wabash. Santa Fe. Chesapeake and Ohio. There were a lot of men around, some with badges, and one, who smoked a cigar that was almost enough to make her sick, told Marjory to get lost.

Marjory just ignored him, and when he wasn't looking she walked along the tracks until she came to the pair of back-to-back diesels a hundred yards south of the crossing. One of the generators was humming on low power. The headlamp was attracting a monstrous swarm of the kinds of bugs you never saw except around intensely bright objects. She walked around to the front of the lead engine, which had a big sooty smudge on it. The odor in the sultry air wasn't only train. Something else, like a barbecue grill that badly needed cleaning.

The family station wagon wasn't there.

It was as if she had been told a fantastic lie. Staring up at the dazzling mirrored headlamp that shone down the right-of-way for more than a mile, Marjory knew they deserved a miracle and one had been forthcoming, her parents were still alive. That's when she began to tremble in a kind of ecstasy. The next thing she knew the diesel engines were throbbing with a reciprocal energy that jarred the roadbed and a man who worked for the L and N railroad had come over to lead her off the tracks. He wore an old felt hat like her daddy wore when he was working in his shop.

"Honey, are you here with somebody?"

"My name's M-Marjory Waller; do you know where my mama and d-daddy are?"

She didn't mind that he was holding her hand; he seemed like a nice man and she was still shaking, teeth chattering. The train began to move and Marjory backed away, stumbling over something metallic. She looked down at her feet and saw it: twisted, blackened, but unmistakably part of the grille of a sedan or station wagon. She looked at the man's face. He slowly removed his hat and got down on one knee in front of her, smiling heartbrokenly. Marjory studied the train going by and with its passing realized the diminishing of hope for the miracle; and she felt a bone-deep nostalgic regret, how she'd felt upon finding out, conclusively, that there was no Santa Claus. A big crazed bug flew away from the train and hit her in the forehead hard enough to stagger her. Marjory's eyes got a little bigger, but it seemed futile to cry. She hated the bug, and she hated God, but she could never get even with either of them.

10

All the bad feeling from her dream had pooled in the tender places of Marjory's psyche. She rose from her bed, went to the windows and looked out. Arne Horsfall had joined Enid in the gazebo, and both were sketching, Arne with secretive head movements and quick glances into thin air, as if he were soliciting inspiration. Marjory went downstairs to the kitchen and ate a peach. She was thinking about calling someone to pass the time of day when the telephone rang.

The prescient bump at the base of her spine tingled warmly; she knew it was going to be Rita Sue.

"Hi, what're you doing?" Marjory said. She spat out the well-gnawed peach pit, caught it with a bare foot, and balanced it on her big toe.

"Nothing. Brenda McClanahan came over to show off her engagement ring. I never saw a diamond that little, it's only about half as big as bugspit. Did you hear Boyce was cleaning out their garage with his daddy and dropped a big old crankcase on his foot?"

"Break any bones?"

"No, but he can barely hobble around and, you know, football practice starts in another week."

"He'll be ready. Want to play miniature golf?"

"I guess so." Rita Sue sighed, bored to distraction.

"Pick you up in ten minutes."

"Marjory, you know I'm not going to ride around in that old car of yours! I'm so allergic to it, it must have come off a nigger car lot." She sniffed emphatically. "Not that I want to hurt your feelings."

"You never hurt my feelings, Rita Sue, that's why I'm still talking to you." Marjory flipped the peach pit across the kitchen, missing the opening of the trash can, twenty feet away, by less than an inch. "Okay, pick *me* up in ten minutes, I probably should get Enid's permission to go out."

"How come?"

"We have company, remember? Wait till I tell you about *him*. But I was acting like a ring-tailed snot most of the afternoon, Enid'll be glad to get rid of me. Oh, can I have my Joplin records back?"

"Do I still have those? Maybe they're under the bed. I'll look for them."

In the gazebo Arne Horsfall was bent over his sketch-pad, hard at work. He drew almost desperately, hand twisted around the pencil as if it had wounded him.

Drawing a barn, or something; but it didn't resemble Crudup's barn across the pond. Marjory, resigned, had the unjustifiable feeling he was like a stray dog that had come to their back porch and was just going to stay on, lurking out of the way and making no fuss.

Enid looked up coolly at her sister.

"I suppose it's all right—even though we have a guest. As long as you're back in an hour."

"I might be an hour and a half. Rita Sue dawdles all over the Pizza-Putt course. Will you be okay?" Marjory glanced again at Arne Horsfall, who paid no attention to either of them. Marjory was convinced that he was more than just a little hard of hearing, as well as speechless. Dissatisfied with what he was attempting to draw, he turned to a blank page.

Enid nodded as if, on Arne's behalf, she resented the question. Rita Sue had pulled up in her red convertible, radio on, Roy Orbison's unearthly voice filling the ear like clouds fill the sky.

"You might trouble to put on a bra," Enid said in a low voice, dismissing her. "This is Caskey County, not Woodstock."

Marjory glanced down at her perceptible nipples. But not all that perceptible—she decided she wouldn't bother with the bra and went running off to join Rita Sue.

"Marjory, doesn't it hurt to have your bubbies bouncing all over the place like that?" Rita Sue asked her.

"*You'll* never know," Marjory said, with a smug look at the nearly vertical front of Rita Sue's sleeveless shirt. She sprawled happily in the seat with her knees up, dialed the volume of the radio higher with prehensile toes.

11

The girls stayed out later than Marjory had reckoned; it was almost dark when Rita Sue drove her home. Daylight had faded to a gossamer pink over the steely pond; hoot owls were starting up in the tall trees near the house. The gazebo was deserted. Enid was alone on the front porch. She came down to the car to ask Rita Sue to lower the volume of her radio; they had a guest, Enid explained, and she didn't want him to be disturbed.

"What happened to Mr. Horsfall?" Marjory asked.

"He got very tired early and went on upstairs. I heard him snoring a little while ago." Enid yawned. "I think I'll go to bed myself. Are you coming in, Marjory?"

"I guess so. Want to watch TV, Rita Sue?"

"No, I need to be getting along home." But they continued to sit in the car for a few minutes longer, listening to the radio, until it was full dark. Rita Sue began an anecdote about one of her redneck cousins. A cat jumped up on the porch railing. Another cat, the one-eyed tom named Zombie, climbed halfway up the screen door after a moth.

Rita Sue broke off the story she'd been telling and said, "That's a big one."

"Huh?" Marjory said. She had been trying out pet names for Tim McCarver to call her, in the most intimate moments of their phantom relationship.

"That moth that's flying around on your porch, see it? There it goes, up by the light."

"Oh, yeh. Luna moth. Pretty."

"There's another one."

"That makes two," Marjory said disinterestedly.

"Anyway, what I was telling you, there's a saying in the family that Aunt Alma is so tight she can squeeze a half dollar until the eagle moults—"

"I always thought it was, 'She can squeeze a penny until the President poops.' "

"That must be one of your relatives, Marjory. *Anyway*—oh, look, isn't that *pretty*?"

A luna moth had touched down on the windshield of Rita Sue's convertible. They stared through the glass at it. The pale green and lavender moth trembled with a delicate energy. There were four prominent spots, like eyes, on the diaphanous wings, darker than the purple margins.

"They're sort of human, aren't they?" Rita Sue said. "You can almost make out a face if you look long enough—there's another one! Where in the world are they all coming from?"

"I don't know. I haven't seen so many lunas in—" Marjory flinched as a moth flew into the car, fluttering an inch from the tip of her nose.

"They don't bite, do they?" Rita Sue asked her.

"Not that I know of."

"Just the same, I think I'm going to put the top up."

Marjory stared at the porch of her house, where the cats were leaping and batting their paws in a blizzard of moths, so many they had changed the color of the light from the single bulb beside the door to a dismal, stormy green. The moths were flocking around the car, too. Marjory shuddered. She liked her insects small or not at all, and the lunas were enormous, some as big as the spread of her hand. The evening had been humid and there was no wind, but suddenly she felt as chilly as if she had opened a refrigerator door and stuck her head inside.

Rita Sue turned the key in the ignition and pressed the button that raised the convertible top. A moth was fluttering in her lap, and she wore another in her pale, bouffant hair. She glanced up as the convertible top rose over them, and threw up her hands in a gesture of panic.

Marjory had only a glimpse of the dark shape soaring down through the moth cloud, picking off dinner, but she knew what it was and grabbed Rita Sue.

"It's okay, that's an owl."

"Marjory, I don't like this!" Rita Sue complained. "Roll up your window!" The edge of the convertible top nudged against the windshield frame and Rita Sue locked it down. No longer enamored of the moths, she batted at one that fluttered too close. Then with a look of shock she pressed the back of her hand to her mouth. "I thought you said they didn't bite!"

There was an edge of hysteria in her voice, and Marjory was concerned; very seldom did Rita Sue lose her poise.

"Rita Sue, why don't we just—"

But Rita Sue had started the engine and was backing away from the house and the moths seething around it. She almost hit the oak at the foot of the driveway but veered off into the street, where the car stalled.

"Hey, c'mon, where're you going?"

"Home! It *bit* me, Marjory, I swear! Are there any more in here?" She got the engine started again.

"Let me see your hand," Marjory said calmly.

Rita Sue held out her left hand, which was trembling. In the light from the dashboard Marjory couldn't see a wound. But a minute icily gray spot was discernible on the deeply tanned skin near the base of Rita Sue's thumb.

"I don't think that's a bite."

"Well, it hurts, it stings me! Marjory, what are you going to *do*?"

"What do you mean, what am I—"

"Just look at your house! Look at all those moths! Some of them are probably getting in."

Marjory looked, and her throat dried up. Now the lines of the house were indistinct within the nimbus of the luna moths; they stained the moon with their shimmering, unearthly greenness.

"Good Lord," Marjory moaned. "I wonder if Enid—"

She opened the car door before Rita Sue could put her foot to the accelerator.

"Marjory, where do you think you're going, hon?"

"I live here, remember? You can leave if you want to."

"Marjory, those moths bite, that's not a lie! It feels like somebody put dry ice on my hand!"

Marjory got back in the car and slammed the door.

"What do you think we should do?"

"I don't know," Marjory said, breathing hard, studying the moth circus around her house. *If it wasn't for bad luck,* she thought, *we wouldn't have any luck at all.* "What are they doing here? What the hell do they *want*?"

"It's probably just a freak of nature, and they'll go away after a while—don't you think? Look at all the owls!"

"Something weird's going on," Marjory muttered, in her anxiety rocking on the seat. "I need to get in the house. Rita Sue, drive around back, and maybe I'll go in that way."

"My car is going to get so stuck up with bugs—"

"Enid's in the house! She could be—I don't know—will you get *going*, Rita Sue!"

Rita Sue backed up and turned cautiously into the driveway.

"Put on your lights!"

Moths appeared by the dithering score in the headlight beams; they flew erratically toward the windshield, then veered off into the dark. Rita Sue drove around to the back porch, stopping five feet from the steps. The porch light was off and there seemed to be fewer moths here, although the Fairlane's headlights had begun to attract them. Rita Sue cut off the lights and the two girls sat in the dark.

"Okay, I'm going in now."

"I don't want to sit here in the car by myself!"

"We'll both go."

Marjory breathed deep, opened the door and ran up the porch steps where earlier she had broken off the heel of one of her good dress shoes. Moths fluttered coldly against her face like enormous snowflakes. Rita Sue was right behind her, gasping. Marjory flung open the screen door, waited until Rita Sue ducked inside, then followed.

"There's one!" Rita Sue said, pointing to the inside of the screen.

"Go on in the house," Marjory told her. She snatched a broom leaning against the washing machine. Another moth was higher than her head, difficult to make out on the unlighted porch. Marjory brought it down with one hard swing of the broom, then bolted into the kitchen behind Rita Sue. Only when she was inside with the door closed did she pay attention to how cold she felt. The girls clung to each other, hearing only the faint music of Enid's stereo upstairs.

"I got bit again," Rita Sue said forlornly. "On my cheek."

"You're right; it doesn't exactly feel like a bite," Marjory acknowledged, rubbing the back of a leg beneath her shorts.

"Do you suppose there's any more of them in here?"

"Let's go upstairs. But don't turn on any lights."

"What happens to moths if they don't have a light to attract them?"

"I hope they'll go away," Marjory said, moving out of the kitchen into the hall. Through the front-door screen she could see plenty of moths; they were, at a distance, spectacular. She didn't know what had happened to the cats. Probably when they began to feel overwhelmed they had crept into the darkness beneath the house. She flipped off the front porch light and went running up the stairs.

"Enid! Hey, Enid!"

"Marjory, what on earth?" Enid said, sitting up on her bed bleary-eyed as Marjory burst into her room. She had dozed off reading a book, which fell from her lap.

"Luna moths!" Now their occurrence was merely bizarre and exhilarating to Marjory, nothing to be frightened of. "Must be a billion of them—they're all around the house."

"Oh," Enid said, yawning and then smiling. "Those are the real pretty ones. Let me see."

"They bite," Rita Sue said glumly. She was behind Marjory in the doorway.

"Moths? I never have heard of—"

She was looking for her flats to slip into when they heard Arne Horsfall scream, more shocking than a boulder falling through the roof.

Enid looked up with a galvanized jerk of her head, mouth opening. Marjory stepped back hard into Rita Sue, turning to stare down the hallway at the door of the room in which their guest had gone to bed. She was, instantly, a mass of gooseflesh, her nipples standing out like round drawer-pulls. Rita Sue, knock-kneed, had Marjory by one arm, and her nails hurt.

But nothing happened to explain the scream. The bedroom door remained closed. Arne Horsfall didn't appear, as Marjory anticipated, berserk, with a blunt instrument or sharp object in his hand to make corpses of them all.

Enid reacted quickly, trying to unblock her doorway by pulling Marjory in a direction opposite the one in which Rita Sue had her going.

"Get out of the way!"

Marjory shifted her weight and shoved Enid back a couple of steps.

"Oh, no! Don't you *dare* go near that room!"

"Marjory, something—he—"

"Call Ted!" Marjory demanded, her voice getting squeaky.

"Marjory—"

Marjory bit her lip so hard a drop of blood ran down her chin.

"Get Ted over here and let *him* go in there!"

They stared at each other for a couple of seconds. Then Enid nodded distractedly and went to sit on the edge of her bed, picking up the telephone and placing it in her lap. She dialed the number of the sheriff's substation while Marjory, holding fast to Rita Sue, stared at the door of Arne Horsfall's room—as if will-power alone could keep it from opening until help arrived.

Rita Sue found her voice and whispered, "Marjory, who *is* that man?"

"A mental patient," Marjory said grimly. She pulled Rita Sue into Enid's room, shut the door, and began pushing the high oak dresser past the door frame. "I could use a little help here," she panted. Rita Sue lent herself to the effort and together they budged the dresser a few more inches while Enid spoke urgently on the phone.

Ted Lufford was there in six minutes, shouting for Enid as two more units from the sheriff's department rolled up right behind him. Red lights washed around the walls of Enid's room. She raised her window and called down to Ted. Marjory, sitting with her back to the dresser, felt too winded and inept to move it back again, but the three of them managed so Ted could get the door open. He had a hand on the butt of the revolver in its holster and a flashlight with a foot-long barrel in the other hand. The upstairs hall was filled with deputies.

Marjory and Enid tried to talk at the same time. Enid said, calmly enough, "Shut up, Marj," then explained,

"Ted, we heard Mr. Horsfall scream. I—we were afraid to go and open the door."

"Charley," Ted said over his shoulder, and one of the deputies moved quickly to the door of the spare bedroom. He rattled the knob. The door was locked. Ted joined him. "Mr. Horsfall?" He knocked sharply twice, then glanced at Enid. "Sorry, but I better do this." Then he kicked hard beneath the latch and the door flew open. Ted went in, followed by two deputies. Marjory and Enid advanced slowly down the hall. Rita Sue stayed behind to call her mother.

Ted came out of the spare room shaking his head.

"Is he dead?" Enid said softly, and Marjory's scalp crawled; Enid had tried so hard for Arne Horsfall.

"You heard him scream?"

"We all did. It was—"

"Bloody murder," Marjory finished.

"He's not in there, Nuggins. The door was locked, and the windows are shut—maybe he was someplace else in the house?"

"Go look," Enid said, leaning against the hall railing. Two deputies hustled down the stairs. Ted went into Marjory's room, flipping on the overhead light. The bathroom door had been standing open all along.

The deputy named Charley appeared at the foot of the stairs and called, "He's not nowhere in the house."

"Let's have a look around outside," Ted suggested.

"I don't think so," Marjory said.

They all looked at her.

"He's gone. That's all. Enid, I don't know how I know, but he's gone. We won't find him."

"He has a hard time walking, his arthritis is so bad."

"Enid, *listen*! I'm telling you he is nowhere around, and—"

Enid said angrily, "I'm *responsible* for Mr. Horsfall, we have got to find him!"

"It's a big waste of time. You'll never—"

"Well, he didn't just vanish into thin air!" Enid said,

focusing her anger on Marjory, as if Arne Horsfall's disappearance were all her fault.

Marjory sighed. "Something like that," she said, aware of how ridiculous she sounded. But she couldn't shut up; she felt as she had once at a brush arbor meeting, when she'd caught the Spirit and just had to testify. "I don't know where all the luna moths are now, either; but wherever it is they came from—that's where Mr. Horsfall went."

JUNE, 1906:

Horsfall Farm

1

In middle Tennessee rain fell almost continuously for six days before the sun broke through and the overflow from rivers and streams began to seep away. The house had mildew, the chickens wouldn't lay, and Birka took to her bed with croup.

Late on the night of June 3, a railroad trestle across the Cumberland River seven miles north of Sublimity collapsed under the weight of a Louisville and Nashville freight train carrying mostly pig iron and coal. Three members of the train's crew were swept away by flood waters, and drowned.

When the roads around Sublimity dried up enough for them to make the trip in their Michigan wagon, Arne's father hitched up his team of horses and fixed a well-cushioned pallet in the wagon bed for Birka, who was slowly recuperating and had requested an outing on this warm and pretty spring day. Arne collaborated with his father on a picnic lunch and the three of them, with Hawkshaw the dog, set out for the wreck site.

It was something to see, an event in their lives: for three quarters of a mile downstream from what remained of the trestle (stone pilings close to either shore) there were jumbled and splintered timbers stacked on slowly emerging sandbars, a few hopper and freight cars high and dry along the embankments or nearly buried, upended, in silt. All that could be seen of the locomotive was a pair of driver wheels where the still-swift current flowed muddily through the gap left by the collapsing bridge. The train had also carried livestock, and the higher air was filled with slowly wheeling buzzards, as if over a battlefield. There were human scavengers along the river, breaking into freight cars with sledges and crowbars.

Birka selected a cove that was nearly iridescent from the light of the sun on wild rhododendron blossoms. Arne's father helped her down from the wagon. Birka had "fallen off" badly during her illness. She looked as pale as the clouds, with flag-blue circles beneath her eyes. But she smiled often; the fresh air had done her as much good as the salve balls with kerosene she'd been swallowing for medicine. She even spoke of having her appetite back. Arne nuzzled up under her arm but he itched to go down along the river and see what he could find.

"Stay away from the boxcars," his father told him.

"And those men," his mother said, speaking of the scavengers as if they were criminals. They could hear sledgehammers battering boxcars upriver.

"Can I keep what I find?"

His father looked at his mother, then said with a shrug, "Anything valuable, it's bound to be at the bottom of the river."

"But if I find something—"

"You call me."

"Okay," Arne said, and he left the cove with Hawkshaw, glancing back once to see his father holding his mother against him and kissing her on the forehead, his mother looking as if she were enjoying a vision of heaven; Arne smiled, grateful that she was going to be all right after three terrible nights that had kept him and his father awake, dosing her with Vicks salve, carrying the heavy croup kettle back and forth from the kitchen.

He was wearing knee-high gumboots, but it wasn't easy getting close to the river. The underbrush that had been flooded over was silty and it was a good idea to keep a weather eye out for poisonous snakes flooded from their dens. Hawkshaw wallowed enthusiastically through hock-deep mud, then splashed across pools left by the receding river to clean himself. They came to the remains of a cow bloated and shimmering with flies; Arne held his breath and took another route to a small limestone bluff with a tangle of uprooted trees piled against it.

Looking down into the tangle, a few feet below the level of the bluff, he saw a large packing crate high and dry and apparently intact, the stenciled markings on it still readable. The crate, about six feet long by three and a half feet wide, had metal handles at either end.

Arne, looking at it, thought: *I can get a rope down there, easy.*

He looked along the shaded riverbank in both directions, hearing voices and the sounds of crowbars and hammers, but no one was near him. Twenty feet below, the river gurgled and splashed around the flotsam in which the packing crate was lodged.

He whistled up Hawkshaw and went back to the cove where his father and mother were laying out the picnic lunch on a tablecloth. Birka wore a white waist, a blue worsted skirt, and a pink rhododendron blossom in her hair; some of the same color had seeped into her cheeks. Her eyes still had the milky cast of sickness, but she hadn't coughed all morning and was gayer, humming to herself as she spooned potato salad from a brown stone crock onto the china plates they'd brought. She squeezed Arne's hand and scolded Hawkshaw for being so muddy; then she tossed him a biscuit with a slice of salt pork in it.

"I found something," Arne told them. "A big box." He described it for them with his hands. "Do you want to see it?" he asked his father.

"After we've et," his father said, pouring buttermilk for them and cold sassafras tea for Birka. She sat on a needlepoint cushion with her back against a wagon wheel, nibbled some potato salad and watched the drifting clouds with a half-formed, contented smile. A strong breeze raked hair across her forehead. The horses ate sweet grass and flashed their brisk tails at flies.

Arne convinced his father to bring with them a hundred-foot length of new rope stored beneath the springseat of the wagon.

"Whatever it is," his father said, as they walked back to the bluff where Arne had seen the crate, "I can't say it's ourn to keep."

"But if we don't pull it up, it'll just fall back in the river someday! Then nobody'll own it!"

"Well, let's have us a look."

From the edge of the bluff his father studied the crate lodged in the branches of the flood-swept trees. Just out of his reach, even when he went down on his stomach with a hand extended.

"I could climb down there," Arne volunteered.

"You could fall in, too." He gave one of the branches a shaking, but the tangled mass didn't budge.

"I'll be careful. Can you make out what that writing says?"

"No. The crate looks to be upside down." Arne was sure that, even if the lettering had been easier to see, his father probably wouldn't have been able to read it. He'd only finished fifth grade, and was often self-conscious about his lack of learning.

Arne took one end of the rope, passed it through his belt, and climbed down slowly, finding the nearly bare limbs scum-slippery and the entire mass suddenly uneasy beneath his modest weight. He realized that if the flotsam shifted and went down quickly into the river, he could be trapped in an underwater maze. But he had a hand on his prize and wasn't about to give it up. He threaded the rope through a handle on the crate. Then came the difficult part: he had to balance himself, feet on a branch, hip against the end of the crate, while he used both hands to tie a good knot.

His father gave him encouragement, then said, "That'll hold. Get back up here now."

He kneeled and held out a hand to give Arne purchase as he climbed up the last three feet through the branches. Arne was flushed with accomplishment.

"Maybe it's tools," he said.

"Might be." His father tightened up on the rope he had belayed around his waist. The crate moved, slipping sideways from its niche.

"Careful it don't fall and pull you in after!" Arne said, admiring the swell of his father's biceps, the arching of his shoulders and heavily muscled back.

"Get ahold of my belt and toe in," his father instructed. His feet were solidly spread. He gripped the rope with both hands. "I'm going to haul it up here now."

They were both prepared for a lot of dead weight, but when the crate slid free of the enclosing branches he staggered slightly backward, Arne dropping to his knees behind him.

"Ain't tools," his father said, taking a new grip on the line and pulling, almost effortlessly, hand over hand. "Don't weigh much more than you do, I'd say not over a hundred pounds." He hauled the crate steadily up over the edge of the bluff and they looked solemnly at it, his father unwinding the rope from around his waist. The water-smooth boards were tightly nailed and caulked with a resinous substance so hard Arne couldn't scrape a bead of it off with the blade of his barlow knife. He put the knife away, brushed dried mud from the black stenciling, and read aloud, slowly.

"Dr. N. C. Ayres, Department of An—Anthro—don't know what that word is—Vanderbilt University, Nashville, Tennessee." He looked up in disappointment. "You reckon it's schoolbooks?"

"Hard to say. Filled with books, that crate ought to be a sight heavier. What we need do is, Birka'll write a letter to the university, recommend this Dr. Ayres come up here and claim his property."

"We don't get to keep it?"

"Wouldn't be right, long as we know who belongs to it. You see that, don't you, Arne?"

"Yes, sir." Arne brushed more dried mud away. His lips moved. He smiled incredulously.

"What else does that say there?"

"Only word I can make out for sure is 'Iceland.' "

"That beats all."

"Mama's from Iceland!"

"Born there; but she were raised up in Maine State."

"I'll bet she can read this."

"Maybe so." His father slapped a mosquito that alighted on the side of his neck. "Time for us to get on home. Let's lug this crate back to the wagon."

2

They put the crate in the barn and, two days later, Birka dispatched a letter to Dr. Ayres at Vanderbilt University. Until the letter went out Arne had been able to tolerate his curiosity, going into the barn only three or four times a day to look at the crate and run his hands over it, trying to imagine what might be inside.

Then he began to dream about the crate. In one dream he was caught in a fast current of the Cumberland River, swimming hard, lunging for a handhold, the crate floating always just out of his reach.

In his spare time, of which he had little now that the rains had stopped and there were a dozen chores to do every day, he hung around the kitchen. His mother, still not fully recovered from her sickness, rested often; but even when she was sitting down her hands were busy, rolling out dough for dumplings, peeling Irish potatoes, knitting the beautiful sweaters that were highly prized in their community. They talked, most often, about Iceland, a country in which Arne had shown almost no interest before the crate.

"We left when I was eight years old," his mother told him. "I know the language well, because, although we were never to return to Iceland, my father had us read from the old books—*Njál's Saga*, the Book of Settlements—every night. But I don't remember so much about the village where I was born."

"Thjórsá?"

Birka smiled and corrected Arne's tortured pronunciation. "That was also the name of the river. It was green along our river, good farming there. But not so far away were deserts of lava, and the Mýrdalsjökull glacier."

"What's a glacier?"

"Like a mountain of ice, but growing, changing, moving very slowly."

Arne tried to imagine this phenomenon. Something huge, alive, threatening. "Why did you come to America, because you were afraid of the glacier?"

Birka handed him a slice of raw potato, and shook her head.

"No. We left Iceland because my father had a terrible fight with a neighbor. There was always bad blood between them; a feud, you might call it. They would quarrel over a piece of land, sheep, over nothing. For the love of quarreling, I think. This is what my mother used to say, in her bitterness. Let me tell you, we had hard winters there, cold and dark—three months of darkness.''

Arne loved the sun, the long days that left time for play after work. He looked bleakly at her. Birka smiled.

"Then in summer, the sun almost never stopped shining. Summer in Iceland is a time of being—reborn, released from that terrible darkness. There are weddings, games, festivals, and always drinking, drinking—so many men, and women, have the weakness for drinking. I know you don't understand, here drinking is a serious sin, so there is no such problem.''

"You mean whiskey drinking? Eugene Collum's pa makes whiskey. Drinks it, too.''

"He is an exception in this community. My father Steinn and his rival, whose name, I think, was Sigurdur, fell to quarreling during *réttir*, the gathering of the sheep. Because of drink they had no restraint. They had fought before, but this time my father crippled Sigurdur.''

"Was he as strong as—''

"As your father, yes.'' Birka smiled fondly. "But Enoch has no violence in him, thanks be to God. Well, it was decided by the village council that Steinn Vilhjálm must pay for the crippling with a nine-tenths share of our farm, and accept banishment. Or else go to jail. With what little money my father had left from the sale of the farm he took us to this country. But he was never successful here, as farmer or fisherman, and finally his drinking wore him down—just wore him down.''

She looked as if she were going to cry from the pain of recalling her father's humiliation and gradual decline. Arne shifted restlessly in his chair and reached for another potato slice.

"Don't you want to know what's in the crate?" he asked Birka.

"The professor will tell us when he comes for it—if he wants us to know. Otherwise, what business is it of ours?"

"But you know where it came from, and you said—"

"I said I have heard of the Ásatrú region. Once upon a time"—Arne grinned contentedly at this storybook beginning—"a time as old as Noah's flood—there was a great forest, covering many square miles, in Ásatrú. But after the Norsemen, our ancestors, came, then little by little the trees were all cut down, sheep ate the grass and destroyed the roots, the winds carried away the soil, so today there are only poor farms left, bare, windswept hills—nothing there."

"*Something* was there—and now it's in the crate."

"Yes. I have wondered—"

"Don't you want to know for sure?" Arne said quickly. "We could open the crate, then nail the lid back so tight nobody—"

"We will wait for the professor," Birka said, lowering her head and rubbing a little color into one cheek. The crate was mysterious. It was something from home. Birka's eyes were sharp from the speculation she tried to hide from him. But she was firm in her scruples.

3

Instead of a visitor a letter, addressed to Birka, arrived at the end of June.

"It says," she told them at supper, "that Professor Ayres is on a field trip to the South Pacific, and will not return to the university until the spring term, nine-teen seven.''

"A *year*?'' Arne said, scowling.

"What do they want us to do with his crate?'' Enoch asked.

"They don't say.'' Birka folded the letter and glanced at Arne with a slight frown. Arne interpreted her look as conspiratorial, and said nothing more as he carefully separated the skin from a drumstick in his chicken and dumplings.

Arne's father shook his head. "Reckon it can just sit there in the barn. Ain't likely to be in the way. Maybe he'll give us a few dollars' storage when he does come.''

"Or a reward,'' Arne suggested, his mouth full.

His father grimaced, working a fingernail between two teeth where something was stuck. "I don't think those professors have a right smart of money. Not much more than we've got, anyhow.''

"If he doesn't have money,'' Arne said, "then how can he take such a long trip to—'' He looked at his mother. "Where did you say he's gone to?''

"The South Pacific.''

"That where China is?''

"No. If you don't want the chicken skin—''

"You can have it.''

"I just don't like leavings,'' Birka said.

4

After supper, with three good hours of daylight remaining, his father took the shay down the road a third of a mile to help a neighbor who was drilling a new well, and Arne went out to the barn to mix whitewash for the fireplace, a chore he'd been neglecting, and to mend old harness with an awl, a hammer, and some brass rivets. While he worked at the anvil in one corner he glanced often across the barn at the crate, until the sun no longer came in the back door and it was too dim inside to make out the stenciled lettering. He said exotic words to himself with each hammer stroke, as well as he could pronounce them, and tried to visualize the land of crags and smokes and glaciers—and scarce, green valleys—where the crate had originated.

At twilight his mother crossed the barn lot with a coal-oil lamp. He looked up despondently from where he sat on a hay bale with a lap full of the mended harness.

"Arne, what's got you like this?"

"It'll be a whole year before we know what's inside!"

Birka hung the lamp on the side of the stall where the family's Jersey cow was overdue to freshen, and sullen about the waiting time. Arne made room for his mother on the hay bale. She put a hand on his knee.

"I need to do a job of patching. Those pants are almost worn through."

"Can't we open it?" he pleaded.

There was a rustling of barn swallows, chirps in the

rafters. The pregnant cow shifted about in her stall, looking morosely at them. The plow horse, Ol' Vol, munched fodder in an adjacent stall. Instead of an immediate "no," Birka was silent. Her fingers tightened a little on Arne's knee. He put a hand on top of hers, making her a prisoner of his intention.

"You know Enoch wouldn't approve."

Arne also knew there'd be a jug after the well-drilling, and his father would drink his part, and come home chewing spearmint leaves so Birka would never suspect. "He won't be back for 'nother hour anyhow. I can pry the lid off and nail it back so slick you'd never guess."

"Arne, it's just like telling a lie." Her tone was, if anything, apologetic, not final, and Arne pressed what he realized was an advantage.

"It isn't if we don't never tell!"

She moved her hand to the top of his head, a familiar soothing gesture, and fingered the hair that was long over his ears.

"Time to take a scissors to that," she said, but her eyes too were on the crate and Arne, glancing at her, saw a pleasurable tension in the set of her lips, a certain mischief in the narrowing of her eyes.

"We'll just take a peek inside," he assured her, "and not say a word."

She hugged him then, and laughed.

"Arne, you're a rascal. But neither one of us could ever wait for Christmas morning. Get the pry bar—*two* pry bars—and the hammer."

Arne was already halfway to the tool chest, saying, over his shoulder, "Maybe you'd better shut the yard door!"

Prying off the lid of the crate without leaving chisel marks or splintering a board was a tougher proposition than Arne had reckoned.

"It's rowan wood," his mother told him. "I knew that right away."

"What kind?"

"It is—special. A wood with magical properties. Here they call it ash, I think. My mother had a little box of rowan wood in which she kept our photographs—the three girls. She believed this would keep us from harm for as long as we lived."

"Where's the box now?" Arne said, fighting a stubborn nail.

"Vigdís has it. But why make an entire crate of rowan wood? That must have been very expensive." A little later she said, "Arne, I've been thinking. Maybe we shouldn't—"

"I've almost got it!" In twenty minutes of careful work, going from one end of the crate to the other, he had raised the cover by half an inch. Now he was sweating in the closeness of the barn. "Mother, help me. Use the other pry bar. Be careful where you set the lantern, you don't want to knock it over." He sounded like his father. Birka, despite misgivings that came and went like gray mice, smiled and glanced at the barn doors.

"Enoch will come along anytime now—and he will be so mad at us—"

Their eyes met. Birka shrugged and picked up the other pry bar.

"Ready?" Arne asked her. "Go."

The long nails made a lot of screechy noise coming out of the tough wood. Arne went around the crate on his knees, prizing, then rose to his feet, seized the lid and pulled it off with one jerk. He backed away from the crate as Birka gasped, crossing her arms in front of her body.

"What's that?"

She said something in the Icelandic language, backing away too, her foot brushing against the lantern she'd set on the dirt floor.

"Mother!"

"My God, my God, what have we done? Cover it, Arne, nail down the lid!"

"But what *is* it?"

Birka picked up the lantern. She held it over her head. The dark thing huddled in the crate, lying on a bed of dry excelsior, leaped into gleaming relief.

"*Huldufólk,*" she whispered, dreadfully, and setting the lantern down again, she fled to the barn doors. Flung them open, listened suspensefully on the threshold. No one was coming. Birka retraced half her steps into the barn, leaving the doors open behind her. She gestured at the crate, speechless. Arne had picked up the nail-studded lid and was holding it like a shield, staring down into the crate. He wanted to see the thing better. He was frightened but fascinated, blood throbbing at his temples. Ol' Vol snorted and stamped in his stall like something had flown up his nose. His mother breathed through her mouth, straining for air as if the croup had recurred.

The body in the crate was the blackest man Arne had ever seen—hairless, rubbery skin that gleamed as if oiled. Skin and mostly bones, prominent beneath the skin. A naked body, complete even to the knobby glans of uncircumcised penis, to reflective toenails, lying on its side in the plentiful excelsior and a litter of what looked like small dried leaves. Cushioned like an egg in the nest. It was apparent to Arne that, whoever he was, he'd been dead for a very long time. But there was a vine twisted around the dead man's neck (not tightly enough to have choked the life out of him), and the astonishing thing was, the vine seemed almost fresh, recently cut—three or four tiny green leaves had begun to unfold as if responding to the nourishing light, the spring air let into the opened crate.

"What's *huldufólk*?" Arne asked his mother.

"Close it!" she demanded, her face averted.

"It's just an old nigger," Arne said lamely, not knowing what to make of her distress; now that his heart wasn't racing and he'd seen all there was to see, he felt disappointed. He set the lid in place and picked up the hammer.

5

His mother said nothing on their return to the house. In the kitchen she put kindling into the stove and lighted the fire to heat coffee. Her hands were trembling and Arne could see the blue veins in her wrists and arms.

"Mother?"

She looked almost unwillingly at him.

"There was a vine around his neck. Did you see that?"

"I didn't have to see it," Birka said, "to know it was there."

"There were new leaves on the vine. How could that be?"

"I don't know. As long as the vine lives, we have nothing to be afraid of."

But she *was* afraid, and her fear made him uneasy. Arne took an oatmeal cookie from a crock and ate it, silently watching his mother rub the skin of her arms as if her circulation had stopped.

"What would the professor want with a dead nigger?"

"It isn't a nigger. The skin is black because of the vine. And Professor Ayres would not want the body if he knew—"

"Knew what?"

"That it isn't dead, can never be."

Arne felt the hairs on the back of his neck stiffening.

Then he laughed at this absurdity, spraying cookie crumbs on the table.

His mother turned and gripped him by the shoulders. Arne nearly jumped out of his chair. Her normally blue eyes looked colorless, as lightning is colorless in a seething sky.

"Arne—it is one of the unwashed children of Eve! How could we be so unfortunate—" Her voice rose. *"I don't know what to do!"* She let him go and gestured, wildly, toward the barn. "We should take it away, bury it where nobody will ever find it. Yes. The rowan wood can never rot, it'll be safe in the ground, of the earth again."

Arne's throat had dried out. He got up and put his arms around his mother, pressing his head against her belly. Trying to quiet her.

"We can't tell Enoch. He shouldn't know. We'll wait for a time when Enoch is away from the farm again. Soon, it must be soon—then we'll be shed of this curse."

"What curse?" Arne said, his skin prickly again. Her hands worried the top of his head, cold fingers stroked his ears. "We didn't do anything! Opened the damned crate, is all!"

"No, no . . . don't be upset. It's going to be all right! But I don't want that thing here another day. Even in the Black Sleep, it might still do us harm."

They heard harness bells; Big Enoch was home. After putting the mare in her stall in the barn and washing up at the pump, Enoch came in bare to the waist, drops of water beaded along the jawline. He sat down, pulled off his boots, smiled at a solemn Arne, then Birka, who placed a mug of coffee, an opened jar of peach pickles, and half a loaf of spice bread in front of him. She started for the cupboard to get the broom and sweep up the traces of mud that had come off his boots, but Enoch stopped her.

"Looks like you took sick again."

"No. But I need to go to bed now. Arne, you, too."

Arne yawned, not convincingly, and didn't look his father in the eye. "I mended the harness."

His father nodded, dunking a piece of the sweet bread in his coffee. "Nathaniel Ballard wanted to know if you'll play baseball with them Saturday."

"I reckon I will," Arne mumbled.

"They need a hard thrower like you. Birka, leave the sweeping up to me." She smiled slightly—it was a rare man who would so much as touch a broom in the house—and bent over her husband for a kiss. Arne followed her from the kitchen. In the big room he climbed a ladder next to the hearth and looked down from his sleeping loft.

"Ma—"

"Shhh." She shook her head dispiritedly, went into the bedroom and shut the door.

Arne pulled off his trousers, was reminded he hadn't visited the outhouse and used the chamberpot instead. Then he lay on his back looking at the stars through the small window of his loft. He couldn't close his eyes. After a while he went on his hands and knees to a leather-covered chest against one wall for a deerskin bag that contained everything lucky and protective he owned: the hind foot of a cross-eyed rabbit, a polished buckeye, dried four-leaf clovers pressed between pieces of vellum. A five-dollar gold piece. He took the talismans and his Old Testament back to bed with him but continued to lie there wide-eyed and weak in the hands, as weak as he'd felt while driving the nails of the crate lid back into their holes. Had he knocked the lid home solidly in his haste? He imagined it thrown easily aside by a tarry hand. He heard his father's tread on the floor below as he made his way from kitchen to bedroom. Arne almost called to him, wanting company, his father's arm around his shoulders. But his father would know the mood he was in meant something was wrong

. . . he wouldn't leave until Arne had told him everything.

6

Arne tossed restlessly on the feather-stuffed mattress long after his father began to snore behind the bedroom door.

The black man was dead, he could believe what he'd seen with his own eyes—but what about the vine around his neck? How could the vine be fresh, even greening, after so long? Maybe river water had seeped into the crate and revived it. But the excelsior and the other leaves that had withered and dropped off the vine were perfectly dry; there was no stench of mildew in the crate.

The unwashed children of Eve.

What children did his mother mean?

Arne opened his Old Testament. His eyes were sharp enough to read by starlight, but he was already familiar with the creation story and the generations of Adam as told in Genesis. Adam "knew" Eve (screwed her, Arne thought, but the Bible couldn't say it like that because it was the Good Book) and she conceived and bore Cain. After Cain, there was Abel. Cain "slew" Abel because he was jealous of Abel's offering to the Lord, the firstlings of his flock. And the voice of Abel's blood (Arne couldn't figure that one out) cried to the Lord from the ground. *God said to Cain—When you till the ground it shall no longer yield to you its strength; you shall be a fugitive and a wanderer on the earth.* Arne shuddered. He knew all this, but it didn't explain the body in the crate, which couldn't be either Cain *or* Abel because they had died so long ago, in Bible times. Even before the Flood, he thought.

Who were the other children of Eve, born on the East of Eden?

Arne wasn't sure. There was Seth, then—the Bible said only that "the days of Adam after he had begotten Seth were eight hundred: and he begat sons and daughters." But what were their names? Arne read slowly, unenlightened. No more names were provided in the text of Genesis—nor were the additional children condemned as "unwashed." But they must have been the children his mother had referred to. Did "unwashed" mean something really bad? Sleepy at last, he fell into a fitful doze.

7

"Arne?"

His mother's voice. She had climbed to the loft in her nightdress and was kneeling beside his straw tick and featherbed.

"What's wrong?" Awake, he could hear his father, still snoring obliviously in the bed she had left.

"I couldn't sleep. I wanted to talk to you."

"About the unwashed children of Eve?"

She picked up the Old Testament that Arne had been holding when he drifted off.

"Their story isn't in the Bible. It's more of a legend—folklore. That doesn't mean they aren't real, that they haven't existed for all the years since Adam and Eve were banished from Eden."

Arne moved over on the mattress and she made herself more comfortable beside him.

"*Huldufólk* means 'hidden people.' When I was a girl, it was accepted by nearly everyone in the village that many of the hidden people were nearby, deep beneath *boelis* of rock, or in natural caves at the edge of the glaciers. Places where they lived in perpetual cold, never seeing the sun. But in the beginning, long before they settled in Iceland, they lived in the Garden of Eden.''

"It says in Genesis that Adam had other sons and daughters, but it doesn't say—"

"—that one day God came to the Garden while Eve was bathing her children. Because she hadn't had time to bathe them all, she showed to God only those who were washed. You know how mothers are. She wanted God to think the clean ones were all the children she had. Of course, you can't deceive God. He was very angry with Eve—"

"He was always angry about something, wasn't he?"

"It seems so. Because God was angry, he cursed Eve and her unwashed children, saying, 'From this day those you have hidden from me shall be hidden from the sight of all men.' ''

"How many unwashed children did she have?"

"No one knows. But there may be thousands today, hidden in the mountains and fjords of Iceland; the survivors who settled in our land after so many were put to the Black Sleep, or driven out of the old countries."

"That's one of them? In the crate?"

"Yes."

"You said he wasn't dead. But he looks—"

"None of the *huldufólk* can die, Arne. They live forever. But they may be blinded or paralyzed by the sun's rays. And the touch of green, growing things puts them to sleep, a sleep like death."

"Is that why the vine is around his neck?"

"Oh, yes. But if the vine is cut or removed, then—"

"He'd wake up?" Arne shuddered against her side. "That's not going to happen. Is it?"

"No, Arne. But I think it would have happened if fate had not seen to it that the crate was delivered into our hands. I'm sure that Professor Ayres would have removed the vine, unless he knows of and believes in the legend. We won't take the chance. We'll bury the crate where it shouldn't be disturbed for ten thousand years."

"Are the *huldufólk* bad? Are you afraid of them?"

"I've never seen one before tonight. Afraid—? Well—yes. It's sensible to be afraid. In some ways *huldufólk* love music, dancing, art. They decorate their caves with paintings and sculpture. My father said he knew of a man who had visited one of their caves, on a night when they were all on the wind—but we heard such stories all the time, there was no proof."

"What do you mean, 'on the wind'?"

"That is the terrible part. They fly. Their wings are made of human skin, dyed the colors of the luna moth— green, pink, lavender. Without these wings they would be condemned to spend Eternity below the ground. That's one reason why they're such a danger to us . . . they seek human skin, flayed from the bodies of their living victims."

"What's another reason?" Arne asked, giving his mother a nudge when she was silent too long. He had goosebumps.

"*Huldufólk* have no living hearts. No breath to cloud a mirror. They may not conceive. Those mortals they choose not to flay they turn into *huldufólk*. I don't know how this is done. Oh, yes—their touch is deadly cold— a kiss freezes human flesh."

Now Arne felt sickened and crept closer to his mother, until he was half in her lap, head on her bosom, which was full and warm beneath the cotton nightdress. Her heartbeat in his ear reminded him of his own origins, the humanness he took for granted.

No longer a baby, still he did not mind being rocked in his mother's arms. Fear was distanced by intimacy; with her assurances in mind, he could think objectively about the thing in the barn, indulge his fascination (*The touch of green, growing things puts them to sleep*) . . . Yes, the Black Sleep—and he would never go near the crate again, remove the lid, without a sprig of fresh-cut vine in his hand.

"Arne," his mother said, as if she were aware of his thoughts, "we must stay away from the barn, until we're ready to bury the crate in the woods. We don't want to look at the Dark Man again."

"But if he's—"

"Even in the Black Sleep, I think he's aware of us. As if we are part of his dreams. He still may have power."

"What kind of power?"

"He might make us do things we know we shouldn't do—cut the vine that's around his throat."

Arne trembled as fear returned like a rush of wind. "How could he do that?"

"I don't know." Her eyes were half closed; she kissed his forehead as if it were a religious object. "As long as we're careful, then nothing will happen."

"Is there another way he could wake up?"

"He isn't going to wake up," she said, her voice still soft; but her heartbeat reverberated in her breast as if an axed tree had crashed there. Outside the house, perhaps half a mile off, they heard bobcats, mating squawls that had begun with the blood-raising spring.

His mother began to sing, a repetitive snatch of song in Icelandic. She had sung to him many times, but he knew he'd never heard this one before.

"What's that?"

She broke off and lifted her head slowly. Her heart was pumping furiously; he felt the heat in her throat, her caressing hands.

"Oh—it's an old song. I don't know why it should

come back to me, after so many years. Well—it is very late, you should try to sleep now. You're not afraid to be by yourself, are you?''

''No,'' he said, and wondered why he should lie. He had only to say ''Stay with me,'' and she would have spent the night beside him. But he was ashamed of his need—he wanted to be brave for her, like his father. *Nothing was going to hurt him.*

But if he hoped to sleep at all tonight, then he had to make sure of that.

8

After he had lain awake for at least another hour, until he was certain his mother had settled down for the night, Arne put on his trousers and went barefoot down the loft ladder, clutching his barlow knife and deerskin pouch of lucky pieces in one hand.

He stood at the kitchen door for several minutes staring at the barn, which he could see clearly against the luminous night sky. Then he put a match to the lantern hanging on a peg beside the door and carried it outside.

Hawkshaw came swiftly and silently out from beneath the steps where he spent all but the coldest winter nights. Arne ran a hand across the top of the dog's flat, bony head, not taking his eyes off the barn. The beating of his heart was in rhythm with the creaking din of cicadas, the peeping of frogs that had appeared by the thousands in the shallow backwater of the flooded Harpeth River three hundred yards south of the farm. The night was warm, too warm for dew, the air still and odorous of rich earth, pear blossoms.

Arne took out his knife and cut pieces of the pea vine trained to a trellis next to the porch. He stuffed the vines into a back pocket.

Hawkshaw realized they were going to the barn and not the outhouse; he trotted ahead and now Arne felt a little foolish, because if anything was . . . *wrong* . . . inside, Hawkshaw would be aware of it. The Dark Man slept, would go on sleeping until his crate was as deep in the ground as Arne could dig. Nothing more to it, and nothing to be scared of—

Hawkshaw went sniffing off after something—possum or raccoon—that had crossed the barnyard earlier, leaving its radiant scent on the ground. Arne looked at his coursing dog, then set the lantern down and opened one of the barn doors. He went in with the lantern held head-high and before he had gone more than a few steps he was shuddering—his feet, the hollow of his throat, his ears suddenly cold. The temperature in the barn was close to freezing.

Amazed, he saw his foggy breath by lantern light, and in the gloomy corner by the harrow and plowstock and hanging harness, the shape of the nailed-up crate.

Something on the lid of the crate that hadn't been there earlier; it was indistinguishable from where Arne stood. A little gray clod of dirt, he thought, and moved closer—

—still shuddering, the lantern at a right angle from his body and jiggling, dancing the light into darkness, throwing his boy's shadow up and back as high as the loft, illuminating—

—a mouse.

Nothing more than a mouse, lying atop the crate on its side, little pink feet outstretched, eyes closed, tail stiff as a nail, dead mouse.

He touched it with a straw. The fur and body of the mouse were unyielding, as if frozen. Where Arne stood only a foot from the crate the air was intensely cold; it seared his nostrils when he breathed. His toes felt as if they were burning on the ground.

Arne backed away, lungs pumping clouds of vapor. Something flew at him like a ghost from the dark of the loft overhead, fluttering in the nimbus of the lantern, which he almost dropped. He saw the fluttering thing first as a shadow, then a small silken kite, and recognized by its distinctive shape that it was a luna moth, one of the largest he'd ever seen. The luna hovered, as if it might be tempted to plunge into the heart of the flame. Two pairs of enigmatic eyes studied Arne, smudges within a veil of the palest green found in nature.

No call to be afraid of a moth any more than a dead mouse—but Arne forgot his resolve to reopen the crate and wrap the shoots of pea vine around the Dark Man's neck. He left the barn in a hurry, barring the doors, shutting in the inexplicable cold as Hawkshaw came circling around to see what he was up to.

9

For the first time in centuries, Theron, seventh born of the first man and woman, is again reminded of his lack of Grace, of the bitterly fallen. Of his mother, twice-shamed. Of the last days of Paradise.

(*After the womb's surge, the child unbreathing in her arms. At her side, the Beau apocalyptic, his mind a fossil of the brain like the bare bones in space, the freezing deities. One child less in Eden; she'd wear mourning to the funeral, if only there were cloth. Her hair could use a rake, yet gray becomes her. Old lion yawns, a pecky bird devours the tidbit of the moon, there is a stillness of depletion, a time of grieving in the napping green.)*

Dissipated, immobile, hatefully bound by a bit of blooming vine, a remnant of damnèd Paradise, Theron dreams of the new Eden he has glimpsed in the minds of the woman and the boy. He schemes renewal, the getting of freedom, mastery of this promising, desirable environment he senses despite the darkness of the prisoning body. He senses fear, and susceptibility. A hidden, unrecognized yearning that matches his own. In his depths, within thicknesses of pitch, the power of Luna glows.

Reach her, Theron commands.

10

Moonlight passes through the chinks of the barn. An owl screeches. On the edge of the crate, a motionless moth.

11

She is restless an hour before dawn; then he is awake.
He slides a hand beneath her nightdress. She is not
wearing step-ins. But Birka, who would customarily
make it easy for him, relaxing, opening her thighs,
tenses this time.

"No," she says. "I'm not ready yet."

It's a lie. She is more than ready, but afraid. Like
Lilith who came before her, Birka has dreamed of ser-
pents.

AUGUST, 1970:

Looking for Arne Horsfall

1

Marjory came out to the front porch after getting off the phone and said to Enid, "That potpie won't be fit to eat if it stays in the oven much longer." For emphasis she gave the screen door a push so that it slapped shut with enough velocity to startle one of the cats.

Enid, still in a funk after three days, didn't look around. She was sitting on the porch railing facing west, her lips bloodless without makeup, circles under her eyes. The light of the fading sun tinted her hair red at the temples. She was taking this whole thing entirely too hard, but Marjory wasn't about to say so again.

"I mean it'll be okay if you want it later, the crust'll get a little soggy is all I'm saying. Just tell me."

"You can go ahead and eat my pie for me, Marj, I'm just not feeling hungry."

"Do you think I was hinting—?" Marjory shook her head. "I'm meeting Boyce and Rita Sue at Dairy Queen after I drop you at work," she said. She scooped up Zombie, who was walking between her feet, and held him snugly against her breast. "They fixed me up," Marjory said with a wry smile, and that got Enid's full attention.

"Oh—that's nice. Who is—" Enid frowned. "You're not going like *that*, are you? On a date?"

"What's wrong with the way I look?"

"You know. That awful bloody rag you've been wearing tied around your head."

"This?" Marjory said pridefully, tugging at a loose end. "I told you, Enid, it's not blood. Red paint. Symbolic. A whole group of us are wearing them until those responsible for Kent State and Jackson State get the chair. Up to and including Tricky Dick."

Enid shrugged halfheartedly, and resumed her lookout, as if she expected Arne Horsfall to come staggering up out of the depths of Crudup's pond at any moment. Although, at her insistence, the pond had been dragged by members of the sheriff's department the day before.

"Enid, you'll be late for work. And you don't need that creep Shelnutt on your back for the rest of the week. His problem is he thinks he owns the store—"

"I'm not working at Buy-Rite tonight; I've got something else to do."

Marjory put the cat down in a cane-bottom rocker and came up behind Enid.

"You know as well as I do—" She sounded slightly belligerent, and softened her tone. "Mr. Horsfall's just scared and hiding out somewhere, and when he's hungry enough he'll turn up."

"That's not what you thought Sunday night."

"I get a little hysterical, that's all. I don't like spooky stuff. Enid, you know there're times when you shouldn't pay any attention to me."

Enid smiled slightly and looked at her sister, without the little critical squinting of her eyes. "Who's the guy?"

"His name's Duane Eggleston. I remember him, sort

of, from church camp three years ago. He wears glasses and collects spiders. Or something like that. Butterflies.''

"Just let me get my purse. I wonder what I did with my purse?''

"Hall table. Would you put the pie in the fridge? Maybe you'll eat it later.''

"I wish I didn't have to go to work," Enid said from inside the house.

"That's okay, don't go to work! I'll have both my permanent crowns melted down and sell the gold! I don't need to chew, I can live on peanut butter!''

"What I meant was, I'd like to drive around before it gets dark again, maybe see if—"

"Enid, *everybody's* looking for him, how can you do any better? You know what I think? He'll drop off a truck in front of the gates of Cumberland State any time now.''

"I just don't think so," Enid said, coming outside, hesitating. Enid could be a little dreamy at times, but tonight it was as if she'd just awakened from a coma. "Do I need anything?''

"Lipstick. Come on, we're—"

"I'll put it on in the car.''

"Good idea.'' The telephone rang. "It's not important!'' Marjory said, suddenly with a case of the jitters for no good reason.

"I think it's probably Ted.''

"Make it quick, will you?''

Enid was five minutes on the phone while Marjory fretted, and called to her twice. Enid came outside looking both puzzled and hopeful.

"It was Ted, all right. Marjory, somebody may have seen him!''

"Oh, yeh, where?''

"Gaithers Lick.''

"That's twelve miles from here! I don't see Mr. Horsfall getting that far on foot.''

"Marjory, let's—"

"No. *No*. Enid. Listen to me—"

"But you don't know how awful I've felt! I've just got to *do* something—"

"You can do something. You can go to work and let the cops handle it. Enid, really, I've got a *date*. Do you know how long it's been since—"

Enid capitulated with a preoccupied nod, and Marjory drove her to the Wager-Symms mortuary, a white Colonial mansion separated from the highway by two acres of immaculate green lawn. Local people called the funeral home Wages of Sin. It was conveniently located across from Balm of Gilead Cemetery, where Marjory and Enid's parents had been laid to rest.

"I don't know about you," Marjory said, dropping Enid beneath the dark green canopy that came down to the drive from the veranda, "first it's loony bins, and now—"

"Marjory? Your morbid streak."

"I'm not being morbid. It's just that every time I come by this place I think about—"

"I know, I know. But Cornell's paying me five dollars an hour to help reorganize their filing system—"

"Why, did *they* lose somebody?"

Enid gave Marjory a stark and possibly unfriendly look.

"Sorry," Marjory mumbled. "I need to have lip surgery. But I'm afraid the zipper will jam at mealtimes."

Enid relented with a smile. "Have a good time, and, Marjory, could I offer you a teeny bit of advice—?"

"No."

"It's just that you have so many *opinions* about everything. Give what's-his-name—"

"Duane."

"A chance to talk about himself."

"I will. I promise. You know I really *do* value your advice. Enid?"

"Yes?"

"Should I let a boy put his tongue in my ear on the first date?"

"You don't need to bother picking me up; Cornell will give me a lift home."

"What a treat; maybe he'll let you ride in that long silver job with the vinyl—"

"Good *night,* Marj."

"Give Cornell my best, but whatever you do, don't shake hands with him."

Marjory was still in a good humor when she pulled into the parking lot at the Dairy Queen. Rita Sue and Boyce Bledsoe were there already. Boyce had a new pair of crutches and a stocking bandage on his injured foot. They were alone in a booth. Marjory didn't see anybody in the place who looked as if he might be Duane Eggleston.

"Marjory," Rita Sue asked, "couldn't you find a Band-Aid?"

"Ha-ha, Rita Sue, that's . . . not bad, for you. This is a *symbol* of our outrage, which I thought I explained—"

"Oh, you know I'm not political," Rita Sue said, flapping one hand in annoyance.

"You will be, when the Tennessee National Guard opens fire on the Tri-Delt house in Knoxville."

"Why would they do a thing like that?" Rita Sue said with a frown.

"How's the foot, Boyce?"

"No fractures. Just a bad bruise."

"What did you do with—"

"Duane's in the little boys' room," Rita Sue said. Elbows on the table, she put her chin on the backs of her hands, her serious gossiping pose. "Marjory, you will never guess!"

"Am I going to faint?"

"I wouldn't be surprised. Brenda McClanahan gave Darden back his ring."

"You swear! Was it that tacky?"

"I don't have a clue. When I called her up about Darden, all she said was 'He was it, and now he's not it.' "

"Maybe Darden is getting a break and doesn't know it. Brenda's always been mean enough to kill Jesus."

"Here comes Duane," Boyce said, and Marjory glanced up and back before sliding over in the booth. At first she thought Boyce was putting her on, because the guy who was joining them didn't look at all like she remembered. He was a lot taller, for one thing. His sandy hair was cut short and his complexion was okay, just a couple of insignificant spots on his chin. He wore glasses with aviator frames that suited his squarish face, which didn't have much going for it. But his eyes were sharply blue; he didn't just look at Marjory, he nailed her. It was a little startling. Marjory also managed to notice that Duane had a good build, almost as good as Boyce's, and Boyce worked out religiously.

"Hi."

"Hi."

"You two remember each other, don't you?" Boyce said.

Marjory was doubtful; Duane smiled and shrugged. "Sure. You still good at playing ball?"

Marjory took a breath and said, "Fair."

"Don't let her kid you," Boyce said. "She hits them out."

"Out of what?"

"Are you a baseball fan?" Marjory asked Duane.

"No." He looked carefully at her for a few more seconds. "Are you protesting Kent State?"

"Yeh. What about you?"

"It made me sick to my stomach. I would, but I can't."

"Protest? Why not?"

"Well—"

"He'd get in trouble," Boyce said. "He's on probation."

"What kind of probation?" Marjory asked, thinking it was probably some school thing.

"For Grand Theft Auto," Duane said. "I stole a car. Me and two other guys."

"You did? What for?"

"Oh—it seemed like a good idea at the time. You know. It was one of those things you don't think about, you just do. We rode around for about thirty minutes and then started to take the car—it was a Cadillac—back where I hot-wired it, but the cops—"

"*You* hot-wired a car? Where did you learn how to do a thing like that?"

"Isn't hard. Maybe we shouldn't talk about this any more. I just feel kind of dumb. It's not something I'll ever do again."

Rita Sue said, "Tell her about all the psychological tests you had to take."

"They found out he was a genius," Boyce said, "so they didn't put him in reform school."

"Lucky for you," Marjory said. She couldn't look away from Duane, and he was smiling at her, ruefully, and it was as if Rita Sue and Boyce had disappeared from the booth in Dairy Queen; Rita Sue was saying something but Marjory couldn't be bothered.

"How long are you—"

"Oh, I don't know—until school starts."

"Well, maybe—"

"I'd like to see you play ball."

"You would?"

"Want something to eat, Marjory?"

"Yes. Yes, thank you, Duane. Just a plain hamburger. No pickles or catsup, you know, I'm trying to watch it. I could lose a few pounds."

"You look fine to me," Duane said.

2

The four of them wound up at the drive-in movies in Rita Sue's Fairlane. Marjory sat with Duane Eggleston in the backseat and in the two and a half hours while she ignored John Wayne in *Rio Lobo* they exchanged life stories in random anecdotes. Boyce and Rita Sue cuddled up front with Rita Sue saying once in a while in a no-nonsense tone, *"Boyce."* But they kept sinking lower in the seat until Rita Sue was quiet, and Marjory couldn't see the tops of their heads any more. She and Duane were together hip to knee as if they had been born that way. She didn't know what was going on with her. She felt light-headed most of the time, and her heart pounded. Finally they held hands, but that was five minutes before the movie ended. Boyce and Rita Sue rustled around in the front seat straightening their clothes, and Rita Sue fixed her hair, which gave Marjory a sneezing fit.

"Thanks a lot, Rita Sue."

"It's only a little holding spray. You are so *allergic*."

"Anybody want the rest of this popcorn?" Boyce asked.

"Not if it's got hair spray all over it."

"What was the movie like?" Rita Sue said.

"It was more fun watching you two arm-wrestle. Or was it his arm?"

"Oh, great," Rita Sue said. "I didn't bring a lipstick."

"I liked the part where John Wayne dropped his gun and blew half his foot off."

"That didn't happen," Rita Sue said.

"How would you know?"

"Because. He's *John Wayne*. Marjory, would you happen to have a lipstick?"

"No. I had a lipstick once, but I loaned it to you. Oh, and while we're on the subject, whatever happened to my Janis Joplin records?"

"Oh, Marjory. You know I've got them *somewhere*." She spritzed the back of her head again. Marjory went into a partly make-believe paroxysm. Duane moved over and opened the door.

"Sorry," Marjory sniffed, thinking she'd offended.

"That's okay."

"Where you going?" Boyce asked him.

"If nobody wants the popcorn, can I have the container?"

"Sure." Boyce handed it to him. "What do you want it for?"

Duane dumped the popcorn onto the ground beside the car and got out slowly.

"Luna moth," Duane said. "Biggest one I've ever seen. I know where I can get ten dollars for it."

Marjory turned and saw the pale green moth on the window of the convertible top. It was larger than her spread hand, a glowing misty green except for the distinctive wing markings, the purplish-red border inflamed by the neon of the concession stand a few car rows behind them. Marjory shied away, although the moth was on the outside, and shuddered.

"Oh, my God," she said. "I just hate it, the way they sneak up on you."

"What's the matter?"

"Duane—don't—bring that thing in here."

"Don't bring it in here!" Rita Sue echoed.

"The larvae can be pests, but the adults are harmless," Duane explained. "All they do is breed and lay eggs." He glanced again, covetously, at the big luna. "This one's early-season brood, you can tell by its markings. I hate to see it get away. There aren't many giant silk moths around any more. Pesticides and herbicides kill them. I wouldn't mind raising a few myself. Just let me try to trap it and I promise—''

''No!'' Rita Sue said. ''They give me nightmares!''

Marjory stared at her. ''You had a nightmare too?''

Rita Sue nodded, fascinated, and bit down on her lower lip.

''Why didn't you tell me?''

''Because you would have made fun of me! You're always making fun of me!''

''I'm not making fun now. I'm serious. Rita Sue— *what did she look like?*'' But Marjory needn't have asked. Because Rita Sue, like one of those idiot virgins in vampire movies who just have to get out of bed and open the window, was studying the luna moth, so unearthly pretty, motionless as a decal in the rear window of the convertible.

''Like that! She looked just like a big old green moth!''

3

When he left the shack to relieve himself, in some dark hour well before dawn, he knew without having to look up that he had company. He knew from the severe chill in the air, the luminous, frosty quality of the light.

Until now he hadn't been sure just where he was: nothing familiar remained except the rivers themselves, the Cumberland and Harpeth, which he had crossed on railroad bridges after dark. At one point he thought he recognized the valley where the Horsfalls had lived along with the Sealocks, the Oakmans, and several other families. The shape of a barn roof against a sunset sky, the flaring of a hundred-year-old tree in a pasture, had excited memories, but barking dogs kept him well away; even if he'd been able to examine the tree for initials carved into the trunk, probably he wouldn't find them any more. Not after so many years—how many? He didn't know. His life since the events at Dante's Mill was vague to him—the years had passed as a sickness, a fever dream.

His blood was thin, his feet were sore, his knees hurt, he had a toothache. He was old. His heart tried, but it couldn't pump strongly enough to keep his hands warm, his brain from fogging. He'd walk for a while, heading west on instinct, then black out on his feet, come to staring vacantly at the sky where the sun had set, the moon had risen.

Like now. Pants open, peter in his hand, but he didn't remember leaving the rotted log-and-shingle cabin, half-buried in thicket and vine, that he'd found on one of the several ridges he'd crossed so far. Since leaving . . . he'd been . . . yes. They'd had chicken for dinner. Then he was given a room of his own, to lie down in. That he remembered quite clearly. The neat, clean bedroom. Taking off his shoes. Lying down. An old radio playing. The comfort. The luxury. His mother saying to him—

Let me go.

Not sounding angry because of what he'd done to her, to all of them. Her tone soft and loving, as if they'd merely been playing a game, and now she needed to finish some chores, get their supper on the table before Big Enoch came in from the field.

Let me go, Arne?

Over and over, never raising her voice. Talking to him on the radio, forgiving him—

No, mother! I can't. Can't go back. Can't let you go, pa said—

Said they would strip his skin off, flench him like a squirrel if they caught him.

But here he was anyhow. Shouldn't have done the girl that way, she'd been so nice to him. He could draw her, but sometimes couldn't remember her name, although she was the most beautiful thing he'd ever seen. As beautiful as his mother. *Enid.* That was who she was. Enid would touch the hand that clumsily held the drawing pencil, guide it. Not afraid to touch him. The difference in their hands—his like a turkey's claw, hers . . . nails clean, rosy with health. Little half-moons like the moon he could see out of the corner of his eye as he was holding himself and, amazingly, stiffening in a way that never happened during all the years he lived in the Place. Shame cramped his heart, panic further weakened his knees.

If you love her, Arne, you can have her. I'll show you the way. You'll be lovers forever. But first you have to do something for me.

He zipped himself up and looked around unwillingly. Her voice so clear, it was as if he were fated to find her there in the clearing with him. No, he was alone except for the lunas. They were as sublime as church-window angels, but with a carnal redness to their burning eyes. They'd been with him since he'd run off—but only at night. They came out with the stars, with the peculiar high-summer frost he remembered from so long ago. Keeping their distance. There was no harm in moths, never had been. But they had too many eyes, bearing witness to his feebleness, his lack of will.

You don't have to be old, Arne. Worn out and short of breath. But there's no time to lose.

How did I get here? he thought. How could she make him come this far, when he didn't want ever to set foot in that cavern again?

(Oh, daddy, didn't we stop them? Was there just one left we didn't know about?)

Silence. He felt the weight of all his years then, like the weight of river stones painstakingly piled on Big Enoch's grave. The weight of a vow he didn't know how to keep any longer.

Trembling, he crept back into the dark of the little falling-down cabin, smelling of decay, sat with his arms wrapped around his sore knees, agonized by cramping feet, and tried to rest, tried to resist her.

Just a little while, Arne. Then I want you to get up. Tonight, Arne, tonight, darling, come to me tonight!

He knew then that she was worried. His hands were clenched, cold and rigid, lacking blood. His heart labored. And he realized, despite the slowness of his brain, what had his mother so worried. There was only one way, but still he had the power to defy her. Just as his father had defied her.

By dying.

4

There was a sheriff's car parked by the porch when Marjory drove up at eleven-thirty.

"Uh-oh," Duane Eggleston murmured, leery of the law since his fling at auto theft.

"That's okay, I know who it is. Come on in for some cake."

"I've got to be back at Boyce's by twelve. That's one of the terms of my probation."

"No problem, Boyce is five minutes down the road. How long are you on probation for?"

"Two years."

Ted Lufford was in the parlor finishing off a big piece of the marble cake Marjory had baked yesterday. Enid was drinking coffee.

Marjory said to Enid, "How was your first night on the job? See anybody we used to know?"

Ted said, "What are you up to, Marj?"

"Oh, we went to *Rio Lobo*."

"How was it?"

"Fabulous. I must have shed a thousand tears. When I wasn't beside myself with excitement. Indians! Buffalo! Bad guys. I especially liked the part where John Wayne's horse sat on him."

"You lie."

"Never! Go see it yourself if you don't believe me. Duane Eggleston, this is my sister, Enid, and Ted Lufford, who's like one of the family. Ted, you look more and more like the Duke every day. In this light. Good gosh, could there possibly be any cake left?"

"Best cake you ever made," Ted told her, his mouth full. "Nice meeting you, Duane. Oops."

"I'll vacuum those crumbs up in the morning, Ted. Duane's from Franklin. He came up here to Caskey County for a couple of weeks to find out what dull and boring is really like."

"Nice meeting you," Duane said, as Marjory took him by the hand and pulled him off to the kitchen.

"Your sister's, uh—"

"You were going to say 'raving beauty'? Faint praise. You ought to see her when she's at her best, she's been off her feed the last few days."

"Just a little piece, Marjory. I get breakouts. Do you have a flashlight?"

"Sure." Marjory put a piece of the marble cake in front of him and took a bottle of milk from the fridge. "Why?"

"I was thinking about all the moths you said you saw. That's real unusual."

"Tell me about it." Marjory poured two glasses of milk but decided to lay off the cake. "You should have been here."

"Yeh. Luna moths are attracted to light, and other lunas. Unmated females. Did you find any dead moths around the next day?"

"To tell the truth, I didn't care to look."

"Well, predators might have eaten a lot of them. Owls, skunks, raccoons. See, they breed twice a year in Tennessee, so because it was only a few days ago, there might be some that haven't pupated yet."

"Poop what?"

"That's when the larvae become adults. They develop reproductive organs and wings. Then they fly and mate and lay eggs."

"We could get more of them flying around?"

"Maybe. If there are any cocoons on the ground with pupa in them, I'd like to have two or three to take home. I've got a few minutes yet. If you could find that flashlight."

"Okay," Marjory said unenthusiastically. Duane was a quick eater, or maybe he was just turned on by the notion of a poop hunt.

"Pyew-puh, Marjory."

"Oh, yeah." She closed a drawer. "Here's the flashlight." She wasn't crazy about the idea of suddenly encountering a flock of moths drawn to the beam; on the other hand, she'd follow Duane almost anywhere. If he liked moths, maybe he'd learn to like baseball. Life was full of compromises.

They went outside by way of the back porch, following the beam of the flashlight Duane focused on the ground in front of them. It was dark in the yard. Marjory kept a hand on his other elbow, walking beside him.

"Why do they only come out at night?"

"They're noctuids."

"I guess that explains it."

"I'm not sure myself. It's probably a defense against their natural enemies. Anyway, they don't bite."

"One bit me. I can't even show you where. The shorts I had on—It just about flew up my—"

"Marjory, they *can't* bite. Their mouth parts are adapted for sucking nectar as adults, but they don't have a proboscis that can break the skin. A few caterpillars like the Io have spines that—"

"I've still got a little spot. It bit me, all right. I think it was after blood. I'll show you the spot, but we have to get married first."

"Is that a hickory tree over there?"

"Uh-huh. Yikes! What was that?" Marjory did a little hop and skip around behind Duane as he switched off the light. Something as big as a bird, but silent, had flown right at them.

"I think it was a Black Witch. Another noctuid. They work their way north from Mexico this time of the year." He stopped suddenly and Marjory bumped into him. "Okay. Hmm."

"What?"

Duane kneeled and switched on the flashlight again. With a twig he turned over a litter of hickory leaves and rotting green hulls. Some of the leaves around the perimeter of the hickory tree were leathery leftovers from other summers, but there was a significant top layer of newer, green leaves with a few clinging husks.

"Luna cocoons," Duane said happily. "But these are empty." He continued looking through the leaves. Marjory watched, a hand on his shoulder. After a while Duane gave up with a sigh and rose, the beam of the flashlight glancing off Marjory's face. She didn't blink.

"I'd better get going."

"Okay."

"Marjory—"

"That's okay, too," she said.

They were only a few inches apart. He kissed her. Marjory had always thought it was going to be a big deal and she wouldn't know what to do. The nice thing was, you didn't have to do much of anything. Somehow it made her feel thin and glamorous. She was impressed.

"Duane? Are you going with anybody?"

"No. I was, but she moved to South Carolina."

"Why did you want to kiss me?"

"Oh, because."

Marjory laughed nervously.

"Was it the same sort of impulse that made you hotwire that Cadillac?"

"I think it was."

"Uh-oh." Because the light had been in her eyes, she couldn't see anything but sparkles. She didn't know if he was smiling. There was just something about Duane: maybe he didn't always do the right thing, but when he felt like making a move he made it, and to the best of his ability.

"Do you want me to come over tomorrow?"

"Afternoon," Marjory said. "I'm busy in the morning." Then, when he just stood there and didn't say anything for a while she raised a hand and touched his cheek, and with dry mouth and thudding heart, kissed him back, beside her fingertips and at the corner of his lips.

5

Getting ready for bed, Marjory bumped into Enid coming out of the bathroom with her newly washed hair wrapped in a towel.

"How was your date?"

"Duane's been lifting weights for a year, don't you think he looks terrific? He's nuts about Janis Joplin, too. And he's real smart. He's going to be a zoologist or specialize in space medicine or something like that. He stole a car once, but it was just a youthful indiscretion. He kissed me and I kissed him back."

Enid put a bare foot up on the railing and with a tissue dabbed at a blood drop over the ankle bone where she'd nicked herself shaving. She gave Marjory a slant look.

"Why, Mar-jory."

"Wasn't time not to," Marjory said, drawling like Duke Wayne.

6

He was awakened in the early morning by a shaft of sun through a large gap between logs of the hillside cabin; by pesky mosquitoes and a louder, intermittent humming. He identified without having to think about it the squeaky-wheelbarrow voice of black and white warblers, the sweeter notes of nuthatch and thrush. He was shaking uncontrollably, jarring his bones. He couldn't remember where he was. He didn't know why he was there.

At the Place it was always warm. In winter the radiators hissed and chattered. Sometimes there were as many as six male patients in his room, usually only three or four. The single bureau in the room, metal that looked like wood, had six drawers. The sheets were changed twice a week, unless somebody had an accident. There was a blanket on each bed. Tears ran down his cheeks now as he shivered and made noises in his throat. He missed his blanket. He missed the routine of the Place. Nothing much to do, really. One day his team mopped floors, on another they cleaned the bathrooms. Breakfast was always at seven-thirty, lunch at eleven-thirty, supper at five-thirty. He liked cinnamon toast for breakfast. That was Sunday. Creamed chipped beef and biscuits for dinner. That was Wednesday. Chili mac, he never cared much for chili mac, always let Rooney have the chili mac off his tray in exchange for an apple or orange. Friday the best day, though, because every Friday his mother baked two pies: apple, cherry, huckleberry, it depended on the—

"Unnnnnhhhhh!" he groaned, and dark phlegm jetted from his lips as he lunged to his feet, momentarily ignoring the pain in his arthritic knees. His brain, already on a low ration of blood, reeled; he saw flashes of light brighter than the sun streaming into the hidden cabin. There was a lot of noise in his ears, like sand rubbing on glass. For several moments he was on the verge of fainting, but clung to the stones of a chimney as if it were the face of a cliff until the homeostatic mechanisms of his brain, for too many years subjected to routinely prescribed chemical abuse, once more stabilized the aging body. The neurochemical flood in re-

sponse to crisis awakened, in its own time, areas of the brain that had little or nothing to do with adaptation and survival.

Arne heard his dog barking. He saw, quite clearly, the hills and fields of home just outside the cabin door. He saw his mother, apron fat with feed, scattering corn to the chickens. He saw his father plowing the straightest furrows west of the Cumberland River. He limped to the doorway, crying, and found himself in the cold, damp passage of a cavern two hundred feet below the earth, the way lighted by emanations from—from giant luna moths clinging to the walls, must be a trillion of them! His dog was barking; he turned and saw a dusty road in red sunlight but Hawkshaw lay in dust with blood spilling from his opened throat. *You come, too,* his mother said, raising a hand black as a thorn, limber as a whip, to rope him in . . .

I'll let you have my apple for some of your chili mac, old Rooney said. He said it every Thursday night, been saying it for—

Arne turned to take the apple but it was his father, eyes drained like the dead, handing him a stone wet from the river.

For my grave, Arne.

Hawkshaw was barking again.

He heard voices.

Morning sun painful to his eyes, that persistent whining in his ears.

"Come back here!"

A girl's voice. Arne's throat constricted. He felt glad and then distressed. *It was Enid*—and she was mad at him for running away, even though it hadn't been his fault. Nothing that had ever happened to him in his life was his fault, and now see the fix he was in! He needed a place to hide. She would look in the cabin first thing, discover him cowering there. Even if she took him back to the Place, they wouldn't let him in again. Somebody else had his bed and bureau drawer now, somebody else had taken his place on the team. Floors Monday and Thursday. Bathrooms Tuesday and Saturday.

Shrill whistling. The sound hurt his ears.

"You get back here right now, I'm done chasing you! We'll just leave you and see how you like it!"

A little dog ran into the small clearing and came to a skidding stop when he saw Arne. Black and tan beagle. Foxhunter. His tail shot up and his throat swelled and he began to bay. Arne backed up slowly, not because of the dog, but because he'd heard Enid coming— no, there were two, perhaps three of them, Enid's blond sister too, with the big body and short haircut, she'd been afraid of him for some reason.

He crept behind low-hanging sumac where he wouldn't be seen. The beagle held his ground and quivered, eyes popped, crooning hoarsely. A teen-aged girl pushed her way through a thicket, followed by a freckled boy, and they pounced on their dog.

"Smarty britches!" the girl scolded, when she had the struggling beagle under control. The boy snapped a leash to the dog's collar. "Just about missed your breakfast, chasing those old squirrels! We got to be all the way down to Texarkana by tonight, you hear that, Gumshoe?"

When they were gone Arne stirred, freeing a pants leg from a sticker bush. His clothes were in sad shape, his shoes muddy. *Cinnamon toast*. His stomach rumbled, his mouth watered. He'd been living off what fruit he could find, a few nuts. The shattering visions had vanished, but his heart palpitated. He listened, hearing the boy and the girl at a distance, the whining sounds which he now identified as truck tires on pavement, a trickling of water not far away. He heard a radio, a car horn. So there might be a town nearby. Had to be careful no one saw him.

You don't know who they are, his father warned him. *You don't know who none of them are, so keep away.*

Arne looked around—and there was his father sitting with his back to a windfall, left arm propped up, the wrist a blackened smoking stub. Ax in his father's right hand. One side of his face shimmering like flies in offal.

Arne grabbed his own face with both hands, fingers digging into his scalp until a little blood trickled down. He couldn't look, he couldn't scream. His unused throat like a dry well crammed with stones. His tongue had healed long ago, but with each passing month it was easier not to speak, easy to forget he ever could.

When he dared to lower his hands he saw a wolf spider on a piece of log where Big Enoch had been. Arne got to his feet, grasping anything he could reach to help pull himself up. Instincts prevailing, he went in search of the water he could hear trickling over rocks. When his thirst was satisfied, he simply followed the little stream downhill. It was the easiest direction to go, and going was better than sitting around, dozing off, having a fit or a spell of Seeing what he never wanted to see again.

Through a gap between ridges he had a glimpse of a wide concrete highway and one big truck after another, windshields dazzling in the sunlight. Even this far from the highway there was a visible gasoline or diesel haze in the air. No wind. Already the morning was heating up. He came to a dirt road that looked well used, heard a car or truck coming, and slipped into shadow. It was a pickup truck, towing a trailer almost as big as the house he'd lived in as a boy. Looked like a house, with windows and a door. He'd seen similar trailers on television, but still he was amazed by the size of this one, it brushed tree limbs on either side of the road. Dust from the wheels set him to sneezing and coughing as it drifted through the woods. The cloud of dust was a long time settling. When he could breathe again he walked on slowly through the woods, staying a few yards in from the road.

Around a leisurely bend he saw a large clearing and the glimmer of a lake through trees. Campground, on a little bluff above the lake. More cars, boats and trailers, mobile homes. A few tents pitched beneath tall trees. There was also a wooden building with a long roofed porch, two flagpoles in front. He heard a radio and smelled bacon sizzling on a grill. Three children were playing with what appeared to be a dinner plate, throwing it back and forth. He hadn't seen anything like it on television. The children were adept at their game. The yellow plate soared as if it weighed almost nothing, dipped, skimmed along inches from the ground.

There was another dog on the campground, big as a wolf. It was called a Rin-Tin-Tin, he knew that from one of his favorite television shows. The Rin-Tin-Tin was on a chain, chewing a bone. Arne was far enough away across the campground so the dog couldn't be aware of him.

A gray-haired woman in plaid slacks served up bacon and slices of ham from the grill and called the children to breakfast. Arne held his shrunken stomach, soured from fruit, and looked around. There were several wooden signposts with symbols and letters burned into them. Arrows pointed in different directions. Arne could read very well, a fact which he had scrupulously kept from the administrators of the Place. He had finished third grade when his formal schooling suddenly ended, but nearly fifty years later, he slowly improved on his long-neglected skill with the help of television sets installed in the patients' lounges.

His lips moved. He sounded out the simplest words. The hairs on the back of his sunburnt neck prickled. At last he knew where he was.

DANTE'S MILL
STATE PARK

Birdsong trickled through the woods. A child laughed, the radio played a country song. A car and trailer drove past him out of the campground. He saw a red squirrel on a chinquapin limb, tail shivering. He saw a whirligig of butterflies in a hot flash of sun. He saw an arrow on a sawtoothed sign beside the road, pointing the way he must go.

Across the road on the tent ground a boy and girl wearing identical khaki shorts and tank tops left their tent. Towels around their necks, they strolled toward the bath house.

When they were out of sight he walked across the road and into the trees, hearing the radio they'd left playing in their tent. No one else was camped nearby.

When he glanced into the tent he could see the portable radio on a little folding stool. He was dismally afraid. But he must have the radio; it was more vital to him than food. Although he would never do what she wanted him to do, he had to hear his mother's voice again.

Nobody was looking; nobody knew or cared that he was there. Arne reached a long arm into the tent and stole the radio. It was heavier than he'd thought it would be, and he almost dropped it. Also there were so many buttons and knobs he couldn't figure out how to turn down the volume; this panicked him. If they came back soon and found their radio missing, they'd be able to follow him through the woods. He couldn't walk fast enough to get away. The young man was muscular and would probably beat him. Arne stood behind a tree frantically working the dials, and although he couldn't turn it off, he succeeded in silencing the radio between stations. Then he unbuttoned his shirt and held the radio against his chest, pulled his shirt over it, and retreated to the woods across the road.

The theft, his mental anguish, his panicky getaway, took a severe toll. Out of sight of the campground, he

couldn't walk another step. Clutching the radio,
which was staticky but not loud, he found concealment in a rhododendron thicket. Woodpeckers hammered at a dead tree nearby. He held the radio in his
lap and stared at it, longing for the sound of her
voice. If she had spoken to him while he was in the
bedroom at Enid's house, why wouldn't she speak to
him now? The sun rose, his mind wandered. After
three or four hours the batteries in the portable radio
went dead. Arne's head slumped in a stupor. The
muscles of his outstretched legs and arms jumped
erratically. His eyes were half-open, but he had lost
touch with his surroundings again. His mind was
elsewhere in time.

(*Arne, get up! We're going now.*

(Sluggish from sleep, gasping at the pain from his
bitten tongue, Arne looks up. The fire is low, the moon
is down; daybreak, the angel-eyed watchers gone, and
his father has risen. At that moment of preternatural
consciousness Arne can smell fear and death as plainly
as any animal.

(He shakes his head vehemently.

(*I need you, Arne. Can't manage without your help.
Pick up that bundle of vine and—*

(Arne opens his jaws in a silent scream. Tracks of
dried blood down either side of his chin. He shudders
as his father drops on one knee beside him. Tears. Big
Enoch wets the fingertips of his remaining hand in the
water of his fiery eyes and attempts to erase some of
the old blood, stroking, soothing the boy.

(*But we got to do it! It's for her sake as much as
ours, can't you understand?*

(Shaking his head again, crying, too.

(Come on. While we're walking, I'll tell you why. Tell you everything she done—and what she done to me. What she'll try to do to you, if you give her the chance. There ain't a choice in the matter, Arne. Believe me. I want it different, but no—just ain't no hope for her now.)

AUGUST, 1906:

Big Enoch's Tale

"Of course she'd had the coughing sickness, so that accounted for a part of it, I mean that Birka was strange to me even after she got most of her strength back. Now I never suspected that she'd been touched by an unclean, an accursed Spirit. What call did I have to believe she'd been deceived in her heart and couldn't love me? I'm sorry I was brought up as ignorant of the Bible as I am, but it's too late to be sorry. Well, you know your verses pretty good, Birka did see to that. I know it says in the Good Book somewheres there is Deceivers that will rise up and preach a different gospel, there is Deceivers will make you believe their torment is another kind of Paradise. Anybody that's looked into his eyes, I'm telling you now of him who turned her, Theron is his name, anybody that's seen him in the flesh and knowed the power of his unclean Spirit, then they know his other name is Torment."

(Saying this to the boy, his voice rough and low; they have traveled less than half a mile from their last camp-site and already Big Enoch's footsteps are ponderous, dragging; he stumbles through the woods as Arne tries to steady him, keep him from falling. But Arne is laden with all of their gear, the handax, the awkward bundle of strangler fig, and the going is treacherous for him, too. Breakfast was meager, and he could not chew for the swollen, excruciating bulk of his macerated tongue. His thirst is enormous, but tears continue to course down his cheeks. When they must stop to rest and his father's eyes close, his head droops, Arne prods him desperately to keep him awake, and talking. He is shocked by the heat of his father's skin, by the fact that Big Enoch has wet his pants and doesn't seem to know it.)

"Well, she took to talking in her sleep, and it was that other language that she knowed, which I understand a word or two of, but that's all. She never taught it to me. I only heard the language spoke those two weeks I was up there in Maine State for us to get married. That were in Zipporah, Maine. Twenty-six miles from Portland, where my brother was there in the hospital just lingering on after he was burnt so bad in the ferryboat accident. Anyway she'd talk in her sleep, which I heard her do, maybe it was three or four nights in a row before she took to getting up and going outdoors, what I reckont was she had a problem for which she needed to use the privy. But she didn't come back, and she didn't come back. I'm a sound sleeper with Birka beside me, but when the other half the bed's empty, that be enough to bother me. That second night she were gone so long, I followed her. The privy was empty, but the barn door was standing open. And she were in there in the dark, talking a blue streak, just a-talking her own language to that damned crate! I'm telling you, the hairs stood out like porcupine quills on the back of my neck. When I called her she wouldn't come, and when I went to drag her out of there she fought me like the devil."

(The boy shuddering at this image of violence between the two people he loves most dearly; he looks at the putrefying marks on Big Enoch's cheek, then touches the decomposed flesh. Big Enoch lurches, howls, throws Arne onto his back with a sweep of his right arm and gets to his feet. He trudges on, muttering to himself, without looking back. It is no trouble for Arne to catch up to him. But he follows behind his father, afraid of both his strength and his pain—afraid that each step Big Enoch takes will be his last. A horse, a mule in his sad condition would lie down, refuse to budge.)

"Before I could get her on into the house, she fainted on me. Carried her to our bed and laid her down. Had 'nother thought, and tied her up so she couldn't leave the room. Because her eyes was open by then, and glaring at me. All she would talk was that language. I knowed she was a-cursing me, even if I couldn't understand exactly. If I'd let that go on, she would have waked you for sure. So I bound up her mouth and hoped she wouldn't choke on her tongue. Once I done that, well, it wasn't like she fainted again because her eyes never closed, she just lied there so still and, oh God, I never did see her again in her right mind! You'll forgive me for doing it, won't you, Arne? Tying up your poor mama thataway? Because I swear to you, warn't no other—you forgive me, don't you?"

(Enoch's strong right hand on Arne's shoulder, squeezing, too close to his throat, and the boy is nearly convulsed. The stump of his father's wrist almost in his face, he can smell it, the vile blackness, the bone-deep rottenness the cautery couldn't reach; he is sick to his stomach. His father releases him and he goes down in a crouch at Enoch's feet, trembling, unable to look up, hearing:)

"I saddled Hob-Nob and I want you to get up now and ride to your great-uncle Carl's and ask him for the borry of his crosscut saw. They'll invite you to stay the night and that's okay, it be too much of a trip for Hob-Nob back and forth in one day."

(Hearing this, and looking around as if he expects to see the saddled chestnut horse right there with them, and then in his weariness and fear remembering: No, I did that already! *Rode the better part of fifty miles up to Long Cane, Tennessee, for a crosscut saw his father could have had for the asking just down the road at the Oakmans'; but pleased that his father trusted him to ride so far alone on their best horse, excited by the prospect of an overnight visit with his red-haired cousins. So excited he didn't notice anything unusual about his father, who dogged his every step until Arne was mounted. Even then his father walked with them a few hundred yards in the brightening dawn, finally reaching up to squeeze Arne's hand before giving Hob-Nob a soft whack on the rump. And the next time Arne saw him—*

(—No, wait! There is more he hasn't heard, more he wants to know:

(Getting to his feet again. Taking his father by the hand. Just holding him, walking him, as if Arne is the father now, Big Enoch the child. Leading his father this way is preferable to the deathlike stillness—the vacancy in Enoch's eyes. Walking. Until, looking down from a ridge through evaporating mist, the modest steeple of the white church in Dante's Mill, the shining, wet twenty-foot wheel in the swishing millrace, become visible to them. Dogs bark. A rooster crows. A neglected cow lows to be milked. There is no human voice but his father's, who speaks up suddenly, loudly, causing Arne to jump.)

"I seen you out of sight, then I went straightaway to the barn. It were cold in there, Arne. Cold as Christmas, just like it will be down underneath. We got to go in there anyhow, because that's where they'll all be in the daytime. Where they all live now, where *she* is. But I was a-sayin', I had to pull on gloves to lift that crate into the wagon bed. I don't know why it was so cold to the touch, on a summer morning. I can't account for a thing that's happened, before or since. All you got to do is believe me, until you see for yourself . . . Well, I did know I had to get it off my property and into the ground somewhere in the woods, where no 'un's were ever likely to find it. That's just what I did. Drove clear t'other side of Coachman to the high hills and into woods so deep there weren't a track no more and Ol' Vol by himself he couldn't haul the wagon past the thickets. I cleared a space of ground with ax and shovel, and put that crate down in a hole I was near four hours digging without hardly a pause. And all the time wondering, What's in it? What's in it to make her act like she did? But I wasn't about to open that crate and look inside. I was afraid. That's the bald truth. Even though it wasn't what you'd call cold no more, or maybe because I piled some cut-off branches on top of it while I was clearing ground. Some white ash and box elder and shumard oak. Done the right thing without I knowed why."

(Sunlight. The trees swaying in a soft morning breeze. Pine warblers overhead; Arne hears the gobble of a wild turkey not far away. His mouth waters. Roast turkey. Hunger in the pit of his stomach like a piece of smoldering charcoal, but he is too despondent to make the effort to find something to eat. Only a couple of bullets for the rifle. Maybe he could get more in town. He has money to buy all the bullets he wants, another rifle if need be. He has a five-dollar gold piece at the bottom of his pouch of valuables and lucky pieces, the gold a christening present from the grandfather in Maine he has never laid eyes on. Maybe he can buy something to eat, down there. He has never been to Dante's Mill. But his father said— His eyes are on the town, the sun-struck pond, the shimmering line of the falls over a rock dam beside the gabled millhouse. It must be almost nine o'clock in the morning, yet there's not a soul to be seen. The breeze tickles the hair on his forehead. His father has slumped down, breathing through his mouth, the vacancy in his eyes again. Arne's shoulders and back hurt. He puts down the bundle of cut vine. The leaves are beginning to dry out. He does not want any bullets. He won't go down there in search of food even if he starves to death. He is terrified of this silent town.)

"I'm telling you I was fair whipped when I was done. All I had left to do then was push the crate into the bottom of the hole and shovel it over with dirt. See, I wanted to go straight home. But I couldn't—well, by then I didn't have no more fear of it. It were just a box I was buryin'. So I had my tools with me and I thought, couple minutes more. Just to satisfy, and not always be a-thinkin' what could it of been in that crate. I weren't meaning no harm. So I fetched the crowbar. If it'd been hard, why, I'd of left off and just piled on the dirt. But it were like sliding open a bureau drawer. No more trouble than that. Like the lid had been pried off once already. Maybe Birka—but I don't see how, with what little strength she had lately. Anyhow. I pried, and off it flew. And, oh God! I looked inside."

(Cold and trembling as his father speaks, knowing that he is the one, he is guilty, if not for him they wouldn't be here, none of this would have happened.)

"It were after dark when I fetched on home. Birka was a-lyin' on the bed where I'd left her all tied up, not moving, she just watched me with her eyes. When I set down beside her she commenced to cry, so I untied her hands and feet and took off the rag I'd stopped her mouth with and the first thing she asked me, 'Did you do it?' And I said, 'It's done.' Then she told me what it was, what *they* was, some poor creatures from way back at the Creation, four thousand and four years ago, children of Eve, and God done give to them a hell of their own. She asked me if I touched the vine around its neck, and I told her I couldn't touch none of it. I didn't want to be a-thinkin' about it ever again. Well. After that we—we done what men and women do when they're married, Arne, reckon you already know about that, we—done it twice, and that finished me off, for the night, I thought.

"But it were still dark when I heard Ol' Vol snort, woke up to the wagon creaking dead slow past the window. I got up and saw Birka on the wagon seat. When I hollered she just raised up the whip and laid it across Vol's back like he never knowed before, and he took off at a run that was bound to kill him before he traveled far. I looked around for my boots but couldn't find 'em—clothes nuther. She'd taken ever' stitch of mine with her. Didn't stop me for long. I just lit out after Birka, naked as the day I was born."

(Something unseen, but big, stirring in the thicket off to their right. Hairs standing up on his neck, Arne reaches for the model 1904 Winchester and their remaining bullets. His father oblivious, eyes on a circling hawk of Heaven, mouth slack, throat muscles working as he tries to put this new ordeal into words. Arne works the bolt, drops a .22 cartridge into the breech of the rifle, closes it carefully. The other, the very last bullet, is clenched in a sweaty palm. The rustling continues. Up on one knee beside his father, he strains to see into the tangle of laurel and baneberry and young vine twisted around a half-fallen and rotting tree. Some little birds, worm-eating warblers, burst from concealment like a blizzard of dirty snow: something coming, all right, coming directly at them—)

"I never should've told her where the crate was at. And she had a good start on me, although the way she was driving Ol' Vol proved to be the death of him. I come across the wagon off the road near the burial place; he was down in the traces, covered with foam and blood, breathing his last. By then it was all I could do to hobble, for the pain in my feet. But she'd left the clothes throwed in the wagon bed, boots, too. I couldn't get my boots on, my feet was swole. By then the sun was up, and I followed her track through the woods. Now she never knowed from me exactly where at I dug, yet she went straight for him. Maybe it had to do with the moths that was still fluttering around, or the cold air in that hollow. There was a frost everywhere. It covered the heap of dirt she'd throwed off the crate with my shovel. The lid was a-lying off to the side, and wasn't nothing left in the crate but excelsior and a piece of old dried-out strangler fig, cut in two with a knife.

"Birka was on her back, still holding the shovel with one hand. Her skin was dead-white, but blue where the bones showed through. I couldn't bear to touch her, she was so cold. She were breathing, but so slow I almost couldn't tell. I knowed I had to get her to a house, put her in a hot bath. Or else—"

(Scarcely listening to Enoch now, all of his anxiety concentrated on the thicket where the unseen beast is blundering, crashing, coming closer, sounding, in the quieted wood, like a steam tractor he once saw on the road to Nashville. He raises the rifle butt against his shoulder, finger on the trigger, thinking of how small the bullet is, undoubtedly all but useless against whatever horror is about to show itself; his left eyelid twitches, his breath is like teeth in his throat, his penis spurts. But he is between his helpless father and the thicket, he will not turn and run.)

"Nearest farm were about two mile, a old hard-scrabbly place like to fall to ruin; only a old couple there, and him with the rheumatiz so bad he needed a crutch to get around. But she was all right, little bird of a woman who reminded me of my ma. Them kinda eyes cold as nailheads that'll send a chill straight through to your backbone. Bless her, she didn't waste words asking no questions, just heated up some water on the cookstove and we got Birka into the tub. That old woman scrubbed with a brush fitten to scrape the hide off a scalded hog, but it were just what Birka needed. By and by some color come back. We poured hot tea into her and she opened her eyes and said a few words. She didn't make no sense, it were more of that damned language, but at least she was a-talking. We put her to bed, and I set there with her most of the day, so wore down from commotion I couldn't move nor eat a morsel of food. Then—*oh God! Oh no! Shoot! Kill it! Kill it, Arne!*"

*(Jolted by his father's scream, Arne fires. It's all a blur
to him, the blackish thing with head like a bear's and
arms of raw meat, human in shape but not resembling
anything he's ever seen before, unsightly, ungodly—it
stumbles, falls out of the thicket a dozen yards away,
lies heaving on the ground and screaming its own
scream, a high-pitched hissing. The little bullet couldn't
have missed, the thing is down and rolling in agony as
Arne pulls back the bolt, ejecting hot brass, and inserts
the last bullet in the breech of the Winchester. Sweat in
his eyes. His father's hand crunching one shoulder, he
shrugs violently. What is it? What is it? he demands
silently of Enoch, tugging at his shirt, mouth opening
and closing like a puppet's, only strangled sounds coming from his throat. Now it looks to him like a man, a
half-butchered naked man crawling with flies and other,
tinier insects visible only as a crowd where his skin has
been sliced or ripped from torso, arms, and massive
thighs.)*

"It's *another* one, Arne. Another one flayed alive,
God knows how he lived this long! Let me tell you—I
must have fell asleep at Birka's side, and when I woke
up she were singing a pretty little song in her language.
Pretty, but it made my flesh creep, too. Just hunched
over me on the bed a-singing like a madwoman, holding
a butcher knife against my throat. It were near dark
then, the sky red as blood and blood dripping down
from the bodies of the poor old man and woman whose
cabin it was, I saw them hanging by their heels from
the rafters 'tween us and the doorway. And outside the
sun going down. And she's singing, the look in her eyes
like she don't have no idea who I am. And that sharp
blade pressed so firm if I'd a swallered hard I'd a cut
my own throat . . . go on, Arne, shoot the poor bastard
in the head this time! Listen to him, I just can't stand
it no more! Put him out of his misery, son, send him
home to Jesus—!"

(Pushed toward the suffering man, Arne is shaking to pieces. Dark curly hair and beard thick with gore, but the worst of it is his nearly skinless body as he is eaten alive by those insects not busy depositing masses of tiny eggs in the suppurating flesh. No: the worst may be his sightless eyes, the pupil of each eye slit, exploded by something sharp as a thorn. His head is raised, there is a dazzle of sunlight where sight should be, he is gasping, but weaker now, and Arne sees, below a naked collarbone, the red oozing pucker where his first bullet struck, doing no serious damage. Shoot, shoot him . . . Arne falls to his knees three feet away and lifts the muzzle of the rifle. One bullet, and he realizes how desperately he wants the precious bullet for himself—he looks back at his father, hatefully, pleading. But Enoch knows his mind.)

"What's the matter? Did I raise you for a coward? If that's so, then God damn you, let him die in his own time—and me—how long can I last without you? Go on, shoot yourself dead, and by the time both of us is lying here just a molder of bones, and nothing to tell who we was, that's not too many months from now I'm talking about—a year—everybody else in this entire state of Tennessee—maybe the whole country—they'll be just as dead as we are, or a part of the plague itself! Which is worse. A lot worse than being dead, Arne! You saw her, didn't you? You saw her, too! Ain't that worse for her than being dead? Well, answer me! Answer me one way or t'other!"

(Trapped between the hideously flayed man and his father's righteous anger, Arne throws back his head and howls. Blackbirds explode like splinters from the tops of trees. Arne points the muzzle of the rifle two inches from the ridge of bone between the eyebrows of the flayed man and shoots him, although he is so numb he doesn't feel himself doing it, and he doesn't hear the report of the rifle. Flies boil into an iridescent green cloud, the shaggy head falls down hard at Arne's feet. A little blood spatters Arne's bare toes as he rises, turns, slings the rifle away. Suddenly he isn't breathing. His chest heaves, but he can't swallow air. He just stands there, twitching and unbreathing with his eyes rolling back in his head, and that's when Enoch seizes him, carries him headlong by the waistband of his denim pants, feet dragging and catching on roots and branches and the bark of deadfalls until Arne too is nearly flayed from ankles to toes; carries him, gasping and turning dark in the face, the shortest way to the brow of a hill overlooking the millpond where he pushes Arne off. It is twenty feet to the surface of the pond. The last thing Enoch sees of his son is the sole of a foot fading deep into dark green water. Utterly exhausted, Enoch slumps down crying.)

"You ain't done, Arne. I know you ain't done. Come up now. You'll make it. Got to, son, got to. Now. *Now.* Oh, God, I can't do no more! Help him live. Help my boy!"

(The sensation of dying, smothering to death. Green smothering woods and the choking in his breast, as if it were packed full of grave dirt. Funerals. Churchside cemetery. The very young children playing at the edge of ceremony, oblivious, a dog barking when the mourners sing. His mother's voice the loveliest he has ever heard. No one, even in darkest sorrow, can help glancing at her when her voice is raised in a well-loved hymn. But he can't sing. He can't even breathe. Just forgot how. Heat and panic. Carried like a corpse undeserving of a decent burial to a precarious space at the edge of the sky, the sun a brand in his eyes, water surface filled with clouds. Spinning down to smack the water broadside. Sharp stinging pain, but still he isn't breathing. Caught by a cold current down there he begins, instinctively, to swim.

(Coming up now through the depths to raw sunlight, breaking the surface, yelling, then at last gulping down sweet air just before he goes tumbling across the slick wall and into the pool of the race below, a few feet from the slowly turning wheel. Missing the rocks that lie beneath the waterfall, touching bottom, bobbing up again, crawling through the shallows and collapsing amid cattails along the marshy bank. Lying there, faceup, teeth bared, lungs gradually cooling, shivering, until his father appears.)

"I'm sorry—sorry, boy. It were the only thing I could do, I reckoned you was a goner otherwise. God knows I thought I was about to die myself, more than once these past few days. That knife pressed agin' my throat, like Birka didn't have the least idea who I was. Like she were just a-doing what she'd been told by the Dark Man. I knowed then he had her; she was possessed entire by that unclean Spirit. That's when I saw him, standing in the dooryard, full-fleshed again. He were a big 'un. The sky was all but dark, but when he raised his arms from his sides it were like rainbows flashing in the sky—like he growed wings somehow. I can't describe it. Thanks be to God Birka took her mind off me for a few seconds, sort of turned to see him, and when I had my chance I just about wrenched her arm out of the socket, got a little cut under my chin is all. Well, she were on the floor screaming and trying to pick up the butcher knife with the other hand and he were in the dooryard, so I went through the window, sash and all, and I run. Run home to wait on you. But you was two days late on account of Hob-Nob's fetlock. So I waited around, figuring they'd come. Come hunting me. Couldn't go to nobody for help, not after the sight I'd seen in the old folks' cabin, the both of them hung by their heels and stripped of their skin. Well. Birka almost got me. Almost tricked me into turning. But now I be a-hunting them. And this is where they're all at. In there, Arne.''

(Lifting his head slowly, a clot of fear moving quick as blood from his heart to his brain, exploding there white as the sun on the watery line of the spillway above them; his eyes going then to the dark windows of the millhouse but no faces there, no eyes like the eyespots of the dreaded luna moth. The millhouse is silent, empty, the huge wheel turning to no purpose, no grains are being ground into meal or flour today. He raises up out of the marshy water and looks around at his father squatting in the cattails, face black with beard, black with rot, eyes sunken and glowing, he seems no less fiendish in appearance than the fiends he pursues. He has brought with him the bundle of strangler fig Arne cut the day before. That, nothing else. Arne looks around again, at the millhouse. His father touches the back of his head, gently, correcting him.)

"No, they ain't in there, Arne. Otherwise I'd just burn it all down and be shut of the lot of them. We got us another ways to go. When you can't believe what you see no more, then just close your eyes and hold on tight to me. I promise if you do just what I say, you'll see the light of day again. If you don't—if you lose your nerve—well, then, reckon neither one of us has got a prayer."

AUGUST, 1970:

Huldufólk

1

"*Potato* salad?" Rita Sue said. "Marjory, I told you yesterday *I* was bringing potato salad!"

"Must have been where I got the idea," Marjory said cheerfully. "Duane, could you give me a hand with all this stuff?"

"Sure," Duane said, leaping nimbly from the back-seat of the Fairlane convertible. In addition to a picnic hamper, there were Marjory's portable Zenith short-wave radio, a folding card table, and a two-gallon cooler on the front porch.

"Potato salad," Rita Sue said again, fuming in the front seat. She was wearing sunglasses and a dab of sunblock cream on her vulnerable nose.

"Doesn't make any difference," Marjory assured her. "We don't make it the same way."

"I can eat me a bluing tub full of potato salad any day," Boyce said. Always the peacemaker.

"Marjory, I don't think that card table will fit in the trunk," Rita Sue objected.

"Yes it will. Have a little confidence, Rita Sue."

"Well, I've got my clothes back there which I don't want all mussed up."

"How many changes of clothes did you bring?"

"Three. What's wrong with that?"

"Nothing. If nuclear war is declared while we're gone, nobody can say you won't be dressed for it." Marjory opened the trunk lid. "Plenty of room. What's in that box, tools?"

"Oh, that's mine," Duane said. "Killing jars and stuff. A can of carbon tet."

"Is that for butterflies? Why do you kill them?"

"To relax them."

"I'll bet it does. So why do you want to—tell me after lunch."

Duane grinned. "I'll show you. There's an art to preserving specimens so they look lifelike, like they could fly right up out of the schmitt box."

"The what?" Boyce said, chortling.

"Stuff it back where it came from, Boyce," Marjory advised him. "Rita Sue, what did you do with the camp stools?"

"Marjory, we're going on a picnic, for pity's sake! Can't you sit on the ground like everybody—"

"That's called roughing it, Rita Sue. I get in a really bad mood when I have to rough it. You know how long I lasted as a Brownie."

"Where're you going now? Marjory, it's already ten o'clock!"

"Enid has a camp stool she uses when she paints outdoors!"

"Rita Sue," Boyce complained, "let me have something to eat. My stomach thinks my throat's been cut."

"You can't eat yet. It's not time to eat! First we get there. Then we go swimming. That's the way I planned it. I don't know why everybody has to go and *ruin* things."

"Just let me have one bread-and-butter pickle, and I promise I won't ask for another thing."

"I'll have one too while you're at it," Duane said, settling down again into the backseat.

Eventually Marjory reappeared with the camp stool and several other items, including a flashlight and a snakebite kit, that she happened to think of at the last second.

"Boyce, can you drive okay with your foot the shape it's in?"

"Yeh, it's my left foot's the hurtin' one, I don't need it to drive." He mashed the accelerator and gave a rebel yell. "We're in like Flynn, and off like a dirty shirt!"

"Well, it's not *my* car," Marjory said to Duane, as they went hurtling in reverse down the drive to the street. "Hey, nice day. There's a pickle seed on your chin."

"No, it's a green pimple. Where're we going?"

"Ask the Tour Director."

"Are you referring to me, Marjory?" Rita Sue said. "Where's the picnic?"

"Oh, I thought we'd go up to Dante's Mill for a change, because Rising Fawn is always so crowded on weekends. And it's nicer to swim there. Boyce, you better had *slow down* for this intersection! If you make a rolling stop we could get hit by a Ready-Mix truck, they come barreling down Beaver Ruin like they own the whole road."

Marjory said, "I suppose you all heard the Feds got Father Berrigan."

"Marjory, don't get *started*. He did break the law, and my daddy says what can you expect from a papist anyway? Everybody knows they're born troublemakers, when they're not drinking themselves to extinction. That's all I have to say on the subject."

"If they put him in jail," Marjory said to Duane, who looked sympathetic about the matter, "that's it. I've had it with this country. I'm leaving. I said, you'll have to get somebody else to pull you through Bio, Rita Sue!''

"Where have I heard all this before? Well, bum voyage, as the French say.''

"Where would you go?'' Duane asked, willing to take Marjory seriously.

"Enid and I are going to Italy. To Florence. She'll study painting, and I'll—I don't know. Must be plenty of things to do there.''

"Next summer I'm going to take a motorcycle trip. The West Coat. Maybe up as far as Alaska.''

"Will you be off probation by then?''

"Yeh.''

"That's a terrific idea, Duane. Well. I probably won't make it to Italy. Not right away. We'd have to sell the house and everything. But we're going. It's a feeling I have in my bones. My sister needs to get out of the rut she's in, and do something with her life. Rita Sue, do you have that tube of zinc oxide handy? My shoulders are getting a little red already.''

"Don't use it all up. I burn like a french fry in hell.''

"You know who I'd like to be?'' Marjory said. "Sophia Loren. *Mama mia!* That beautiful olive skin. I'll bet Sophia doesn't get sunburn. If you could be anybody else, who would you like to be, Duane?''

"I don't know. Nobody. I guess I haven't been me long enough yet to know what it's like.''

Marjory and Duane had done a lot of talking during the past four days, but still she was surprised by the way his mind worked; she thought he was the deepest person she'd ever met. Rita Sue said, "You do have a resemblance to Sophia Loren in one department, Marj.'' Marjory, smiling sheepishly, said, "She's talking about my—'' And Duane, also smiling, said, "I caught that right away.'' Marjory took the tube of sunblock from Rita Sue, uncapped it, and looked at Duane again. He spread the ointment on her shoulders, and then, even though she was wearing her baseball cap, which shaded most of her face, he dabbed a little on the end of her nose. Marjory went on smiling. Somehow it was sexier than kissing.

2

Dante's Mill State Park, seventeen miles west of Sublimity, had been created in the early sixties with the flooding of eleven hundred acres to create a lake popular with both fishermen and swimmers. Large powerboats were banned. Slow-moving houseboats were acceptable, and could be rented for the day at the state-run marina near the spillway. Thousands of tons of rock had been dumped to ensure a clean shoreline. There were three campgrounds, each with a swimming beach and boat landing, a cafeteria in the park's headquarters, and a children's petting zoo. The centerpiece of the park was the restored old settlers' town, more than a dozen frame buildings, four of which had been built before the Civil War; a stable and smithy; a mill that still functioned; and a covered bridge.

It was known before the land was purchased for a park that there were caves around and perhaps directly beneath Dante's Mill, as there were throughout the region. Some had been explored by cavers who thought there might be a link, a vast almost endless succession of deep chambers extending north and east to Dunbar Cave near Clarksville, Tennessee, and the famous Mammoth and Great Crystal Caves of Kentucky, a distance of more than one hundred miles. The ground due to be flooded was gone over thoroughly, and one previously undetected cave entrance the size of a rabbit hole was plugged after examination by members of the National Speleological Society revealed nothing but three muddy, middling caverns connected by umbilicus passages and containing only a few commonplace bats and transparent crickets.

Geologists concluded that the limestone subsurface of the land to be flooded could hold the lake; there were already dozens of really large man-made lakes across the Cumberland Plateau. Perhaps entrances to caves of incalculable significance had already been covered by the dammed waters of Barren River, Percy Priest, or Guntersville. The chance that anything really worth exploring lay in the vicinity of Dante's Mill was remote, although previously undetected entrances to caves turned up all the time, betrayed by a puff of steam, a stream of bats at dusk, a newly created sinkhole, or an oddity like the Gochen Hollow Sucking Fire Pit in Alabama, so named because it inhaled the smoke from surrounding campfires.

"My mother must have found a dozen new caves," Duane said. "All over the south."

"She was a spelunker?"

"Cavers don't like to be called spelunkers. Spelunkers wear tennis shoes and write on the walls and leave Coke cans lying around. Cavers are serious explorers. My mom was stuck in a cave for three days once. A rockfall pinned her down. She never lost it, though. That's one thing she taught me: never lose it."

"What's 'it'?" Marjory asked him. They were driving through the cool woods toward the lake that came and went from view as the road curved through the hills of Dante's Mill State Park. They had put the top up on the unpaved road, which was a little clouded from gritty red dust raised by the tires of other vehicles.

"I guess she meant whatever it is you need to get through whatever's giving you hell right then. She took me down once. I was about three, but I'll never forget. We just went straight down into this dark cave, two hundred and fifty feet on a rope. She had me under one arm.''

"Good Lord. Were you scared?''

"I thought it was fun. They named a cave after her, in Missouri I think it was. I haven't seen her for a long time. Three years and two months. My dad divorced her when I was just a kid. He said all he wanted from a wife was dinner on the table every night when he got home. She wasn't too great about getting dinner on the table.''

"Where is she now?''

"France. She married a, I think he teaches mountain climbing. She took that up, too. She writes me every month. In French, because she says she wants me to learn French. I'm learning it pretty good. When I was ten I hitchhiked to the airport and hid on a plane and they didn't find me until we were halfway to Washington. I just wanted to see her.''

"Does she want to see you?''

"I don't know. She's got two other kids now. Maybe she doesn't. But she keeps on writing, so I know she thinks about me.''

"Won't your dad let you go see her? You're old enough.''

"He said if I could pay for my own ticket, okay. I had a job last year and I was saving up money. But he took it all to pay for the lawyer when I got in trouble.''

"Do you get along with him?''

"Yeh. I just do what he says. He's not that bad. Neither is Nannie Dell. My stepmother.''

"What's she like?''

"She wears pigtails. She organizes prayer groups. She's a good cook.''

"Here we are!'' Rita Sue announced, as Boyce found a place to park the Fairlane in a graveled lot that was almost full. "Who's going swimming?''

Rita Sue and Marjory changed in the women's bathhouse and joined the boys on the sunny strip of beach where they were having a chin-up contest on the exercise bars. Rita Sue wore a skimpy two-piece fire-engine-red suit with a long-sleeved lace shirt that came down to her knees, and a Mexican straw hat with a brim the size of a birdbath; Marjory wore a dark blue tank suit and matching short-sleeved top. She tried not to look down to see how much she was shading the sand with her hips.

Boyce complained about being out of shape after his week on crutches and dropped out of the contest. Duane had broken a sweat but wasn't breathing hard after twenty-seven chin-ups.

"You going in?" he asked Marjory.

"Oh, I don't know."

"Race you to the raft."

"Oh, I don't want to race."

Boyce laughed. Duane looked at him and looked at Marjory. "Why is that funny?"

"Race her and you'll find out," Boyce said.

Marjory was sitting on the side of the raft that wasn't overpopulated by kids when Duane finally showed up. She felt happier when he grinned at her.

"Shouldn't have done all those chin-ups first," he said.

"Don't you think Rita Sue's darling in that little suit?"

Duane turned for a look at the beach. "She's okay. No butt and, you know. You look a lot better."

"Maybe a little better than Namu the Killer Whale."

"Marjory, why don't you just shut up and stop criticizing yourself? Hey, you want to know something? Nannie Dell was seventeen when she married my dad, right? She looked just like you do: the same build. She says it was all baby fat; kind of laughs about it now. Nannie Dell turned twenty-four last Thursday and she's had offers to model, but she won't because she's too religious."

Marjory looked at the sky for a few moments, then

at Duane's face in the water, and said, "I guess I kind of lost it there, didn't I?"

"No harm done. Let's swim."

3

After diving and swimming for an hour, they changed and joined Boyce and Rita Sue in the shade of the picnic grounds for lunch. Then Boyce and Rita Sue took a siesta in the macramé hammock Boyce strung between a couple of pines. Duane got two of his lethal jars, a small butterfly net, and a pair of binoculars from the trunk of Rita Sue's car. Marjory carried her Zenith shortwave radio and they went off down a nature trail, then left the trail and found a big log to sit on.

Duane took a two-inch joint rolled in Saran Wrap from his shirt pocket.

"Oh, do you smoke much dope?" Marjory asked him, mildly alarmed.

"No. Once in a while. There's a steel player down the street where I live, he used to be in Tammy Wynette's band. He has pretty good pot. Want to try a toke?"

"I, uh. Well. I never."

"I didn't think so. This is good stuff. If you want to try it."

"Sure. Why not?"

Duane lit the joint and showed her how to smoke it. "Suck in the smoke and hold it down as long as you can."

Marjory did as she was told, and managed not to

choke. When she was red in the face she exhaled. "Yeh. So what?"

"Wait." Duane toked and passed the little joint back to her. They sat smoking for a while, not saying anything. Duane picked up his binoculars between tokes and scanned the trees overhead, the sun coming through in flashes. Marjory noticed a swarm of butterflies and nudged him.

"There's some." It seemed to her that each of the butterflies—there must have been fifty of them—stood out from the woodsy background with exceptional clarity. They were yellow with brown stripes and scallops of dusky blue. Their wings were serrated. Marjory felt an affinity for butterflies she'd never known before. She was in awe of them. She nudged Duane a second time.

"Tiger swallowtails," he said, and raised his binoculars again. "There's a painted lady over there. Nice specimen. Maybe I'll—no, there she goes."

Marjory nodded solemnly, holding down what felt like a furnaceful of smoke. She exhaled, looking at her feet. The radio played softly, a melancholy Judy Collins song. Marjory felt the urge to take off her sneakers and play with the pretty butterflies.

Duane handed her the binoculars and got up with a relaxed smile.

"Excuse me, Marjory. I need to go."

"To the little boys' room?"

"No, I'm just going to take a whiz in the woods."

Marjory laughed and laughed, rocking on the log. She thought it was one of the cleverest things she'd ever heard.

He glanced at what was left of the joint she was holding between thumb and forefinger. "You can finish that, I've got another one."

She nodded and took another drag on the diminishing joint as he walked away. So here she was, sitting on a log in the woods smoking pot with a car thief and amateur lepidopterist who she thought she might be in love with. Life took some funny turns.

There was a mosquito on her wrist. Marjory just gazed at it benevolently until the mosquito was full and staggered into the air so slowly she thought it was going to crash-land. She imagined the mosquito big as a bomber and smashed on the ground, spilling quarts of her blood. She shuddered and felt less mellow. But another, last deep pull on the roach restored her blowsy good-humored equilibrium.

Judy Collins had segued from "Winter Sky" to one of Marjory's favorite songs, "The Last Thing on My Mind." She sang along until the music was obliterated by a blast of static. Then, even more annoying, the radio seemed to go dead, although she'd changed the batteries the night before. Marjory picked up the radio and balanced it on her knee while she searched the AM band trying to find something. She heard voices, but faintly. Dry whispery sounds, in a language she didn't think was English. A woman, or a child, sobbing. She knew instantly it wasn't a program. The sobbing gave her a chill. She dialed higher up the band and came across it again. She turned the radio off. She felt uneasy. She looked at the roach that had almost burned itself out on the log beside her, one tiny spark remaining. There was a pain behind her eyes, as if the day had become too bright to bear. She had feelings of guilt, of obligation denied, that she couldn't make sense of. She looked up with a stricken expression when she heard Duane's footsteps in forest litter.

"What's the matter?"

"I don't know. My radio's acting weird."

"Is it?" Duane took the Zenith from her and turned it on. A riot of music from a polka band caused Marjory to yelp and laugh in surprise. Duane turned the volume way down and found the Beatles. "Sounds like it's working okay."

"I guess so. I'm not sure what I heard. Maybe I was

on the shortwave band and didn't know it. Could we go someplace else?''

"Sure. Where?"

"Dante's Mill isn't too far. It's a restored town, the way it was a hundred years ago, or something like that. There's a general store where they sell drinks and ice cream."

"Let's go."

He gave Marjory back the radio, which was behaving, and they took a marked nature path to the town, approaching by way of the little bluff overlooking the millpond. Weeping willows fringed the pond. In an open grassy area near the mill house people were sitting and sunning themselves, eating ice cream from the store. Duane and Marjory followed the footpath toward the cluster of town buildings a hundred yards west of the mill.

A slim girl in a halter top and smudged yellow short-shorts came out of the woods above them, skidding a little in her sandals the last few feet down to the path, causing Duane to stop suddenly and reach for her with a steadying hand. The girl was so dark it was as if the sun had dirtied as well as tanned her. Her smile was a replica of the necklace of shark's teeth she wore around her neck.

"Hey, thanks." She also had a portable radio, which she held protectively in both arms. She glanced at Marjory's radio, still smiling. Her eyes were almost perfectly round; a cast in one of them seemed to make it difficult for her to focus on whomever she was looking at. Also she was stoned. "Did you hear it, too? Man, I thought at first it was some really bad ganja, you know? But Wiley's my witness. That was before he got so bombed on Bud I couldn't move him with a fucking cattle prod. You know? Deke and Smidge, they've been out of it since like a week from Thursday. Hey, this is Saturday, right?"

"Right," Marjory said. "Hear what?"

"My name's Brittany," the girl said. "This year. Hey, glad to meet you guys. Hold this?" She thrust her large shiny radio at Duane, who already was carrying his box with the killing jars and carbon tetrachloride under one arm. "Is that a butterfly net? Cute. Listen, are you holding any good dope? What've you got? I'll pay you. I've got twenty bucks here somewhere." Brittany poked a couple of fingers beneath her halter top; after a lengthy search she came up with a twenty-dollar bill folded to the size of a spearmint Chiclet. She also left exposed to the air a nipple surrounded by suck marks. Duane turned around with a little shrug to Marjory until Brittany noticed the faux pas, muttered "Oh, shit," under her breath, and snugged the loose breast back into the knit top. "You didn't see that," she informed Duane, who shrugged again, guilelessly. "Twenty bucks enough?" Brittany asked, peering up at him with her gleaming sharky grin.

"I've only got one stick," Duane said. "You can have it. You don't need to pay me anything."

"Hey, thanks!" She was very quick to reinsert the compacted twenty into her top. "Who knows, we'll probably need this, something else goes wrong with the fucking woody. I should have known when I set eyes on it we wouldn't get all the way to fucking Chicago without *major* difficulty."

"Where're you from?" Marjory asked.

"You mean this week or last week? Last week I was in Sanibel. Next week maybe I'll be in Mount Horeb, Wisconsin. Isn't that nifty? My brother's part owner of a dairy farm there. I haven't seen Max in, Jesus, I don't know how many years. You tell me." She gave Duane an expectant look. He handed the portable radio back to her and reached into his shirt pocket for the other Saran-wrapped joint. Brittany accepted it with her free hand. "This is really great of you guys."

"Don't think anything of it," Marjory said. "I like your radio."

"Sure, it's a Grundig. Got it at the PX in Frankfurt. This is the one thing I won't part with no matter how tough times get. Not that I'm worried. I'm an Army brat. I know how to take care of myself. Wiley, well, he's not so bad when he's straight. I think I'll drop him when we get to Chicago, though. Call my brother for bus fare. I mean, can you imagine *Wiley* in Mount Horeb, Wisconsin?"

Marjory looked up at the woods, wondering where Brittany had left her traveling companions. "What was that you were saying about your radio? You asked me—"

"Yeh, oh yeh! If you heard it, too. What did you say your name was?"

"I'm Marjory. This is Duane."

"Well, Marj, talk about fucking *creepy*."

"It was somebody like, crying, you mean?"

"That, too. But I meant *her*. Over and over. 'Puff. Come and help me. I need you, Puff.' "

"Puff?"

"Yeh, isn't that *too fucking much*? Maybe five people in the whole world ever called me that. Did you hear her, too? Am I wrecked, or what?"

"Well—"

"Your radio's working okay. I'm afraid to turn mine on again, I kid you not. Hey, let's go down there by the pond and pass this joint around. Get to know each other better."

"What about Wiley?"

"He'll be okay where he is. Honestly, he's a lot of fun when he's sober. Plays great cocktail piano. The Holiday Inn in Mo Bay held him over for fifty-seven weeks. But that's what did it. I mean, how can you sing 'Yellow Bird' every night for fifty-seven weeks without truly fucking up your head?"

4

Brittany ("Why don't you call me Puff; I'm going to change my name again anyway") said she was nineteen but seemed younger to Marjory; maybe it was the chatter that fell on them like rain, and which seemed oddly disconnected with anything actually going on in the girl's head. Maybe it was her famished-waif look, as if she hadn't had a square meal lately. And whenever she looked at Marjory there was that lameness in one eye, as if her mind had taken a hard fall and couldn't get up. Puff seemed compelled to give them a full reading of her life to date. Her father had been one of those middling career officers in the Army who hadn't attended West Point. Also he was the kind of luckless gambler who would have bet on the Trojan horse in a two-horse race. There was some unpleasantness involving misappropriated commissary funds in Texas that had earned him a dishonorable discharge. Now he was in Mexico, or maybe Guatemala. Puff was inclined to blame her father for her lack of purpose in life, her footloose ways.

"Do you get along with your mom?" she asked Marjory.

"I did, but she died."

"Oh, tough break. Mine did too, when I was twelve. On the threshold of puberty, as it happens." Puff cast around for a comfortable spot, and sat down in the grass where there was some shade and a breeze coming their way. Thunderheads had appeared in the east, rumbling but far enough away so that it seemed unlikely there would be a shower. Ducks coasted on the placid mill-pond. Nearby a couple of small children were eating hot dogs and smearing mustard on their sun-flushed faces. "God, we sure have a lot in common, Marj."

"Uh-huh," Marjory said, doubting it. Puff still had the wrapped joint between her fingers. Marjory wondered if she intended to smoke it there and glanced around uneasily, afraid of spotting someone she knew.

But Puff was looking at her radio in a brooding way.

"I ought to turn it on, find out if she's still there. But I'm afraid of what she's going to say next."

"Who?" Duane asked. He had plucked a long blade of grass and was tying it into knots, only using the fingers of one hand.

"My mother, who else? She's trying to contact me from beyond the grave. I mean, she called me Puff, didn't she? That was a family thing."

Duane looked at Marjory, then at the ducks on the pond while he absently continued knotting the blade of grass. Marjory admired his dexterity.

"I'd call my brother and tell him," Puff said. "But Max thinks I'm nuts as it is."

"Why don't we get some ice cream?" Marjory suggested. "How about you, Puff?"

"Ice cream? That's a fabulous idea! Now that I think about it, I'm really hungry. Where do we get ice cream around here?"

"Oh, the general store. It's over that way."

Puff, her Grundig radio between her legs, hugged herself and looked wearily back over one shoulder. "That far? I don't know, I'm really wrecked."

"We'll bring you a cone."

"You would? God, that is so nice of you! Chocolate, with, you know, lots of sprinkles? Two scoops." She dipped fingers into her halter top again. "Where'd that damn twenty go? I put it back, didn't I?"

"We'll treat," Marjory said hastily. Duane was staring at Puff as if waiting for her nipple, flat as a half-dollar, to pop out again. Marjory nudged him, hard. Puff stopped searching for her money and scratched the top of her breast instead, leaving livid streaks on her tan.

"I like ducks," she said, eyes on the pond. A slight childish smile came and went. She played with the necklace of shark's teeth. "I wouldn't wear these, but they're supposed to be lucky. The guy who makes them only had one leg, though. I wonder if a shark got the other one?" She yawned and lay back in the grass, giving her head a shake to loosen and fan her hair, which was several shades of color, from tawny blond at the temples to a russet with darker streaks that looked unclean. "I like kids, too. But not if I have to have one growing inside of me like a mushroom. Or a toadstool. Sometimes I think about that, and then I can't come. Bummer. Why don't you leave all of your stuff here, I'll watch it for you."

"Well, I think I'll take my radio, I like to hear music while I'm walking."

"I'd go with you, but. You know. I'm just not feeling that great. Probably my blood sugar. Jesus, it's a scorcher today but I'm still cold. The hotter it is, the better I like it. Even in this weather I don't sweat. I wonder what Wisconsin is like. I'm probably making a mistake going there. Mount Horeb. Is that a hoot? Definitely not the sort of place where I can do my nails in church."

Marjory carried her radio in her left hand, and held Duane's hand as they walked up the rise from the millpond toward the Dante's Mill general store. There were a lot of people in the village, wandering from the smithy and stable at one end of the street to the white frame church with its modest steeple at the other. Picnic benches circled the trunk of an oak tree in the churchyard: the oak's branches provided a full dusty canopy for the fenced cemetery.

"A couple of my relatives lived here," Marjory said to Duane. "You know those pictures in the parlor? Third old party from the left, the one with chipmunk cheeks and a crumb-catcher. I don't remember his name. My mother knew; she was the family historian. Funny thing about Dante's Mill. Now that Puff has me in the mood for ghost stories.''

"What about Dante's Mill?"

"They all left one day. Seventy-four people. Men, women, children, just picked up and vanished."

"Why?"

"Nobody knows what happened to them. There's a plaque in front of the church with all their names on it. Rewards were offered; famous detectives investigated. Sherlock Holmes.''

"Sherlock Holmes is a fictional character."

"I know that. I mean the author, whatever his name was.''

"Arthur Conan Doyle."

"I think he wrote a book about Dante's Mill. There's a commemorative grave in the churchyard, but nobody's in it. Anyway, I'm surprised you never heard of the place.''

"Is that line for ice cream?" Duane asked, looking at the tourists packing the covered porch of the general store.

"Or the pottie."

"Looks like a good half-hour wait."

"Probably not that long. It's hand-cranked ice cream. What do you make of Puff?"

"Maybe she'll be gone when we get back."

"Yeh, that's what I was hoping, too. If she does split, you'll have to eat two ice creams."

"Chocolate? I'll break out. I always get a sore bump right here, next to my ear."

"You broke out already, when Puff dropped her top and flashed the bubby."

"Did not."

"Did, too. You wouldn't, would you?"

"Wouldn't what? You mean with Puff? *Uh-uh.* She's worse than a turpentined cat."

"Okay, I like you again."

5

They were on their way back to the pond when the screaming started.

Marjory looked at Duane and said, "Sounds like good ol' Puff."

"Who else do we know would say 'fucking' three times in the same sentence?"

A child began to wail. They hurried. Puff saw them coming down the slope from the village and waved frantically to them. She was below the spillway opposite the mill house, up to her ankles in the race. A few people, including the mother with the red-faced squawling child, had gathered on the bank behind her.

Puff pointed at something below the spillway. She had a rock in her other hand. "That's where he went! He took my radio! Isn't anybody going to *do* something? I want my fucking radio back! It cost a hundred fucking dollars, and I *want it back*!"

"Hey, Puff!"

"Hey, you guys! Come on, come on, he's in there, let's go get him!"

The mother of the crying child said to Marjory, "He went right *by* us. He almost stepped on Bubba. Scared us half to *dayeth.*"

"Who?"

"The man. The one took your friend's radio? He just up with it and ran—I wouldn't call it running. He couldn't go very fast. He went straight down to the dam there, and through the waterfall.''

"He's hiding back there!" Puff yelled, jogging up and down in the shallows of the race. "He didn't come out! I'll bash his fucking head in! You better come with me, Duane. Here." She backed out of the cattails at the water's edge and handed him the rock. "*You* knock him in the head! I'll grab my radio. He's already got it wet! It's probably ruined by now."

"Here's your ice cream, Puff," Marjory said, looking at the curtain of water that fell ten feet from the top of the spillway. She couldn't make out anyone lurking behind the silvery curtain. "Maybe we ought to get some help. He can't go anywhere, can he?"

Puff took the ice-cream cone, hesitated, then handed it to the curly-haired boy huddled in fright on his mother's shoulder.

"Here you go, little boy. You eat it. I'm sorry I yelled so loud and scared you."

"Oh, look, Bubba, she's giving you a ice cream! With sprinkles on it. Now you say 'Thank you for the nice ice cream,' and don't get any on mama's good blouse."

"Thank you," the boy mumbled, taking his thumb out of his mouth.

Puff smiled edgily and looked at Duane. "Hey, you coming?"

"Okay," Duane said. But he tossed the rock into the water.

Puff nodded. "He was just an old guy, from what I saw of him. A bum. He probably won't give us any trouble."

Marjory said, "Why would he run under the waterfall? That doesn't make sense."

"Let's go see," Duane said, and handed Marjory what was left of his own ice-cream cone.

"Maybe I'd better get some help," Marjory suggested. "There's always a sheriff's car or the Highway Patrol around on weekends."

"Wait a minute," Duane said. "I just want to have a look. If he's back in there hiding, then he can't get away."

"Watch out he doesn't pitch a rock at you."

"Yeh," Duane said, and went off around the edge of the race to the rocks at the foot of the spillway; Puff was behind him, a little unsteady on the wet rocks, twice grabbing his belt in back to keep her balance. Duane took her hand and they plunged through the downpour. Marjory could see them pressed against the spillway wall behind the waterfall, edging slowly toward the middle.

"This is scary," said the woman with the curly-haired boy. "I don't think those children should be doing that. I'll tell you what, we're leaving now, but I'll stop at park headquarters and inform them of what's going on over here."

"Thanks," Marjory said, keeping her eyes on Duane and Puff, who were now hard to see through the torrent. Obviously they hadn't come across the man who had taken Puff's Grundig radio; but how could anyone hide between the dam wall and the overflow anyway? But now they were only ten feet from the opposite bank and the foundation of the mill house, the slowly turning wheel. It was dark in that nook, where a storm-split willow drooped thickly over the pond and spillway, one branch rubbing against the blank west wall of the mill. But the acoustics were pretty good and Marjory heard their voices, although she couldn't make out what they were saying.

Then she couldn't see them any more, as if they'd stepped back into a crevice in the wall, and their voices sounded hollow before fading entirely.

Marjory sat on the grass partway up the bank and waited. Some clouds hid the sun, and it was darker still where she'd had her last glimpse of Duane and Puff, who was proving to be nothing but bad news; Marjory had sensed she was some kind of hoodoo the moment she laid eyes on her.

What were they *doing* back there?

"Hey, Duane! Puff! Where are you?"

Not that she expected them to answer; but confirmation that they were no longer within earshot gave her a bad case of stomach flutters. She didn't want to leave, but no help had arrived.

A familiar horn honked three times on the road on the other side of the mill.

"Marjor-yy!"

Rita Sue sounded annoyed. Marjory, still keeping one eye out for Duane and growing more anxious by the minute, waved and then beckoned. Rita Sue didn't get the message. Boyce honked the horn of the Fairlane again.

"I can't—" Exasperated, Marjory picked up Duane's butterfly net and other collector's paraphernalia. She carried the stuff, along with her radio, up the slope to the wooden bridge that arched across the millrace. Glancing down at the waterfall from this elevation, she couldn't see much. There were no bodies floating facedown in the turbulence around the mill wheel. Duane and Puff could not have emerged at the other end of the waterfall where the willow hung low and climbed the slippery rocks to the walkway that surrounded the mill. She would have seen them from the bank. There were some people on the walk with cameras, but no Duane and no Flibbertigibbet. *Damn it!* They had simply vanished, along with the radio thief.

Boyce backed up alongside Marjory.

"Where've you guys been?" Rita Sue asked.

"In the woods."

"I'll bet *that* was a lot of fun," Boyce said.

"Shut up, Boyce." Preoccupied, Marjory dumped everything, including her purse, into the backseat. Then she retrieved her purse and pulled out the flashlight she'd brought along. "Duane's missing. I don't know what happened to him. He's with some girl we met. Her radio got stolen. When the Highway Patrol comes, tell them—'' Marjory shrugged. ''I don't know what. Just tell them to stay here.''

''Who called the *Highway Patrol*?'' Rita Sue asked. ''Marjory, where are you—''

''Down there. Behind the waterfall. That's where they went. I want to see what's back there.''

Boyce said, ''You think he got hurt or something? I'll go with you.''

''You can't, Boyce. You can barely get around on one foot. Just don't go anywhere, you guys. Please?''

''I wish I knew what was going *on*,'' Rita Sue complained.

Marjory shook her head and walked quickly back across the footbridge with the flashlight in her hand, then made her way down the bank to the race. It was a good flashlight, supposedly waterproof, although she'd never had occasion to test that claim. The race and most of the waterfall were shaded now; sunlight slanted across the side of the mill, bright windows hurt her eyes. She looked at the rocks at the base of the dam where the water came down hard; already her shirt and hair were damp from spray, she had gooseflesh on her bare thighs and arms. Marjory took a deep breath, walked past the rusting sign that said Danger! No Wading or Swimming, stepped into the torrent. And through it.

There was a space between the waterfall and the old stonework of the dam, a narrow wet path littered with indestructible flotsam: beer cans, disposable diapers caught on tree branches cemented greenly to the rocks at her feet. She saw a waterlogged duck with a broken neck. The uneven wall of the dam, which slanted out at the top by as much as two feet, leaked everywhere above her head, through small crevices between stones. To Marjory it seemed poised to fall down.

The air was so full of spray she almost choked at

each breath. This was even less fun than she had thought
it would be. Although Marjory had superb balance, each
step was an ordeal. She slipped twice before she had
gone a dozen feet, and the sharp tip of a water-hardened
limb gouged the calf of her right leg. She was drenched,
and her teeth chattered.

Still there was no sign of Duane or the girl.

She could see well enough because of sunlight reflected down from the mill windows to the surface of
the race, then through the watery curtain, but the farther she got from the bank the unhappier Marjory was.
Something moved lumpishly on the path ahead of her
and she froze, lips tight against her teeth. Turtle. She
was willing to put up with turtles. At the first sign of
rats, though, somebody else could do this.

There might be a deep hole concealed by the boil of
water at the fall line. If Duane had slipped and dragged
Puff down with him—no chance to yell, just pulled deep
beneath the creaking old mill wheel, then to God knows
where. On out into the lake several hundred yards away.
She'd heard a lot of freak drowning stories. Her own
daddy—

Marjory paused and bit her lip. She thought she was
going to cry. But she couldn't stop and go back and
maybe not know for a long time what had happened to
them; uncertainty was worse than fear at this point. She
pushed on cautiously, one hand on the stones of the
dam, face averted from the rush and tumble of the waterfall, enough power to knock her flat if she stumbled
into the middle of it. What a lousy idea. Picnics. She
disliked the outdoors anyway, unless there was a back-
stop and a good playing surface handy.

The face of the dam was rounding toward the bank
and the stone foundation of the mill. Just inside the
waterfall, close enough to reach out and touch, was the
turning wheel. Her feet were cold in the soggy sneakers. It was darker here. She edged past the wheel and
into the crevice, twice as wide as she was, between the

dam and the foundation wall and the dripping roots of the willow protruding like fingers where the wall had cracked, and that was it, nowhere else to go. But she turned on the beam of the flashlight in the misty dark just to have a quick look before retreating.

From what seemed like a long way off she heard Rita Sue calling her.

Then she heard Duane's voice, sounding almost as far away.

"Hey, Marj! Is that you out there?"

She was so relieved she could have killed him. She flashed the light frantically around the cramped walled space until the beam suddenly lengthened, reaching into what seemed like infinity.

"Duane!"

At the extreme end of the flashlight's beam something shadowy stirred, and she was reminded of the circus, total darkness and then the slash of a spotlight, a tiny figure high above the arena floor poised on a trapeze platform. But Duane was dead ahead of her, at eye level and probably a hundred yards away. She saw him wave.

"Hey! Here I am!"

"Here you are *where*? You scared the—" She was shouting. "Where's Puff?"

"She's here. She's got a little stone bruise, but she'll be okay."

"What are you—"

"Come on in! It's safe. It's a big cave. The biggest one I've ever seen. There's probably more of it, a lot more. I want to look around."

"Are you *crazy*?"

Puff's voice said, "Listen, Duane, there's my radio! He's playing my radio again, the sonuvabitch. Hear it?"

"You're both crazy! It's dark in there! Maybe he's a murderer. You better get out while the getting's good!"

"It's not that dark! It just looks dark from there!

Light's coming in from somewhere, and that's not all— come on, Marjory, you've got to see this!''

"No I don't!"

"Okay, we're going to explore, see if we can find the radio. There's probably another way out if we look for it."

"Duane!"

"What?"

"I'm coming! Just wait, don't go anywhere! And don't try to hide and then jump out and scare me! I hold grudges for life. Nobody ever gets off my grudge list, Duane!"

The entrance to the cave was just a waist-high hole in the wall, then a passage like a big drainpipe or slightly sloping well that she could shuffle through while bent nearly double. The floor and walls were rock and rock crystal, it was like being in the hollow of an enormous geode. In places Marjory was dazzled by her own light. The floor was covered with something dry, crisp, almost papery, that rustled unnervingly underfoot: layers of parchmentlike leaves or husks. She couldn't identify what it was and didn't care to pick anything up, but the pallid carpeting took on a spectral glow in the beam of her flashlight. Some of the litter looked suspiciously like old snakeskin, she thought. *God*. Fear ran up the backs of her legs like an icy blowtorch.

"Duane!"

"Yeh, I'm here, I can see you."

"I'm t-t-terrified of snakes, Duane!"

"There aren't any. Some salamanders. They won't bother you. No bats either, it's not a bat cave. But it was used for something once."

She reached the end of the passage, banging a knee painfully on a crystalline outcrop. Duane was there, reaching up to help her down into the cave. In the sweep of the flashlight beam Marjory saw Puff sitting casually on a boulder with one leg cocked over her knee, drawing slit-eyed on the joint Duane had given her. Puff's hair was sleek around her head and combed down over her breasts. She'd removed her halter top and wrung it out, but she still wore the necklace of shark's teeth. In this setting, essentially naked, round eyes elated as an animal's, Puff looked coarse and threatening, a Paleolithic princess.

"Hi, Marj! Take a hit, and you won't mind being so wet. If you turn that flashlight off, then you can really appreciate this place. Maybe you ought to wring out your shirt, you could catch a really bad cold. I'm getting the sniffles myself."

Marjory turned off the flashlight and stood breathing in a room in the ground, jolted by every pulse of her body. At first she couldn't see a thing except the glowing tip of the joint between Puff's thumb and forefinger. Then there was a hint of light, like the sky before dawn. The walls around her were a rough grayish-green, but with many chinks and fissures that revealed quartz crystal. Gradually Marjory could distinguish both Puff and Duane, dark but dimensional against a background of subtle colors: lavender, ochre, a deep glowing pink.

"Fuckin' fantastic," Puff said, exhaling. Marijuana smoke was shockingly pungent in the thin, odorless air of the cavern. "But this isn't all of it." She looked over one shoulder. "He's back there, somewhere. Way back. Every now and then I hear a blast from my radio. Scout's honor. Duane heard it too, didn't you, babe?"

"H-how could there be any kind of reception d-down here?" Marjory said, keeping her voice low. She disliked the ghostly quality of their echoes.

"Good question. Mostly it's static. Definitely heard some voices, though. Just like when I was up there in the woods. Here's what I think. There's probably a bunch of them, like gypsies, living in another part of this cave."

"I'm not so sure," Duane said.

"Makes sense to me. They rob stuff, and hide all the loot in here."

"And go in and out through that waterfall each time?" Duane muffled a sneeze with his one hand. "Not worth the trouble." He sneezed again.

"Bless you," Puff said, and for some reason made the sign of the cross in the air with the glowing tip of her joint. "Well, like you said, there's probably another entrance. Which I hope we find real soon, because I don't intend to get soaking wet again."

"Maybe g-getting wet's not the worst thing that could h-happen to us," Marjory said.

"Marjory, you'd better take that shirt off before you get pneumonia."

"Can't. I'm m-modest."

"Leave your bra on then. Here, have a toke; then we need to come up with a plan."

Marjory unbuttoned her shirt, turned her back on them, wrung the shirt out and put it back on again.

"We haven't heard anything for a while," Duane said. "I know a little about caves, and this one could go on for a couple of miles. I think you ought to kiss your radio good-bye, Puff."

"Thanks a lot!"

"Look, we're probably near the surface and that's why there's some light, but the sun will set in another three hours, and then it'll get pitch-black in here. Do you know how easy it is to get lost in a series of caves?"

"Yeh, I guess," Puff said dispiritedly.

"That's settled, let's go," Marjory said.

"Not yet," Duane said.

"You just said—"

"This is a very interesting cave. It might even be valuable. Like the one up in Kentucky where they kept this guy's body in a coffin with a glass top. Floyd Collins, I think his name was."

"What happened to F-Floyd?" Marjory asked.

"Buried alive in the cave he discovered. Anyway, I want to take a look around here while we have time. As long as we can hear the waterfall we won't get lost."

Puff and Marjory just looked at him. Duane shrugged.

"Okay, I'll go by myself. Meet you all outside. Marjory, could I borrow the flashlight?"

"Duane, what if this place *is* full of gypsies, or—worse."

Duane grinned. "What's worse?"

"I don't know. Come on, let's just go."

"Ten minutes. I'll look around for ten minutes, then I promise I'll be back. Or if I find a better way out, I'll call you."

Puff got up. "That makes sense. I'm not getting wet again. I'll go with you."

Duane looked at Marjory.

"Okay. I don't want to get wet, either. I hope you know what you're doing, Duane."

6

He could find no music.

The radio played, but only voices he wished not to hear.

Why had he taken the radio in the first place, in broad daylight with people around? The girl screaming, calling him names . . . because the desire to take it, the third radio he'd stolen in a week, was like a hunger that surpassed the need for food.

Because music quieted the voices. But now he could find no music.

Arne?

No. I won't listen!

They're coming, this time. They'll find us here. And then they'll take you away, and what will *I* do?

Not only his mother's voice. The others, moaning, pleading. But she silenced them. Only his mother had the right to speak to him.

You have to go now. Don't let them find you here. Don't let them find me. Come, now. Come to mother. You know I'm the only one who cares about you. I'm not angry because of what he made you do. You know I'm not angry. Come a little closer, Arne.

Can't!

Darling. Why?

On . . . on his grave. Made me swear . . . !

So awful of Enoch. So cruel! That this should happen to us, to you and I, Arne. But there's still a little time. I can make it right again. In your heart you know this is true. But they're coming. (Stop! You're confusing him. Not another word from anyone!) Men, Arne. Murderous men, they will hang you when they see this place! How can you explain? They'll drag you by your heels and hang you by the neck unless you— Quickly. Save yourself. Save me, too. Just reach out, take me in your arms. My boy. Oh, my lovely son . . .

"Mamaaaaaa!"

7

The blond young man in the tie-dyed T-shirt said, "We're looking for a friend of ours. Maybe you guys saw her? She's about five six. Good tan, like us. We're from Florida. And, uh, she's probably got her radio with her, it's a Grundig. One of those big jobs. What's she wearing, Smidge, do you remember?''

"Shorts, I guess. Unless she changed into something else while we were zonked. Yeh, and the necklace probably. I've never seen her without it, have you, Deke?''

"Oh, yeh, yeh, her shark's-tooth necklace. You'd know her right away if you saw her. Name's Brittany, but she likes to be called Puff.''

Boyce looked at Rita Sue, who shook her head.

"No, sorry,'' Boyce said. "Actually we're looking for somebody ourselves.''

"Oh. What happened to your foot?''

"Dropped a crankcase on it.''

Deke looked around blearily. His eyes were bloodshot. He wore Levi's with his tie-dyed shirt, and needed a bath. He hadn't shaved for a while. He was half bald; the rest of his hair was gathered into a ponytail that sagged over one shoulder. The girl, Smidge, had a raggedy mane and the starkly hungry eyes of a pretty werewolf. Despite their tans they had the shy, baffled demeanor of subterraneans who hadn't ventured out into the light recently. They fidgeted and looked lost.

"Don't know where we can get something to eat around here, do you?'' Deke asked Boyce and Rita Sue. "When's the last time we ate, Smidge?''

"Tallahassee, I think. But Puff has all the money. She's got the gasoline card, too. She better not have taken off with somebody, I'll ream her liver.''

Rita Sue said, "There's a general store up the road where they sell ice cream and stuff.''

"Thanks, but we're fucked until Puff shows up. Might as well go on back to the woody and wait on her there, Deke.''

"Hey, right,'' Deke said brightly, as if it had been his idea. He was a little unsteady on his bare, dusty feet. "Listen, how long you guys going to wait around for your friend?"

"Not much longer," Rita Sue said, spacing her words meaningfully.

"Well, okay, we'll, uh . . . if you see Puff, you know. Wouldn't happen to have a can of beer in your car, would you, partner?"

"Fresh out," Boyce said.

"Those are the breaks. If you're in the mood for blotter, I've got some. The best. Just look us up. We're parked, uh, where'd we leave the wheels, Smidge?"

"Up that hill there behind the millpond."

"Some what?" Rita Sue asked, frowning.

"Blotter, dear," Smidge said, looking keenly at her and then showing her overbite in a smile that caused Rita Sue to fold her arms defensively across her breasts. "Acid. Guaranteed good trip. Want some?"

"No, thanks."

"I love what you've done with your hair. Or is it natural?"

"Yes."

"Well, come on anytime you're in the mood for a swinging party. I'd like to get to know you, what did you say your name was?"

"Rita Sue."

"That's darling. So, we'll probably be here another day or two. Who knows? Bring your buddy when she comes around, if she's as good-looking as you are, Rita Sue."

"Smidge, I'm not feeling so hot. Let's move on, huh? Nice meeting you guys."

When the two were out of hearing Boyce said to Rita Sue, "She sure was looking at you funny."

Rita Sue said, "There wasn't anything funny about it. Boyce, you can be so dumb."

"How?" Boyce said, injured.

"Never mind. Now my back's starting to burn up because you didn't rub enough sunblock all over. I want

to go home. If Marjory Waller isn't standing right here
ten minutes from now that's *exactly* where we're going,
and she and Duane can hitchhike.''

''Want me to spray your back?''

''I can't take my shirt off here, there's a million people.''

''We'll drive up the road some and see if we can find
Duane and Marjory. Then where there aren't any people I'll pull off and spray your back for you with Solar-
caine.''

''Okay. It hurts like the dickens. The backs of my
thighs, too.''

''I can take care of it.''

Rita Sue looked at Boyce for several moments, then
lowered her lashes.

''Let's get us some ice cream first. Then we'll find a
place.''

''What if Marjory shows up here?''

''She can wait. She's kept *us* waiting long enough.''

8

''*Mamaaaaaaaaa!*''

''Ye Gods, what was that?'' Marjory said, unsure
whether the calamitous whinny was human or animal in
origin. They were all bunched up in a passage of the
caverns as confining as a broom closet. Duane's breath
was on her cheek, and Puff's ragged fingernails were
digging into her forearm. She had the flashlight in her
other hand, the beam wigwagging, inflamed ripples
snuffing against bare, blank walls as far as they could
see. ''Puff, let go!''

"Sorry. It was *him*, wasn't it? Must've been him."

"I don't know," Duane said. "It could have been the radio. But you hear some strange sounds in caves. Sometimes you'll hear voices that are a mile away on the surface. If you let yourself imagine a lot of stuff—"

"Duane, would you scrooch back a little so I can get by you?"

"Where're you going, Marjory?"

"Out of here. Back the way we came. I've had enough. It's like being toothpaste in a tube."

"Marjory," Puff said, still hanging on to her arm, "don't be a poop. Actually I think this is kind of fun."

"Here, take the flashlight," Marjory said, and she worked her way between Duane and the wall an inch at a time. She didn't feel anything like toothpaste; she felt overblown in these close spaces, hippo-dumpy. Their downward progress had been slow to this point; they couldn't have come far, she was sure of that.

Their faces were almost together; they exchanged breath like oxygen-starved divers. She wanted to rest on him, like a featherbed. Dream a little dream, awaken to trees and rain. But she would have to earn her way out of this unenchanting place. Suddenly Marjory had the hiccups, and Duane started laughing. Marjory popped free of him, feeling vaguely humiliated but giddy herself.

Duane said, "You and Puff could wait here. I just want to take a quick look a little farther down the bend. I hear water dripping; that might mean a big cavern."

"Uh-uh, I'm going with you," Puff said.

"Marjory?"

"No, I've—*hup!*—h-had it."

"Five minutes, Marjory. Sure you'll be okay?"

"*Yes*. It's just—*hup!*—up there." She took deep breaths. Duane's hand found her shoulder, squeezing. "I'm okay," she insisted. "No, actually, *mick!* make that a little panicky. But I promise I won't l-lose it."

Puff said tolerantly, "I lost it when I was eleven and a half years old."

"I'll bet that stung, but it's not what we're t-talking *abup!* about."

"Thanks for the flashlight. Holler if you need help."

"Helllllp," Marjory said, squealing like a mouse, and they both got a laugh out of that. The laughter was distorted in a way that sounded ominous to Marjory, who found no bliss in inky darkness. She feasted on the beam of the flashlight as Duane turned himself and Puff the other way. Then she started up the passage, fingernails scraping rock and veins of crystal, vision smothering in her eye, the suppressed hiccups burning in her throat, erupting spasmodically despite her best efforts at control. Weary of walls, of darkness, unable to see anything of herself, fingernails dragging but failing to strike a spark. After a few seconds she thought she detected the mild glow of the chamber they had recently left. This cheered her considerably. She heard Puff and Duane conversing, she heard all the nuances of their passage deeper into the cavern. When she looked back she saw only the momentary glow of the flashlight beam reflected from a cloudy aggregate of quartz. Faint as fireflies. Puff was still rattling on about retrieving her radio. Puff, Marjory thought, was demented, but she was most concerned about Duane. At least his interest in exploring further was understandable. He'd been in caves before, and had no fear of them. Maybe Puff wouldn't be able to talk him into something foolish or dangerous.

Marjory kept going, slowly, looking down at her feet as if she could see them. Looking up again, at nothing. It was one of those rare times when she felt used up, devoid of energy. Almost sleepy. Duane and Puff had stopped talking. Marjory heard instead the flowing of the waterfall beside the mill. She knew she was going the right way . . . but there was only one way she *could* go. Wasn't there? The hiccups continued. Marjory

stopped a couple of times and rubbed her eyes, which
felt dry and smarted. After rubbing she saw flashes,
trifling visions, like outtakes from forgotten dreams.
But any light, even false light provided by the optic
nerves, mysterious impulses of the brain, was welcome.

Marjory fetched up a massive shudder, then trembled
almost continuously as the muscles of her body twitched
furiously to keep her warm. Her mind was wandering.
It seemed to her she was heading down again, not up;
but that couldn't be possible. How much longer? The
waterfall was louder, she had to be dead on course. She
didn't recall hearing it so loud before. But all sounds
were magnified down here, and maybe a mild but persistent anxiety had sharpened her senses. Marjory shivered and yawned. Then her head jerked up with a start
and she bumped, hard, against a wall of the passage.
Dozing on her feet? She yearned for the spit and fury
of the sun. Marjory was not an underground person—
if ever there'd been a doubt. When she died she was
not going to be buried. Put that in her last will and
testament. Great-aunt Lillie Day Wingo had insisted on
a funeral pyre in *her* will. But she'd been one of the
more conspicuous loonies in the family. Aunt Lillie
Day. Hard-boiled as a hanging judge. Buried three hus-
bands. And two of them were just napping. Ha-ha,
where had she heard that joke, on *Laugh-In*?

Much lighter up ahead. The waterfall pouring in her
ears. Almost like daybreak, with little flecks of nearly
transparent birds wheeling in a slate-gray sky. Enormous. *Thunder.* It was, God, had to be, the hoped-for
waterfall; but it had never sounded like that. She felt a
draft in her face, a freshet of depths and secret places
with no end to their astounding darkness.

Oh no. Please. I'm not. I can't be! I can't be lost!

That was when she saw it, not too far away, drifting
so high she had to raise her eyes, the thing illuminated
by many moths clinging like shroud cloth but with an
excited flutter of all-over wings. Svelte, gleaming, but

with a gruesome head, nearly featureless, knobby as a ball of tar. The eyes electric red, as startling as an exhibit in a carnival's chamber of horrors.

The vision cured Marjory's hiccups on the spot. But she peed down both legs.

9

When Rita Sue had her breath she lifted her damp blond head from Boyce's shoulder and said deliberately, "Boyce, if you ever say a word to *any*body about this, I mean if you let on to a living soul, what I'll do is I'll get daddy's shotgun out and blow the ears off you, son."

"I won't say anything. I love you, Rita Sue."

"I love you, too." It was darker in the cove of Dante's Mill State Park where they'd found privacy; either the sun was setting or it would rain soon. Marjory's radio played beside them in the backseat. Rita Sue's bare bottom was still molded to his lap. She couldn't, and didn't, move. "Don't be putting your hands where it's all sunburnt. My lip's swollen. You must've bit it. I am going to be such a *mess* in the morning." Now she moved, experimentally. "You like me doing this?"

Boyce took a deep breath and said, "Yeh, just like what you were doing before. It don't hurt you none?"

"There was just a little hurt at first. It wasn't as big as I thought it was going to be. It's still like a hot dog, only without the bun."

"Well, the only thing small about me is my pecker. My daddy's got a little one too, I reckon it runs in the . . . uh, Jesus! The family."

"I like it just fine," Rita Sue assured him, running

her fingers through his strawberry-blond hair. ''Reckon
it's going to stay like this all the time now?'' she teased.

''Only when I'm with you, sugarpie.''

''That better be the whole truth and nothing but. Tell
me how it feels, now.''

''Oh. Rita Sue! It feels so *fine*.''

''Maybe you just better . . . hurry. Because I think
I'm way ahead . . . of you, hon.''

Wind rushed through the trees outside, turning the
leaves silver. Rain spattered down on the convertible
top of the Ford Fairlane.

''Boyce!''

''Huh.''

''Say the F word to me again while we're doing it.''

10

What was it she saw, or thought she saw?

Nothing less than Arne Horsfall, stealing a nigger's
mummy.

And what seemed to be a billion luna moths fluttering luminously within this deep cavern of fluted, hollowed limestone, following him like the tail of a comet
through interstellar space. Remarkable. He had to be at
least a hundred yards from Marjory, and climbing, carrying the thing in his two arms, but she recognized him:
there was no mistaking Arne Horsfall, she could never
forget him.

Through a deep cleft in a wall what amounted to a
river poured twenty feet or more to a churning pool in
the floor of the cavern, and this was the waterfall she'd
heard, while thinking it was the spillway of the mill-

pond. There was no telling how she had so easily lost track of where she was going, but she was lost, all right.

But not frightened so much any more, even of the lightshow moths: they came close to her, eyespots like drops of blood, stirring the air with delicate wingbeats. The adrenaline surging in her body seemed to produce a wave of heat, a field of energy that kept them from clinging to her the way they shrouded the red-eyed mummy Arne had in his arms. So after twenty seconds Marjory was able to breathe without screaming, and as for flooding herself, she'd needed to go anyway and it didn't matter, because sooner or later, before she got out of there, she was going to take another cold shower.

Arne was moving very slowly as he climbed through what amounted to a limestone beehive, solid rock carved as intricately as a Chinese puzzle box by the action of water that dripped and flowed apart from the fuming torrent of the underground river. As Marjory watched him, he almost lost his balance; the eyes of the black moon glowed furiously for a few moments and Marjory heard a scream of outrage that made her cringe.

She heard—

But that was impossible; the roar of water pouring into the cavern was too loud. She couldn't hear anything like a scream because she knew good and well no one would hear *her*, even if she let go at full lung power.

Without thinking, she did it, took a deep breath and hollered until her throat ached. She couldn't even hear herself. Arne Horsfall failed to react. He stumbled on in the midst of a cloud of glowing moths that turned his skin a vivid lime-green shade. Some aperture in the beehive afforded him passage, and he disappeared, although a seething afterglow remained.

What turned them on? Marjory wondered, but she didn't stand there thinking about the luna moths. Maybe Arne knew where he was going, and the chances were fifty-fifty he was headed out. Better to follow him, and

the trailing moths, than to blunder around on her own
and eventually get so lost no one would ever find her.

The rush of adrenaline had receded, and she was
shaking again. There was a way to cross the cavern
above the river: haphazardly slanted flowstone ledges,
like stairsteps through transparent, hanging formations
that looked as delicate as wind chimes: they actually
moved in the drifts of spray from the falls. The steps
looked forbidding, treacherous. As long as she could
see where she was going, okay. What if the moths suddenly left, drawn off like smoke through some small
passage she could barely get a fist into? Or else died—
just like that. One timid glow after another, fading into
darkness. Marjory had a fleeting impression of herself
welded in fear to some high pinnacle, unable to see, to
move, until her bones were indistinguishable from the
spiny limestone. A hundred years from now, just a
quaint photograph on the wall of one of Enid's great-
grandchildren.

If nothing happened to Enid, that is.

Why should she suddenly be more worried about
Enid than herself? Marjory was the one who had to go
poking around holes in the ground; *Marjory* was the
dummy, not Enid!

But it was Enid who had brought Arne Horsfall home
from the asylum; that had been the start of all their
troubles, and the end was not in sight.

Not as long as he lived.

This thought got Marjory moving, and fast: no longer afraid for herself, but perilously concerned about
her sister, about something that was going to happen,
and soon, to the unsuspecting Enid, if Marjory didn't
keep track of Arne Horsfall. If she didn't—couldn't—

Stop him.

11

"What are those things?" Puff said, behind Duane's back. She was holding his left hand, squeezing it nervously. He had Marjory's flashlight in the other hand and was slowly playing the beam around the walls of the chamber they'd entered. "Some kind of bat? I'm not going another step if they're bats."

"Luna moths," Duane said. "Giant silks. These are the biggest ones I've ever seen. Take it easy, Puff." She was digging her nails into the heel of his palm.

"Sorry. Do they live down here?"

"I don't know how. The adults don't feed, but they lay their eggs on tree leaves so the larvae have something to eat after they pupate. Puff, close your eyes a minute."

"Put your arm around me first."

"Puff, get serious. I'm going to turn the flashlight off, that's all."

"Are you sure that's all?"

"I just want to see something."

"Okay. Tight shut." She also had a tighter grip on his hand. "No tricks. I hate it when people play tricks on me. I go bananas. Are *your* eyes shut?"

"Yeh."

"Duane, tell me something. How old are you?"

"Sixteen."

"Wow. I could've sworn you were older! You act older. Most of the guys I've met up with lately, they're twenty-five going on twelve, if you get what I mean. You must still be in high school."

"Yeh. I'll be a junior."

"Wow. Well, I guess it doesn't matter, if you're attracted to somebody. I mean, you're old enough. You've probably got it on with a couple of girls already, haven't you? I was wondering if you and Marjory—"

"You can open your eyes now."

"Uh-uhhh, you have to kiss the sleeping princess before she'll open her eyes! I used to play that game with daddy." She put a hand to her face, fingertips touching her forehead; sullenness and pain showed through the partial mask. "Of course it was only princess time when he wanted to cop a feel. When he needed his boots polished, I was 'Corporal Puff.' " Eyelids twitching, she lowered her hand and grazed Duane's forearms. "You've got goosebumps. Did I give you—my God!"

"They glow in the dark. I've never seen anything like it. Moths must have been the source of light we had in the chamber back there—it passed through the rock crystal in the walls."

"This is so fucking beautiful! It's fairyland. How many do you think—"

"No way to count them all. This chamber's maybe sixty feet across, twenty feet high—"

"Cobwebs! All over, the floor's covered with—it looks like, you know, what do they call it, angel hair? Or maybe cotton candy—"

"I think it's silk. But not cobwebs. I don't see any moth larvae. That's amazing. The lunas must come back here after they pupate. Wait a second—"

"What do you see?" Puff asked nervously.

"I'm not sure." Duane went down on one knee and turned on his flashlight, carefully pulled apart a cloud-like mass of pale silken thread.

"Hey, there could be something under there, like spiders?"

"Spiders didn't spin this stuff." Duane held up what appeared to be a transparent twist of papery material, several inches long. He frowned. "Could be part of a cocoon, but—"

"You have such a beautiful back," Puff said, leaning over him and then on him, fingertips caressing the nape of his neck. "Did you ever think of letting your hair grow and wearing a ponytail? Men's ponytails are so sexy."

"A ponytail would get me stomped to death where I go to school. Could we just stop talking about sex?"

"Am I embarrassing you?" Puff teased.

"No." Duane folded the papery strip and carefully placed it in his damp shirt pocket. "As long as we're here, I'll just look around and see what else—"

"You're not going to walk through that hairy shit."

"Why not? It's only silk. But that's the weird part."

"What do you mean, weird?"

"Lunas aren't true silk moths. So I don't know where this stuff came from. Maybe somebody's been raising silkworms down here, where it's dry and cool and there aren't any predators. But they eat a ton of mulberry leaves, and I haven't seen even a piece of a leaf anywhere. Of course it may have been years ago . . ."

"Duane? Look!"

"What's the matter?"

"Where you were about to step!"

"Oh—yeh." He turned on the flashlight again, tracking damp depressions in the glossy, matted-down silk. "Right. Somebody was here. Not too long ago." He dipped a finger into a footprint. "Mud."

"The kook who stole my radio!"

"Probably." Duane looked as far as the beam of the flashlight would throw. "Went that way."

Puff lowered her voice to a whisper. "He might still be here."

"I don't think so. I think he was just passing through."

"Let's find out where he went!"

"Marjory's going to be wondering—" Duane bit his lower lip. "Well—okay. Follow me."

"I wasn't thinking of going first. You're right. It's beautiful, but it's really—weird. Where did you say the silk came from?"

"Uh—silk moth larvae."

"Are you sure you didn't say 'worms'?"

"They aren't actually—"

"Oh, they just *look* like worms. If you see one, bud, you better let me know well in advance, because if I step on a fucking worm I am going to spend the rest of my life getting even with you."

"Come on if you're coming."

"How long do you think it took to make all this stuff?"

"Oh—one strand of silk can be more than a thousand yards long. But that's another thing: silkworms spin cocoons, sort of oval-shaped."

"Duane?"

"Yeh?"

"Well—when you look at it—this cave is, it's definitely, like, oval-shaped."

"I guess so."

"So maybe—what we're walking through—is one big cocoon." Puff lurched against Duane suddenly, and they almost fell.

"Hey, watch your step."

"Sorry, I got hung up. The silk clings; it just grabbed my ankle and wouldn't let go."

"Step where I step."

"You know what, I feel like I'm tripping out. I am not shitting you, Duane boy. All those butterflies, the colors are fantastic—"

"They're luna moths."

"And this cocoon, or whatever it is. Like a big dreamboat of a bed. So soft. I always wanted a bed like this when I was a little girl. There aren't any worms, are there? We'd have seen some by now."

"No. I'm sure there aren't any worms. Haven't been any for—who knows how long this stuff has been here?" Duane felt a tug on his hand, halting him. He turned.

"Hi," Puff said, grinning. She had thrown her long hair back over her shoulders, exposing her breasts. There was excitement in her good eye; the other looked forlorn, a little weepy. Twins with radically different temperaments. Puff stood almost to her knees in billowy silk, shivering, pruny nipples erect.

"Puff, come on."

"Come and get me," she said, moistening her underlip with the tip of her tongue. She unbuttoned her shorts and pulled them down. "I'm numb all over! It's so cold in here! Warm me up, Duane." She gathered up a double handful of the silk, playfully hiding her pudenda, the hair of which had been shaved down to the size of a small arrowhead.

She turned then and went prancing off the path they had made and out into the cloud of silk that surged up around her brown naked body and threw herself down, laughing, kicking up her heels, settling slowly out of sight.

"Duane, this is a gas! It's so soft. I can't describe what it feels like. You've got to try it."

"Puff, I don't think that's a very good idea."

"I won't tell on you! Just between friends, right? Hurry up."

Duane took a breath and rubbed his throat where the pulse was hammering away and felt a little shabby for both of them even as he dropped his hands to his belt buckle.

Fortunately, or unfortunately, that's when Puff started screeching in mortal terror, like a housecat being vacuumed off a carpet.

12

Marjory heard thunder again, a dull rumble as if somewhere in the succession of caverns she had wandered into and couldn't get out of, a ceiling had collapsed.

She had never been afraid for her life before. Even the awful night of her parents' death she had not brooded on her own mortality. But now she had lost track of Arne Horsfall, and the moth-shrouded mummy he carried laboriously through one lookalike passage after another, so totally familiar with this underground world he didn't need to look for landmarks, or else guided by some mysterious radar. He had moved slowly, an old man with unreliable legs and little stamina, but never as if he were unsure of where he meant to go.

Marjory's left knee hurt her badly. There were times when the pain almost took her breath away. She had slipped off the narrow path in a small cave and tumbled, wrenching the knee. She could barely hobble. Arne, unaware of being followed, had moved on, the radiance of luna moths fading, finally vanishing abruptly. And here she was, her worst fears doubled: not only in the dark, but hurt. Listening to thunder and shaking at the thought of pulverizing tons of rock, choking clouds of dust, entombment.

"Arne! Arne Horsfall! It's Marjory! Marjory Waller! Where are you? I need help! Pleasssse helpppp meeee!"

After her third try at raising Arne, Marjory was strangling on tears and knew it wasn't any use. He was gone. She heard nothing but her own panicky breathing and the repetitious, distant thunder.

And saw, very far away in the dark, a little flicker of light, abrupt as a struck match but almost colorless. She held her breath as if a yogalike suspension would sharpen her perceptions. *What was that?* A sound like the wind. But she'd heard it before; apparently there was a current of air flowing from outside, channeled through the many chimneys and tight corridors of the caverns . . . more thunder, and Marjory decided to breathe, slowly, massaging her bruised knee. If it actually was thunder and not a rockfall, then—*there*, thank God, that pulse of light again, in the same place as before! She hadn't imagined it. She had to be close to the surface, where a summer storm was at full power. All she needed to do was keep her eyes open, make her way toward the intermittent lightning, inching along through the dark, and if she didn't fall again and kill herself this time, maybe she'd get out of here . . .

13

"God! Duane! Oh God! *It's got me!*"

Duane saw Puff trying to lunge out of the nest of spun silk she'd made for herself, reaching high with one hand, her head arched back; but she couldn't get her feet under her, or slipped, or was pulled back by something or someone, and fell more deeply into the cocoon, almost vanishing from sight despite her struggles. Screaming. He tried to run to her, but the strength of the voluminous silk resisted hurry. He lurched as if drunk, trying to get some footing, trying to get to her, the short hairs on his head frizzled by the tenor of her screaming; it was as if she were being eaten alive.

Then he stepped on something leathery and bony, lost his balance, dived awkwardly in Puff's direction and made contact with her. Her fingers dug into his left arm above the elbow. Her other hand, flailing, hit him hard enough on the side of his head to welt an ear. He grabbed Puff, got one foot down on solid floor and yanked her full upright. Her face was about six inches from his own and it was as if he'd never seen Puff before, fear had made her crazy, distorted her features.

Other than that, she didn't seem to be hurt. She was a handful, but he was a strong boy. He turned her sharply and looked at her naked back and glossy buttocks with the flashlight. He saw nothing hideous, no wounds, only a couple of yellowed bruises on one hip where her skin tone was a shade lighter than elsewhere.

"Puff, stop! You're not hurt." It was kind of interesting. He'd never seen a woman flat-out hysterical before, spitting up and with the whites of her eyes showing like those of a horse that knows it has broken a leg. His own self-control was a little wobbly, she'd given him a real scare. He was powerfully aroused by her nakedness and total vulnerability. But Puff put a quick stop to that by accidentally jamming a knee close to his groin.

"Oww! What's the matter with—"

He saw it then in the glance light of the flash, lying half uncovered on the cavern floor where Puff had been thrashing around. Puff was now twitching all over and trying to climb on him, giving out little whimpered yips while spraying him with saliva. Duane pulled them both away, finding it hard to believe his eyes, and aimed the flashlight more precisely while holding Puff against him with his other arm, squeezing as hard as he could. Duane could squat-lift close to four hundred pounds, more than double his weight. Puff suddenly had no room to breathe. Her head fell laxly against his shoulder, air hissing noisily through her teeth.

His first thought was, *Dead nigger.*

The severely emaciated body was black, all right, from the roots of its hair to the patent-leather toenails, with a faintly rusty sheen where the flashlight beam struck hotly. It was a nude male, one knee drawn up in a relaxed attitude, hands at its sides. The glans of the penis like a small onyx egg Duane's mother had found in a Mexican cave and given to him. He had buffed it to a high gloss in his rock polisher.

"Grabbed me—" Puff said. He could feel her heartbeat, and her teeth on his neck. He was afraid she was going to bite him. Duane said with a trace of scorn, although he could understand now what had touched her off so violently, "It can't hurt you. It's just a . . . like a mummy. God knows how long—"

"Duane—"

"You okay now?"

"Uh-huh. Ohhhh Duane . . . There's another one!"

"Where?"

"Don't let go!"

"Take it easy." He relaxed his grip on her.

"I'm not a sissy! I saw a soldier who was run over by a tank once. When I had my abortion I didn't cry. But that thing—those—horrible—"

Duane trained Marjory's flashlight on the other body, the one he had stepped on, not knowing what it was, as he went to Puff's rescue.

"God!" Puff said. "It's a woman! Isn't it?"

"Yeh."

"Do you see that? Around her neck? They both have something tied around their necks."

"Some kind of dried vine."

"You know what I think? They were killed and left down here. Duane?"

"What?"

"I'm not in the mood to fuck any more. Maybe later when we get out of here. I want to put my shorts on."

"Okay."

"Come with me?"

"Yeh, just a minute," Duane said, casting around with the light. He left Puff and took a few gingerly steps into the spiffy silk and bent over to part some of the strands.

"Guess what?"

Puff started to laugh. "Man, I just really don't want to know."

"Three of them." Duane straightened and looked around the cavern. "Maybe if we look hard enough—"

"*You* look. I'm getting out of here. In a minute. I need to find someplace to go to the bathroom first. Can I have the flashlight?"

"Sure," Duane said, preoccupied with their discoveries; he casually tossed the flashlight to her. Puff was not at all athletic. Instead of catching the flashlight she fumbled and batted it into the middle of the cocoon, where it struck something with a metallic *clunk*.

Overhead there was a noiseless stirring of wings, an agitated light show rippling through the congregation of lunas.

They heard a burst of static from Puff's hidden radio. Then the voices began.

14

Marjory crawled out of the cave into a lashing rain, and nothing had ever felt so good. *Weather*. She relished it, as someone recently entombed. Cool and dry and monotonously dark below. What death might be like: Marjory occasionally had worried about that. Despite her religious training she was reasonably sure the afterlife would not be choirs of angels in open-toed sandals singing on cloudtops somewhere. While some saint or other read out loud from a Book of Judgment with her name on it in gold. Like going to school forever; talk about monotonous. She'd prefer more of a carnival atmosphere. Wouldn't everybody have earned a joyride or two just by getting to Heaven in the first place? And if she had to be judged, then what about a funhouse filled with mirrors called *This Was Your Life*? Here I am at the age of three tarring the cat's tail. There I am at thirteen—*I know I'm going to die someday, but just don't bore me.*

She bit down on her lip trying to control the shakes and wondered where Duane and Puff were. Wondered where *she* was, wincing at a pitchfork of lightning tossed at some windblown trees nearby. Rain in her face mixing with the hot saline of tears; she hadn't known she was crying. Between flashes of lightning it was pretty dark, but not night yet.

The cave entrance, or exit, slanted into a low hill and was barely three feet wide at the base. There was a thick tangle of rhododendron all around. Even if you knew exactly where it was, you still might have trouble locating the seam in anything but broad daylight.

The glossy rhododendron leaves kept the worst of the rain off her as she huddled a few yards beyond the cave, gently massaging the knee she had twisted. Might as well wait it out here. She wasn't going back inside. The lightning didn't scare her. Much. Until it flashed with a jarring violence, perhaps hitting the hill behind her, revealing something that, ordinarily, she wouldn't have paid much attention to. Under the circumstances, it seemed unnervingly creepy.

It was a shoe. A man's black shoe, slowly filling up with rainwater. The style of cheap loafer Arne Horsfall had been wearing the Sunday he came to Enid and Marjory's house. For all she knew, it was Arne's shoe. If so then he had come this way, carrying—no, he would

have had to drag it behind him through the laurel slick—
the mummy with the fierce red eyes.

Marjory hiccuped forlornly, and a taste of something
bitter rose to her tongue.

Why think about it now? She didn't care about Arne
Horsfall. Or want to know what he was doing stealing
radios and skulking through caverns with a nigger's
body—

But that was the hard part to accept. The thing he'd
been carrying couldn't be dead. Not with those eyes,
which had seen, down below, what Arne couldn't see:
they had seen Marjory.

Something damp and clinging swirled out of the
tangle of rhododendron branches overhead and clung to
her cheek. It was too delicate and papery to be a leaf;
she brushed at it and saw, briefly, printed on the back
of her hand like a tattoo, a drowned luna moth. Shook
it off with a cold sick feeling in her stomach. She was
quick, on hands and knees, to find a way out of there.

Now which way?

The sky full of lightning, not dramatic thunderbolts
but a tracery, briefly luminous and as delicate as the
webbing of cracks in eggshell. She wasn't afraid of it.
The rain seemed to be slackening where she was, falling straight down.

She reckoned that she was still in Dante's Mill State
Park. Walk in one direction and she would come to the
lake shore; another, and before long she must cross a
road or marked trail.

Shivering, Marjory pushed aside some drenched
limbs of second-growth trees and followed a descend-
ing course from the modest hill where she had emerged
from the caverns. It wasn't hard going by the intermittent glow of the sky. Thunder kept its distance.

Marjory?

Spoken so softly, she couldn't be sure she'd heard
anything. Marjory paused, on tiptoe, then her heels settled to the sodden ground. She looked around, looked

behind her last with a hard shudder and saw . . . no one.

Whipped her head forward with a sudden creepy lurching of the heart, but there was nothing ahead of her except for a mild pulse of lightning in which a thick-bodied chestnut tree stood almost alone on a cresting acre against the sky, a tree right out of an illustrated children's book, *Swiss Family Robinson* or *Treasure Island*: you could climb into the gnarled but cloudlike boughs and be pleasantly lost for an afternoon's reverie. This was a tree for hiding out and secret clubs and feats of daring—how high would she dare to climb in such a tree? Marjory had plenty of time to look the tree over and speculate, because the pulse of light had become a steady glow in the sky around it, as if the tree radiated from its own source of power, contriving a mysterious but attractive aura that had (more obvious the longer she stared) a tincture of color, partly gold, also a little of the green of weathered courthouse bronzes. At least, she was sure, the huge tree must bear some sort of charm or enduring force, or else the power of storms would have torn it apart long ago in its singular, exposed location.

Yes. This way.

That was good for a start, and some large goosebumps; easy to imagine that the tree, intriguingly in motion in a renewed spate of hard rain, had a voice. The thrill of imagination: but Marjory, although she could daydream with the best, wasn't particularly creative. Talking trees? Fairy stories had never appealed to her.

Good God, she thought, *it's dark and you're lost in the woods so don't get spooky! Just get out of—*

"No, Marjory! Over here!"

This time Marjory jumped and tried to run; pain in the knee she had twisted in the caverns hobbled her and she went sprawling over a stob of a nearly buried windfall, taking some of the skin off the instep of her right foot. Fell heavily but in forest litter that cushioned the fall, with nothing sharp lying there to punch through her.

"Oh, Marjory—no!"

—She said mournfully, sympathetically, and with that accent that might have been Danish or something, Marjory didn't know. She only knew she was frightened, and resentful because one of her fears was she might be losing her mind and would wind up in the most dreaded place of all, Cumberland State Hospital; and she was shaken because she was floundering around and clumsy—God, how could she take a fall like that? Physically out of rhythm, no more control than a boulder rolling downhill, in a way that was more disturbing to Marjory than the Voice.

"I'm here. I'm real. I want to help you."

Marjory sat up sniveling in the dark, brushing her face, which felt spider-webbed all over.

"*What do you want? Who is it?*" she yelled, and wiped ropy snot from her upper lip with a knuckle.

"The tree, Marjory. Come to the tree. I'm caught. Get me loose, then I'll help you."

The woman sounded calm, but sad. "Who—" Marjory said, then stopped, because there was a kind of pressure on her tongue, and in her mind, a sensation that speech was unimportant, even useless, in this communication. *Who are you?* That was easy, the thought just flowed; as she felt it going—somewhere—she sensed its reception and leaned back on her hands, gazing toward the dark towering tree and the faint pulsing cloud of sea-green light.

"My name is Birka. I'm concerned about you. Are you badly hurt? Can you walk?"

"Yes, I—" Oh, forgot. No need to talk. *I'm all right. Scraped my foot. But what happened to you?*

"You'll see. Hurry, please."

"Coming." I mean, *Coming.*

Marjory wiped her nose again, sniffed as she started to get to her feet, but froze and was appalled. In sniffing she had smelled something: strong, almost fresh. She smelled blood.

Oh, my God! No . . . wait, I'm not hurt, I just scraped my foot, I can't be bleeding that much. As her hands were frantically busy, searching her body, looking for wounds, for an outpouring to account for the odor. No wounds, thank—

"Marjory! What is it!"

Uh, give me a minute. Could be menstrual blood, she could have started her period a little early. Marjory checked. Uh-uh. And usually when she was upset about something or other, she got it late, not early. *I smell blood.*

"I know you do. I'm afraid that it's me, Marjory. Could you hurry now?"

A flash of concern for Birka, brighter than the lightning, and Marjory was off unthinkingly, running up the modest hill toward the standout tree, to her new friend. New? But it was as if they had known each other as intimately as soul mates in places far from here—shared every thought, loved chastely, exchanged vows of loyalty. *I will give my life for you.*

Birka! Where are you? I can't see you!

Running into a wall then, her footsteps slowing. The smell of blood like a countryside hog-butchering, all this rain but the rain couldn't wash away *that* smell.

God . . . what is it?

Birka was silent, almost coldly silent. But she didn't have to speak, because by then Marjory was beneath the tree and they were almost in her face, the dangling bony feet with blackened nails, one foot bare, the other still shod in the nondescript loafer that was a twin of the one she'd seen filling up with rainwater in the laurel slick. Except for his loafer Arne Horsfall was naked and nearly skinless to his shins and dripping on her before she could draw back and try to smother the sight of his flayed corpse with the heels of her hands, grinding them into her eyes, punishing them as if her own vision was at fault for this horror, this outrage. Marjory screamed.

"Birka!"

"I'm over here," she said. Aloud this time, because they were so close; some compassion in her voice but not as much as Marjory might have wished to hear from her old, dear friend.

15

The voices.

They clamored on the radio like some ghostly call-in show, such a babble that few words were intelligible to Duane and Puff, although the emotions were clear: suffering and desperation. Puff held her hands over her ears, grimacing.

"Turn it off!"

"I can't turn it off," Duane said. "I don't even know where it is. And I don't want to go look for it."

"I want my radio, and I want to get out of here!"

"You go find it."

"No! It's *them*. I *told* you I heard my mother before!" She took her hands from her ears and circled him around the waist with one arm, her other hand pushing against his ribs as she tried to move him backward, out of the cavern. Duane, more fascinated than frightened, held his ground easily. Puff looked at him, chin bunched, her mouth pushed into a tight bow. "Wha-what is this, Duane? Is it hell? All those bodies, is that wha-what we'll look like whuh-when we're—"

"Hey, Puff, it's just the damn radio."

"MAKE IT STOP! Please, Duane!"

"Okay—okay, stay here, I'll find the radio. Let go?" With a little prying on Duane's part, she loosened her grip on him. Her lips also loosened and quivered, her chin relaxed, and while she continued to stare at him, all expression drained from her face like water squeezed from a sponge. She looked very childlike, except for her peachy breasts and large nipples, dark as bruises and pebbled. He put a hand between her breasts and felt her heart trying to jump into his palm. She swallowed, Adam's apple bobbing. Duane felt a corresponding emotional bobbing. Half the time she was like a sister he had to put up with, and half the time he wanted to fuck her. Down here he wanted to. Outside, well, he just wouldn't be interested. He couldn't explain that to himself. Her eye with the cast looked glum, a little dusty, like the eyes of all the trophy heads in his father's den. His father had even stuffed a raccoon, as if it were as rare and dangerous as a white tiger. It was a weird time to be hating his father, but being in Puff's company for so long had finally started to unstring him. Then she closed both eyes, head tilting back almost blissfully, and he felt the slackness in her body as her breathing slowed. But she was steady on her feet.

"You okay?" Duane asked. The din from the radio

was fading, only two or three voices now, down to whispers. But even without the voices acting as a beacon he wouldn't have much trouble locating the radio, out there in the middle of this big cocoon. The beam of the nearby flashlight reflected from veins of quartz in the roof. "Be right back," Duane said, reluctantly taking his hand from her heart. Puff swayed almost imperceptibly, breathing through her mouth, and didn't answer him. She had rebounded from hysteria into a trancelike state. Maybe that was normal . . . if anything about Puff could be called normal. Or maybe it was something to worry about, a deferred acid trip she was just now catching up to, but Duane liked her this way. Once he recovered the radio, then he'd simply take docile Puff by the hand and walk her out of the cavern. With luck he wouldn't run into Marjory, leading a naked Puff around. Duane grinned, picturing that encounter. *I don't know what happened to her clothes, Marjory, she just kept taking them off and leaving them places.*

This had turned out to be quite a day. There wasn't half as much buzz in stealing cars.

Puff sighed deeply and seemed to ease still further into stoned privacy.

Duane stepped around her in the soft tangle of silk.

"Mom?" Puff said, as if she were talking in her sleep. A muscle fired beneath the bad eye, crinkling the skin. Both hands were clenched at the level of the shadowed dent of belly button, tendons standing out in the slender wrists. Her head was still tilted back as if she might be gawking at something overhead. Eyes closed but the tiny muscle twitching like code. Puff frowned. The tip of her tongue appeared between parched lips, withdrew. Duane hesitated, watching her, uneasy now. Wanting to say something to snap her out of it, but concerned about the consequences. Better to leave her alone, retrieve the radio, get the hell out of there.

He heard only one voice on the radio now. A child, in tears.

Don't you whine, Ethan!

Shit, Duane thought, who said that? The rebuke wasn't on the radio, the voice seemed to come from inside his head. Duane felt a cold streak down his breastbone, a freezing knifepoint deep in his bowels. Thinking now about what Marjory had said earlier, concerning the unknown fate of the population of Dante's Mill. *They all left one day. Seventy-four people. Just picked up and vanished.*

Why?

There were no more voices on the radio, he heard only a mild humming as he waded deeper into the cocoon to find it.

He stepped on a hidden head the size of a croquet ball and jerked away with a cry, almost lost his balance to go sprawling deep into the nesting of mummies. Now they seemed to be everywhere underfoot as he picked his way cautiously toward the beam of the flashlight pointing up at the roof, thick as casualties on a battlefield. Looking down, he couldn't see much. But kept stepping on them no matter how he danced around trying not to. Desiccated limbs tough as beef jerky, not yielding underfoot. Not breaking off, either. His throat locked but too late, an instant later he threw up.

When he could breathe again he continued to wade grimly through the nearly waist-high drift of the cocoon to the place where the flashlight had struck Puff's radio—there it was, resting atop something dark, another mummy but small. *God, a kid,* Duane thought, reaching down to get the radio, his nerves half shot from the vomiting, heart accelerating.

Something shriekingly painful went through his head, ear to ear; his eyes closed involuntarily and he gritted his teeth, hands hovering above the radio: it was worse than a high-gain blast of static. A scream, maybe, but inhuman in range and intensity: inhuman in the relief, the joy expressed. He looked down at a closed tarry face, the face of a mummified child. Long dead and with a twist of dried vine deep in the wasted throat. But he could swear, in those moments of contact, of unexpected empathy, something stirred beneath the surface of that satiny shrunken face like a burrowing worm, that the eyelids of the mummy were about to open.

Duane seized the radio and groped for the flashlight, lying deeper, thrust aside a stiffened hand, the shrieking in his head causing him to cry out too, an outpouring to relieve the pressure of the unrelenting interior sound. He picked up the flashlight and straightened, throwing the beam in Puff's direction.

But she wasn't there any more. Puff had vanished. And as the radio in his hand vibrated again with the babble of exultant voices, Duane had the dreadful feeling that Puff, wherever she was, had just done something irredeemably wrong.

16

Ted Lufford finished cutting the grass in the rain and came into the kitchen dripping after he put the Toro away. He was wearing only a pair of grease-stained denim cutoffs and ratty sneakers; Enid could count eight of his toes through the holes in those sneakers. Grass cuttings clung to Ted's slightly bowed legs almost to his knees, which were a little smoky from the exhaust of the old lawn mower. Enid smiled as she slid a Pyrex dish filled with breaded pork chops into the oven.

"You're a mess," she said.

"Let's take us a shower."

"I don't need a shower," Enid said, wrinkling her nose at him.

Ted went to the sink and leaned over to drink from the faucet.

"That is a habit of yours I'm never going to get used to," Enid said mildly.

Ted straightened and wiped his mouth. "Saves dirtying up a glass. What else are we having for supper?"

"Marjory's warmed-over scrapple."

Ted nodded approvingly. "It don't get to tasting just right anyhow until it's warmed over two or three times." Enid closed the oven door and adjusted the temperature. "Better cook those real slow," he suggested.

Enid took off her apron and glanced at the wall clock. "You ought to be half-starved after cutting all that grass." Thunder rumbled. Rain poured onto the back steps, overflow from a clogged gutter.

"I need to do something about that gutter the next time I'm over."

"I know you do," Enid said, smiling, her eyes on him melting like honey on a hot biscuit.

"What time's Marjory coming home?"

"I don't have any idea. I would've thought with the rain they'd be here by now. Or maybe she's over at Rita Sue's."

"Think we'll have the house to ourselves?"

"No telling for how long," Enid said. She folded the apron across the top of a ladder-back chair and glanced over one shoulder at Ted.

"I know what that look in your eye means," he said with a tough well-satisfied grin.

"Maybe you just think you do," Enid said.

"Reckon I'll get rid of these shorts."

"The shoes too while you're at it."

Ted went as far as the doorway and unbuttoned his shorts and pulled them down and kicked them over the sill, then kicked off his sneakers and turned back to Enid in a flash of lightning, a little potbellied and bronzy naked and still shining from rainwater and sweat and plastered-on grass. Enid took off the gold bracelet that had belonged to her mother, and the sleeveless top she was wearing, and her bra.

Enid said, "I caught mama and daddy doing this once, right here in this very kitchen when they thought I was minding Marjory somewhere else. I guess I was about six years old."

"What did you think, Nuggins?"

"Well, I remember thinking, 'I wonder what he does with all that.' "

"Did you find out?"

"Oh, no. Not then. I didn't keep on looking or anything. I respected their privacy."

"Well, when did you find out?" Ted asked teasingly.

"Oh, I expect you know the answer to that, you were there at the time."

"Were you that innocent?"

"Not enough to matter." Enid pulled her green Bermuda shorts down, wriggling a little, then treated him to an impudent pelvic twist and thrust as soon as the shorts dropped to her ankles.

"Boy, I just never suspected about you," Ted said admiringly.

"Never suspected what?" Enid said, hipshot and naked too except for a slim ankle chain and sandals. She rubbed across a breast with her knuckles. "I know I don't have anything to be bashful about, or do I?"

"What I meant was, how you don't like to wear underpants."

"I do when it's cold. I don't when it's hot. And Lordy it's been hot."

"Baby baby," Ted said fervently, coming toward her, a hand on his joystick.

Enid playfully put a thumb in her mouth, forefinger curled against her nose. Ted cozied up to her, plucked the thumb from her mouth and licked it, all the way to the inside of her wrist, watching her nipples pucker.

"Daddy, what do you do with all that?" Enid said dreamily.

When Ted picked her up in his arms she put her thumb back in her mouth and closed her eyes.

Fifteen minutes later Enid dropped off to sleep. She always did, even in the car, although they'd stopped doing it in Ted's car six weeks ago. Ted lay there in Enid's bed for a while, a little drowsy himself, watching the rain on the bedroom windows. Then he got up, brushed some of the grass off the sheets, and went down the hall to the bathroom. Marjory wasn't home yet. But he'd taken a few showers in their house and he was fairly certain that Marjory, who was a chore to be around sometimes but sharp as a tack, knew what was going on anyway. He'd left his change of clothes in the spare room. After he was dressed he took a washcloth soaked in warm water and half wrung out and a towel back to Enid's bedroom.

She woke up while he was giving her a sponge bath and put her arms around him.

"Umm. What's that good smell you're wearing?"

"It's just some new stuff I bought at Sears. Like it?"

"I like all of your smells. Your after-shave and shampoo. I like your sweat. I like the way your fingers smell when you've been playing with our things." Her eyes wide-awake and staring solemnly at him. He didn't know what to think when Enid talked like that. It was the last thing he'd ever expected from her. He liked sex talk during sex, oh yes. But sometimes when they weren't doing it, when they were out on a date or just chatting on the phone, she would come out with a remark that, although she never used vulgarities, would jolt him, then giggle at his reaction. She had said, for instance, one night while they were having dinner at the DQ, "Which part of my meat do you like best, the brown or the pink?" He'd nearly strangled on a bacon cheeseburger when she came out with that. And then she'd said, "Gravy or plain?" Or, over to his folks' house for an evening of porch sitting and Fourth of July fireworks, leaning over to whisper in his ear, "I was thinking about you today shopping at K-Mart, and I just had to get out my hanky." Well, actually, it was Ted's handkerchief, which he had loaned to her after that first time in the car when neither of them was prepared for what took place, and she had kept it, and not washed it through subsequent usings. Enid claimed she took the handkerchief everywhere with her, though she stoutly refused to produce it on demand. She didn't need to carry his picture, Enid said, but she liked to be close to his smells. Plural. Maybe she was just teasing; still, the notion gave Ted a definite kick, but made him uneasy, too. Enid was a little strange. Fiercer than he'd ever thought a woman could be in bed, the rest of the time as demure as if she'd never been kissed. Not exactly down-to-earth. As his mother said, not approvingly, "You just never know what's on that child's mind." Maybe that was the creative artist in her. Most girls he'd been at least half-serious about, once you knew them for a couple of weeks there were no surprises. They were as predictable as migrating ducks. Ted thought of the way his mother used to wrap Christmas presents before her arthritis got too far along, you could look at one of her packages and be convinced you knew what was in it, then on Christmas morning a toy truck would turn out to be a Hopalong Cassidy holster and gun. Enid wrapped herself new for him every day and dared him to guess, and that was a part of what kept him engrossed. Oh, and he liked her smells just fine, too.

"Guess I'd better change these sheets," Enid said, giving him a kiss and getting off the bed. Ted watched her bending over stripping the bedcovers and was a little sorry he'd been so fast to get dressed.

Enid straightened slowly, the linen-changing half done, and walked away with a forearm crossed under breasts, as if something mean and gloomy had come over her. She went to the windows where the rain was pelting hard and stared at the drowning tree outside, the unseen road.

"What's the matter, hon?" Ted asked. "Looks like you've got a stomach gripe."

"I do," she said almost inaudibly.

Ted felt both a thrill and flash of anxiety. Her cute belly was rounding out just a little more than he'd ever noticed before. "Don't imagine you're—"

"No," she said, matter-of-factly, "I surely would know if I were going to have a baby. Anyway I can't while I'm—"

"Well, I thought you might've—"

"No, I'm real good about taking them. You know I don't want a baby anytime soon. Not while Marjory's still the baby of the family." Enid tensed, then nearly doubled over. "Oh, God," she said, looking up and out at the dark with fearful eyes Ted saw reflected in the streaming glass.

"Nuggins, what is it?"

"Just this hollow feeling. Like, at mama and daddy's funeral when I realized for certain I was never going to see either of them again." She turned. "That was the first time. Up until then I just thought it was all a mistake. Like it was not actually happening."

"But what's the matter now?"

"We're never going to see Mr. Horsfall again," Enid said, with a woeful sideways fall of her head and a sniffle and then tears.

"Oh." Ted relaxed his grip on a bedpost. He had expected it was something really bad going on in her mind. He put an arm around Enid while she gasped and shed tears, then sat them both on the edge of the mattress. "Nuggins, I know you feel responsible that he ran off, but you shouldn't be carrying on like this because somebody took advantage. How were you supposed to know?"

"What I know now," Enid said bleakly, "is that he's

lying dead somewhere." She looked at the wall by the door where she'd tacked up a portrait Mr. Horsfall had done, for the most part smearing the heavy paper with white liquid shoe polish. Ted thought the portrait was ugly. A woman, sort of, with big screechy looking blue eyes but no hair. Holding out a clawlike hand that had only a thumb and three fingers. There was a black smudge where the little finger belonged.

Ted said something meant to be comforting like, Time will tell, and cuddled Enid, and presently she dried her eyes and smiled forlornly at him. He changed the sheets for her while she got dressed, blue walk shorts but still no underpants, and they went downstairs to supper.

Once the dishes were cleared Ted continued with his efforts to teach Enid the strategies of blackjack, and they listened to the radio. By nine o'clock Enid was demonstrating her version of the fidgets: staring eerily into space, fingers of her right hand clenched as she cocked and uncocked her thumb. She still couldn't seem to remember which pairs to split, although she tried to get interested in the card game.

They took a break. Enid called Rita Sue's house. Then she poured another cup of coffee and came back to the kitchen table.

"I don't know where they can *be*. Isn't that boy supposed to be on probation or something? I've never known Marjory to act like this over any boy."

"Well, she's getting to be the right age. I told you I ran his sheet. He was a first-time offender. They all were. His probation officer says he's got a stable home life, a good academic record, and regular church attendance. No trouble since he wired that Cadillac. Hell, I was in a little trouble myself that age, but nothing ever got on the books."

"This just isn't like Marjory, to be late and not give me a call. It's almost quit raining. Do you feel like taking a drive?"

"Where to? I'm on the eleven o'clock shift tonight."

"I don't know. I'm not sure if they went to Rising Fawn or Dante's Mill."

"Whichever, you don't want to be chasing after her while she's out on a date. Marjory's got good sense."

"So do I, but it didn't take you long to make a card-playing sinner out of me. If the preacher dropped by and saw a deck of cards on my kitchen table, he'd have a stroke."

"Being as how I'm in law enforcement, I could tell you a few things about Preacher Goodbright that'd knock your dick in the dirt."

"You could?"

"But they're mainly allegations."

"Daddy used to say Baptists are like cats. You know they're raising hell, but you can't catch them at it."

"He got caught this one time. With his pants down around his ankles after hours at the Southern Baptist Convention a couple years ago."

"You swear? Are you going to tell me about it?"

"Well, give me some sugar, and I might."

Enid tilted her head back a little and showed him a quarter of an inch of the tip of her tongue.

"Come and get it," she said.

17

She should have run away. That much was obvious to Marjory, even as the balance of her mind fell into a kind of dismal funk. But the longer she stood there gaping at the body of Arne Horsfall, jammed between tight branches of the chestnut tree ten feet off the ground, the less important he seemed. The fact of his death was no longer important. He'd been old, of no further use to—

"Marjory?"

Birka was calling her. Marjory's face, stiff with shock and distaste, relaxed enough for her to smile. She continued to shudder. Thank God the cold, sifting rain was ending. She turned her head one way, then another, looking for her friend. There was a light in the eastern sky, rays of the rising sun illuminating smoke from the mile-high volcano that dominated lava fields only a few kilometers from their green—and treeless—valley. Marjory looked up again, slow-witted, and had a surprise. There was no chestnut tree where she was standing, no dangling man raw as a leg of mutton. How could she have dreamed such a thing? And there weren't any dark, ancient caves underlying the smoothly contoured pastureland where five families lived. Beneath the occasional fertile valleys and lava deserts of Iceland there were only chambers filled with steam, rivers of glowing magma. In a past century the subterranean heat had been high enough to bake potatoes in the fields. No human thing could survive down there . . . but that was part of a melancholy dream that seemed to have lasted as long as winter. Now the reddening sun, which would remain above the horizon for the next four months, was full in her face; blinded by the unaccustomed light, rainbows in her eyes, she was ecstatic. All summer long the six of them played outdoors until they were exhausted. The children Marjory's age were Páll, Gudný, Vigdís, Lun. And Birka, eight months older than Marjory, who was nine. Always the leader among them.

"I'm caught, Marjory! Help!"

Birka's distress sounded real enough. But where was she, and where had all the others gone? Were they hiding? Despite the reappearance of the sun the constant wind was still cold, burning Marjory's ears and the tip of her nose. She felt a little bump along her bones, like an earthquake's signal, accompanied by a subtle displacement. She had, mysteriously, moved, from grassland to a colder place near the crest of the last lichen-covered hill that lay below the ashy tor of Hekla, which in the length of its fissured sides resembled a fallen dinosaur. Here the wind was punchy, boisterous, it stalked her. Behind Marjory, almost four kilometers away, red roofs, the smoke of homefires. Sheep grazing.

"Where are you, Birka?" Had she ever been this far before, unaccompanied? And what was Birka doing on this hill, treacherously rocky and long uninhabited except for—

"*They* did it to me, Marjory! They brought me here! You have to get me loose before the shadow covers me!"

Marjory's eyes watered from the light and the wind, which sometimes flung grit so fine it couldn't be seen even on her fair skin but stung, invisibly. Nevertheless she climbed higher to where the hill was broken, bearing only scattered shrubs in deep lees where the wind couldn't reach them. Rifts underfoot, some so wide she had to jump across; they were packed with old snow and ice turned nearly black from drifted, ingrained volcanic ash. Here the stones had vague statue shapes, as if once the hill had been a wild sanctuary, or sacred ground. Still sacred, perhaps, to the *huldufólk*. Marjory trembled, her chest tightening painfully with each spasm. She was instinctively afraid—but they were the Hidden Ones, as God willed: the pure light of day was death to *huldufólk*, turning them darker than the lava flanks of Hekla. She would be safe as long as the sun— A loose stone caused Marjory to slip; she shrieked but didn't fall.

"I hear you!" Birka called out. "This way!"

Birka began sobbing, which made it easier for Marjory to find her, at last.

"Oh!"

The shock. Like another warning shiver of the earth, prelude to a destructive upheaval. The sight of Birka lying wedged faceup in a green cleft of the rock naked as a pea in a pod except for the rope of horsehair wrapped three times around her ankles. Her nakedness somehow unchaste in this mean and desolate setting. Her belly white as marble, plum-colored nub of navel. Marjory had always cherished Birka for her spirit, for her soul, like that of a crystal angel. Now she looked cast down, punished—but why? Her pale blue eyes shimmered from overflowing tears.

"Who did this?"

"Páll. Gudný. They left me here for the *huldufólk* to find. That's what they said! They think it's a big joke!" But she blinked and her eyes darted nervously. The shadow of Hekla was approaching with the sideways movement of the sun. Who could tell what creatures crept with the shadow, anxious to claim Birka, and make her one of their own?

"They took off—your clothes?"

"They're *mean*! They should have come back by now! Oh, please, Marjory, get me out of here! Untie the rope."

(Gesturing; but if her hands were free, why hadn't she untied herself?)

"Are you—going to tell on them?"

"I don't know. I don't think so. I'll get back at those two, don't worry. I'll steal *their* clothes when they're swimming, and they'll have to walk home with nothing to hide their backsides. Come on. G-get me out of here! I can't move my feet. I have a cramp.''

"Where are your things? Did Páll—did Gudný—they touched—''

"No. They aren't stupid. Just mean. And I'm lying on my clothes.''

"I—maybe I'd better get your father.''

"Have *him* see me like this! He'd kill them both. I'm not *that* mad at them. I don't think. Just untie me, all I want to do is go home, I'm so cold.''

"B-but, your hands—''

Birka held up her hands, fingers drooping, as if confessing a lack of strength, powerlessness.

Marjory understood, or thought she did. She kneeled, touching Birka's knees, then a shinbone that felt like a blade of ice. Odd that Birka wasn't trembling. Now that Marjory was doing something about her predicament, the last of Birka's tears trickled down her cheeks and she seemed in control of herself. Smiling in spite of her discomfort. Marjory wondered how this could have happened to Birka. They had never played a game remotely like this one before. Birka would have been quick to condemn the suggestion, and her disapproval was always a mandate. Páll and Gudný were not mean, as far as Marjory was concerned. They teased and taunted, like all boys, but this act of near brutality seemed beyond anything their minds could conceive. It was also inconceivable that Birka would lie . . . thoroughly confused and scared, Marjory focused on the danger in this lonely place. What if the *huldufólk* had found Birka first? She shuddered so violently that her vision blurred.

Birka said impatiently, "Stop fumbling! Get me loose!''

"The knots—under your ankles—I can't—"

"Oh, you idiot! No. I'm sorry. I didn't mean that. You know you're my dearest friend, Marjory."

Marjory sobbed; she couldn't help herself. She kneaded her stiff fingers and tried again. It seemed so dark here, where had the sun gone? And the vine he'd bound her with was wet and slippery.

(The vine? Wasn't it horsehair, a horsehair rope? She could've sworn—)

Birka's eyes, so blue they burned. Burned right through the center of Marjory's forehead, causing not pain but a terrible sensation of loss. Loss of will, of hope.

But you have everything to live for, Marjory! And you're going to live forever. Darling, what do you think of that?

"Don't . . . know. It's . . . not possible."

Oh, Marjory. You know so little. And I have so much to teach you! Now the knots . . . there!

Choking. Marjory wanted to swallow. Couldn't manage it. Birka's eyes twin blue suns, her breasts so unlike those of a child . . . but what had happened to her beautiful pale shoulder-length hair?

"Did they cut off your hair, too?"

Birka's eyes flashed, losing all color, flashed as white as lightning; Marjory felt as if she had been turned inside out. Weightless, her skinless self sizzling, reeking of ozone, she was swept up brutally, thrown through the air, and came crashing down hard on sodden ground.

I should have run away! Now I'm dead.

Still sizzling, but not on fire, Marjory raised her head, which wobbled erratically. She was sick to her stomach. Her eyes focused slowly. The huge chestnut tree flared where lightning had struck, sending a heavy limb to the ground. In spite of the rain the body of Arne Horsfall was outlined in flames. She could see his eyes, then greasy smoke from his own body obscured his face.

But where was the mummy he'd carried from the caverns?

Marjory retched. She felt so terrible it was an effort just to sit up. God, she had been *talking* to it! Just before the lightning bolt struck only a few feet above her head. Now she was a good forty feet from the tree, swept aside by the falling limb, tumbled down the slope of the hill into a scrub thicket. Smarting all over her body. Her lower jaw felt displaced, it hurt terribly when she tried to close her mouth. It hurt to take a deep breath.

(Talking to it. As if—)

No, no, that was wrong! It wasn't a mummy, it was a naked ten-year-old girl bound hand and foot like a sacrificial virgin on a gloomy hillside in Iceland. Her best fr—

Her best friend was Rita Sue Marcum, and she'd never been to Iceland, and she wasn't going to sit here in the mud and go crazy if there was any other possibility. That meant getting up and walking away, fast.

Marjory was able to cover a dozen yards downhill before sinking to her knees, shockingly depleted. Never in her life had she been so lacking in stamina. Marjory sniveled and closed her eyes. When she looked up the sun was shining and Birka was running down the hill with her multicolored dress in one hand, the material streaming in the wind like smoke and as lovely as the plumage of rare birds; free again, she was laughing. Marjory called futilely to her, *Wait, wait*—secretly afraid she'd been tricked into doing something all of the children would soon be laughing about, taunting her. *But what's the joke? I don't get it.* Tears in her eyes from the wind, her vision obscured, Birka seemed no longer to be running, but flying. Marjory pouted. Maybe Birka had deserved to be tied up and left forever on that barren hill. But nobody ever told her *anything*.

Marjory wiped her tearing eyes and saw the top-of-the-world sky, saturated with the vivid colors, lemon to heartsblood, of Birka's special dress, which she now wore as a pair of voluminous, undulating wings that lifted her lazily into the clouds. Marjory was pained and furious and bereft.

—Lightning flashed, shocking in the blue, the sky fumed and darkened and poured and there she was again, looking up at what was left of Mr. Horsfall, smelling him as he flickered and charred, turning as black as the feet and ankles, encircled by vines, of his mummy.

(But it was only her feet that were tied and blackened. The rest of her was alive; and oh the wicked, entrancing blue of her eyes as she promised

You're going to live forever.)

Didn't seem likely. At the moment Marjory felt so rotten she wasn't sure how she was going to make it through the night.

18

Duane's heart started beating properly again when he saw Puff's head lift slowly above the muzzy drift of silk that covered the cavern floor.

"Puff, what're you—"

"Oh, Duane," Puff said, in a calm, hushed voice,

staring at something in the cocoon maze, "come see this!"

"Uh-uh, I really do think it's time to get out of here."

Puff didn't answer him or look around. The flashlight in Duane's hand danced a little as he put the beam on her. She appeared totally absorbed, excited, breasts rising and falling quickly as she breathed through her mouth. Something dangled from her right hand. To Duane it looked like a piece of the dried vine which all of the mummies had in common. He didn't like that; he didn't want to think about where it might have come from. Duane's skin was crawling. He'd heard that expression before, "made my skin crawl," and by God it was the literal truth, it did crawl. It also puckered pretty good when he heard a thin, fussy, wailing sound, like that of a newborn just beginning to breathe. Like the first sounds of his baby sister, whom his stepmother Nannie Dell had given birth to three weeks early in their mountain vacation home. He'd more or less helped his father deliver the baby, along with a part-time midwife who worked at the Minnie Pearl's in Gatlinburg, and he didn't want to ever have to do that again.

Puff was still breathing heavily through her mouth, which she closed in order to swallow and talk. In the light he held on her she trembled, flesh appearing to ripple like muddy water, jogging the numerous shark's teeth on her breast. "Duane? You know what?"

"Puff, damn it, come on, we've got to—"

"No. Hurry! It's . . . he's . . . alive!"

"Jesusssss!"

"Duane," Puff said, seemingly the calm one now despite the husky heaving of her breast, "bring the flashlight over here so I can see this better."

She turned her face then, full into the beam, eyes wide and unblinking, one of them vibrant with precious rings of color, the other marred and moody, it looked scrawled on her face, an afterthought by a careless totem artist. When she grinned her large sharp canine teeth appeared even more prominent than usual. Not just nerves on his part: seeing that grin, as hostile as a killer dog's, Duane realized dismally how Puff could be so agitated in the flesh, jerky as a tribal dancer, while talking to him in a near monotone. Her brain had cracked, her mind flung all over the inside of her skull messy as uncooked egg. Now he had real problems.

The wailing at her feet again. Puff looked down slowly and said, "It's happening. It is *really* happening! I always knew he wasn't . . . they didn't just throw him away! Oh, no, don't you see—this is where they put *all* of them, Duane, isn't it? Oh, God. Now I don't have to feel guilty any more. Duane, would you bring the light over here?" She held up the length of tough shriveled vine. "Mama wanted me to untie her first. But it was on too tight. So I did *him*. What do you think I ought to call him, Duane? Huh?"

Duane didn't reply, and couldn't move. The flashlight in his hand dipped. The absence of the beam distressed her.

"Don't leave me! I told you to bring me that fucking *flashlight*!"

On "fucking" she gave a leap, astonishing because she was nearly up to her hips in silk, and charged high-stepping through the frothy cocoon, shark's teeth flying as high as her ears, arms working like the erratic limbs of a capering marionette. He backed up only two steps before she dropped a fist hard as a hammer on one of his collarbones, snatching at the light with her other hand. Duane was driven to his knees, and as Puff turned frantically to go back to the nesting place, she inadvertently smashed him in the jaw with an upshot knee.

Duane went over sideways in a burst of sparks and comets that thinned drastically in a gathering fog. Dark gray, but not black: he didn't totally lose consciousness. He was numb and bleeding inside his mouth, but he could hear exceptionally well. Voices on the damn radio again, the baby's wail, now Puff babbling and calling to him, Duane, just as if she hadn't put him down for the count moments ago. His fingers, digging through silk, found bedrock. He pushed himself upright, tilting, wobbling. He'd bitten his tongue. His jaw was still numb but the back of his neck hurt like hell.

For the first time since they'd made the discovery of mummies in the sepulchral cavern, Duane was very much afraid they weren't going to get out of there alive.

Puff was back, standing over him, shining the light in his eyes.

"What's the matter?" she asked him.

He couldn't say anything. Puff reached down, took him by the arm, and set him on his feet. He couldn't believe how strong she was, how weak he felt in her grip. His knees weren't supporting him too well. Fell off the garage roof when he was eight, didn't hurt any worse than this.

"Come look," she said happily, and dragged him into the midst of the cocoon. "I was three months along. They told me, it doesn't look like anything at three months, not as big as a mouse, even; but that was all lies. Huh? It was no fucking *mouse,* it was my little baby boy! I had it done in Puerto Rico, you know. They speak English there. In Puerto Rico. They rob you, too. It cost five hundred dollars, but she wasn't even a regular doctor. I don't think."

"Jesus, Puff, let go of me!"

"Three years ago. Huh? I thought he was dead. Wait till everybody finds out about this!"

"No, Puff, *no,* this place—I'm not sure *what* it is, but I know we have to get—"

"There! There he is! Look, isn't he *beautiful?*"

Where she aimed the beam of the flashlight Duane saw something shapeless—to his unaccustomed eyes— not only shapeless, but dark and writhing like a bucket of eels. Making those chilling human sounds of anguish, birth pangs. One glance, and he didn't want to see or know any more. The voices on the radio, all of

them screaming now, like a mob at a prizefight. Locked
in her maniacal grip, he looked at Puff, and she was
chewing her lip in a frenzy, making it bleed. Blood just
flowing down her chin. He was cold and dizzy from
horror. There was a fog rising from the matted-down
silk where the whippy thing struggled to live, or die;
their own breaths were condensing. And now some of
the luna moths, eyespots aglow like small lanterns, had
begun to flutter around their heads, as if taking a keen
interest in the spectacle, the abomination, the horror
. . . Duane tried to draw back, to pull Puff with him as
if from the brink of an abyss, but she was immobile
except for the thrilled antic workings of her face, the
sharp teeth piercing her lip.

"He's coming," she muttered, as if what she was
watching were pornographic. She wiped her swelling
lip with the back of the hand that held the flashlight. At
least she had stopped biting herself. Duane shot another
look at the floor as something popped up darkly, slick
with fluid, through the fog and silken haze: something
with a gaze as stark and stunned as his own. The round
hairless head of a kinetic tarbaby. It was still not clear,
from the expression on its face, if it was struggling to
live, or dying in agony.

"Damn you, Puff, why did you take that vine from
around its neck?"

She looked at him in surprise, and responding to the
pressure of his fingers on the back of the hand she held
him with, relaxed her grip.

"Mama told me to!"

"Your mother's not here!"

Puff did her little joyous, herky-jerky dance. "Look,
look at him now!"

It was sitting up, he could see that much. The wildly
contorted limbs, once twisted like the length of vine
Puff was still holding, had straightened. Fingers were
recognizable, and toes. So was an immature penis, half
the length of Duane's little finger, and erect. Tremors

still ran through the small body in waves, but the screams had become sobs. And its—his—skin tone was softening, turning from pitch thick as a tar road to a dark gray, with faint pinkish highlights which at first Duane thought were reflections from the wings of the moths flocking to the beam of the flashlight. As the child breathed and its own vapor formed like a blanket around its head, the tremors and upheavals lessened.

"He'll get his hair back. Won't he?" Puff said, smiling deliriously. And she reached down to run her hand over the crown of the well-shaped head, a milder gray than the rest of him. His skin continued to lighten, to soften everywhere. At Puff's touch he held up his arms to be taken. "Ohhh," she said, rapt in motherhood. She handed Duane the flashlight.

"Puff, don't!"

"I'll take him with us. We'll come back to get mama. I need something to cut away all the vines. I don't want to leave any of them like this." There was a squawl of protest on the radio, and Puff hesitated as she was bending over to pick up the child. She frowned. "It's all right," she said. "I said I'd come back. You can depend on me." She listened. "You can depend on *him*," she said, but with less conviction, and although Puff didn't look his way, Duane felt a warning pang around the heart. "I'll leave the radio on for you," she said then with a note of finality, and turned her full attention to the waiting child, who watched her solemnly, arms still uplifted. Duane thought he might be five or six years old, but it was hard to tell—that hairless head.

"Don't," Duane said again, but he was drained of protest; there was no reasoning with her.

She lifted the child and brushed away some of the cobwebby silk that clung to his moist, wrinkled, repugnant skin and held him against her breast. His head was on one of her shoulders but his eyes, elliptical and filmy, didn't close. He looked steadily at Duane, without curiosity or any other sign of intelligence.

"I'm going to call him Alastor," Puff said. "Do you read Shelley? Do you know that story?" She spoke happily to the child. "How do you like your new name, hmm?" A moth sat exquisitely on the child's head. Alastor gave no indication he knew it was there. He was perfectly quiet except for breathing. Duane reached out slowly and touched a boyish shoulder, jerked his hand back. The child's flesh was impossibly cold, as if he'd been plucked from the waters of a well.

The eyes moved, following Duane. A small hand clutched Puff's arm above the elbow, and Duane realized something was wrong with that hand. The little finger hadn't turned, it was still carbon-black. And tapered; it came to a point as sharp as a thorn's.

"Puff," Duane said, his voice cracking, sounding childish, "put him down."

"What?"

"Just put him down, and let's go. We don't have any business—"

"We're going, all right, but Alastor's going, too."

"No."

"What do you mean, no? What do you have to say about it, shithead? He's mine!"

Another luna alighted on the boy's skin, now a spoiled-looking whitish-gray. Two more. With their wingspans, three of them were nearly enough to cloak the inert Alastor in alluring moths. They gave him, with their beaming eyelets, both stature and menace.

Duane swallowed. He'd nearly lost his voice. He looked at Puff's eyes and knew there was no sense in yelling at her. But maybe he could save her. He trembled in his guts. His chin wrinkled.

"I think . . . he's used to being down here, belongs here, and . . . if you, we . . . take him outside, who knows what'll happen?" *To us.*

Puff gave her head a toss and laughed; Alastor's thin hands clutched her arm tighter, and Duane looked at the thorny little finger denting her skin.

"You're crazy!" Puff said. "Nothing's going to happen to him. Now what're we waiting for?"

"Feel how cold he is, Puff. He shouldn't even be . . . alive."

"He isn't cold! He feels fine to me! He's probably hungry! I want to get him something to eat and some clothes and stuff. Toys. He wants some toys to play with, don't you, big boy?" Puff jogged Alastor up and down a couple of times; the child rode glumly on her shoulder. The faintly luminous moths fluttered but settled down as if they'd become attached to him. "I'll call my brother Max collect in Wisconsin. When I tell him the good news he'll wire me a hundred dollars right away. Then . . ."

Puff, having fixed a course of action in her bombed-out head, pushed her way past Duane. After a few steps she looked around wearily.

"That's the way we came in, over there. Isn't it?"

"Yes."

"I can't get out without the light, Duane. Help me?"

"Oh, Puff."

"If I can just get a little help from my friends now and then, I'll do fine." She was crying.

The hairless child on her shoulder, on his bed of shark's teeth, closed his eyes. He seemed to have gone to sleep. Maybe his hair would grow back. Maybe there was nothing to be afraid of, after all. The radio was as still as a stone. If he wasn't afraid, Duane thought, then why didn't he stop shaking? If he'd gone crazy too, down here with mummies that came back to life, then somebody would recognize that right away when he reached the surface; they'd put him in a safe place until he got sorted out. He yearned for that safety. It was a craving much stronger than hunger.

"You go first, Puff," Duane said. "I'll light the way."

19

The telephone in the kitchen rang at five after nine, and when Enid answered she heard a thin high voice made less intelligible by crackling static on the line. "I haven't seen Marjory for hours and I can't find her anywhere! I don't want to speak to her, I just want to know if she's home!"

"Rita Sue?"

"Yes, it's Rita Sue!"

"Where are you, baby?"

"Dante's Mill State Park! Phone booth! Campground! Everything's closed here! I think she went behind the waterfall, that's why I'm—"

Enid took the receiver away from her ear and said sharply, "Ted!" He was under the sink with his tool box taking another crack at a leak that had resisted his previous efforts at repair. He backed out and glanced at her, reaching for a grease rag to wipe his hands on. Rita Sue was still talking. Enid gave Ted a baffled look, shook her head worriedly, and got back on the line.

"Rita Sue—wait—tell me that again. Where did you see her last? Who was she with? That boy—"

"No. We didn't see Duane. She had some of his stuff with her, you know, that he uses to collect butterflies. She put it in the backseat and said—what was it she said, Boyce?"

Enid said quickly, "Rita Sue, put Boyce on and let me talk to him."

"Hi, Enid, this's Boyce."

"I know. What's going on over there?"

"Beats me."

"You're not being much *help*, Boyce. Now think about it calmly and tell me everything Marjory said the last time you—what time was that anyway?" Enid looked around at Ted and pointed upstairs, telling him to get on the telephone in her bedroom and listen in. He nodded and went at a jog to the stairs.

"I reckon it was a little past four."

"Where was she?"

"By the millpond at the old town."

"She's not there now?"

"Well, they close the road over there at sundown."

Enid heard Ted pick up the receiver of the phone in her room. "You saw Marjory a little after four, but Duane wasn't with her."

"No. I don't know where that booger's got himself to, and if he's not careful he's gonna violate his probation—"

"I don't care about him," Enid said sharply, "I'm worried about Marjory. What did she *say* to you?"

"She said—near as I can recall—'Duane's missing. He's with some girl.' And, oh yeh, her radio got stolen, that was it, Duane was helping the girl get her radio back. I think. They had to go behind the waterfall after it."

"*Behind the waterfall? At the millpond?*"

"That's right." Boyce paused, apparently to listen to something Rita Sue was saying urgently in the background. "Oh, yeh. Marjory must've called the Highway Patrol, she said they were coming. But they never did. Then she took her flashlight out of her shoulder bag and said she was going to go look for Duane behind the waterfall."

"Oh, good Lord! How deep is that water there? *Ted?*"

Ted asked Boyce, "Did you see Marjory go behind the waterfall?"

"No, sir. Me and Rita Sue stayed in the car until we decided to go have us a ice cream—"

"Boyce, how could you let Marjory—"

"Nuggins, calm down. I can barely hear him."

Boyce said, "Well, I was gonna go with her, but you know, because my foot's all wrapped where I dropped that crankcase, I can't get around so good."

"I heard about it. Where'd you say you're at now?"

"Oh, you know, the big campground where the park headquarters is."

"I want you to stay right there with Rita Sue," Ted told him. "There'll be some law officers on the scene in just a few minutes—"

Enid lowered the receiver of the telephone between her breasts and put a hand over her mouth. She was still standing there like that when Ted came running down the stairs, peered at her in exasperation from the doorway, then came quickly to hang up so he could make a call.

"We don't know it's anything; maybe they—" He was dialing.

"She's been missing *five hours*? How could she go behind the waterfall? Isn't there—it's like a big wall! There's no way—"

"Hold on. Hi, Loretta, this's Ted. I'm over at Enid Waller's. Her sister's up at Dante's Mill, and she and maybe a couple other kids have been missing since right after four o'clock this afternoon. Marjory Waller. Her date was a boy named Duane—" Ted snapped his fingers a couple of times until it came to him. "Eggleston." He spelled it. "Yeh, do that first, and also notify the Wingo County Sheriff's Department, have them meet me at park headquarters. Oh, and give ol' Rhubarb a call, ask him to take my shift tonight . . . I *know* that, but the horse show's rained out tonight, they don't hold hunter-jumpers in a dang downpour. There's one more thing." Ted turned away from Enid and walked toward the back porch as far as the telephone cord would reach, but he couldn't get his voice low enough not to be overheard by Enid. There was thunder outside, going on and on like a bowling ball rolling downstairs.

"Tell Wingo County we may be needing their tracker dogs. And enough men to drag that pond up there at the old mill. Yeh. Leaving right now."

When Ted turned around Enid was facedown in a heap on the floor. Because of the thunder, or the pressure of blood in his ears, he hadn't heard her fall.

20

Birka was finding out that coming back from the Black Sleep was no bowl of cherries. She was having the devil of a time holding on to the Marjory-human, and in Birka's present circumstances, Marjory was the only hope she, or any of the *huldufólk* colony, had left.

Killing Arne had been a mistake: purely an accident. After the deeply painful minutes of awakening from the Black Sleep, Birka had been too easily enraged to discover she wasn't free at all. Arne (unrecognizable, to be sure, as her son, except in distant neurons of the hypothalamus where primitive structures of human emotion survived vestigially) had prudently tethered her feet to the tree with strangler fig. Petulantly she reversed the polarities of his brain, rendering him unconscious. No harm in that, ordinarily, but then, because he was biologically antiquated, perhaps, he suddenly stopped breathing. Birka had a lot to learn about mind-tempering, the harmful effects of misfires on hormonal balances, although she couldn't have put any of this into words. Theron was the learned one, surrounded by fledglings, but he'd had little time to instruct Birka before Enoch and the boy caught up to them and banished them all to limbo with nooses of fig. She had never taken Enoch seriously enough, Birka lamented, and that had been their downfall.

Once she was certain Arne was dead, instinct fifty million years old took over: no sense wasting a human, so Birka skinned him. (Uh-oh; she visualized this a little carelessly, and the Marjory-human jumped nearly a foot off the ground where she was crouched partway down the hill. Birka turned on the childish tears again, loading up the cortical belief-systems of her own mind with images of kinship. Her enormously sensitive, telepathic pineal "eye" distributed these diverting images and messages to priority systems in twinkling thickets of the Marjory-human's hierarchical brain, preempting, but not with complete efficacy, conscious awareness of her present surroundings and circumstances.) All that aged, mottled skin might prove to be of no value in Birka's renascence, but it was something to start with. Theron would have criticized her for not taking advantage of the opportunity. If she ever saw Theron again.

Heaving Arne's skinned carcass high into the fork of a limb was no more difficult for Birka than lifting, in her former unsatisfactory incarnation, a pot of beans from the back of the stove. Even though she couldn't stand on her numbed, poisoned feet. Nor touch the knots of strangler fig without instantly losing the use of her fingers. She had persuaded the Marjory-human (must think of her only as "Marjory"; the leak-through, the currents of cross-imagery, disturbed the basic, reptilian brain that wanted to scuttle, and save the irreplaceable body) to untie her, continually eliciting sympathy through imagined kinship: a taxing exercise in Birka's present state of development and difficulty. Now she continued the exercise, but Birka felt drained, incapable of Turning the girl, even if she could position her for this effort. Such a malignant fate: almost free, then lightning striking the tree just as the stubborn fig-knots came loose in Marjory's hands. Fortunately Marjory wasn't killed, but Birka lay trapped in a cage of limbs, a welter of green leaves. Not the type of leaves to send her off to the Black Sleep; only a vine around the throat could do that. But the greenery sapped the vital energy of the pituitary gland, caused an annoying mist in her mind when she most needed all of her faculties.

And the steady rain had thinned the flocks of messengers, the luna moths; she had no idea what was going on down below where Theron waited, entombed. The force of his mind had remained potent even in the rigors of the Sleep, although she couldn't hope to tap him now, through layers of limestone and deeps of pitch. What would he say, advise, in these moments of crucial helplessness?

He would say that her fear of dying was vestigial, unworthy of her status. Her flesh was so cold marauding animals or vultures would not care to touch her. The sun, of course, was a different matter: to be illuminated unpityingly at dawn, quickly banished by the hated orb of God; oh, the smoking horror of the unhidden which preceded the Sleep! A noose was bad enough, she never wanted to undergo the torture of sunlight. But she might have hours left, before dawn. And what else could harm her? *Nothing*.

Her immediate needs were clothing and shelter. A farmhouse, a barn would do. Was Marjory from a farm, or town? Birka preferred the isolation of a farm; not so many humans to deal with. Marjory was all she could handle, for now.

Birka's other option was to return immediately to the cave and free the others. With Marjory's help, of course. Only a human could release the Sleepers. But this might put too much of a strain on Birka's efforts to maintain their relationship. She couldn't afford to lose Marjory, but controlling another's primal fears was ticklish, even at this range. The child was so afraid of death (Birka sensed without crystallizing the event a catastrophic loss of parents). For now wherever Marjory went, Birka had to go.

"Oh, Marjory! Are you hurt?"

"Yeh. I hurt all over."

"Can you walk?"

"I think so. Did you—why were you running?"

"I was afraid of the storm. I'm still afraid! Take me home."

(Marjory's eyes darting to the sky where lightning flickers, then to the damaged tree. No trees in their Icelandic valley. Marjory sees instead the tumbled stones of a sheepcote.)

"I'm pinned down! Hurry, Marjory, get the stones off me!"

"I'm . . . coming, Birka."

A long way up the slope for her, slipping and sliding. Breathing hard. Struggling through the wet leaves and myriad branches of the huge chestnut limb lying half on the ground. A raw wound in the side of the old tree visible as lightning flashes again. (All of this recast by Birka as tumbled sheaves of hay under a fallen shed roof. The lightning is very useful to Birka because it is something else Marjory dreads, reducing the activities of her brain to basic survival alarms.) Marjory cringes, and sees Birka lying helplessly in mud, looking up at her.

"That stone . . . so heavy. Can you lift it, Marjory?"

"Don't . . . know. Trying. Leg . . . broken?"

"No. I can move it. A little more—there! Give me your hand."

"What happened . . . to your pretty dress?"

"I don't know. I don't care. Let's get out of here. We'll go to your house. I want to take a bath. You'll lend me a dress, won't you?"

"Sure. Birka . . . I saw you flying. How . . . ?"

"Marjory, don't be ridiculous. Which way?"

"I don't know. I'm . . . lost."

"Well, then. There must be a road. We'll have to walk until we find it."

"Walk until we find it."

"We'll tell each other stories. Keep our spirits up. It can't rain forever."

"You're so cold."

"But I like being cold, Marjory."

21

The girl called Smidge had looked in Puff's luggage twice for the gasoline card, but she couldn't find it. Sorting angrily through raunchy underpants and other items of clothing sprinkled with reefer dust and Johnson's baby powder, paperback copies of *The Origins and History of Consciousness* and the poems of Shelley, autographed photos of trash gods and already obsolete rock icons of the fast-diminishing Love Generation, and *beaucoup* empty containers for Tuinal and Quaaludes, she found, the second time around, wrapped in aluminum foil and stuffed in the toe of a lizard-skin shoe, the only thing of value Puff owned that was immediately accessible to them: some jewelry that looked old enough to be genuine gold. It might, Smidge estimated, be worth a fast hundred bucks at the right place, a pawn shop or jewelry store that specialized in such stuff. So she took the jewelry without telling either of their male traveling companions, Wiley and Deke. Smidge had, after an initial infatuation on the beaches of Sanibel, just about given up on Puff, who wouldn't let Smidge fuck her unless she was so high she didn't know what was going on anyway.

In Smidge's opinion Puff had, at some point during their last few hours in the backwoods of Tennessee, come across a guy with a good-looking bike or something who appeared to be a better deal than she had with *them:* maybe she'd met up with her very own "exterminating angel," which she claimed a fortune-teller in Europe had told her she was destined to meet. Smidge had thought Puff was so cute, she'd just hung on every word there for a while until it came to her that most of Puff's philosophy was rock-hipster bullshit right out of *Crawdaddy.* Because the woody wasn't acting right, burning gallons and gallons but getting no significant mileage, Puff probably figured they'd have to camp out for a while, and she could spin by and pick up her things in a day or two once she was comfortably relocated.

Smidge was still reeling a little from the aftereffects of a mescaline high two days ago, feeling mean as a dog with a thorn in its paw. They had no money and nothing to drink. Wiley had thrown up in the woody while she and Deke were out scouring the countryside for the treacherous Puff. The rain had been heavy and she could only crack the windows and try to get used to the rotten smell—not that it had been smelling all that good in there before he chucked his guts. Wiley, conscious now but not much help, was huddled under the canvas the two guys had pitched above the popped hood of the woody while Deke tried to get the carburetor cleaned out, or whatever, so they wouldn't be stalling every thirty feet and jerking along at twenty miles an hour. Deke was a whiz at electronics: he could take apart a malfunctioning guitar amp and reassemble it in the dark onstage while fifteen thousand teenyboppers were screaming at a concert. But he wasn't much with cars. Wiley was no fucking good with anything but a cocktail lounge piano and Puff's pussy, at least to hear her tell it.

Both of them had vetoed ditching Puff the first time she brought it up. Give me one good reason, Smidge demanded, and Wiley, the asshole, racked his putrefying brains and said with a smeary grin, "She knows how to have some fun," putting Smidge down again and shoving her farther to the outside of their little group than before. Smidge was of a mind to outboogie both of them. Her little romantic schemes involving Puff having collapsed like the castles on the sand they'd built together while they were still friends, what was the point of hanging out any longer? She didn't mind hiking with her backpack through a little rain, once the lightning abated. She was scared silly of lightning, those flashes that lit up her skull like X-rays, followed by a *crack* that seemed to jolt the heart loose from its moorings.

Wiley was holding a flashlight over Deke's shoulder while Deke worked, and the smell of gasoline in the station wagon was almost enough to overcome the stench of beer puke. Smidge concealed the stolen jewelry in her backpack, put on her Seminole poncho, and opened the tailgate of the woody. Wiley was jiving and making jokes under the square of tarp that sagged in the middle from accumulated rainwater. What's the difference between a clever midget and a venereal disease? Do you know the difference between a genealogist and a gynecologist? That kind of joke. Good old Wiley. You could dress him up, but you couldn't take him anywhere. Smidge decided to say good-bye to the fellas after all.

"Where you goin', babe?" Wiley said, when she had their attention.

"Find a place to sleep tonight. Get myself a bath. My hair smells pukey."

"Hey, yeh, listen, I'm sorry about that, it was just an accident." He was flicking the flashlight on and off in her face.

"Yeh, well, sure. Anyway, I'm gone."

Deke said, "What do you want us to tell Puff?"

"Tell her I'll be around the old campground," Smidge said vaguely. "Wiley, don't shine the damn light in my eyes like that."

"I'll get this thing going in a little while," Deke promised. "We'll drive over in the morning and pick you up."

"Do that." Rain was running down her neck. Smidge felt an unexpected pang, thinking about Puff. A clever midget is a cunning runt, and Puff's a runny— She said to Deke, "Which way did we walk to get to that town?"

"Just pick up the trail over there and follow it," Deke said. "Then you come to the road we drove in on, and it's all downhill."

Smidge looked over her shoulder and saw nothing, and shuddered.

"How the hell am I going to get there in the dark?"

"I thought maybe you noticed that already. It's dark, and it's raining."

"Well, I could use the flashlight."

"Well, we only got one and we need it here." The wrench he was using slipped from Deke's hand and fell to the ground underneath the woody. Deke uttered a blasphemy.

"Can't you swear and leave Jesus out of it?"

Wiley laughed. "Preacher's daughter," he said.

Smidge said, "There's some things I'm sensitive about, believe it or not."

Deke grabbed the flashlight out of Wiley's hand and got down to look for the wrench.

"Wiley could walk me as far as the road, there's probably some lights on in the town. Okay, Deke?"

"Yeh, hell. Go on. I'm sick of this shit anyway." Deke came up with the wrench in his hand and scowled at it, then banged the hood down as Wiley jumped back with a laugh and did a little of his Jamaican dance, the one he said appeased the crocodile gods. "We got anything left to eat?"

"There's some Cokes, and peanut brittle."

"Peanut brittle! Whose idea was it to boost five pounds of fucking peanut brittle?"

Wiley said, "There wasn't much else to boost, except all that shit made out of seashells, and postcards and stuff. But that's a good idea. Maybe I can get us a couple six-packs in this town. Smidge, we'll work it the way we did at that convenience store, you know, where the old lady looked like Granny on *Beverly Hillbillies*? I could've walked out with half the store, and she—"

Wiley abruptly stopped talking and licked his lips and looked off with a slow sideways movement of his head. He was doing that a lot lately. The flashlight in his hand dipped, shining on the bumper of the woody and the faded sticker that read We Want the World and We Want It Now! Smidge reached out and took the flashlight from his hand. Five seconds later Wiley came around, eyes blinking rapidly, and said, "*Beverly Hillbillies*. That show fucking cracks me up. You going somewhere, Smidge?"

"We're taking a hike down to the town. Except it's not a real town, Wiley. Nobody lives there any more. It's an exhibit. Come on if you're coming."

"Right on, babe. Back before you know it, Deke."

"Yeh, swell. I'm gonna crash."

"Smidge, you know the difference between a genealogist and a gynecologist?"

"No, and I don't care," Smidge said, shining the

light up the wide firebreak they had followed off the
road and into the woods, staying far enough from the
road so the occasional park ranger wouldn't come across
them and make them leave. Two days already. They
could've been in Chicago. There were friends of friends
in Chicago, at the university, who she knew she could
put up with.

"Where did you say Puff's got to?" Wiley asked her
as they trudged up the path in the rain. Lightning off to
the north, or what she thought might be north, not close
enough to be really scary. The flashlight had a good
strong beam, like a headlight almost. She was wearing
her muleskinner's hat, which kept the rain off her face.
Wiley, as usual, was barefoot. His striped railroad pants
were sodden and muddy, his vest of unborn pony hide
gleamed wetly when she swung the flash toward him.
He'd been a husky guy, well-built, but beer was turning
him to a pile of suet. He couldn't be more than thirty,
but there was gray in his scimitar sideburns. Well, he
was better than no company at all.

"I didn't say. I don't know. She took off about four
o'clock, I think, and didn't come back."

Wiley was silent about that, and then he began singing "Lovely Bunch of Coconuts," jumping around on
the path, behind her, in front of her, leaping into the
air and holding his balls. Inevitably he slipped and
crashed down and lay there on the trail, muddy and
with a look of pain in his triangular eyes.

"Wiley, get up."

"Can't," he said, wincing.

"Knock the breath out of you?"

". . . Yeh."

"What you get for being such a—" Smidge offered
a hand. Wiley grasped it and raised his head slowly,
but then he was deadweight.

"Don't think I can get up yet."

"What'd you do?"

"Back, feels like."

"Oh, great."

Wiley slowly inched to a sitting position.

"You gonna be okay?"

"I think so. You can go on if you want to. Maybe I better go back to the woody."

"Can you walk?"

"Yeh, sure. In a minute."

"Look, I'm gonna take the flashlight, because—"

"That's okay. *No problema.* I'll get back okay. See you in the morning, huh?"

"I feel like a shit, man, leaving you here."

"No sweat."

"Okay, then."

Smidge actually did feel, at least momentarily, bad about leaving him sitting there, but on the other hand you could never tell about Wiley. Maybe he was faking it. Maybe he only wanted attention. She felt better about his situation when he started humming "Malagueña." His back couldn't be hurting all that much. She resumed walking uphill along the firebreak, averting her face when lightning streaked low off to the left. The trees were a dark oceanic blue, rolling like combers in a surge of wind that hadn't reached her yet. The rain quickened, or else it was just runoff from the drenched boughs overhead. Smidge paused to adjust the straps of her backpack.

She heard Wiley call out then, full-throated, "Smidge!" Like that, his voice sounding hoarse and high, and as she whipped around awkwardly another bolt fired off at tree-top level, dazzling her. Thunder came at her like a jet flying six feet off the ground, breaking the sound barrier; she grabbed her ears with both hands and the flashlight slipped, glancing off her hip on the way down. Smidge bent over to pick it up. Something about the tone of his voice. *Scared.* Wiley scared? He had the trust of a two-year-old that nothing bad could ever happen to him. A true moon-in-

Aquarius. Maybe he'd tried to walk, and slipped again, and was just sitting around spaced-out in the mud.

Smidge aimed the light down the firebreak but didn't see him. She didn't think she'd come very far, but in the dark and rain she didn't have her bearings. She walked back slowly, following her own boot prints.

"Wiley?"

Smidge looked right, then to her left at the undergrowth ten feet on either side of her, thinking Wiley might have become bored and was going to—well, if he tried anything cute, she'd give him a fat lip to go with his lame back. The rain was beginning to make her miserable. Goddamn Wiley! Lightning. Cringe. Thunder. Cringe again. Flashing her own light around. Boot print, boot print, she couldn't have passed him by, boot prints, footprints, yeh, Wiley's big feet, size twelve or better but he hated shoes, this was where they—

But whose footprints were *those*?

Smaller, narrower, a feminine foot. They came from the left, down from the woods, two, then almost three feet apart as if she'd been running, running to this big mud wallow in the middle of the firebreak. Depressions filling with rainwater, a big churned-up area as if they, there'd been—

And then sort of a fresh path going off diagonally the other way toward the fullness of woods on the other side, and alongside that dragged path the womanly footprints began again, all the way to—

She was starting to turn to stone. Interesting reaction. She'd heard of people petrified by fear and had never thought that much about it, yet it was exactly what happened, beginning with her knees. They turned to stone, they wouldn't work. Then she was stone up the back and across the shoulders and the throat, yes, the tongue too . . . she could still feel her heart beating, though, and the rain dripping from the brim of her hat onto the hand that held the jittery flashlight. Smidge was making noises like a blind kitten trying to find its mother when something came crashing in a panic out of the brush twenty feet away with a deep sob of anguish, and stopped dead in the beam of the light.

Not that he could see it. What was left of the pulp of his eyes was running down his cheeks. And what was left of the skin of his torso hung off the pegs of rib bones, the keel of his breastbone, like a yellowish, blood-stained toga. Blobs of fat undulated at his flayed midsection. His hands rose and fell uselessly in the streaming light spread out across the mass of understory shrubs behind him.

That's when the coldly, unnaturally white, hairless, naked woman with the shimmering blue eyes stepped calmly from concealment, glanced Smidge's way, then seized Wiley by his abundant hair and, uncovering the nape of his neck, stuck him there with something in her other hand. Hard to tell what it was. Not a knife. Just a weapon of some kind, about three inches long, slender and black and jutting at a slight angle from her fist.

God, she had to be strong, because without much effort she jerked Wiley, a two-hundred-pound guy, backward by the hair and off his feet and into the brush that, almost instantly, swallowed them both.

Smidge blinked once and her lip curled as adrenaline-laced blood went pounding up into her head and through all the stone parts; she ran without feeling a thing—the ground, the rain—ran back up the firebreak with hell going off like fireworks behind her, thunder smothering her cries. She was a good runner and at peak stride just as someone came leaping out at her from the underbrush, knocking her muleskinner's hat off and grabbing her by the arm.

"Got you!" Smidge heard, words and then breathless laughter, but her right hand was already in motion as her momentum was slowed; she came spinning around with the flashlight in a hard chop to the side of the head and heard a good solid *thock* even as the girl's grip loosened. But Smidge was unbalanced by the force of her swing and the weight of the backpack; she fell down on top of her assailant, swinging again with intent to kill but missing. For several seconds they were both motionless, Smidge on top with a knee on the girl's considerable chest, her breath searing her throat, unable to get away because the girl, her nose bleeding, hung on to Smidge with both hands.

Smidge flashed the light in her eyes. Blue eyes, like those of the apparition glimpsed in the woods below, but filled with pain and bewilderment.

"Owwww, God, get off me!" Marjory cried.

"Who're you?"

"Who are *you*?"

"Smidge. If you don't want that maniac to get hold of us, you'd better hop up and get running for your life and I mean . . . right *now,* asshole!"

"What maniac?"

"I said *run!*"

Smidge lurched up with a quick look behind her, the abused flashlight putting out a splintered beam in the rain. She had a lump in her throat that wouldn't go down, a blaze of terror in her breast. Marjory ran a hand across her bloody nose and cried out, but she was so quick getting to her feet that Smidge, in the way, nearly was upended.

"What am I doing here?"

"Later," Smidge snarled at her, and without knowing why—maybe it had been the totally bewildered tone of her voice—grabbed Marjory by a lapel of her dirty wet shirt and dragged her a couple of feet uphill. "Will you *run*?"

Marjory didn't need further coaxing. Before Smidge got going again even half as fast as she wished she could run, fleet Marjory was nearly out of sight; Smidge would have lost track of her, except for the lightning. What the hell had she been doing out here by herself? Stoned, Smidge thought, just stoned out of her gourd. *Got you.* Pleased with herself, playing some kind of stupid game while less than a hundred yards away Wiley was getting dressed out like a deer slaughtered in the woods.

Or maybe Wiley was part of the same game. And there were a lot of other players, all over the place.

Devil worshipers, Smidge concluded, running hard despite a cramp in her stomach, but mortally afraid she was going nowhere. Afraid to look back. *Human sacrifice*. Shit like that. Last year's ritual murder of a pregnant actress and four other people (Smidge couldn't recall any names) was very much on her mind.

Oh, God. My daddy's a Methodist preacher. Don't let them! Jesus, I'll come back to you! I'll preach if you want me to. I won't do drugs any more. I swear on the cross, just don't let it happen to me!

22

"I think we should go this way," Puff said, pausing to take a breather where the shaft they were following turned into a narrow cone-shaped chamber that angled up so high the beam of the flashlight barely grazed the reflectant chandelier formations beneath the roof. "Alastor, what do *you* think?"

She'd been going on like that for several minutes, chatting with the sleepy-eyed boy and all but ignoring Duane, except to snap at him when she thought he was doing something wrong as they made their ways up from the lower chamber filled with moths and silk and mummies. Duane already with the low, sick feeling that they were seriously lost, but he didn't have a clue as to how they'd gone wrong. Maybe from the very beginning: the mummy chamber like the inside of an egg, points of reference scarce, numerous holes in the walls, and then the boy—if that's what he was, and Duane wasn't so sure about that any more, about his humanness—had come to life in an unforgettably ghastly manner, which had really cold-cocked all of his senses. Now he was concentrating most of his mental energies on just trying to keep cool and objective and ignore Puff's rambling madness. The lunas fluttering around their heads were of no help. They were probably lost, too.

Some water was trickling over translucent ledges of stone into a pool and Duane, sampling cautiously, concluded that if the water was deadly he didn't really care at this point, and drank his fill. Puff sat down and shifted Alastor's weight into her naked lap with a grimace and a sigh, and rolled her head to loosen stiff neck muscles. Alastor had the indentations of shark's teeth all over his chest and belly. The lunas would swoop toward him, alight briefly, then take off again. He stared at the necklace, then reached up slowly with the hand that had the thorn and touched it. Puff smiled.

"Puff, do you want to get a drink?"

She looked over at Duane, and at the little waterfall.

"Here, you hold Alastor."

"Puff, I don't think I want—"

"Hold him!"

"All right, just take it easy."

"And don't drop him," she added, getting up and crossing the floor to Duane in her flappy sandals.

Duane's glasses were misted from the waterfall. He took them off and set them beside the flashlight on a shelf of stone and accepted Alastor gingerly. It was like taking a snowman in his arms. He began to shudder right away, his teeth chattering. Alastor's legs clamped him at the waist. Puff went down on one knee to drink. Her hair hung off one side of her head, across the left shoulder. Without his glasses she looked a little blurry to Duane, but because of the angle of the flashlight beam he couldn't miss the thin line of partly dried blood from the nape of her neck and along the pebbled track of her arched spine.

"Puff? Did you know you were bleeding?"

"Where?" she muttered, cupping her hands to her mouth.

Alastor's head came up slowly and he stared at Duane.

"Looks like it's right in the middle of the back of your neck."

"Oh." She reached up with a wet finger and touched the spot. "I did feel something a little while ago. Alastor had his hand on my neck and he must have scratched me."

That's when Alastor went for Duane's left eye with the thorn where his right little finger should have been.

Duane jerked his head back instinctively, and the thorn missed, gouging the bridge of his nose instead, burning like a hypodermic needle. Duane let go of Alastor and cuffed him on the side of the head. Alastor screamed, lost his grip with his legs and fell at Duane's feet.

Puff jumped up at the sound of the scream, Duane cursing contrapuntally, and reached for Alastor, who was sitting spraddle-legged on the floor.

Alastor scrambled away on all fours, and Puff went after him. She stubbed a toe on the uneven floor and pulled up howling and limping.

Out of her reach, Alastor paused, looking around, looking up. Then he got to his feet and went running to a wall and began to climb. Within seconds he was out of Puff's reach.

"Alastor! No! Come back, you'll fall!"

Duane retrieved his glasses and with the flashlight illuminated Alastor on the inslanting wall. He showed no hesitation in climbing, although finger and toeholds were scarce. He moved like a fly, not in a straight line but zigzagging quickly over the rock face, continuing upward until he was more than halfway to the top of the cone-shaped chimney. A fall from there would have killed an ordinary child, but Alastor didn't fall, confirming Duane's hunch about him: but if he wasn't human and he wasn't an animal, what was he?

"Get him down!"

"How?" Duane asked reasonably, shining the light almost straight up through a whirligig of luna moths accompanying Alastor. For a few moments he paused as if searching, hanging upside down on the rock, then altered his course, scurried out of the throw of Duane's flashlight and vanished in near darkness.

"Oh, no, oh, no," Puff moaned. Her foot was bleeding where she'd ripped a toenail. "He's gone! We've got to find him!"

Duane sat down slowly and hung his head, flashlight dangling between his knees. He didn't have even a spark of energy left.

Puff, hopping mad, started kicking him with her uninjured foot.

"Get up! Get up! We have to get out of here and find Alastor!"

"I can't, Puff," Duane said, tears running down his cheeks. "I can't move. Leave me alone."

She tried to rip the flashlight from his hands. Duane resisted her. Her spit flew in his face. Duane buried his head and held on to the flashlight and took a few blows until Puff was too tired to keep it up. Drained of frenzy, panting, she slumped down beside him. He turned the light off.

"Why—did you do that?"

"Save the batteries. I don't know how long it's going to take us to find the way out. Maybe Marjory'll send help."

She crowded closer to him like a denning animal. The cold of her flesh set his teeth on edge. How she could be that cold, and not shaking to pieces?

"I don't feel good," Puff said.

"I don't, either."

"If Alastor got out of here, there must be lots of ways. I'll find him. Won't I?"

In the dark Duane remembered Alastor, clinging to the walls. *I hope not*, he thought. He said, "We'll rest a few minutes, then get started again."

23

The stable in Dante's Mill was clean, for a stable, and dry. Smidge kept a close eye on the girl who said her name was Marjory. She was bigger than Smidge, bur seemed harmless. Maybe a little off in the head. Smidge had found a couple of horse blankets that'd probably never been on a horse, and they were wrapped in those. She had changed from the skin out. Marjory was soaked too, but wouldn't take her wet things off. Her teeth chattered rhythmically. She was pale and there was a swelling bruise on one cheekbone where Smidge had slugged her with the flashlight, which had a steel barrel. The lens was cracked, but they still had some light, though Smidge was cautious about turning it on, not wanting to give away their hiding place to whoever might be looking for them. Marjory's nose had bled a little. Her hair was a blond bird's nest. Smidge might have felt sorry for her, but she couldn't forget that image of a half-skinned Wiley being tossed around by a grotesquely nude woman nowhere near his size. The strangest sight Smidge had ever seen, and she'd been in some tough places where far-out was the norm when it came to personal style and adornment. She—they—had stumbled into a witches' coven, all right, and this kid might well be a part of it. Or an intended victim. Smidge couldn't get much out of Marjory, but who could talk with such a case of the shudders?

"Hey, listen, Marjory? I don't think I'm going to stay here too long." Smidge kept her voice low. "If you tell me you weren't involved in that, okay, I believe you. Somehow you don't seem like the type. And I think you're pretty fucking scared like I am."

"W-what?"

"You saw what happened to Wiley, didn't you? But why were you trying to grab me?"

"W-Wiley?"

"Oh, come on! You know what I'm talking about."

Marjory hunched her shoulders, bracing herself for a chill that threatened to tear her apart. She was sniffing, but not fast enough to keep some of the snot from running out of her nose. She looked like she'd been raped by the Turkish army.

"W-who're . . . you?"

"I told you, my name's Smidge! Yeh, I know, that's not a name. I just didn't grow until I was almost thirteen, then I got my period and like, wow, all of a sudden I shot up a foot. Kovellis. Paula Kovellis. Akron, Ohio. Do you live around here?"

"Yes."

"They stuck Wiley in the eye with something. Blinded him. The poor dumb son of a bitch. That wasn't the worst thing that happened to him. Jesus, I can't stand thinking about it. So why *did* you grab me, what were you trying to do? You acted like it was some kind of fucking *game*."

"You've g-g-got . . . a dirty m-m-m—"

"Excuse *me*, sweetie. What church bus did you ride in on?"

Marjory shook her head, swallowed hard. "I didn't— I think I—c-came with Rita Sue-Sue-Sue. Boyce. And, uh, uh, Duane. B-but h-he's—"

Marjory put her hands over her face, grinding away.

"Hey, Marj, easy."

"Is Duane—still down there?"

"Down where?"

"C-cave."

"There's caves around here?"

"Big one. I s-saw—"

"You saw what?"

"Mr. Horsfall."

"Who's that," Smidge said impatiently, "your fucking Sunday school teacher?" She got up and prowled around. The stable doors were open at one end. Rain fell outside, but thunder was far away. There was a gaslight in front of some building or other halfway up the single wide street—now a muddy lake—of the town. The whole town looked like *Bonanza* to Smidge. Just a stage set, and deserted as far as she knew. She'd picked out the first doorway they'd come to. But Smidge was worried. The hairless woman had gotten a good look at her. Funny about that. Maybe if you were a woman you could get weird enough to shave your head, but she didn't have a trace of hair on her cunt, either. That look in her eyes—wander through a zoo and distract a predator from its meat, that's the look you'd get. As if she were preparing to eat Wiley. Smidge's throat filled, she couldn't shut it off in time, and she coughed some exceptionally bitter vomit. Mescaline. Pills. She put both hands hard against her stomach where the pain was intense.

"Matter?" Marjory asked, hearing Smidge gag.

"*Deke*. He's back there. They must have got him too by now. Look, I'm getting out of here. I mean, somebody has to go for help. You'll be all right, don't you think?"

Marjory rose slowly to her feet. "Is Puff . . . a friend of yours?"

"Puff? Hell yes! Where did you see Puff?"

"She was with us. Duane and me. In the c-cave. See,

Mr. Horsfall s-stole her radio, and took it into the cave.''

''Uh-huh. So that's your story? Well, I'm not worried about Puff right now, she never gave a damn about *my* ass. I just don't want anybody coming after me, you understand?''

''No.''

''Why don't you go way back in one of those horse stalls, nobody'll know you're there unless you make a lot of noise. See you around like a doughnut, Marj.''

''I . . . I've got to find Duane.''

''Suit yourself. Good luck. Just don't tag along, I don't feel like company.'' The pain in Smidge's stomach wouldn't quit. All the chemical abuse, catching up to her. Stoned since she was fourteen practically, twenty-two now. Twenty-three, don't lie. One year all but erased from memory. According to her passport, she'd been in Greece, Minorca, Bimini, other sunny ports of call. No reliable memories of anyone except a grossly fat, ever-smiling, apparently rich woman called Punk-A-Doodle. Or maybe that had been the name of her yacht. Cold turkey now at the worst possible time, the ripping twitches starting up all over Smidge's system. Hot flashes behind the eyes, ears ringing. Ring, ring—maybe she could get daddy on the phone, at the manse outside Akron. Maybe he'd be willing to listen, one more time. Daddies never gave up on their little girls, did they?

Smidge put on the backpack, draped the horse blanket from the top of her head and added her muleskinner's hat. The blanket hung to her knees. She walked out of the stables, bearing right, eyes on the flickering gas lamp up the street. The flashlight in her hand kept her out of the worst of the mud and the pooled water. She turned once for a quick look at the stable and smithy, but the doorway was blank, no sign of Marjory.

As she turned back the way she was headed, Smidge saw something, or somebody, scamper across a porch

of one of the buildings on the other side of the street. It
gave her a jolt that made her forget, momentarily, the hot
wires twisting ever tighter throughout her lean body.

It had been low enough to the porch floor, below the
railing, to be a dog. Instinctively Smidge flashed the
light that way to see if she could pick it up again. She
made out the gold-leaf letters "MERC" on a dark window. There was something of human shape motionless
behind the glass; she needed a few moments to realize
that it was an old-fashioned dressmaker's dummy. Full
satiny skirt. White gloves. No further movement on the
porch. There was a slat wooden bench under the window, but she couldn't quite—

Smidge held the flashlight at arm's length and ventured a little farther toward the middle of the street,
boots sucking mud. The rain down to a drizzle now,
lightning farther off, giving the sky a dusting.

The object of her search was under the bench. Huddled with knees up, head bent, eyes just above knee-
level and locked on her in the wisping beam of light.
She took another mucky step. Human eyes and sticking-
out ears . . . not a baby but a child, without visible
eyebrows or hair. Not even a rain-slicked coating of
pale down on the head.

"Hey!" Smidge called, bolder now although she
couldn't imagine what a kid was doing there alone and—
as far as she could tell—practically naked. Maybe he
(the shape of the face looked wrong for a girl, somehow) belonged to a caretaker family living in the town.
Upstairs over the store? But there were no lights in the
row of windows above the slant porch roof.

When she took another step the kid changed position, began to creep out from under the bench without
taking his eyes off her. A boy, all right, he was sporting
a tadpole-size whang. He looked poised to go off on a
tear.

"Wait a minute! Don't run off. If there's a phone
around here, I need to . . ."

Smidge's voice trailed. She had a sickening inspiration. The kid in her light was a scaled-down version of the woman in the woods, the one who apparently had done some unbelievably ghastly things to Wiley. Mother and son? Lord have mercy. She wasn't waiting around to find *that* out.

Something large and smudgy-wet arced out of the night just within her peripheral vision and smacked coldly against her cheek. Smidge jumped with a shriek and lost her footing in the mud, sat down squarely and hard clawing at her face to get it off. Insect wings, a big bug of some kind—she heard high-pitched childish hooting.

Smidge staggered to her feet. The flashlight, jarred once too often, had gone out. She worked the button. Nothing. He was still making fun of her distress, sounding as shrill as Smidge herself. There was enough illumination from the yellow chimney of the gaslight two buildings away to reveal him crouched on a step of the porch, a froglike posture. Smidge began to run, slipping badly but maintaining her balance.

When she looked back there were luminous moths swirling in the saturated air; her cheek felt quick-frozen where the other luna had touched her.

And the boy was following: running a few steps, stopping, crouching, stalking. Mud to his hips, but he was as swift and surefooted as she was clumsy.

He ran right up behind her and jumped high on her back, clinging to the mound of the bulky backpack. He rode her facedown into the mud.

Smidge thrashed and cursed and tried to turn over, to throw him off. He was like a forty-pound blanched spider. She felt icy hands in her hair, uncovering the nape of her neck. Then something sharp as a needle jabbed her a little more than an inch above the occipital bulge and entered deeply through the cerebellum, slipping up under the bone shelf. Smidge saw a couple of flashes of intense blue light like the onset of a migraine, and gradually stopped struggling. Tears streamed from one eye. Her blood seemed suspended in her arteries, bubbly, frothy, intoxicating as wine fermenting in a vat. It was not like any rush she was familiar with. She experienced a cloud-cozy lassitude. She continued to weep softly.

When she came around, aware that his weight was off her, Smidge sat up. She wiped mud from her face. The pin-prick on the back of her neck where he'd jabbed her felt electric. She cleaned a couple of fingers on her shirt and touched the spot. There was a trace of blood. That was all.

He was sitting a dozen feet away in the mud with his knees up again, gazing at her. Some of the luna moths were keeping him company, in spite of the slow rain. He watched one of them, balancing it on the back of an outstretched hand. The little finger of that hand was so dirty it looked black in the available light.

"What the hell did you do to me?" Smidge whined.

With a slight affectionate casting of his hand he put the luna in flight and studied it wistfully. He extended both hands from his sides and made languidly graceful flying motions. Smidge got up, dropping the sodden horse blanket, and took off her backpack. The boy stopped imitating the air show of the comely lunas and got up too, facing her. Smidge felt woozy, not too strong at the knees. Her heart was swollen like a hot-air balloon, a crisis in the making. She came up with the precious reds she'd been hoarding, worked up some spit and swallowed them. What she wouldn't give to be ripped to the tits right now—but she knew that wasn't smart. Smidge located the other item she wanted: a belt-buckle knife which she clenched in the palm of her right hand, two-edged, two-and-a-half-inch blade protruding between the fore and middle fingers.

"Get away from me!" she said. "I mean it, I don't want you hanging around."

The boy stared at the dagger, then looked at her face,

unafraid, a little puzzled. He appeared to shrug, or it might have been a sudden case of the willies. Then he turned and walked off, taking a detour to splash-kick his way through a large puddle. He stopped and slowly looked around, and made an unmistakable gesture. *Follow me*.

"What?" Smidge said. The root of her tongue felt numb. There was a buzzing at the back of her head she couldn't account for.

This time he gestured with both hands.

"Come on!" he said. The first time he'd spoken. It sounded disarmingly Southern. *Come aww-unnn*. He was like any other kid sneaking out of the house to play at night in the rain. But something unpleasant had happened to this one, sickness perhaps. He was altered in a way that wasn't immediately obvious but seemed pathetic to Smidge and put a dirge in her heart.

"I'm *not* coming. I'm getting out of this—"

"Don't you wanta play?"

"No!"

He was blank-faced at the rebuff. Considering it, he scuffed in more mud, then strolled toward a picket fence and a churchyard. The shrug again, saying more than he could put into words. His laughter.

"You will!" he said buoyantly, and cleared the fence in a bound. Smidge glimpsed him among tombstones for a few moments, then he was gone.

24

"I don't want to go home yet," Boyce said. "Not till we locate Duane. I'm kind of responsible for him, because he's on probation and all."

Boyce and Rita Sue were on the porch of the log building that served as park headquarters. Ted Lufford and Enid Waller had arrived at Dante's Mill ten minutes ago, ahead of the deputies from the Wingo County Sheriff's Department. Low-key, no flashing lights to disturb the tucked-in campers. They had a photo of Marjory which Enid kept in her wallet.

Rita Sue said, "I am *so* uncomfortable from this sunburn, Boyce."

Enid said in a low voice, "I'm not believing you, Rita Sue. Marjory's missing and you want to go home! You two were the last ones to see her."

Rita Sue squirmed a little. "If you ask me—"

"What, Rita Sue?"

"She's not *missing*. I mean, they're probably somewhere, together. You know."

Enid looked as if she wanted to slap her face. "There's something strange has been going on here, from what you all've told us. You've got to stay and help us look for them."

"We have to stay," Boyce said emphatically to Rita Sue, who backed off without another word and sat heavily in a rocker on the porch, hands clenched nervously in her lap. She looked both sullen and guilty about something. Enid didn't bother with her; she'd always more or less disliked Rita Sue anyway.

"Ted!" Enid called.

The Wingo deputies left the porch and Ted came over.

"They're gonna ask around here, show some people Marjory's picture—"

"Isn't that a big waste of time?"

"Okay, now, listen, Nuggins, the four of us'll drive down to the mill where they saw her this afternoon. Maybe they're just holed up because of all the rain."

"What about the waterfall?"

"That's what I'm gonna do next, have a look behind there."

"Oh. Oh!"

"Come on, now, let's don't be expecting the worst."

"I thought they were going to bring dogs!"

"Well, Wingo's bloodhounds was off on a prisoner chase the last couple of days and they're not too fresh. It ain't for certain we need them yet anyhow."

Ted took her by the elbow and guided her to the steps, Boyce limping along behind. Rita Sue got up from the rocker with an elaborate sigh and patted her hair.

"I'm going to be skinned alive if I'm not home by eleven-thirty."

"Rita Sue, hush," Boyce said.

"Your car's more comfortable for the four of us," Ted said to Rita Sue. "Just let me get a couple things out of my Firebird."

"Is that Marjory's radio?" Enid said when they got into the Ford Fairlane. "She left her purse, too? What's all this other stuff?"

"Oh, that's Duane's. I don't know what all's there, he collects butterflies. Boyce, put that junk in the trunk so we have a place to sit. Is that top leaking again?"

"Looks like."

"Shit," Rita Sue said under her breath. "I'm getting tired of this old car already. I *told* daddy I wanted a Trans Am."

Boyce drove and Ted sat in the front seat, flashlight

out the window in the steady light rain, the powerful beam raking the woods on his side of the road. Boyce drove slowly and operated the side-mounted spotlight. Enid sat in the backseat with Rita Sue and shivered silently.

"Oh," Rita Sue said quietly, "I honestly don't think there's anything to be scared about, Enid."

Down the road a hiker appeared in the headlights. Floppy-brim black hat, a blanket or poncho draped to the knees. Too far away to tell if it was a man or woman. After a couple of seconds' hesitation, the hiker took off at an angle into the woods.

Ted was out of the car waving his flashlight. "Hey! I want to talk to you!"

The hiker didn't stop or even hesitate, and Ted followed on the run, crashing through underbrush with considerable momentum, lighting up a wide patch of the woods in front of him, keeping the hiker in view. The hiker was less mobile in the thick understory. The hat went first and Ted saw that he was chasing a woman. Then she got hung up in a tangle of epiphytic vine and floundered, plastering him with gutter language as he caught up. She had a knife in one hand. Her teeth were bared. Nearly blinded by his light, she stabbed ferociously at the air.

"Cut you! Get away!"

"No, hey, take it easy, what's the matter with you? I'm not going to hurt you. I'm a deputy sheriff. I just want to ask a couple of questions."

Smidge sagged helplessly in the webbing of vine that had caught on her backpack, ensnared one arm, and tangled her hair.

"You better not be . . . lying! Not be . . . one of them!"

Her face was muddy. Her pupils, he noticed, were large, and slow to react to the bright flash beam. He whisked it far enough away to examine her by sidelight.

She was convincingly terrified, not just putting on an act for him.

"You'll be okay. Who you running from, puddin'?"

"Johnny Law?" she asked.

"I'm not lying. Look here at this." Ted held up his shield and flashed the light on it.

"Take off your cap!" she demanded.

Ted hesitated, then lifted the black baseball-style cap with "Deputy" inscribed on it in yellow block letters.

Smidge stared, then nodded, her panic ebbing like the tide leaving a beach. "You've got hair. Okay—can you help me get loose, I'm hung up like a bastard."

"Ditch the knife first, sweetness."

"Sure. Here, you take it."

Smidge reversed the blade and handed it to him carefully. Ted tested one edge of the blade with the ball of his thumb. Plenty sharp. Boyce was calling from the road.

"Okay!" Ted yelled back. "Stay there." He used Smidge's knife to cut her loose. She went slowly to her knees, leaving a lot of hair behind on a sticker vine.

"Better hurry," she mumbled.

"Want to tell me your name?"

"Smidge."

"I'm Ted."

"I saw—them do it. One of them anyway. Got Wiley. He's dead for sure."

"Who's Wiley? Who got him?"

"Friend of mine. I don't know—they must be some kind of demonic cult. Human sacrifice."

"You stoned, Smidge?"

"No! I had a couple of reds, that's all, I was—look, there's another guy, Deke, he stayed with the woody so maybe they didn't get to him yet! Please! You should've seen Wiley! She blinded him, and she—I don't know, like his skin was all hanging off, God. God!"

Ted put the flashlight under his arm and lifted her to her feet with one hand. "Okay, come on, show me."

"What? Are you *crazy*? I'm not going back there ever! They must be all over the fucking place."

"You're gonna show me, Smidge. You don't have anything to be scared of." With his free hand Ted reached inside his poncho and took his .38 Special from the holster on his belt. She was cold to his touch, Ted noticed. So cold, even after the exercise, that her teeth should have been chattering hard enough to chip them. But he had a lot on his mind and didn't make anything of it. "Let's walk."

Smidge ran a hand distractedly over her head and more hair fell away. "I don't think so. If you want my honest opinion, I don't think you can handle them. You don't know what I *saw*. Why don't you just leave me out of this."

"Smidge—what kind of name is that, nickname?— I'm not letting you out of my sight, sugarbun, so you better cooperate, or I'll cuff you."

"Shit," she cried bitterly. "*Shit*. I can't *remember* the last time I had any luck."

"Lucky if you don't get pneumonia, you're soaked through and cold as a witch's tit." She was also extremely pale, a pallor beyond tired blood.

"I'm not cold! I don't feel anything. Just the back of my neck's a little numb. That damn kid—" She looked around at Ted warily, as if she didn't trust him to believe anything else she might have to say, and folded a bloodless underlip between her teeth. Ted signaled the way with his flashlight. Smidge made adjustments to her backpack and trudged ahead of him to the road.

"Let me have that backpack, and you get in the front seat," Ted told Smidge when they reached the Ford.

"What happened?" Boyce asked.

"We need to drive back to the campground. Smidge here seems to have a problem that needs checking into."

From the backseat Enid wailed, "I thought we were going to look for Marjory!"

Smidge turned and squinted to make her out. "Who did you say?"

"My sister, we're looking for my sister! Her name is Marjory Waller."

"Tall and sort of hefty? Blond kid?"

"That's her," Ted said.

"I know where she is. She was there too, with me. She saw it, what they did to Wiley."

Enid was out of the car in a moment. *"Where's Marjory?"*

"Look, I think she's okay. I left her in the barn in that quaintsy town back there. Told her to stay put while I—"

"Ted!"

"We'll get over there in a minute, I need to talk to the Wingo—"

"No! I want to go now!"

"Enid, you have to let me handle this and do just what I tell you. Get back in the car."

"No! What's going on? Why don't you want to tell me? Is she hurt?"

"I think she's okay," Smidge said, in a tone of voice that left room for doubt. Enid's jaw dropped. "She was like, in shock. I guess I was, too. We just ran like hell when—"

Without a word Enid began to run down the road toward Dante's Mill.

"Enid!"

"Hey," Smidge said to Ted, "I don't think she ought to go by herself."

"Get in the car!" Ted snarled. "Boyce, you get out. I'm driving. *Enid, goddammit, would you wait for me?"*

When Boyce was out from behind the wheel Ted thrust the flashlight into his hand and said, "Boyce, I know you've got problems with that sore foot, but do you think you can make it back to the campground and tell those Wingo deputies I want them over at the village right now?"

"Yes, sir."

"Go." Ted climbed into the Ford. On the other side Smidge was a little slow getting settled. Ted reached out and yanked her into the seat, changed gears and took off in a splashy sideways slide after Enid, who was still visible in the headlights. They caught up quickly but Enid wouldn't yield the road or look back as Ted honked the horn. Ted hung out the window.

"Enid, come on, Enid, we'll be there in two minutes!"

She stopped then, out of breath; Ted leaped out and grabbed her. Enid just stared at him, rain dripping down her face, hair matted on her cheeks.

"Ted . . . Ted . . . Ted!"

Rita Sue had opened the door on her side and Ted put Enid in the backseat. Enid's hands moved distractedly, she gasped, she tried to talk.

"I knew. I knew. Something b-b-bad—"

"You don't know anything yet," Smidge said grimly. "Just wait."

"That's enough," Ted told her, and drove straight to the barn at the far end of Dante's Mill. The doors were still open. He parked with the front end of the Fairlane inside and the headlights on high beam.

"Marjory!"

"Over there," Smidge said, pointing out the stalls opposite the smithy. "That's where I left her."

Enid got out of the car slowly as Ted tore through each of the stalls. They were all calling Marjory as he emerged from the sixth stall, shaking his head in frustration. He had a damp horse blanket in his hands.

"You mean she's not in there?" Smidge said apprehensively, looking up at the loft. "Uh-oh."

Enid ran to the doors at the far end of the barn and wrestled with the crossbar, groaning and sobbing.

Ted started up the ladder to the loft. Smidge drifted that way, then saw something flutter from a nail, disturbed by the momentum of his climb. She picked it loose from the nail.

"I remember *you*," Rita Sue said, crossing through the wash of the headlights to Smidge. "You were down by the mill this afternoon, looking for somebody—God, what *is* that?"

"Never mind," Smidge said, turning away, balling her find in her fist. She looked back over a shoulder at Rita Sue, face heavily shadowed, eyes glittering. "I remember you, too." She smiled, a mildly flirtatious smile. "Small world. Or maybe it was just meant to be, huh?"

Enid pushed one of the doors open and screamed Marjory's name. Ted was walking around cautiously in the loft. Some chaff drifted down through the light. Rita Sue shuddered slightly, looking at the fist Smidge had made. There was a little smear of blood on the base knuckle of her thumb.

"What have you got there?" Rita Sue said. "Is it something of Marjory's?"

"Listen, it's none of—it's *nothing,* so back off."

Ted was coming back down the ladder. Enid was out in the rain again, calling, calling.

Rita Sue took a deep breath. "Ted, this girl's got something in her hand I think belongs to Marjory."

Smidge started to run and Ted caught her. He held her wrist in a monkey-wrench grip and squeezed. Smidge ranted and spat. Her fingers uncurled slowly. In her palm was a golfball-size wad of tissue and blood.

"What the hell is *that*?"

"Ssskinnn!" the girl hissed. "I found it, and I'm keeping it."

"Oh, Lord," Rita Sue moaned. "Oh, Lord! What kind of skin?"

Smidge's expression changed then, a flash of uncertainty and bewilderment canceling all savagery. Looking into her eyes was like watching a squirrel go from tree to tree. She glanced at the shiny viscous wad of human tissue. Then with her free hand she plucked it from her palm and hurled it wildly across the barn.

"Let me go! I can't stay here! Something terrible is *happening* to me!"

Smidge's hair was hanging in her face. When she tried to thrust it back behind an ear some of the hair, a shaggy thick handful, came loose from her scalp and fell to the barn floor.

25

Duane dozed and dreamed of the midnight corridors of the Williamson County jail, where he'd been held with the other boys following their one-night fling at car stealing. Only this time he was alone: Orby Upshaw, Robert Joe Poston, and Style Nichols had vanished. He was not dreaming in color right now. His dream-purview was of shadows, bars, and concrete with the rough texture of stone. A light flashed here and there in his dream, poking around, and he heard sounds: wailing, gurgling. The lidless toilet in a corner of his cell was like a fat porcelain toadstool. Most of the scary gurgling came from there. The water level was rising, soon it would overflow. He knew, as one knows things in dreams, that it would come in a gush and fill up his cell like an aquarium; he would drown, although one wall of the cell was nothing but bars. The barred door wasn't even closed. But if he went out there, into the corridor—

Better to climb to the top bunk in the cell, out of reach of the coming flood. His stepmother Nannie Dell was lying there naked. That was reasonable, and desirable. He'd glimpsed her naked once, flushed and sweaty, exhausted from childbirth. The slack, emptied belly, the size of her purple-veined breasts, was astonishing. But, no, that wasn't allowed. His father would punish him severely if Duane saw Nannie Dell naked again. What was he supposed to do with the baby, though? That was the way things happened in dreams—suddenly he was holding Nannie Dell's baby. The baby was crying pathetically. The trouble was, it was black. If he showed a black baby to Nannie Dell—Duane felt like crying, too. All the guilt was his. He had stolen a baby, not a Cadillac. That was why he was in jail.

No . . . it was a courtroom. A long way off the judge was sitting in black robes, rapping judiciously with his wooden gavel. Peals of thunder. Duane couldn't make him out very well. He spoke loudly, in a language Duane had never heard before. Marjory sat on one of the benches for spectators, trying to clean something that had stained her shirt. It might have been a big luna moth. He recognized the colors, so he was dreaming in color again. *"What did you do with the carbon tet?"* she asked, as if she were mad at him. *"It's the only thing that gets them off."* He looked from Marjory to Puff, who was somewhere else in the courtroom draped in rattly shark's teeth and nothing else. The shape of her ass got Duane with an incredible erection. It was so embarrassing. Nannie Dell, wearing her church straw hat with the periwinkle band and sleeveless aqua blue dress he liked so much, smiled at Duane from her pew as if she hadn't noticed his excitation. The organist played a familiar hymn, but the congregation sang in that same perplexing foreign tongue. The altar was decorated with a profusion of green vines that writhed unpleasantly when he noticed them. He tried not to take notice of the coffin in front of the altar with his father lying faceup on the pearl-gray satin, a twist of dried vine around his neck.

"Just bend over," Nannie Dell said behind him. Her

fingers were on the nape of his neck. Her touch felt wonderful. But he couldn't look at his father's choked face, that awful blackness. "Don't be afraid. He won't hurt you. We are love, not death. Untie the vine, and you'll find out." The organ was thundering. The choir sang hosannas. Nannie Dell wasn't tickling the back of his neck any more. She was scratching it, like a cat, with needle cat claws. This was mildly hurtful, and mournfully exciting. The sun coming through the middle chancel window was full in his face, its heat and power as much of an aphrodisiac as the cat-scratches on the back of his neck. Unable to control himself, he turned around to thrust his penis thankfully into Nannie Dell, but she wasn't there. Nothing was there but the blackness and cold of a cave. He came anyway, groaning fiercely with the effort, sobbing as the spasms ended. The heat in his balls a vivid contrast to the icy palm on the back of his neck.

"There," Puff said in the dark, "feel better?"

Tears flowed down his cheeks. He couldn't speak.

"Hell of a time for a wet dream," she said. The flashlight flicked on. "I unzipped your pants for you. I guess I could've helped you out, but it's funny, you know? You just don't want to any more, Duane. It was *all* I wanted to do, most of the time, but now I don't feel a thing down there. The only thing I want to do is—"

Duane got awkwardly to his feet and tucked himself in. Awake, he was shivering, his teeth chattering.

"We—we've g-got to f-find a way out of h-here."

"Oh, we don't want to do that yet. There's something else we have to do first."

Puff got up behind him, shark's teeth rattling on her breast.

"W-what?"

"We need to go back where the people are."

"P-people? You m-mean those f-f-fucking m-m-mum—"

"Don't say that, Duane! They're my people. *My* family. But I can't help them, the way they are. It's too late. I need you to let them go."

He backed away, from the sound of her voice, from the pool of light burning on the rocky floor between them.

"S-s-saying? C-crazy, Puff?"

"Fuck no. I'm not crazy. Do I *look* crazy?" She laughed softly. The flashlight in her hand turned, the beam crossing her smudged bare feet, narrow and so full of bones, the big toes bulging and callused and ugly as fat uncles, moving up her flat prominent shinbones past knees like wrinkled faces without eyes to the smooth strength of thighs and tuck of narrow waist, the humanness of shaved pudenda, navel, thick glossy appendectomy scar, to breasts flattened by a buckler of overlapping shark's teeth. He held his breath, because everywhere, except for the hard walnut-colored burls of her nipples, she was as white and glistening as if modeled in wax, whiter than the array of teeth hung around her neck. And something else: the teeth moved slightly with the movement of her arm as she bathed herself in light, but not from the movement of her breast. Because Puff wasn't breathing, and she let him dwell on the fact that she wasn't, the light centered on her torso and illuminating her throat, the faintly pudgy underside of her chin, the longbow curve of jawline to the lobes of ears slightly akilter on the ivory, almost hairless skull. Puff had a few strands of hair left, dangling to her shoulders. She didn't look sick; her skin was taut, the flesh firm. Obviously she wasn't dead. As he gaped in astonishment and terror, she raised her left hand to rub across shut lids, and what remained of her eyebrows and lashes drifted down across her face.

"I don't need to breathe any more," Puff said. "I don't need food, or water. I don't need any of the things *you* need, Duane. But as long as you need them, I guess you'd better do what I say."

26

"Come away from the window, Marjory."

Marjory obediently took a step back and let the damask curtains fall, turning her head to look at Birka. They were in the parlor of the parsonage of Dante's Mill, a tiny single-story house, one of four similar houses across from the church at the other end of town from the stables. The lights passing on the main street that had briefly turned the rain-spotted glass a dawnlike rose shade faded as the sheriff's patrol car drove on to the stables.

The boy whom Puff had named Alastor remained where he was on the deep window seat, just the top of his hairless head and his eyes above the sill as he watched the patrol car out of sight.

"Lookit that!" he said. "What is it, Marjory?"

"Police car," Marjory said.

"I think these clothes ought to fit you, Marjory," Birka said, smiling, holding out black shoes, trousers, and a collarless white shirt she had found in the bedroom closet. The parsonage, which was open to the public during the day, was completely furnished down to the ladies' unmentionables in a bureau drawer, but Birka had opted for men's clothing, because Marjory was larger than the average man; the average man in 1906 . . . Birka had been wondering about that, and it seemed like an appropriate time to ask.

"What year is this, Marjory?"

"Nineteen seventy," Marjory said, taking the clothing. The shirt was stiffly starched, the trousers a heavy wool. She frowned.

"It's better than what you have on now," Birka reminded her. "And we don't want you catching cold."

"Thank you," Marjory said, but her nose was already running, and had been for a while.

"Could I see a nice smile instead of a frown?"

Marjory's lips twitched forlornly as she tried to please, and then she looked down at the piled clothing in her arms. Behind her the windows lightened, there was a flush of scarlet on the papered walls.

"Here come *another* one," Alastor said gleefully. "Gosh!"

"Don't be seen," Birka advised.

"Won't. How fast can it go, Marjory?"

"Souped up, maybe a hundred twenty-five miles an hour."

Alastor looked baffled, and suspicious, thinking she was pulling his leg. "What kind of soup?"

"Marjory, change out of those wet things now."

"Why does she have to put clothes on?" Alastor said. "Ain't she going to be one of us?"

"Not yet, and hush."

Marjory turned and looked at Alastor on the window seat. She didn't say anything.

Birka observed that the scarlet light shining through the parlor windows was stationary and said, "Marjory, why don't we hurry just a little bit? We have a lot to accomplish before the night is over."

"All right," Marjory said, and she unbuttoned her blouse, took it off, then tried to undo the snaps on her Cross Your Heart bra. Birka had to help her. Marjory flinched at the icicle touch of her fingers. Birka admired the construction of the bra and wondered where to hide it, and the other items of clothing Marjory was taking off: "panties"; "Bermuda shorts."

Marjory stood naked in front of her and said, "I need—"

"Yes, I suppose the trousers will be itchy without something underneath. Why don't we try the preacher's drawers? As for your breasts, well, you can't wear this soggy thing any more. Hmm. I noticed some men's undershirts, one of those might do."

Birka hid Marjory's clothes and the towel she'd used to dry her hair in the bottom of a cedar chest in the bedroom and returned with the other things. Marjory pulled on the undershirt, which reached to the top of her thighs, and the silk drawers. The shapeless, uncuffed wool trousers were at her ankles, loose around the waist but not so loose she had to hold them up. The high-top shoes were narrow, she could barely get them on. But Marjory couldn't be expected to walk barefoot through the caverns without seriously damaging her feet.

Marjory was sitting on the edge of a sleigh-shaped couch tying one shoe when they heard Enid calling outside.

"Marjorrryyyy!" Her voice was amplified by a police bullhorn.

Marjory looked up slowly, growing tense. She glanced at Birka, her lips trembling.

"We can't go out and play right now, Marjory. You agreed. We have far more important things to do."

"Can we show Marjory the robes?" Alastor asked.

"We'll show her everything. Now get down from that window seat! There're more of them now, and obviously they're going from building to building."

"Yes, ma'am," Alastor said. "But what about—"

"Who?"

"I don't know her name. But I turned her."

"You little wretch! Who told you to do *that*?"

Alastor looked humbled. He bit a knuckle on his right hand. "Just playin'," he muttered. "Besides, ain't we supposed to turn *everybody*?"

"No! And you had better learn two things quickly. Everyone can *not* be turned, because some humans spoil

on you. And if we turn them all, what will we do
for robes? And without our beautiful robes, *what are
we*?'' Oh, now she was becoming shrill. She was tiring,
and that was serious. Birka looked at the tinted windows and then quickly at Marjory, who had risen from
the couch. ''Sit down.'' Marjory sat, trembling. Birka
felt the scissoring pain at the back of her head that
meant she was putting too much effort into keeping Marjory docile. But there was the problem of the other one,
out there somewhere in the midst of humans. That was
dangerous, no matter what the results of her turning,
but Birka had no solution to this unexpected problem. Her principal obligation, she reminded herself, was to protect the rest of them until Theron,
reborn, could resume the leadership of all *huldufólk*.

''We're going,'' she said. ''Now.'' And was gratified
that Marjory rose, without urging, to follow her.

27

They were getting into the back of the Ford Fairlane
when Smidge went into convulsions.

She fell down in the road jerking uncontrollably, teeth
grinding, saliva dripping from one corner of her mouth,
eyes not quite closed but only the whites showing: it
looked to Ted and the other deputies like a classic epi-
leptic seizure. Her skin was chalky. The seizure lasted
thirty or forty seconds, and then, as two of them held
her, Smidge's body went slack and she gasped. At least
she hadn't swallowed her tongue. When Ted spoke her
name she responded vaguely. There was a nasty bruise

on her right cheekbone he hadn't noticed before. Also an odor of corruption on her breath. Some of Smidge's hair came away in Ted's hand when he and one of the Wingo deputies laid her on the backseat of the Fairlane.

"What if she throws up in my car?" Rita Sue said indignantly. "Can't you take her to the hospital in one of the cop cars?"

"No," Ted told her, and looked at Boyce, who had come down to Dante's Mill in the second Wingo County car. "Park superintendent show up yet?"

"He's off fishing somewhere. One of the rangers is on his way, he's just five minutes from here."

"Okay, you all drive back to the lodge and wait on him, he'll call an ambulance." Smidge groaned and rolled her head side to side.

Rita Sue said, "Oh Lord, she's fixing to have another fit! Boyce, I want to go home!"

A disheveled Enid, bullhorn in hand, heard this and crossed the road with a deputy behind her. She looked at wit's end. "You *can't* go home. Marjory's missing. If you're a good friend to Marjory you'll want to stay until we find her."

"But it's not my fault she's missing!"

"We all have to do our part," Enid said, calmly enough, but there was a wildness in her brown eyes, which moved quickly, not settling on anyone for very long. "You go with that poor girl and try to make her comfortable until she has medical attention."

"Enid, maybe you should go with them too, and—"

"I won't hear of that, Ted! I won't hear of it. Why are we just standing around? I want to look in every one of these buildings for Marjory! I want to go down to the waterfall."

"We need keys, Enid, everything's locked up." Ted looked at Boyce, who put an awkward hand on Rita Sue's shoulder. She shrugged it off but got into the Fairlane anyway, glancing apprehensively at Smidge sprawled faceup in the backseat, as inert as if she were sleeping. But her lips were pulled back in a doggy sneer.

"I don't even *know* her," Rita Sue murmured. Boyce hopped backward, trying to keep his bandaged foot out of the mud, and got in behind the wheel of the Fairlane.

Ted put an arm around Enid's waist and conferred with the four Wingo County deputies. One of the newcomers he knew from high school football. Low Cow Jones had put on thirty or forty pounds but still looked as if he could tear the bumpers off a pickup as easily as other men peel a banana. His partner had the build of a cheetah, slim-hipped and high in the shoulders, with a couple of bad facial scars and perfectly round, black eyes that made him seem more astute than he probably was. His name was Wayne Buck Vedders. The deputies on hand when Ted and Enid arrived at the state park were a couple of old-timers. Moon Milcock had a heavily pocked, brick-red complexion, hands that reached nearly to his knees, and the kind of ears that early in life had earned him the nickname Flappy. Lee Winkfield was a tall, thin man with a sour, grapey mouth; he chewed kitchen matches and was related to Ted by way of a great-uncle who owned a tire dealership in Tonto Springs.

"So what've we got here?" Milcock asked. "Two kids missing?"

"Maybe it's a little more complicated than that," Ted told him, and explained his encounter with Smidge, and the gob of what might have been human skin which she'd found, and been possessive of, in the stable. Enid shuddered against him and was silent.

Milcock scratched a hairless temple and said to the other Wingo deputies, "Reckon we ought to kick this 'un back to ol' Wimp and see if he wants to take a run out thisaway."

"Hell, Moon," Wayne Vedders said, "the Old Man's granddaughter got married today over in Hazelrig, and right about now you'd have to pump a half gallon of

Sani-flush through his liver just to get him standing straight up on his feet.''

''Yeh, I forgot,'' Milcock muttered.

''Let's split up, then,'' Winkfield suggested, taking the matchstick out of his mouth so he wouldn't inhale it when he yawned. ''Why don't me and Flappy check the high ground over there back of the lake where the girl said that Satan cult was operating, and you all see what you can come up with around here. Low Cow, you want to make us the loan of your ten-gauge?''

''What for, you figuring on raising the devil?''

''Buddy, I'd rather raise the devil than some outlaw biker's been gargling crank or some other kind of shit, with his eyes spinning around in his head the way they get. You'd have better luck stopping a locomotive with a .38 than one of them kind.''

Low Cow Jones donated the shotgun from his patrol car and the other two deputies drove slowly out of Dante's Mill on the curving road past the millpond. Enid drew a long harsh breath and looked up at Ted, who smiled, trying to be reassuring.

''We know she's alive. Anyway, she sure didn't drown, if Smidge was telling the truth, and we can be thankful for that.''

''No reason for her to lie, but where *is* Marjory? And why was she acting so strange?''

''Shock, maybe. Hard to say.''

''Somebody might've taken her away, Ted! Before we got here. But that was only—how long?''

''Smidge could've walked from here to where we met her in ten minutes, maybe less. If she didn't stop to powder her nose.''

''So where could Marjory have gone to, in a quarter of an hour or less? She has to be around here!''

Wayne Vedders said, ''The only way out of Dante's Mill by car is the way we come in. Maybe, if your sister's with somebody she don't want to be with, and they're just laying back in the woods looking to make a run for the highway, then we ought to be looking to block off the park entrance down by the highway.'' He glanced at Ted for confirmation.

''Good idea. Who all have you got left tonight?''

''Nobody in this end of the county. I reckon we could call THP, but that's got to go through the undersheriff, with Wimp unavailable. You know, it's a whole can of worms.''

''Yeh, I know,'' Ted said. ''Let's do it anyway.''

28

''Glad that storm decided to move on,'' Lee Winkfield said as he and Milcock, who was behind the wheel, drove slowly up into the woods behind the Dante's Mill pond. Winkfield operated the spotlight mounted on his side of the patrol car, raking the understory that came down to the edge of the narrow road, which was part shale and afforded some traction despite the recent heavy rain.

''I don't much care for them electrical ones,'' Milcock admitted. ''I knowed a boy once was standing on a post and wahr fence when lightning went through it, burnt all but his big toes off. He lived through the experience, but he was a funny-looking sight after that.''

''Kinda reminds me, you remember Clinton Tuggle, was the U.S. Marshal in Apworth before he retired to go into the cattle business?''

''Allow that I do. Wasn't a man alive could take him in a five-card stud game until he married that feisty little church-going woman. They tell me she could hear a deck being shuffled five miles over in the next county.''

''Well, Clinton, he had enough winnings tucked away to spend maybe forty thousand upgrading a herd, took him quite a few years to accomplish. Owned two Brahmin and two Limousin bulls he bred his heifers to. Then along come a lightning storm that hit one of the big sweetgums in his pasture, with most of his cows standing under it. You know how a sweetgum is, them bare roots going ever which direction on top of the ground, and most of his herd was grounded on the roots.''

''Uh-oh.''

''Damn near wiped old Clinton out. Want to hold it right here, Moon?''

Milcock throttled down. Winkfield held the spotlight steady on a firebreak that ran uphill from the road. Water was running down one side of the break in a succession of waterfalls only inches high.

''What you got?'' Milcock asked.

''See it? Vehicle parked up there. Station wagon, looks like.''

''Yeh, I can make it out. Appears to be good bedrock along that firebreak, I ought to be able to drive up there.''

''Let's have us a look, then.''

The station wagon was parked with its back end to the road, and the hood was up. There was a tarpaulin suspended from low boughs of a pine tree over the guts of the wagon. Both deputies carried 10-gauges as they approached. Milcock stayed behind the wagon and Winkfield looked inside with his flashlight.

''Ain't nobody,'' he said.

''This here one's a real old-timer.''

''Looks like a forty-six, forty-seven model.'' Winkfield took a fresh kitchen match from his shirt pocket and put it in a corner of his purple mouth. He opened the door on the driver's side. ''Somebody's been sick,'' he said disgustedly. ''Too much beer, from the smell of it." But he continued to look around meticulously before backing out.

"Puke," he said. "But no blood."

"Listen," Milcock cautioned, turning his head.

Winkfield listened, but his partner had the sharper ear. "Yeh, what?" he whispered after twenty seconds.

"I don't know for sure. Animal, maybe."

"Where's it coming from?"

"Yonder," Milcock said, pointing up the firebreak.

Neither man said anything else. They went up the firebreak five yards apart, Winkfield several steps behind Milcock. Water gurgled softly in the little trench on one side. They heard thunder, but it was a long way off. And, gradually, Winkfield heard something else. Sobbing. Milcock left the firebreak and went into the trees, shotgun in one hand, flashlight in the other. Winkfield followed cautiously. There was a modest path, no more than a deer trail. And something that glistened in the light. It was snagged on a thornbush.

"What've you got there?" Winkfield said, on his toes trying to see over Milcock's shoulder.

"Jesus," Milcock said, in a tired tone of voice. "You look."

Winkfield added his light to the scene. He saw a bloody patch of well-tanned hide with a few bleached, sun-crisped hairs on it, but he wouldn't have known exactly what he was looking at except for the unmistakable, if shriveled, human nipple off center on the patch. Man or woman, he couldn't say. Somewhere up ahead of them, there was a sobbing in the woods. Winkfield felt vulnerable; he felt as if he were standing on a whole mess of sweetgum roots with a charge of lightning building in the humid air inches from the fuzzed-up back of his neck.

Milcock peeled the cellophane from a pack of Lucky Strike. He broke off a dead twig from a birch sapling and gently removed the pierced doily of skin from the thorn. He placed it in cellophane and put the packet

away. They heard a hoot owl. A large luna moth floated
into Winkfield's flashlight beam and was all but motionless for a couple of seconds before drifting away.
The intermittent and anonymous sobbing continued in
the drizzling, seeping wood.

29

Puff had the flashlight and wasn't about to give it up,
so Duane had no choice except to follow her while he
tried to think what to do. Followed her back down to
the mummy room (as he thought of it), where, he was
sure, she expected him to unknot the dried vines from
all the throats of the strange blackened sleepers. He
knew what would happen next, because he'd already
seen one example. Then, after he'd done what she
wanted—

Duane stared at the back of Puff's head, as bald as
the cheeks of her behind, and tried to imagine himself
like Puff, although there was no way to describe exactly
what she was like, had become. Terror caused him to
lag behind her, stumbling across a chamber floor littered with breakdown, slabs of rock, some as big as
doors and thicker than his body, that had fallen from
the ceiling in a long-ago subterranean cataclysm. During the last few minutes he had learned a lot about
himself, and about the activities of fear. He'd been
scared a few times in his life, momentary jolts, like
grasping an electrified strand of wire around a cow pasture. When the hands sweated, the jolt was worse. He
wasn't sweating now, it was too cold down here—the
temperature in most caverns was a constant 56 degrees,

his mother had told him—and terror was nothing like a quick flashy jolt up the arm to the back of the head. Terror had an acid odor; he could smell it on his skin. Terror was a horrid destructive wasting process, as if there were termites at work throughout his body. Eating him from the inside out. Terror was literally eating him up. As long as he kept moving he could deal with it, but his movements were increasingly clumsy as he crawled over rockpiles. He only wanted to think about his mother. Any moment now she would glide smoothly down out of darkness on a thin strong rope and gather him in, hold him close to her breast; laughing, she would signal for them both to be lifted out into the blue of day. Later they would go canoeing. Swim together. The terror would stop. It was all he would ever ask for, as long as he lived. Mother! *Just make it stop.*

There was a pall of rock dust where they traveled, and it packed Duane's nostrils, the back of his throat. He choked and halted, trying to clear his throat. His nose and eyes were running. The beam of the flashlight centered on his face momentarily, then lifted.

"Look, Duane. That's why I came this way. I wanted you to see this! Look up now."

Gasping, wheezing, his pulse running wild, Duane did as Puff asked. Not far overhead there was a fluttering reminiscent of the flight of moths in the mummy room. He had noticed a few stray glowing lunas in this chamber, but what he saw wasn't moth wings. The colors were similar, pale purples, reds and greens, but the materials were more like cloth, cloth he could see through. They hung from nearly invisible strands of silk. Puff walked around slowly with her light, admiring the display.

"These are our robes," she said. "The robes we wear. And when we wear them—"

Duane leaned against an oblong of rock, and it seemed to tilt slightly, noiselessly. The movement was subtle enough that he thought it might have been a tremor of his own body he was feeling. He pressed again. No, the slab moved. It was nearly eight feet long on one side, and perhaps two feet thick, part of a larger slab that had fallen ages ago and broken into several pieces. The largest section was balanced on one of a series of rounded boulders that might have been part of the cavern floor subject to the eroding, shaping action of water (the floor was dry now, but smoothed and etched in channels that suggested it once had formed the bed of an underground river, dried up or diverted millennia before dinosaurs disappeared from the region).

A giant teeter-totter, weighing several tons.

It had been a favorite game in first grade to creep up the green-painted board on hands and knees, to see how precisely he could balance the seesaw without tipping it to the ground on the other side.

Ridiculous to think that he could do it here, that this much stone would budge more than a millimeter.

But if it happened, if he got it moving—

Because his mother wasn't coming, nobody was. And if he got out of here, or if he died, whatever the outcome it would be better than going down to the cocoonlike mummy room with Puff, hearing their voices on the radio again, seeing them . . . Jesus, *wake up.*

He raised one knee, grasped an edge of the slab, pulled himself up as slowly as a lizard looking for an angle on a fly. His heart was beating so enormously he couldn't be sure the slab had moved at all.

"I guess," Puff said, looking up, absorbed, "you want to know what the robes are made of. Well—that's what makes them so special. It's all skin, Duane. Human skin."

Duane crept another foot up the slab and this time he was sure it moved. His own weight was a hundred and eighty-six pounds. There was an angle of declivity to the cavern floor, too shallow to reckon in near darkness, but it might be enough. And more of the smoothly rounded boulders between him and the beam of the flashlight.

But when it went, if it did, the huge slab was going to make a lot of noise, deeper than thunder in the small cavern.

Duane caught his breath and lunged almost to the uptilted end of the slab and felt the low end coming up, silently: but what if it was webbed with cracks, and just broke into pieces?—no. No! Now it was moving, sliding, beginning to rumble, he held on with outthrust arms, and Puff, ten feet away, turned without haste, bringing the flashlight level, shining it behind her.

Duane and the flat-sided rock picked up speed faster than he'd thought possible as the beam of the flashlight shone at an angle in his eyes, but the distance was too far, all she had to do was step out of the way. The beam slashed suddenly to one side, to the deep end of the cavern and maybe Puff screamed, but he couldn't hear her for the rumbling and grinding of the stone slab across the jumbled stairsteps of boulders, some of which rolled along with the slab like a set of clumsy wheels. Then something wet and cold came bouncing over the forward edge of the slab and lodged momentarily against his shoulder. Duane let go and slid backward just as the slab came to a massive jarring stop against a wall of the cavern and a shower of rock, from bits and pieces to fist-sized chunks, pelted him. He rolled off one tilted side of the still-intact slab and came down hard and painfully on his butt. His glasses fell from the end of his nose but landed in his lap.

There was a lot of dust in the air, he could barely breathe without gagging. But at least he could see the dust, because the flashlight was still working, the beam remote but steady, aimed at the drifting robes overhead.

"Puff!"

He got to his knees and crept over debris toward the source of the light. The dust was thick enough so that he didn't see the necklace of shark's teeth until his right hand hung up in them. He backed away, shaking the hand with a growl lingering in his throat. There was something on the heel of his hand as red as blood but viscous, half-frozen, like a melting popsicle.

The light was a few feet behind the slab, and her body was wedged down between some boulders, sheared at the neckline, the red glop having spilled over in a kind of ruff like that of a turkey buzzard's, oozing down between her breasts.

He was cold and tingling himself. He couldn't feel his fingers as he pried the flashlight from Puff's hand, expecting her, headless or not, to sit up at any moment and battle him for it. He was sick with horror and felt himself sliding down a long spiraling windless tunnel, getting farther and farther from the light he craved. He had to stop gulping air; he knew that was the worst of the problem. Just get the precious light and back away, put his head between his knees. He saw why she had not escaped from the path of the huge slab. One foot was wedged in a crevice of the floor, the body turned precisely a hundred and eighty degrees from the angle of the foot, the knee exploded like a kernel of popcorn. If he fainted now the batteries of the flashlight would fail while he lay there unconscious; then, even if he woke up he might as well be dead. Like Puff. Or had she been dead hours before the hurtling slab ground her head off? It was a question he didn't feel like debating. All he wanted was the chance to see daylight again, once he got that far he would have a whole lot of time to think about the rest of it.

30

The Wingo County deputies Moon Milcock and Lee
Winkfield discovered the half-skinned body of the man
they subsequently identified as Gene R. Wiley, age
twenty-seven, last address Key West, Florida, propped
against a bur oak in a partial clearing fifty yards in from
the firebreak. They found another young man, who
identified himself as "Deke" but was otherwise incoherent, some fifteen feet off the ground in another tree
nearby. He would not climb down when ordered to do
so by Deputy Winkfield. When Winkfield climbed up
to try to force him down, Deke howled and kicked furiously at him. Winkfield retreated to the ground, and
Deke sat sobbing, more quietly, in the sanctuary of his
tree.

Winkfield chewed the end of a kitchen match and
walked over to his partner, who was studying the corpse
by flashlight. Already the skinless flesh and blubber had
attracted an amazing variety of tiny insects and a few
nightcrawlers. There was an unmistakable stench of
slowly putrefying flesh in the still damp air.

"What about the wild man?" Milcock asked, getting
up, his knees creaking. He took out a cigarette. "Let
me use the business end of that match."

Winkfield took it from his mouth, wiped spit on his
sleeve, and handed it over. Milcock struck it on a
thumbnail as hard and rough as a concrete block. Winkfield said, "Stoned or crazy or both. I ain't gonna mess
with him until we can get a line on him and yank him
down from there."

"Reckon he did this?" Milcock said with a glance at Wiley's remains. He inhaled and blew streams of smoke through his nostrils.

"I don't know. His hands don't have no blood on them. And that there looks like a bloody job, front and back."

"It's a good job, though," Milcock said, like a connoisseur of the bizarrely maimed. "They didn't miss but a little patch or two. He weren't just butchered for the fun of it. And both his eyes, did you notice that, they're pierced straight through the middle of the pupil."

"Reckon what the point of that was?"

"Some goddamn ritual or other. Blinded him so he couldn't run off. It's all drugs, ain't it? I ain't never seen such abuse to human beings since we got all these fucking drugs." Milcock glanced at the tree Deke was in. "Maybe that hairy old Easy Rider boy didn't do it, but I'll bet cash money he got a look at who did."

"Yeh, he sounds more scared than anything. I'll tell you what, first time I've seen a man halfway skinned. That's a disgusting sight. A bear would've been kinder to him."

"How about that Willie Wigfall they found in the corncrib back of Cudsey's long about sixty-three, sixty-four?"

"Well, now you're talking nigger, and a commonness agitator to boot. You want to get old Low Cow up here, help us rope down the kid in the tree?"

"Fair 'nuff."

"Looks like we done pulled us an all-nighter, partner."

"You look out for yourself while I'm gone."

"Shit, that won't be hard," Winkfield said, smiling and patting the barrel of his Seneca 10-gauge.

31

Ted Lufford came out from behind the waterfall by Dante's Mill wearing only his Jockey shorts and said to the watchers on the bridge, "It's a cave back in there."

Enid called, "Did you see Marjory?"

"No sign of anybody. I hollered."

Low Cow Jones came in a shambling trot from the patrol car parked in the road and said to his partner Wayne Buck Vedders, "They need me up the road apiece. You wait here for the Highway Patrol and the boys from the TBI." The TBI was the Tennessee Bureau of Investigation.

"No shit, the TBI? What's going on?"

"Found a body."

Enid drew a sharp breath like an indrawn scream. Low Cow said hastily, "No, ma'am, it's a male Caucasian, but that's all I know for sure." He returned to the patrol car, jumped in and went off with tires churning, mud and pebbles rattling in the wheel wells.

Down below Ted had waded to the sedgy shore with his flashlight. Enid crossed the bridge with his clothes and held the light while he turned his back, stripped off the wet Jockeys, and pulled on his pants.

"If that's where Marjory went this afternoon—I mean, into the cave, why was she way up there in the woods when that girl saw her?"

"We don't know where she went, or why. We don't know much of anything yet."

"Aren't you going to look in the cave?"

"Not by myself. Who's this?" There was another car

on the road, a forest-green sedan. It stopped by the mill and a park ranger got out with a flashlight.

"One of you Ted Lufford?" the ranger said.

"That's me." Ted crossed the bridge buttoning his shirt. "This's Wingo County Deputy Wayne Vedders. And Enid Waller."

"How y'all doin' tonight? My name's Tilghman." He was a short man in his sixties, with slicked-back white hair. "What the devil's been going on? Those two kids up at the lodge—well, no, there's three, counting the one had the seizure, they said it was—those two kids claim they lost somebody this afternoon. Where you been, in swimming?"

"No. Did you know there's a cave back of that waterfall?"

"You don't say. What kind of cave?"

"I didn't look."

"Well, there's caves all through this region. Some that ain't been explored but a little. Let's see. There's Big Spangle and Griffee and Bluefus—"

Enid interrupted. "Do you have keys to all the buildings?"

"Yes. What do you want keys for?"

"My sister's the one who's missing. We thought she might be—might be hiding in—"

"If she's inside one of the town buildings, then she either broke a lock or a window to get in. What do you mean, hiding? Who's she hiding from?" Tilghman looked at the revolver in the holster on Ted's belt. "You a deputy, too?"

"Uh-huh. Mr. Tilghman, reckon you can let us have a quick look around, satisfy my curiosity Marjory's not in the church or someplace else?"

"What I'm here for," the ranger said, jangling his key ring. His radio was squawking in the green sedan.

"Can you get some more help?" Ted asked him.

"Saturday night? Hard. What for?"

"We need to be sure nobody leaves the park until we know they're okay."

32

At first there were only a couple of the luminous moths in the dark hole in the ground and Marjory hung back, shivering. Birka's eyes had a certain luminosity as well, the intense scathing blue of an arc welder's flame.

"What's the matter, Marjory?"

"I don't—think I want to go down there." She almost said "again," although she was confused about that. Had she and Birka been playing in the root cellar already today? But the concept of *today* was vague to her as well. Today, yesterday, she had no sense of time; Birka was keeping time for her. But Birka couldn't overcome Marjory's sense of dread, of wrongness, guilt for having wronged God. "We shouldn't—play down here. I don't think." Marjory squirmed uncomfortably. Her skin itched. Everything was miserably wrong, including the clothes she wore, but she was powerless to express her feelings. Birka was always right, so it was futile to argue. She bit her nails and avoided Birka's gaze, concentrating instead on the moths. She counted six of them—no, now there were eight. They were multiplying, out of nowhere, shedding a delicate webbed glow of light around the roughly hewn rock walls. She saw the shining hairless head of Alastor bobbing in a corner as he played with the giant lunas, leaping in artless imitation of their roundabout flight. He couldn't fly, but he could do other things that astounded Marjory. Like cling, upside down, by his fingers and toes, to a cellar facing.

"Stop that," Birka said indulgently to Alastor. "You'll fall."

"Won't fall. Anyhow, it don't hurt me none if I do."

"Well—you must learn not to be quite so sure of yourself, because there *are* things that can hurt you. But you are an agile little man. I hope you can be of some help in getting Marjory down."

"D-down where?" Marjory stammered.

"Oh, Marjory. I told you not to worry. I'm going to show you our very special place. Not even Páll or Gudný have seen it."

"Has Rita Sue—seen it?"

"Damn Rita—! No. *No,* Marjory, and I really want you to stop thinking about her . . . that is my fault, of course. But I wish you'd try to appreciate the strain I've been under. It's very hard to keep you with me, so close, all the time."

"But I—I just wondered what happened to her," Marjory said, cringing, sniffling, wiping her nose on the handkerchief of a long-ago preacher. She had tremors again, that abject fear of displeasing Birka, who meant everything to her. So much more than— Marjory felt a slight but definite tightening of the mind, as if every thought, all memories except those Birka wanted her to have, was being wrung out. Which didn't leave many. But not thinking made Marjory less agitated. Content to do whatever Birka wanted. Even to play down here where the air was old and musty and smelling, just a little, of rotten potatoes, the breath of an alcoholic.

Birka was smiling again, thinly; Marjory smiled back and tenderly rubbed her swollen nose. She could see a lot better. The cellar room was thick with luna moths, a floating church window that glowed with supernal light. Birka turned away and looked around as if trying to remember just where she was. Alastor lost a toehold on the wall he was exploring like a fly on sponge cake and tumbled down, laughing. Birka gave him a no-nonsense hand up and pulled him along with her.

"Now that's enough; we don't have time to play. Hmm. I think this may be it."

One wall of the small cellar of the parsonage was natural rock, loose but not quarried, as if it had been piled up following blasting. Birka picked through the lesser chunks of rocks like a fox picking through chicken bones, putting some back where she'd found them, setting others aside. She had a thoughtful expression, as if she were playing a game involving a code, or distinct strategies. Some of the rocks she lifted and put elsewhere with no show of effort were so large Marjory would have had trouble rolling them across the floor. Marjory watched dumbly by luna-light until Birka had uncovered a slit of passage through which more pastel moths streamed like wine through a bottleneck.

"She can't get by there," Alastor said of Marjory. "She's too fat."

"I'm not *fat*," Marjory said, wiping her eyes, unable to hide her feelings. "I just have b-big bones."

"We will simply have to try," Birka told them impatiently. "There's no other way for us. And we can't leave Marjory behind. Come over here, Marjory. What do you think?"

Marjory peered into a closetlike aperture, unable to see much for the moths fluttering around. "What's in t-there?"

"Oh, Marjory, we only have to climb down a little way. I'll go first, then you, and Alastor will follow." She touched Marjory's bruised cheek, lightly, but Marjory jerked away as if singed by a torch.

"That *is* a problem," Birka said. "I'd forgotten how quickly human flesh freezes. Enoch's face . . . well, for every problem there is a solution. The two of you stay here, and no monkeyshines." She directed this admonition to Alastor, who shrugged. Birka went swiftly up the cellar stairs, paused there to listen, then opened the door and disappeared.

Marjory and Alastor looked at each other. He stuck his tongue out at her.

"S-same to you, b-brat." Marjory had a headache. It wasn't so bad when Birka was nearby. Now that she wasn't, Marjory experienced such a brainstorm of confusion, so much emotional churning in her breast, that she was dizzy. This odd little boy she had to deal with, mud all over his vividly pale body. Her brain reeling and stuttering, he seemed to be a part of that. "Stop," she said crossly, turning away.

"Stop what?"

"You know w-what. What you're doing."

Not doing nothing.

"Yes you are. That." Marjory put a hand to her breast and throat. Panic; the urge to run. She had run once before, and it was coming back to her, but confused, murky as an ominous dream. The girl she'd been with, in the barn. What had happened to her? Marjory wouldn't look at Alastor, but she felt him grinning. A big mind-grin, and she shuddered violently. Little as he was, he'd done something unpleasant, maybe hideous was the word, to that girl, and he wanted to do it to Marjory as well.

You'll get in trouble if you run away again!

Marjory made no reply. She was trying hard to squeeze him out, but his thoughts were oozing everywhere down private pathways of her mind. Colorless, formless, nonsensically childish, yet an occupying force as frightening as a Mongol horde. She hated him, and was powerless. The seductive urge to run, the hopelessness of flight, increased the velocity of her trembling, until she thought she would fly to pieces.

There, there! What's all this?

Birka was back, on the creaky cellar steps, and Marjory turned a woeful tear-streaked face to her.

Birka came toward her, and the storm in Marjory's mind blew itself out, replaced with the tranquillity of a twilight summer's pond, only the faint reflection of Alastor remaining on the surface, sulky and watchful.

"This is what you need," Birka said, handing her a pair of long kid-leather gloves. She also had a length of rope with her.

Marjory looked with a mild expression of apprehension at the rope, but Birka smiled at her so winningly, with such confident good cheer, that Marjory was able to smile, too. This was going to be *fun*.

Just slip into the gloves, Marjory, then tie the rope around your waist. We'll be there in no time.

"Where?"

Oh, below. You know about Eden, don't you? Of course you do. Well, that's where we're all going: to Eden. Now isn't that a nice surprise?

33

"Help."

Rita Sue looked up, startled, and the magazine she'd been leafing through disinterestedly, an old copy of *Field and Stream* with a tattered cover that featured springer spaniels and flocks of pheasant, fell from her lap. She was sitting with her feet under her in a chair cleverly made from deer antlers, and she had nodded off smarting from sunburn and drearily wondering what she was going to do if she was pregnant. Drown herself in the stock pond, more than likely. She'd always been able to control Boyce, only to find out at a really crucial moment that she couldn't control herself. This revelation, that her slender body had its own sense of direction, of destiny, was depressing. Her sister Rosemary had run off at nineteen to get married; Rita Sue now had more insight as to why she'd been so impulsive, but already Rosemary had three kids and was a total wreck. No fair! Even more depressing, now that she'd gone all the way with Boyce, Rita Sue really didn't have all that much interest in him any more. They hadn't spoken ten words to each other in the last couple of hours. What if she had to marry him? But wait a minute, Rosemary had once confided that a woman was aware the *very instant* she conceived. Rita Sue didn't know any such thing, she was just worried about the possibility, because for now she was stuck here and there wasn't much else to—

"Help!"

It was that girl, Smidge, the one who'd had a fit and was lying down on a daybed in an office. The blond fuzz on the backs of Rita Sue's reddened forearms prickled. Rita Sue was alone at the front of the one-story log building where they had a small museum and large framed maps of the campsites and hiking trails. Boyce had gone somewhere with a park ranger. Twenty minutes had passed since they'd brought Smidge to the park headquarters building, and an ambulance was supposed to be on the way for her. But nothing was going right tonight.

Now the girl was crying. Rita Sue got up slowly, grimacing, looking at the front door of the building, hoping Boyce would appear. Or anyone else. Rita Sue didn't want to go into the office, answer the frantic plea for help. What could *she* do? Even before Smidge had fallen in a jerky heap with foam on her lips, Rita Sue had been—well—scared of her. The unkempt hair, the carnal mouth, the slight cruel jut of teeth, the way she stared at Rita Sue—she was just outright trashy, dirty, and *suggestive*. Rita Sue was properly contemptuous; but at the same time she was weak in the knees, pierced through the heart, a submissive, love-doomed hurt she'd never experienced with Boyce, even when giving in to the urge to screw him until his teeth rattled.

"Oh, help. Help. It's happening. No. I don't want to. Want to. No, no, don't let me die."

Rita Sue trembled. She stared at the office door for a few moments, then walked toward it. Smidge wasn't screaming; her voice was weak. She sounded delirious, out of her head. No threat in her. So fetch her a drink, talk to her a minute or two. Tell her help was coming.

The office was small, ten feet square. A desk, two metal folding chairs, the shabby daybed with a plaid cover. Smidge rolled carelessly into an olive-drab blanket on top of the daybed, shoeless feet sticking out. Quivering lumpishly, her face to the wall, to the formless humped shadow of herself cast by a gooseneck lamp on the desk.

"Hi—it's me—Rita Sue. C-can I get you anything? Smidge?"

"God. What's happening? Don't don't. Let me die."

Rita Sue couldn't see her face. There was a powerful odor in the room. Putrefaction. It locked Rita Sue's throat, she couldn't breathe or speak.

Smidge sat up suddenly, wildly, casting aside the blanket. When she tried to scream something came out of her mouth that wasn't sound.

Rita Sue backed out of the office as if impelled by the muzzle of a shotgun thrust right between her eyes. She remembered to close the door. *As if that would keep it in.* She breathed then, more or less clean air acting like rockets to the brain, walked herself to the front door of the building, tripping over a woven hemp rug by the entrance but not falling, went outside, took another big lungful of air, leaned on the railing, looked at the hint of a three-quarter moon in an inky sky, and then, with her head still back and her eyes rolling, began to howl like a dog beside a newly filled grave.

34

Just when he was about to give up, and submit to the fear grinding against his heart like abrasive stones, Duane thought he heard voices.

He had no idea where he was, or how long he'd been searching for a way out. By flashlight, caverns and passages all began to look alike after a while. He wasn't wearing a watch. Having so thoroughly lost track of time, he couldn't be sure that he had not doubled back on himself, trekked the same way two or three times. He was cold to the marrow and nearly exhausted. Thinking was difficult; his brain was occupied mostly with childhood memories that had a dreamlike gloss and, frequently, confounding twists and turns of hallucination. Dreaming on his feet, shuffling, climbing laboriously, the gradually weakening beam of the flashlight sliding aimlessly through bowels of rock, glittering in teardrop geode palaces. The voice he heard was feminine but unidentifiable, and in a cramp of fear he imagined that Puff had risen, ghostlike, and was pursuing him. How? He had smashed off her head like an overripe peach. Nothing much left above the collarbones. But probably more than one of these caverns had its ghost; mummies, he knew, were everywhere, and, morbidly, he often watched his feet as he walked. He didn't like the idea of coming across more mummies,

but precious light hovered over them, like sun through
misty stained glass .

the moths. He would have
given anything for a few luna moths bumbling along
with him right now. Instead he had disembodied voices,
at an unguessable distance.

Or a radio.

Could it be? Puff's radio? Still operating and report-
ing in an obscure language the laments of the chambered dead—or not so dead, as it had turned out. If it
was the radio, then his fears were realized, he had not
made any progress, and he was so tired, footsore and
aching, he didn't think he could go another hundred
yards, even on a downward course. On the other hand,
the voices might mean cavers, searching for him.
Duane's blood raced, his throat swelled. He inhaled
shakily and was about to call out, but changed his mind.
It wouldn't help just yet, the way sound traveled here
and became distorted, blurring like a mirror when you
breathe on it.

Better to remain still and listen hard, because the
voices, occasional but not growing fainter, might serve
as a beacon in this convoluted void. He dared to hope
that they might even be coming his way. Faces: light,
warmth, food—Duane began to cry, softly, struggling
to hold most of it in.

He didn't know how long that went on, pawing his
face, gulping, sniveling, his cheeks wet and salty, but
he dried up suddenly when he heard a familiar voice,
although neither his heart nor his head believed until
she spoke a second time.

"Birka, you're going too fast! I need to stop and rest."

Marjory.

But where was she? Sound still had no locus. Duane held his breath, listening, but his heart was going so fast, pounding blood to the temples and his ears, he couldn't hear anything else but his heartbeats. He skidded down from a pedestal of rock where he'd been crouched in the dark, not wanting to wear out the waning flashlight batteries, and thought he saw something: not the tiny intermittent flashes that occurred behind closed lids when he tried to relax his overstressed eyes, but a dawnlike glow in the darkness. He lowered his head for a few moments, looked up again.

"All right, if you're sure it's not much farther," Marjory said reluctantly, as if she were replying to a question Duane hadn't heard. The glow was still there, tinted, and seemed to be in motion, like light on the surface of mildly rippling water. *Luna moths*, he thought. He didn't know how far away they were. He turned on the flashlight, aimed at his feet, but tried not to look at the beam for more than a second or two at a time. Without his own light he wouldn't be able to follow the slowly drifting moth-cloud. Any kind of fall down here (he reminded himself again), a twisted knee or broken ankle, could be disastrous, even with help nearby.

Maybe he should have yelled to Marjory, told her to wait. She was looking for him, wasn't she? Duane was frantic to catch up. He held his breath and swallowed, staring into black space at a single small pulsating galaxy across a chamber of unimaginable proportions. He was about to call her name, when he heard the unmistakable chatter of alien voices over Puff's radio. The uproar like that at a World Series game when somebody hits a home run. The crowd cheering for a hero, and Duane had the creepy iced-over sensation that the cheers he was listening to were all for Marjory, just as the illuminating moths somewhere overhead were for Marjory too, lighting her way to the chamber filled with lying-in-wait mummies. Pain stitched through Duane's stomach: *Who was she with?* He didn't want to think about Puff again—crushed, headless Puff. Puff was out of the picture. *Don't think about Puff. Just go get Marjory.*

It wasn't a bad floor, where he was. Trickles of water everywhere, much of the rock crushable from centuries of softening, no matter how carefully he walked he left footprints. And came eventually to other footprints in the sedimentary bottom of the cave. Someone was wearing narrow shoes. There was a second set of footprints, bare, womanly feet, too small to be Marjory's, tracking with the first set up a slope and into a passage, the entrance of which was beneath a trickly curtain of very cold water. There were a few neon-green moths along the way, perched on outcrops, wings swaying gently in the current of air from the passage. He didn't need them any more. The chattery radio was beacon enough; so were traces of finely spun silk in the air, brushing against his wet face. Mummyweb. Cocoon thread. His blood was thin, sluggish, cold.

Marjory said, in a surprisingly childlike voice, "Is that Páll? He looks funny lying there. Who tied him up like that?"

"Just untie him," a woman said, in an accented voice, and the hairs on Duane's forearms spiked as if he'd stepped suddenly into an electrostatic field. He paused, letting out some light through fingers spread over the lens of his flashlight, seeing in the fragmented yellow glow the passage crooked left and slanting down. He couldn't be more than a hundred feet away from the chamber he'd never wanted to set foot in again.

"Okay," Marjory said, in that same high-pitched, slightly squeaky voice, "but we have to go home after this. I'm tired of playing, Birka. It isn't any fun. It's a dumb game."

"The vine, Marjory. Undo the vine from around his neck."

"But it's on too tight."

"Try again."

"*You* do it."

"I told you, Marjory; now for the last time: *I cannot.*"

"Why?"

"Those are the rules."

"Who made up the rules?"

"Who indeed?" the woman said, with a faint distressful sound. "Try again, please darling. Oh, I see. There are two knots. Damn Enoch! Never mind that. Simply give it—a good hard—yank."

Duane walked into the chamber and saw what he thought was Puff, only with her bald head intact, then realized it wasn't, and saw a man bending over one of the silk-wrapped mummies, but realized it wasn't a man: it was Marjory in old-fashioned men's clothing. He blinked his light on both of them and croaked, "Marjory. No. *Don't.* Get away from it."

Just as the bald woman flashed a stormy blue look at him Duane heard a chortling sound that froze him worse than the rage in the woman's face; he looked up and back with the wavering beam of the light and saw Alastor crouched on a side wall of the cave a good ten feet above his head, Alastor's own grinning face hanging upside down. Then Alastor came unstuck from the rock and plummeted straight toward Duane, hands outstretched. On one of his small hands, the little finger missing. In its place, the sharp black thorn he had nearly driven through one of Duane's eyeballs the last time Duane saw him.

As Duane ducked, most of Alastor's weight landed on his shoulders and the back of his neck, and they both fell into the midst of the cushiony silk cocoon.

35

The park ranger named Tilghman aimed his flashlight at the back door of the Dante's Mill parsonage, across the street from the churchyard with the white paling fence. He said, "Looks like the padlock and hasp was pried clean off."

Enid said quietly, "Marjory's here. Or she was here."

"Then she had company," Ted remarked, studying the muddy footprints on the steps of the unscreened back porch. "Two of them were barefoot. Those little prints, what do you make of them? Whoever it is can't be more than six years old."

"Well, it's plain they broke in. Might better find out if they done any more damage."

Tilghman opened the door and Enid, behind him, said sharply, "Marjory! It's me! Where are you? Are you all right?"

No answer. Enid looked at Ted, who touched her arm, a stay-put gesture, and said calmly, "Let us have a look around first."

He and Tilghman went in through the kitchen. There was a small dining room, a front parlor, two bedrooms, and an indoor bathroom. Traces of footprints on the flowery parlor carpet, up and down the polished oak floor of the center hall. A wardrobe door stood open in one of the bedrooms. There were no closets, only cupboards and chests. No one was concealed, or lying dead, under either of the walnut beds. Nothing appeared to be disturbed. All of the windows were closed;

the front door was still padlocked, from the outside. Tilghman shook it to be sure.

"They came in; then where'd they go?"

"What's underneath?" Ted asked.

"There's a fruit cellar. Trap door in the kitchen floor."

"Okay." They returned to the kitchen. Ted motioned to Enid on the porch, and shook his head as she came inside.

"Where can she *be*?"

The kitchen table had been pushed up against the stove, a black iron brute. Tilghman held his light on the ringbolt of the trap door and Ted lifted it slowly on creaking hinges. A short flight of steps went down into musty blackness, to a dirt floor crossed and recrossed. The footprints were more distinct, easier to read than those left on the back porch.

"That one there," Tilghman said, moving the beam of the flashlight slowly, "looks to me like a woman's print, or maybe it's a man with an uncommonly delicate foot. Those are the prints of a child, I'd say. And the others, looks like a man wearing shoes or dress boots." He nodded for emphasis, enjoying his detective work. It beat checking fishing licenses and campground permits.

"We didn't see any shoe prints on the porch," Ted pointed out.

"That's true. Maybe somebody was waiting on them, here in the parsonage."

"Oh, God, what is going *on*?" Enid moaned.

A car went by quickly in the road, with a signature splash of red lights against the side kitchen window. Ted looked up, frowning, then again at the cellar.

"I'll have a look," he said, and started down the steep unrailed wooden steps.

"Ted—!"

"Nobody's here now, we'd of heard something. I just want to get some idea of where they all went."

"Could those bare prints be your sister's?" Tilghman asked Enid.

"Oh, I don't think so. Marjory's foot is bigger than that. Like mine. We both have daddy's feet, unfortunately. Not much arch, and—"

"What made you so positive outside that she's been here?"

"A feeling," Enid said vaguely. "Mr. Tilghman, could I—I just want to have a look around the house myself."

"We already made a thorough search." Enid just stared at him; she had to see for herself the house was empty, except for them. "Sure, go ahead," Tilghman said sympathetically. "Take my flashlight." Tilghman returned his attention to the fruit cellar, which glowed from the light of Ted's torch. "You okay down there, Deputy?"

"A lot of loose rock's been moved, and there's a cave entrance. I'd bet that's what it is."

"You don't say! I must've been in this house a hundred times, but I never knowed there was anything down in that cellar. Maybe it's part of the same cave you located behind the waterfall."

"Like I said, there was a pile of rock in the way. Some chunks too big for me to tote without throwing my back out. But that's where they went. They had a rope with them, and it's at the bottom of this shaft."

"A mine shaft?"

"I don't know. Doesn't look dug out. Probably it's a natural shaft, or chimney is what I think they call them. My guess is it's about sixty feet. A hell of a climb down there in the dark."

"What are you aiming to do?"

"Carry any rope in your car?"

"Tow chain, but there ain't no sixty feet of it."

"I better think of something else, then."

Enid called loudly, almost hysterically, "Tedddd!"

Ted came scrambling up the rickety steps on all fours

and followed Tilghman to the room where Enid kneeled beside a cedar chest at the foot of the high bed. She had uncovered some damp clothing—a short-sleeved shirt with Marjory's monogram on the pocket, and walk shorts—and a pair of filthy, wet sneakers. She cradled a sneaker as if it were an abandoned child.

"Oh, no. Oh, no."

"Marjory's things?" Ted picked up the other sneaker. "Are you absolutely—"

"Yes! They were at the bottom of this chest. *Somebody hid them here! Why?*"

"Honey . . . listen, Enid—"

"If she's not walking around naked, then maybe they—they've—"

Ted had already looked for bloodstains; didn't see any. "Don't go jumping to conclusions."

Enid jumped at him instead. "We've got to do something! Find! Marjory!" He was impassive a moment too long, thinking, and Enid hit another conclusion head-on, at two hundred miles an hour. She twisted violently in his arms. "You found her! In the cellar! *They put Marjory in the—*"

"No. She's not dead. I'm not lying." Enid slumped. Her eyes dropped, her mouth trembled. She raked her lower lip with her teeth, and two tears fell.

"I think she's all right. I do. *Wet* clothes, Enid. Sure! Marj was out in the rain, we know that. So she had to change. Probably borrowed some of the things that were in this cedar chest."

Enid looked up, gazing abstractedly, eyes swimming. "You think?"

"I found out where they went. There's a cave. I don't know what's down there, but I'm going after them right now."

Tilghman said, "Don't know that I'd go alone, if I was you. Caves is plenty treacherous, in my experience."

"Get me that tow chain," Ted asked him. "And anything else you might have in your car that would come in handy.''

36

Smidge said from behind the closed door of the office at park headquarters, ''Don't come in. I don't want anybody to look at me except a doctor. When's the doctor coming? Did somebody call me a doctor? My hair's falling out. I'm—''

Her voice, already thick with grief and phlegm, ended in a choking sound; she coughed and strangled.

A portly man in an undershirt and Bermuda shorts, one of many campers aroused by Rita Sue Marcum minutes before, knocked on the door and then tried to open it. The door wasn't locked, but Smidge had barricaded it, probably with the park superintendent's desk.

''Miss, I'm not a doctor, but my wife's a registered nurse and she can help if you'll—''

His wife, wearing a plaid bathrobe and hair curlers like rolls of baling wire, said encouragingly, ''Just open the door, hon, and let me have a look at you. It's probably something you ate.''

Smidge was vomiting, gasping for breath between spasms.

In a corner of the lodge Rita Sue's pert face twisted and she said to Boyce, ''I'm gonna throw up, too! I can't help it. When I hear somebody being sick I get sick.''

They heard a siren. Boyce said, ''Maybe that's the ambulance.''

Someone near the door spoke up. "It's the Highway Patrol. Two of 'em. But they ain't stopping here."

Smidge continued to retch horridly. Rita Sue's face was enflamed, but her blue eyes were so washed out they looked colorless. "Walk outside with me, Boyce, I'm going to heave. Then you better take me straight home."

The portly man and his wife both knocked on the office door. "She sounds real sick," the woman murmured.

"Wonder if we should try to knock this door down," he said. "But I hate to take that responsibility on myself. They could get me for destroying state property."

Smidge moaned.

" 'Scuse us," Boyce said, walking Rita Sue through the crowd at the entrance and outside to the porch. Rita Sue hobbled meekly in his grip, holding her stomach.

"Rita Suuue! Where are you?"

Rita Sue paused and looked around, alarmed, a hand going to her mouth.

"Rita Suuue! Don't leave me!"

"Oh God," Rita Sue muttered, digging her nails into Boyce's wrist. "Get me out of—"

The office door suddenly flew to pieces, as if dynamited, and the woman in the plaid housecoat screamed as she was flung backward to the floor. Her husband staggered and tripped over his own feet, hands groping a face stuck full of splinters.

Smidge came flying off the desk jammed up against the shattered door like a projectile from a circus cannon—half clown, with a naked skull and huge encircled eyes and a vivid red mouth, half battered carcass of something foul and unidentifiable. There was no smoke, only a fine spray of blood from Smidge's throat as she howled and tumbled across the body of the prostrate woman. An assaultive odor accompanied her, expanding like a cloud of thick coal smoke to fill the large room.

On all fours, the Smidge-thing was nearly motionless for a few moments, searching for Rita Sue. The nose drained, the ears ran blood and brain fluids, her bare scalp literally crawled, as if there were frantic worms beneath the skin, which had turned all shades of bruises from pale green to deep purple. Her arms, like Popeye's, were deformed. The fingers of the left hand resembled a leper's: clubby, stubby, decaying. On the right hand there were no fingers at all, but sprouted, spike-hard thorns. She had destroyed the door with one swipe of this hand; now she gouged the solid floor, routing it by the handful like a cat trying to cover up its droppings.

"Rita Suuuuue!"

One eye bulged hugely in the blotched, thunderously discolored face; it appeared to zoom in on the cowering Rita Sue, then, alight with anguish, exploded with a soft plopping sound and drained like a slow jelly tear from the socket. Smidge stopped digging up the floor and made for the door, wobbling like a baby on inefficient appendages, with a slathered-on smile for the object of her desire.

A sound went around the room as people shrank from the dismal sight; not a concerted scream but the kind of stressful moan one hears from sleepers locked in a nightmare.

"Not like . . . others," she gasped, protesting, denying. "Can't make me . . . one of them. I won't. No-nonono. Just get me . . . doctor. Huh? Need a shot. Sleep. Be all right . . . in the morning. But stay . . . stay with me, Rita Sue. I need you . . . Precious."

Smidge was having locomotion problems as she crawled through the doorway; no one limb of her body cooperated with another. A hand wanted to claw; a leg wanted to kick ferociously. There was a froth of lung tissue on her swollen lips. She coughed and sobbed. Parts of her skin were bubbling like thick mud in a thermal spring. The stench had more shock value than her grievously misshapen and untidy appearance; the porch emptied of all but a few of the more rigidly fascinated.

"Precccioussss," Smidge hissed adoringly, lifting the needle-tipped hand that could go through hardwood like a spinning mill saw. Rita Sue was pressed against the sturdy railing of the porch as if welded there, pale knees resembling little globes of fruit and well within reach. On Smidge's cheek the flesh erupted like a sunspot, widened smilingly.

Boyce, holding on to Rita Sue with one hand, pivoted in grinding pain on his injured foot, reached out with his other hand and seized a golf putter from the hand of a camper who had been slowly backing up out of Smidge's way. He swung the putter up and back and got all of his shoulder and plenty of wrist into the downward stroke. The blunt end of the putter hit Smidge dead-center in the forehead and disappeared up to the shaft. There was an implosion, of sorts: everything just caved in except for her intact eye. which was fixed on him. All else about her was freakish and awful except for that one sane, normal, sweetly reproachful eye. Nobody else did anything or said anything except Rita Sue, who started bawling. Boyce stood there holding the wrapped handle of the putter, unable to let go or willing to believe he'd killed her, held Smidge with the strength of his arm like a gaffed fish until his lips began to get numb and twittery and he felt like he was a thousand miles away from there, yawning and wanting to go to sleep.

37

Marjory was concentrating on the last stubborn knot of the dried vine around the dark and wizened throat of the mummy, thinking all the while that it was Birka's childhood friend Páll who was lying there so still and making her uneasy (what a dumb game, everybody tied up like this), when she heard something that made her jump.

"Marjory. No. *Don't*. Get away from it."

His voice low and hoarse, sounding funny, but she thought she recognized—

As she turned for a look over her shoulder all she saw was Alastor, hanging from a wall with a big grin showing in the light of Duane's flashlight, then Alastor detached himself and kicked away like a swimmer and went almost straight down, plunging on top of Duane, and by her side Birka said sharply, "Get rid of him!"

There was a violent, nearly silent scuffle in billowing silk, the flashlight beam muffled, vanishing, reappearing as Duane rolled over and over trying to fight Alastor off. Moths were everywhere, in a light-storm frenzy. Marjory, astonished, glanced at Birka.

"Who's—"

"It doesn't matter, they're only playing." Duane cursed and Alastor squealed, from the fun of it and not from pain. He could never feel pain, even when Duane hit him twice in the head with his fist. In turn Alastor drew blood pointedly, from an earlobe, a shoulder, Duane's breast above the heart, but missing the vital

spots he was instinctively intent on penetrating: either
eye, the back of the neck, the depths of an armpit.

"I want to go home," Marjory complained. "I'm
tired."

"Not yet. Not *yet*. Look, it's almost finished. The
knot, the knot, Marjory."

"Oh, all right," Marjory said crossly, kneeling again
to her task, picking with cold fingers at the last knot,
her vision a little blurry.

"Marjory!" Duane gasped, but she ignored him. She
hated being around boys when they were acting like
roughnecks. If only she had fingernails, the knot would
be easy. Why couldn't she stop biting her nails? There.
It was coming. *There,* it was off. Wake up, Páll. Stop
the silly—

Alastor, squealing loud as a rat, came flying into the
middle of the cocoon as moths scattered, leaving random little comet trails in the air.

Next to Marjory, the long mummy began to squirm
like eels feeding in ink, startling her, filling her with
dread.

"Birka?"

Birka went slowly to her knees at the mummy's head,
hands poised above the closed but twitching eyes, a
look of rapture on her face.

"Oh, shit," Duane said, looking down over Marjory's shoulder at the mummy. She looked back again just
as he reached out with a blood-stippled arm and
snatched her to her feet. Duane almost wrenched her
arm out of its socket; it hurt, and Marjory burst into
tears.

"Stop!"

"Come *on,* Marjory!"

The mummy began thrashing horridly against her legs
and Marjory backed away, staring at it with her mouth
open. Staring at Birka, seeing her. Seeing all the horror
at once as Duane got a better grip on her and hauled
her through the clinging silk. Marjory wailed.

Duane took the nearest exit with Marjory, not knowing or caring, for the moment, if that was the way he'd come in. Marjory, on instinct, kept up with him. But, unfortunately, the passage he chose seemed to be narrowing too abruptly, he was forced almost into a crouch. He couldn't speak; each breath was like a sob. And Marjory, bumping awkwardly along in tow behind him, just wouldn't stop her high-pitched wailing.

Duane wormed his way around a bend where a drip of water hit him in the face. He stopped, breathing through his mouth, and aimed his flashlight, which bounced off a water-smooth, precipitously steep surface: the end of their passage.

"What's that?" Marjory gasped over his shoulder.

"Water slide."

"Where's . . . it go?"

"I don't know!"

"Don't . . . yell in my ear."

"Sorry."

"Duane."

"What."

She rested against his back, breast heaving. "Who were . . . those?"

"Don't know."

"Well . . . do you have any idea where we—"

"No."

"Excuse me," Marjory said. She turned away and retched, although nothing much came up.

Duane's fingertips were coming back to life after being half-frozen; they stung like hell. Fighting with Alastor had been like wrestling a chunk of dry ice. He glanced at Marjory; her head was hanging, her mouth open as her throat worked convulsively. When she got it under control Duane said, "Let me have one of those shoes."

"Okay. Duane—"

"Just don't ask me anything right now, I told you before *I don't know*!"

He took the shoe she handed him and crept forward toward the slab of rock on which water fell in a ribbony stream and drained into darkness. He pitched the shoe and tried to follow it with the beam of the light. After the shoe disappeared he counted slowly: two, three, four thousand—and heard a remote splash.

"That's it," he said. "Let's go. You hold on to my waist."

"Duane—we don't know what's down there!"

"Well, we can't go back."

"Why?"

They heard Alastor laughing in the dark; Duane trembled. He pointed the flashlight and turned her head with his other hand. They saw Alastor's baby face. He was crouched on all fours a little distance behind them, grinning. Just waiting.

38

Ted Lufford rappeled down the shaft beneath the Dante's Mill parsonage and Wingo County Deputy Wayne Buck Vedders followed him. Ranger Tilghman had opened the mercantile store for them, and they were well equipped, although the rope which the store had stocked in 1906, the year the people of Dante's Mill vanished overnight, was too thick and heavy for efficiently exploring caves. The best thing they had was two cans of fluorescent spray paint from the trunk of Tilghman's car, and a dozen flares to augment their flashlights. Between them they carried axes, a pickax, and shovels. Both men had brought their revolvers.

"What now?" Vedders said, when his feet were on

solid ground. He'd had a rough descent, twisting and banging against the sides of the shaft. He didn't like heights. He wasn't crazy about caves, either. When he was eight years old a friend of his had been bitten by a bat, necessitating a painful course of rabies vaccine.

"We'll try to keep up with their tracks. You blaze a trail with those aerosol cans so we don't wind up enjoying our old age down here."

"Lufford!"

"What?"

Vedders had his nickel-finish Smith in his hand, hammer cocked. "Saw something fluttering around over there. Man, I have to tell you, I can't tolerate bats. I'll take a nigger with a razor any day."

"Doesn't smell like a bat cave to me."

"You mean you can smell 'em?"

"You can smell batshit. There's none on the walls or floor here. Look, that's where they went. Heel marks, from hard shoes."

"Jesus Christ."

"What now?"

"It's some kind of big moth up close to the ceiling! Now there's two of 'em. Hell, they're near big as string kites."

Ted checked with his own flashlight. "Yeh."

"Look how the light makes them glow. You ever see anything like that?"

"No," Ted said disinterestedly. "Want to spray an arrow on the wall there, and we'll get going."

39

The dark cave chute was as slick and cold as ice, and although Duane held the flashlight with its waning batteries tightly in both hands they couldn't see much except jagged stalactites flashing by, some only inches overhead. Marjory had begun their lightning descent with her legs in a tight scissors around Duane's waist; but after the first slippery bend in the chute they were only in precarious contact with each other, and totally out of control. Marjory screamed all the way down. Duane, leading, flung from side to side by velocity and with his hands unusable, was scared soundless by the glowing stalactites in the chute: if he ran into one at the speed they were falling he could crush his knees or lose half his head. But there wasn't time for thinking, or regrets; they just *went*, helplessly, through that jagged toothy maze, drenched by waterfalls, as if they were being sucked down the long throat of something that was swallowing them alive. Duane was riding mostly on one cheek of his behind, feet up, hands and elbows high, one of Marjory's feet in an armpit, her other bare foot loose, the heel hitting him painfully on his left ear.

The chute seemed, momentarily, to be leveling off; Duane was thrust back on his shoulders and then propelled, with a dizzying torque that turned him nearly on his stomach, sprawled helplessly and flying. Two seconds went by before he realized there was nothing more beneath him, he'd been launched and was beginning to drop, with Marjory almost right on top of him. He had a glimpse of her in the beamed-up light, mouth

wide, screaming, but faintly, like a scream from the
other side of the world. Wherever they were, the heights
were beyond the reach of the flashlight. He heard water
cascading into water, a torrent, and then he was in and
under himself, shocked nearly senseless by the cold. He
felt a stabbing pain on the side where he'd hit the water.
His face went numb, as if slapped by a plank. Then
Marjory crash-dived, hitting him in the chest and hands,
bearing him down in a flurry of bubbles momentarily
visible by flashlight. That's when he lost his grip and
the flashlight turned over slowly, a vague smear of light,
and sank out of reach while his instincts sent him flailing and kicking toward the surface marked by an as-
cending trail of ghostly, illuminated bubbles.

40

"We're in danger," Theron said, the first words he
was able to speak to Birka.

The seventh child of Adam and Eve looked slowly
around the cocoon, pained by the voices in his head:
the demanding voices of the still-entombed, the
shrouded mummy-litter, for whom he could do nothing.

Resurrected from the Black Sleep, his skin tone by
luna-light was gray but his eyes were clearing as mu-
cus dripped from the corners. His eyes, widely set in
his face, were as blue as Birka's but had pronounced
epicanthus folds. His limbs, sadly twisted and shrunken
in the Sleep, now were long and stronger-looking,
though unable to support him yet. He had a deep chest.
The build of an ancient foraging man, the smooth hairless surfaces of childhood. She covered, in a few mo-

ments of communion and tenderness, the crown of his head with both of her hands. The thorn where her little finger had been twitched like a dark vein overlapping the damp wattled skin. Theron had been lifeless pitch, and now he was excitable clay.

Alastor came skipping through a passage and rolled in the tufty cocoon and said unconcernedly, "They're in the pool. If'n they don't know how to swim, reckon they're goners."

"The water's too cold for them anyway," Birka said glumly. "I think I should have let you turn them."

Alastor's head popped up. "But what if they went and spoilt after I done that? You said—"

"Well, it doesn't matter now."

"We're in danger," Theron repeated, as if it were all he could say.

"I suppose," Birka conceded, "others will come, looking for Marjory and the boy. I was virtually all alone and in a hurry, and I had to use the parsonage entrance. But there are three of us now, and if I can just fetch Marjory back, we will soon be a hundred."

"Who is Marjory?" Theron said, wincing.

"Someone I just met, outside, and whom I became very fond of. She was so afraid of death; but we all were, once."

"You were . . . outside?"

"Yes, thanks to Arne."

"Your son?"

"Yes. He was very old. I did him a kindness."

"After what he did to us."

"That was his father's influence. Does it matter now? We're back."

"But we—"

"Let them come. Anyone. Let them all stumble around, lost, in the dark, trying to find us. In our place, *our* home. You'll be safe here, for a little while. I'd better try to recover Marjory."

"I'll bet she drownded already," Alastor said, with a note of glee.

"Why don't you just shut up?" Birka said impatiently. "And look after Theron while I'm gone. Don't nod your head and pull a long face. It's 'Yes, ma'am,' and 'No, ma'am,' from now on when you speak to me, is that understood?"

"Yes, ma'am," Alastor said, but he wasn't paying close attention to her. He had lifted his head and was listening to what Birka had also overheard. Sound traveled amazingly well through the passages.

Voices.

"Followed you," Theron said, placing a hand on her forearm. He had huge hands. His thorn was nearly five inches long. Birka trembled slightly at the memory of his power.

"That changes things."

"Then we have to . . . protect ourselves."

"Yes. Can you—?"

She helped him. He stood up, leaning this way and that, erratic, unbalanced. He was more than a head taller than Birka. Gaining in strength slowly, but perhaps not fast enough. For the first time since Theron's resurrection Birka felt worried.

"I can fight 'em!" Alastor said. "I'm a good fighter."

"Yes," Birka said, allowing him a smile. "You come, too."

"You gonna get Marjory out of the pool first?"

"No, there's no time now. She will just have to die where she is."

"Good," said Alastor.

41

In total darkness Duane and Marjory floundered and choked and clung to each other in the cave pool.

"Get me out of here! Get me out of here!"

"Marjory!" Their voices came back to them, hollowed and reverberating, above the steady downpour of the waterfall, and the part of Duane's mind that wasn't concerned with panic and drowning noted that this cavern was far larger than any he'd come across so far.

"Get me out of here!"

He couldn't see her but she had a grip on his belt underwater, and she was close enough to be choking and spouting in his face.

"Marj . . . shut up . . . stay afloat . . . we'll be all right!" But he didn't believe it himself. He took in water and his own throat locked. He was most afraid of both of them going down and losing their sense of direction—swimming, fighting to regain the surface but going deeper, disoriented, swimming down instead of up until their lungs burst.

"Geh . . . me . . ."

"Marjory. Just. Tread water. Relax."

"Dark." But she was listening to him, not so frantic, her instincts as a fine swimmer taking over. Face to face, they bumped knees. He put an arm around her. His face grazed hers.

"Stay. Like this. A minute. Don't talk."

". . . see."

"I know . . . you can't see."

"God. Oh God."

"No, don't. Be okay. Promise." She was gasping in his face. He wanted to keep her like that, almost nose to nose. It wasn't so difficult for Marjory to stay afloat. She was well endowed for that. He put his free hand on one of her bobbing breasts.

"Good. We've got. Life raft."

"Duane. You asshole. No joke."

Her knuckles were digging painfully into his stomach where she had a grip on his belt. Now that they had stopped thrashing so frantically Duane could tell they weren't in a current, being slowly pulled along somewhere they might not want to go.

"Why . . . you make me do that? Run away. Now look."

"Marjory. Did they . . . did one of them . . . do something to you?"

"Mean?"

"Like . . . stick you in the back of the neck?"

"Stick me?"

"Your hair's . . . not falling out. Is it?"

"Gone crazy?"

"No. I guess you're. Okay."

"*Okay?* Uh-uh. Wet. Cold. We're . . . Duane . . . oh. Ohhhh!"

"No. We're going to be. We'll. Get out of here. Didn't I. Promise?"

"How?"

"Don't know. Yet. Tired of. Treading water. Swim?"

"Where?" When he didn't answer right away she said sharply, "Duane!"

"Was looking around. I think I see . . . I don't know." Duane touched his glasses, which had stayed on even while he was submerged. Then he placed his hand on her cheek. "Turn. This way. See anything?"

"No. Uh. Maybe."

"What?"

"Like . . . something sparkling. High up. Comes. And goes."

"That's what I—"

"There. Wait. Maybe two of them. Like stars. Stars?"

"I see it, too. Geodes. I think."

"How high?"

"I don't know. Come on. Swim that way."

"Duane, I'm."

"Uh-huh. Me, too. We have to swim. You know you're. Better than me. Just do it."

"I don't want to die!"

"Then swim, Marj. Swim to the stars."

42

"Wait a minute," Ted Lufford said, going down on one knee, casting his light along two diverging umbilical passages, the walls of which looked sheared; they glittered hotly in places like animal eyes by the side of a rural road.

"What is all that stuff?" Wayne Buck Vedders said.

"Quartz crystal, most likely. My daddy and uncle and me used to go looking up around Cordell Hull for geodes. You ever see a geode?"

"Sure, I had me a couple when I was a kid. Jackson County? Fished up that way now and again. There's a little cafe on the south side of the courthouse square in Gainesboro has the best buttermilk pie I ever put in my mouth."

"I know the one. Crawford's."

"Yeh, ol' Smiley Crawford. Long gone now, I hear. One-armed, he was still the best short-order cook around the lake." Vedders moved out from under an almost invisible drip of water from the roof of the passage and said uneasily to Ted's back, "What happened, we lose 'em?"

"I don't know yet. Listen."

Both men were quiet. They heard the far-off sound of falling water. And something else, perhaps a voice: thin, unidentifiable.

Vedders shivered. Ted rose slowly, handed back the flashlight, which gave Vedders two of them to hold, and cupped his hands to his mouth.

"Marjory!"

His voice wailed down seemingly limitless spaces in the earth, echoing dimly a couple of times.

"Jesus," Vedders whispered, spooked. They waited to hear something back. "How big you reckon this cave is?"

"No telling. It's probably a whole lot of caves, strung together for miles." Ted felt a pinching in his stomach, concern for the fate of the girl. No telling who she was with, or what they had in mind. He held out his hand for the flashlight and sprayed the walls again, then the rough floor. "I don't know," he mumbled. "I don't know."

"Just pick one, I reckon," Vedders said.

"Marjory!" Ted hollered again, frustrated; he took a couple of deep breaths.

"I know where she's at," a childish voice said, and there was the sound of a muffled giggle.

Ted and Wayne Vedders looked different directions at once, because there was no clear indication where the voice had come from. The beams from their flashlights crossed each other's startled face.

"But she's drownded already."

Ted swore under his breath and took a couple of steps down the left-hand passage, to the delight of the unseen boy.

"Where are you?"

Silence.

"What's your name?"

"Pudd'n and tame," Alastor sang. "Ask me again, I'll tell you the same!"

Vedders charged a little way down the other passage with his flashlight and stopped suddenly.

"Lufford," he called, in a strangled voice.

Alastor giggled again.

Ted ran into Vedders as he was backing out.

"What's the matter?"

"Jesus. I don't believe it. He's . . . I don't know what it is. Have a look."

Ted aimed his flashlight along the passage, lighting up a display of crystal studding both walls.

"No. I mean—up there." Vedders used his own flashlight. There was Alastor, clinging upside down on the roof, between clusters of glistening stalactites. Fifteen feet up.

"Fuck is *that*?" Vedders said, breathing heavily.

"You talk?" Ted said to the naked, hairless boy.

Alastor did a couple of bird calls instead: his hooded warbler wasn't bad, Ted thought. The hairs on the back of his neck still felt as if caterpillars were crawling there.

"Tell me something, how'd you get yourself up there thataway?"

"Ask me no questions, I'll tell you no lies."

"Smart kid, huh? Ain't you afraid you're gonna fall and hurt yourself, Big 'un?"

"Don't get hurt," Alastor said unconcernedly.

"That so?"

"Watch me," Alastor said with a grin, and suddenly sprang from his perch to the wall closest to Ted, sticking there just out of reach. A wave of cold air came off him and Ted instinctively backed up a step, treading on Vedders's toes.

Ted swallowed and forced himself to smile. "Hey, real good. Like to know how you do that."

"You can't anyway."

"I sure don't intend to try, Big 'un."

" 'Cause you got to be dead first."

"Oh," Ted said, unable to remember when he'd felt so cold. The tip of his nose, his lips tingled.

"Jesus fucking Christ," Vedders groaned behind Ted's back.

"Listen, Big 'un, you can pull my leg all you want, uh, but I need for you to tell me something—"

"What's *your* name?" Alastor said with his wide gap-toothed smile. "Funky butt?" He snickered.

"No, it's . . . Ted. What I want to know from you is, do you . . . live down here?"

"What's it to you?"

Ted exhaled, seeing his breath. But he couldn't see Alastor's breath. He felt something picking at his mind, *chink, chink,* and looked into the strange boy's bright unholy eyes, knowing it was him. Rummaging as idly in Ted's mind as if it were a mailbox. A sensation he'd never experienced before, but unmistakable. He put a hand on the checkered butt of his holstered Smith Special and Alastor's eyes flicked nonchalantly, taking in the movement.

"I'll show you where I live," he said unexpectedly, and failed to laugh.

Ted thought, *Afraid of the gun.* Then he thought, *No, he's not afraid of anything.*

Vedders said, his own breath puffing out, "Partner, I just got me a bad feeling. Let's us get out of here. Right now."

"No. I want Marjory."

"Can I see your gun?" Alastor said. "Is it a six-shooter?"

"Yeh, it's a six-shooter. Yeh, I guess you can see it. But I want you to tell me—"

"Already told you about Marjory! She and him probably drownded in the pool."

"It's *probably* now? That mean you saw her? What pool?"

Ted drew his revolver and swung the cylinder out, dropping .38 cartridges into his other, cupped hand, holding on to the flashlight by his fingertips and thumb. He closed the gate and held out the emptied revolver to Alastor, tempting him with it. All boys, even dead boys, liked guns, he thought. A muscle twitched in Ted's throat, another in his face. His extended hand felt almost numb, as if he'd dipped it into a pool of ether. Alastor looked solemnly at the blue-steel revolver, and at Ted. Trying to make up his mind about him, but not trusting him.

"Go ahead, Big 'un," Ted urged. "Look it over, son."

Alastor let go of the wall with his right hand, which Ted noticed looked deformed, but he was calculating other matters. As soon as his chance was apparent he let the flashlight drop from his left hand and snatched Alastor's wrist, yanking him away from his perpendicular perch on the rugged crystal wall face, stepping to one side and slinging Alastor like a dangerous breed of cat to the rocky floor.

The cold shocked him again, numbing his palm and fingers as if he'd grabbed onto a live wire. He wasn't prepared for Alastor's resilience and powers of recovery; the boy just bounced off the floor undamaged and turned on Ted, slashing with the hooked little finger of his right hand, cutting through Ted's pants below the knee. Ted let go of Alastor and the boy leaped away from him to a crystal rock face, clinging there, making a keening noise only a little more audible than a dog whistle.

That's when Vedders took aim with his revolver and cut loose, missing with the first shot, taking off part of the side of Alastor's head, including all of one ear, with the second shot. The roar and reverberation in the passage nearly collapsed Ted's eardrums; he grabbed his own head in pain. He was spattered with bits of skull and a mucilaginous mess cold as sleet but Alastor scarcely seemed aware of the gunshot as he scampered away on the wall, on all fours, and grabbed the ceiling. Vedders, shouting something, fired again, drilling Alastor cleanly through the side but barely slowing him down, and in another instant he was beyond the reach of the erratic flashlight in Vedders's other hand.

"Jesus! Christ! Stop it! Firing your piece down here, you crazy or something, we could catch a goddamn bullet coming back!"

"I hit him! Know I hit him twice!"

"Saw what good it did!" Ted glanced at the rip in the khaki below his knee, a small stain of blood. He was dazed by the action, the ferocity of Alastor's counterattack. His ears rang; if he didn't have permanent damage it would be a miracle, he thought. Vedders, smoking gun in hand, pushed past Ted, wild of eye, whisking the beam of his light around. The passage was stinking from powder.

"Gonna tell me I didn't kill him! He's dead already, let's go get the little—"

Ted grabbed him from behind. "Listen!" He pressed a hand hard against his left ear, released it. "You hear that?"

"Hell, I'm half-deaf!"

"No. I heard it. Kids."

"Talk louder!"

"I said *kids*! Yelling. It was Marjory. She's not dead!"

"Where?"

"The hell would I know? Down there. Where Big 'un went."

Vedders was staring at the front of Ted's jacket. He reached out tentatively with the hand that held the Smith and picked up a fingerload of slushy jelly, which he promptly slung away.

"That blood? That what he was made of?"

"I don't know."

Vedders stared at Ted, his eyes perfectly round. Unexpectedly his teeth began to chatter.

"Partner? What's d-down here?"

"I don't know that either."

"If there's m-more of them, we have done g-got ourselves in a real mess." Vedders wheeled suddenly, crouching, hearing a rock fall somewhere in the passage. He looked both ways with the flashlight, brooming the walls. Ted unloaded the knapsack he was carrying and opened it. He took out a flare and popped it with a twist of his hands, planted it in a crevice. The flare sizzled and broadcast harsh pink light.

"Feel better?" he asked the other deputy.

"H-hell no. What was it? You g-got any ideas what it was?"

"Yeh. I think it was a vampire. Kind of. I don't care. I want Marjory. You have anything to stuff your ears with?"

"I don't know." Vedders searched his pockets and came up with a crumpled pack of Marlboros. "Filtertips might help. We gonna go down there shooting?"

"Not going anywhere." Ted took the cigarettes from him and twisted off filters. "Plug your ears and get down low, I'm gonna let off another round."

"What for?"

"I'm trying to locate where it was they were hollering from."

"Doesn't make any s-sense. You don't expect me to believe in vampires, that's kid stuff."

"Explain it any way you want, Vedders. You shot his head half off, and he went right on with what he was doing. Hug the floor."

Ted plugged his ears, reloaded his revolver and got down, looked along the uneven passage with his flashlight and hoped he wouldn't get lead back between his teeth. Then he pulled the trigger.

43

"Marjory?" Duane said. He said it again. Then he shook her.

"Go 'way," she murmured.

"Marjory, don't do that. Don't go to sleep."

"Tired."

"You can't go to sleep. It's because you're so cold. If you do, you'll die."

"Leave me alone."

"No," Duane said, as peevish as she was, and nearly as numb. He breathed in her ear. No response.

They had pulled themselves from the water onto a shelf of rock that was barely wide enough for the two of them lumped together like seals. Water dribbled down from somewhere but Duane scarcely felt it any more. Once he had stopped swimming lassitude set in. It was an effort to keep his eyes open, particularly with nothing to see. Utter, final blackness everywhere. Marjory so cold to the touch, and seldom moving. Barely responding when he pinched her arms, her thighs. He had another idea. He felt for a breast inside the soggy clinging shirt. Fingered a nipple and twisted it, cruelly.

"Stop!"

"Did that hurt?"

"Yes." She tried to push away from him.

"Don't. You'll go back in the water. I won't find you."

"What are you doing?"

"I'm making a fire," he said desperately, alternately rubbing and licking her nipples. Right, left. Breathing on them. No amount of agitation made them stand up. "Stop that, Duane," she complained.

"What are you going to do about it?" Duane panted. "Get hot, Marjory. Get hot." He felt no lechery himself, no stirring of interest. If he couldn't get himself up, what was the use?

"Quit," Marjory said. "Couldn't if I. Wanted to. And I. Just don't want to. I'm going to sleep."

"No, you're not." Duane stopped belaboring her nipples, raised up, tried to fill his lungs. He screamed.

"Matter now? Get off."

Duane screamed again, and almost immediately he heard what he thought might be a gunshot.

"Marjory!"

"I'm so *tired*."

Duane raised his head from Marjory's breast. "Didn't you hear that?" He looked around, directionless, wiped a drip of water from his face. And saw something, a wan pink glow. Almost directly overhead. He closed his eyes, shuddering, looked again. It was still there, faintly, like firelight reflected from low clouds.

"Marjory!"

"Uhh."

"I see something! I think somebody's . . . looking for us." He took a full, deep breath, and screamed "WE'RE DOWN HERE!" As befuddled as he was, he knew that might not mean anything. "Marjory!" He shook her, and she didn't respond. Terror gave him needed strength. "I SEE YOUR LIGHT!" Duane screamed it again, then fell, exhausted and sobbing, on top of Marjory, who did not move at all.

Seconds later, he heard two more gunshots, in quick succession.

He didn't know what that meant, or if it meant anything. And he was too far gone to raise his head again, to see if the angelic glow was still hovering somewhere above his head.

44

While Wayne Buck Vedders kept watch, Ted attacked, with the pickax they had brought, the wall of the passage that was thickly studded with quartz crystal. He kept the bill of his cap pulled low to afford some protection from flying shards and splinters of the glasslike rock, but his hands and jawline soon leaked blood from several nicks and cuts. When he paused to rest his aching shoulders and arms, he called Marjory and Duane. There was no answer.

"Man, that vein of quartz could be a quarter mile thick," Vedders said.

"No. You heard. 'I see your light.' They must have meant the flare. If light got through—fuck it—I'll get through." Ted kneaded his fingers and resumed with the pickax, driving the bit with savage grunts of effort into a seam he had opened.

Without warning a small section of the wall flew apart, a draft of cool air streamed through a hole the size of a watermelon.

Ted dropped the pickax, the handle of which was slick with his blood, and scrambled atop a small pile of rubble to peer into darkness. He heard the splashing of a waterfall.

"Give me a flashlight!"

He turned and seized the light Vedders handed up to him and thrust it through the opening.

"Duane! *Marjory*—it's Ted! Where are you?"

The beam of the light played off a ghostly acre of stalactites, some hanging in blue tapering bundles, like collections of knuckly pickled fingers, others as delicate as crystalline needles that looked as if they would shatter at a touch. His light dipped almost vertically to the glossy black surface of a rippled pool. There were stalagmite formations in the water, some neatly pyramidal and very much like the remnants of cypress trees in a swamp, others barely above the surface and resembling the worn, gnarled heads of trolls—the shocking, naked head of Big 'un, who crept on walls and grinned mischievously and survived gunshot wounds at close range. Ted coughed out something thick and bitter that had lingered in his throat. He located the waterfall that was making the noise, and other, lesser drips. But the powerful flashlight beam could not reach all the way around the cavern. With his other hand he pitched a chunk of quartz, and counted: three seconds to splashdown, a faint echoing splash. It was a long way to the pool from where he was. The size, the depth of the cavern intimidated him. And still he didn't know where the kids were.

"I see your light."

The voice so feeble he couldn't tell who had spoken.

"Who's that?" he called into the cavern.

". . . Duane."

"Duane, this's Ted! Ted Lufford! Are you okay, you hurt, what's going on?"

"Cold."

"Marjory? Where's—"

"Here with me. She's . . . Marjory, Marjory, wake up."

"What's the matter?"

"Too cold. Breathing. But . . . needs a doctor."

"Listen, Duane. I'm coming down."

Ted scrambled back from the hole in the wall and reached for the pickax. "You have to go back," he told Vedders. "Round up all the help you can find. Get a doc and an ambulance out here. Leave me the rope and some flares and—let me have your jacket, okay?"

"Yeh, okay, no problem. I'll be back in twenty minutes."

"Try to make it quicker."

"Unless I run into the big 'un. Next time I'll just keep shooting until he's in so many pieces he can't find all of himself. How do you plan on getting down there?"

Ted turned and began attacking the wall again. "Rope's a hundred foot. It'll have to do."

"Take care. I'll be back."

"You, too," Ted said, smashing another large chunk of quartz out of the widening hole in the wall.

45

In the robing chamber Theron looked at the remains of Puff near the slab of rock that Duane had ridden over her and said, "She was one of us. Where did she come from?"

"The boy turned her," Birka said. "There was one other, he claims."

Theron frowned. To Birka he still seemed disturbingly insensible, disoriented; he'd had a painful awakening.

"Where is the boy now?"

"I don't know," Birka said. "He may have surprised our visitors. Yes, he would be quite a surprise to them. With luck he might turn them. It doesn't matter. He'll find us. Can you climb?"

Theron looked at the robes made from human skin, patiently chewed to near transparency and woven together with strands of silk, that hung a safe distance above the cavern floor. There were so many luminous moths in the cavern it was difficult to distinguish them from the robes.

"I can climb," he said. Without another word he began creeping up a near vertical wall, and Birka followed him. The moths were rioting, delirious. Soon they would have important company, the nightflying *huldufólk*.

"We have to consider leaving here right away," Birka said. "It may still be night out there."

"What if it isn't?"

"Then when the resurrection is finished we'll go deeper into the caves and complete our cycle there."

"You know we don't have enough robes for everyone. That's the reason your husband caught up to us. It's always been a struggle, Birka. We have never been safe." Birka was lagging behind. Theron paused, hanging on grimly to the rock. "What's wrong?"

Marjory. She's alive, but weak. Weaker than you are.

Then she'll die.

"No. I don't want her to die. If I can get to her, I can turn her first."

"What difference . . . does one more human make?"

"I feel . . . motherly. Isn't that odd?"

"Yes."

"Theron?"

"What now?"

"I liked being outside."

"We all do. There's nothing wrong with that. As long as we can go to earth for our cycle."

"I want nice clothes again. I'm tired of my own skin already. I want to hear music and go dancing. What's the good of living forever, if we can't dance? He didn't take that away from us, did He?"

"No. He only took away the sun."

"And air. Air is no good to us, except it's hard to

learn to speak without breathing. He took away hunger, and sex. But those aren't good things. They were good enough, when you could do something about them. Flying is better. And music: I would rather not have the sun than not have music. Oh, Mozart! If only one of us had turned him, he would still be composing that glorious music.''

"No he wouldn't. It's one of the rules of our state. We can create our robes, which are necessary to sustain our existence. But everything else we borrow from humans. Their language, all of their art. We can never have a culture of our own. Or a permanent home. Let's get on with it.''

"Theron? It's good to be us, isn't it?''

"Yes. But then I don't know any other way to be.''

"Theron?''

"*Why* do you keep rattling on?''

"Because I haven't seen you or talked to you since— Theron, did you see Him? On the East of Eden?''

"No. I wanted to look out, from where we were hidden. But I was afraid to. I only heard His voice.''

"What did He sound like? Like heavenly thunder? Like mountains cracking open?''

"Like a schoolmaster with a boil on his ass.''

"Theron! He did not. Well. At least you have your sense of humor back.''

"Then why am I not laughing?'' He paused again, thirty feet above the cavern floor, reached out and plucked a robe, saffron and gold and sizzling pink. "This one suits you,'' he said, and graciously passed it down to Birka.

"Thank you.''

"And this will do for me.''

"Yes, I think so. I like you best in blue.'' Birka shrieked, plunging toward the cavern floor, then swooped and turned over on her back with the colorful robe fluttering translucently around her. She floated there, kicking up her heels like a child, smiling up at

Theron as he slipped into his own robe and came down more gracefully, trailing giant glowing moths in an imperial, fluttering train. For a few moments they lay side by side in air, luxuriating, the tissue-thin robes crafted from human skin swelling and receding over their marble-white bodies like iridescent waves of the sea.

"He gave," Birka said at last, "more than He took away."

"Sometimes," Theron murmured, "I think so, too. Even though I should know better by now. Humans are quite inventive, when it comes to new horrors to plague us."

46

Duane, looking up at the flare, like a smoky sunrise, in the cavern wall, saw Ted work his way through the hole which he'd cut and dangle on the rope wrapped once around his waist until his feet were braced. Then he rappeled efficiently down to a narrow ledge that was like a rim of unbaked piecrust a few feet above the ledge where Duane and Marjory were marooned: Marjory on her side and with her eyes closed, Duane straddling her.

Ted tested the piecrust ledge to see if it was going to hold him, then popped another flare.

"You all right?"

"Weak," Duane said, all but blinded by the abundance of light after hours in near darkness.

"Marjory?"

"I can't . . . wake her up," Duane said, and began to sob.

"Just take it easy, Duane, we'll get you out of here."

Duane, squinting up at the heights from which Ted had descended, shook his head hopelessly. "How?"

"More help on the way." Ted peered down at the lower ledge; Marjory took up most of it. There wasn't room for the three of them. He pitched the remainder of the rope down.

"Come on up here with me. Pass that rope under one arm and then around your waist and through your crotch."

"I did some rope climbing in gym," Duane said. "But—"

"You'll make it. Just hang on, I'll pull. How much do you weigh?"

"One eighty-four."

"Give me some help then, bubba."

Duane looked at Marjory; his glasses were badly smeared with calcium carbonate and her features were indistinct, but her pallor was frightening in contrast to the black water inches below. Duane took two deep breaths, then grasped the hairy rope with both hands and started to climb, as Ted leaned back and hauled. Part of the frangible rim of the ledge crumbled, bits of rock falling on Duane's lowered head.

Ted let go of the rope he had belayed and reached for Duane's wrists, then his elbows. Duane wormed over the edge and lay exhausted, still crying, at Ted's feet.

"Reckon you don't want to try the rest of it yet."

"No . . . sir. I can't."

"Okay, rest here. I'm going down to Marjory."

He was there in a jump, and felt the clamminess of her skin. "Duane! Did she drown?"

"No, sir. She's . . . just cold, that's all. Too cold."

Ted sat her up and worked frantically to tear the sodden half-buttoned shirt off. "Marjory? Marjory!" She made a sound, a protest of some kind, but her eyes didn't open. He rubbed the palm of one hand between her breasts, trying to stimulate the heart. He took Wayne

Buck Vedders's jacket from the knapsack and dressed
Marjory in it, still talking to her. He tilted her head
back and pumped his breath into her lungs. There was
a pulse in her throat, extremely faint.

He was frantic about Marjory and unaware of the
gradual lightening in the cavern, the approach of the
luna moths and the two creatures in their midst: huge,
smooth, gliding quieter than a whisper across the dim-
pled jet-black pool.

Marjory.

Marjory gave a start in Ted's arms, a little flutter kick
that almost rolled her away from him and into the pool.
Gasping, he raised his head and looked into a pair of
eyes so blue they were near to colorless, so cold they
could not be human.

"There's nothing you can do," Birka said. "Let me
take her. It's what she wants. If you could ask her, she
would tell you. Marjory wants to be with me."

47

Someone was coming.

Enid got up slowly from the box she'd been sitting
on in the fruit cellar of the parsonage, her shadow
growing huge by lantern light on the jumble of rock
that formed one wall, merging with the dark cleft in the
wall where she had last seen Ted, just before he and the
deputy went down into the cavern.

She heard the sound again, a skittering of loose rock
below.

"Ted?"

She had been waiting there for the better part of an hour. There was a lot of activity outside the parsonage: she heard vehicles, the static of radios on high gain as lawmen talked to one another in short laconic bursts she could not quite understand at this distance. Tilghman, the park ranger, had been in and out, keeping an eye on her and the entrance to the cavern. Now he was upstairs, on the back porch, she thought, with two other rangers.

"Mr. Tilghman? I think they're coming back!"

Maybe he was out of earshot. Enid picked up the lantern and walked slowly toward the cleft in the piled rock. Just wide enough for the two men to have slipped through sideways. Enid, not going in, called again. This time she heard her echo. which made her uncomfortable. She listened, tense and disappointed as the echo died away without a response. Well, if it wasn't Ted, or the deputy, then it was nothing. Nothing human. Rats, bats, what else lived underground? Enid didn't want to know. She had never possessed much nervous energy. Her system was already on overload. She had a vision of something dark and feisty shrieking at her, getting tangled in her hair. She would just as soon die as go through an experience like that. *Take me now, Lord, I don't have the strength,* their mother used to say. Fear of loathsome flying objects was the major reason Enid had stayed close to the fruit cellar steps and away from the rocks during her vigil.

"Ted? Is that you? Did you find Marjory? Ted, answer me!"

Enid edged a little closer to the cave entrance, extending the lantern with its multiple halos of yellow flame, and saw the climbing rope, tied to spikes driven into the hard-packed cellar floor, move slightly, stretching tighter as if someone were on the other end, coming up. She reached out with her free hand and felt a faint vibration.

Too heavy for a rat; if it was Ted or the other deputy, why—

"Ted . . . please?" She gave up on Ted. *Who is it?*

Enid glanced at the fruit cellar steps, but Ranger Tilghman didn't appear, and the voices above had faded; it was sepulchrally quiet in the cellar. The thick climbing rope shifted again under her hand. Enid's heart vibrated sympathetically. She moved a little closer to the shaft, going slowly to her knees for balance, then creeping near the brink, pushing the lantern ahead of her inches at a time, blood drumming in her temples. She filled the cleft between shaft and cellar like a cork in a bottle. Earlier she'd watched both men straining, working themselves sideways to force their bodies into the same space. Poor Ted, heavier since she'd met him, Marjory was just too good a cook—

The metal base of the lantern scraped on stone as she pushed it to within a foot of the shaft. As far as she intended to go. The rope was quiet between her knees. She smelled something, an odor she hadn't been aware of before. Nothing she could be definite about, it was just . . . unclean. She was poised between fear of what might be there, and an intense desire to see what lay at the bottom of the shaft. Ted had warned her, just before starting his descent, not to try to follow, the shaft was deep. If Marjory had made it down, Enid thought, then she was, had to be, okay. Enid made sure of her grip on the lantern, almost belly down now as she wormed closer, her other hand on the rope. Fingers reaching the point where the rope made a right angle and disappeared over the edge.

A grubby set of childish fingers, stunningly cold, slid up the rope and closed on her hand.

Enid reacted as if she'd reached into a wolf trap, trying to jerk free, shrieking in horror. She almost lost the lantern in the shaft. The bleak white gunshot face of little Alastor bobbed into the light, his mouth open

wide as if he were screaming, too; but no sound came
from his airless lungs. Enid, heaving backward, swung
the lantern, breaking it on the earless side of his head.
Still he clung to her, coming up, coming out of the shaft
with a bowlegged bound as Enid scrambled backward
on torn knees into the fruit cellar.

The lantern flame was snuffed out. In the hard grip
of Alastor's small hand, Enid beat on him in a frenzy
with the remnants of the lamp, soaking them both in
dashed kerosene. Her right hand, her wrist, burning
from cold. His right hand flailing, she was stabbed on
forehead and cheek, low on the side of her neck, but,
anesthetized by fright, she felt nothing. They rolled together, pummeling each other, Enid screaming until she
choked on the old and evil-tasting dirt.

The darkness of the dust-filled cellar was pierced by
flashlight beams, she heard men shouting. Suddenly she
was released by the naked boy; he seemed to fly away
from her body, a leap that took him nearly as high as
the cellar roof. He came down in a crouch in front of the
gang of men, right hand up, blazing in their lights, then
jumped into the midst of them. Someone was slashed
as if by a razor and reeled from the pack, spurting blood
from a torn wrist. Enid saw a revolver in another man's
hand. Flashlight beams crossed through the haze,
searching like lighthouse beacons; a beam nearly
blinded her just as she glimpsed Alastor on the steps.
The cheeks of his behind, thin little wings of shoulder
blades, the human crease of backbone . . . and the head,
so hideous, like a gargoyle's. She had a glimpse, no
more. He was up the steps in another bound, knocking
another man off balance, pitching him sideways to the
cellar floor.

Enid tasted kerosene, and retched. It was one anti-
dote to frenzy. She was on her knees with her head low;
as blood flowed back into her face she felt wasp-stung.
Revulsion, weakness, she was beginning to tremble violently when two men lifted her.

Their voices, just babble to her ears. More men crowding down into the cellar. Bitter dust everywhere, in her eyes, her mouth. She couldn't forget his lashless and faintly glowing eyes as he gazed at her from the brink of the pit, his grip that could grind her bones. So that was what was down there, where Ted had gone: hell was down there. She didn't want to be touched any more, but she couldn't fight them off. *Just leave me alone,* Enid thought, as she was half carried across the cellar to the steps. *My God. Isn't it enough yet?*

48

They were adult versions of Big 'un, Ted observed, trying to be calm and rational and not succeeding; both of them naked as original sin, fully, almost obscenely human in appearance (the male particularly, level in flight with long arms outstretched, his genitals hugely hanging) but with skin so white it took on the subtle coloring of their diaphanous wings—if they could be called wings—as full as parafoils, as vivid as auroras, that held them in suspension above the pool in which they were so precisely mirrored he also felt threatened from below. They were a little like angels he remembered from a Sunday school comic book long ago: picture stories from the Bible. But the skin of Ted's face felt as if it were shrinking two sizes too tight from the cold radiance surrounding them almost as visibly as the billowing, floating tissue that clung to their bodies and kept them aloft. Angels or fiends? His breastbone ached from shuddering, as if it were splitting in two. What-

ever they might be, he desperately did not want them
to see him shudder.

Their eyes seemed unusually large, perhaps because
of the shorn skulls or the fact that, like the eyes of
animals, they didn't blink. He could see, reflected in
the blue pupils of the female, the fluttering of moths as
large in flight as his two spread hands. What did moths
have to do with these creatures? The moths were a be-
nign presence. For now the strangers kept their distance, but not as if they had fear of him. Bald heads
seemed innately savage to Ted, but they were not immediately antagonistic, although both the male and the
female had needle-pointed, ebony thorns in place of the
little fingers of their right hands, like the smaller thorn
which Big 'un had slashed Ted with below his knee.
There was a hard, immaculate beauty about the female
(he couldn't think of her as a woman) that fascinated
Ted, but he couldn't look at her for very long without
feeling as he did when he was in the dentist's chair,
relaxed and aware of his surroundings but sort of
dreaming at the same time, numbed along the jawline
and between the eyes as well. He was not particularly
imaginative and had no superstitions; "vampire" had
conveniently come to mind to describe the startling appearance and preternatural agility of Big 'un, but here
were two more of the same species, and now he wasn't
so sure of his appraisal. Although he couldn't name
them, he was inspired to speculate about where they
had come from. Cave dwellers, or just the opposite?
Within moments speculation became conviction. Ted
was more awed than frightened.

Eight months after he had joined the sheriff's patrol,
Ted responded to a not-very-specific complaint from a
woman who lived on a farm in northeast Caskey County,
remote from her neighbors. She had called about someone shining bright lights in her windows. When Ted got
there the woman was trying to coax a couple of hounds
out from under the porch. The dogs wouldn't budge,

even for food. The woman had an ancient double-barreled shotgun in one fist and a lump of chewing tobacco in her jaw. She spat with particular vehemence and said, "Reckon if you didn't take half the night to get up here you'd of seen 'em. They was in my cornfield nigh on twenty minutes, just a-strolling around like they had a purchase on my place."

"Who was?" Ted asked.

"They wasn't no friends of mine! And I ain't a-talking about the Second Coming. Reckon I'll know Jesus when I see him. No sir. They was outer-space people."

"Space people? What did they look like?"

"They was maybe twice as tall as you, wearing them silvery-looking suits like the moonwalkers. Heads as skinny as carrots and nary trace of hair. No ears neither, that I could tell."

"What about their eyes?"

"Well now, they had plenty of eyes 'tween 'em. They had more eyes than Old Glory's got stars, all the way around their heads, kind of little eyes and glittery, without much color to 'em. You think I'm a born liar! Just come on with me, then, Deputy. I can show you right where at they come down, making a whistling noise so the dogs foamed at the mouth and crawled on their bellies. The corn's blowed over like a cyclone hit it, and blanched. Now I don't know what we'un's is supposed to do for a crop this year. The pond was partial frizz too, it had ice all round it, and this here is July, not December."

"Come down in what?"

"What do you think? Some kind of space ship."

"How big?"

"Big! I didn't get that close a look, it hurt my old eyes. Give off rays, is what it done. My eyes's still a-smartin', can't you tell? They don't make water like this otherwise. What I'd like to know is, how many other folks seen it tonight. Don't know how anybody could miss that dang thing. It come down quiet enough, till it shined them bright lights through the house, but the dogs didn't bark like they might've. Right away they just cowered and whimpered and crawled off to hide. Dogs, they know when something ain't natural."

. . . *When something ain't natural.* There was tension in Marjory's body, and Ted responded by tightening his grip on her. The female hovering a few feet away in the pink glow of the flare on the ledge above him was staring at Marjory. Ted was in an awkward position on the narrow ledge, left arm cramped against the rock so that he couldn't reach the holstered revolver on the other side. But it probably wouldn't be any help, even if he could get to his gun.

"Don't let them take Marjory," Duane said hoarsely.

"Don't intend to," Ted replied, looking into the eyes of the male. "Where do you come from?" he said.

The male seemed uninterested in answering him.

"Tell me this. Do you live down here?"

The female turned her head, glancing at her mate, then looked at Ted and smiled.

"We're not from the stars. Live here? We live wherever we like."

I don't care for this human. He's a yokel, but dangerous. Like your yokel husband. Take the girl from him and let's go.

No, have patience, Theron. They both know too much about us, don't they? Can't you read the boy?

Of course I can read him! I didn't plan to leave these two alive. Perhaps . . . the boy should come with us, too. There is something about him . . . he's intelligent, not like the pious, ignorant dirt farmers of the town. Like that other boy. All he wants to do is play, and be a nuisance.

No. I'm against it. I think you're still too weak to take him.

And I think you're jealous. If you have the girl, why shouldn't I have someone? Young enough to fashion in my image?

Ted said to Birka, "Well, what are you doing down here, then? I suppose there's a bunch of others like you. How do you do that, anyhow? Just float up there that way? Kind of like a big moth yourself."

Saying that, Ted felt a little bump of the heart, a tweaking of intuition—he suppressed the idea immediately, because he had the uneasy feeling that either of them could see inside his mind if they tried. ("We're not from the stars." But he hadn't said anything about his trip out to the cornfield, the strange footprints, the bits of metal some agency of the U.S. Government he never heard of before had confiscated by sunup.)

The creatures were drifting apart now, the big male rising as if in a subtle draft of air. Ted licked his dried, numbed lips, and tightened his grip on Marjory, who had become agitated, moving her head against his breast as if to see for herself the circusy spectacle; but her lids remained shut.

Duane said, "Don't let them get close to you, Ted! See those thorns they've got? They'll try to stab you in the back of the neck. That's what happened to Puff! Then she turned cold"—Duane whuffed a full cloud of breath—"and her hair fell out. She wasn't breathing. I swear! She just stopped breathing, but she was walking around, she *talked* to me, she wasn't dead."

Maybe I won't keep him after all.

It certainly doesn't matter that he knows. There's nothing he can do to stop you from turning him.

How are you going to get the girl away from the other one? Don't forget you're at a disadvantage. Those jagged rocks . . .

I'm leaving that up to Marjory. Watch.

''I don't know what Marjory has to do with you . . . people, but if you have any decency in you then you'll help me get her out of this cave, and to a hospital before she—''

The female was smiling at Ted, gently, but her eyes, so sharply blue moments ago, became vague, as if she were no longer listening, or even aware of him.

Marjory suddenly tore herself away from Ted and stood, teetering on the brink of the ledge.

''Birka!''

''Here, darling! Reach up.''

Ted tried frantically to get a firm grip on Marjory as she lifted her arms toward the hovering female, but something happened, like a furious burst of static in the mind that jammed his will and made him powerless to do anything but turn his own eyes slowly to the male, now staring him down with a ferocity that was enough to petrify his heart and bleed marrow from his bones.

I thought you could use some help.

Thank you. Just hold him there a little longer while . . . Theron, look out!

Birka's fingertips were on Marjory's own trembling fingers when Duane, rising from his knees on the ledge above Ted, grabbed the spiked flare from the porous rock where Ted had anchored it and dove toward Theron, blazing a smoky red path through an air carpet of moths and landing on Theron's back. For a few moments Theron wallowed helplessly, silently, as Duane clung to him with an arm locked around his throat; then the precious fabric that held them both in suspension blazed—first in little jet puffs, then a great gauzy flare. Singed and howling, Duane loosened his grip and plunged head-down into the pool. Ted, freed from the grip of Theron's mind, made a grab for Marjory but was too late; Birka had her, and was bearing her away.

Help me—I'm burning!

I'll burn, too!

Moths, Ted thought, looking at Theron as he tried to stay aloft on his crisping, shrinking wings, and then at Birka who, with Marjory limply in tow, pulled slowly away from the ledge on which he stood. He was astounded by her strength, the power of wings so easily destroyed: *Ain't nothing but overgrown moths, is all, and the worst thing that can happen to moths is to fly too close to an open flame.*

But there went Marjory, and what could he do?

Ted smelled human skin scorching, and Theron plummeted right in front of him, missing the ledge by a few inches, trailing sparky ribbons of tissue, residue of charred luna moths. He fell silently and made a deep pocket in the black water just as Duane's head appeared several feet away.

Without the flare, now dead in Duane's hand, the level of light in the cavern sank to the greenish glow of moths, like blips on a radar screen. Ted tore into his pack for more flares. Below him Theron struggled in the water, lips pressed tightly together, eyes furious. Ted popped another flare and looked down in the sizzling pink light. Theron was trying to get his hands on Duane, who kicked frantically away, looking up and around for Marjory. Theron, missing Duane, sank. It was obvious to Ted that the male couldn't swim and had no buoyancy. Something else he'd observed: in the cold they had brought with them his own breath had turned to vapor, but though the female had spoken, twice, she'd left no trace of breath in the frigid air around her. Cold, airless creatures. With no air in their lungs, unable to swim, they should be no better off than stones cast into the water. He waited, almost too long, for Theron's head to reappear and cancel this hunch, then called out to Duane.

"Marjory's going in! Get her!"

He popped a second flare and looked out over the

glaring pool where Birka seemed to drift without resistance, like a giant balloon aloft on the wind; now she was apparently holding Marjory around the waist. But it was difficult for Ted to distinguish a human form out there. They both were fringed with fluttering moths. The moths glowed supernaturally like a big green storm cloud twenty feet above the pool and just below the tips of clustered stalactites.

There appeared to be open water below the cloud, over the center of the pool. He knew he was about to risk Marjory's life, but what was the alternative?

Ted heaved a flare end-over-end into that pulsing cloud and saw the moths scatter precariously, some exploding in little bursts of flame as the thin fabric that gave the female power over gravity billowed from heat and burned in a flash. Within moments the fabric turned dark and vanished, except for flakes of char and another sickening odor as Birka, clasping Marjory, turned over once and fell head down. Unnaturally silent as they fell, together they made a huge splash—not the small splash he was dreading, which would have meant they'd fallen on something solid just beneath the surface, crushing Marjory.

Ted, already without his jacket, pulled off his sneakers, then stripped his pants and holstered revolver. He jumped feetfirst from the ledge, the way he'd been taught in life-saving classes, to protect himself as much as possible from unseen obstacles in unfamiliar water. He had nerved himself for cold water, but it was cold beyond his expectations. He came up gasping and struck out toward the middle of the pool. He heard Duane ahead of him, his voice echoing frantically through the cavern.

"I can't see! I lost my glasses! I don't know where they are!"

Theron, where are you? I'm in the water! Sinking! I can't

"Duane! I'm coming!"

can't swim   heavy   help   me

Birka   let the girl go   let her go!

Swimming furiously, Ted plowed into Duane and for a few moments both treaded water, face to face in the light of swirling moths. Singularly frail and mild in luminescence, by the hundreds they formed a storm-green tornado just above the surface and a dozen feet away from the heads of the swimmers. The draft from the flutter of all those wings was enough to nearly freeze their faces.

"That must be . . . where they went under!"

Ted didn't reply; he took a couple of hasty breaths and dived. Frog-kicked twice and found himself direc-tionless in ink. He bumped something hard with his left shoulder, veered and scraped by it painfully: a big sta-lagmite, perhaps, but in total, horrid darkness panic almost did him in and his left side was on fire, as if he'd scoured most of the skin off his ribs. On the other side of the stalagmite he had butted into, the water was translucently pale below the seething surface, a pillar of light cast into the depths and brilliant as moonbeams. Light fading into deathly quiet, melancholy depths, painted surrealistically with the shadows of other sta-lagmites, an underwater forest of knurled, fluted stone-work. He had the sensation of being in a vast aquarium. He saw, in the dreamy, phantom light, a wavering hand. It appeared—eight, perhaps ten feet down at the begin-ning of jet darkness—like an oddly shaped fish, then vanished as he kicked toward it. Ted couldn't be sure how deep he was. He felt pressure on his eardrums. He was more than a little out of shape, and, throat filling with liquid fire, already needing to breathe.

Sorry   little Marjory   I can't keep you   sorry you must die   and never know   us

Ted felt something on his ankle, a failed attempt to grasp, and with a jolt of fear he turned convulsively, quickly using up more of his precious store of oxygen.

It was Duane. He gestured emphatically where he meant to go and stroked away, powerful and fluid at these depths, a better swimmer than Ted. Duane was heading for one of the stalagmites, mountainous to Ted's eyes, faintly aglow at its tip where there was a murky disturbance in the water. Ted couldn't make out anything more, his lungs were bursting. He went straight up, to the surface.

Theron   sinking   why

No air   in our lungs   too heavy to float   hold on to something

Can't see   there's no light   so dark   worse than   the Black Sleep.   Save me   Theron

Ted's head broke the surface of the pool near the icy whirligig of moths; one of them stuck to his forehead and fluttered there; colder than the water itself, it made him feel as if he were being branded to the bone. His limbs were heavy, his mind lethargic, he couldn't seem to breathe deeply enough to get all the air he wanted. But Duane was still down there, somewhere, and so was Marjory. And so would they all be, if they stayed much longer in the water. The cold, he knew, killed with great subtlety. First the lack of focus, then the loss of momentum: unable to lift an arm for one last stroke . . . frightened and angered by his frailty and fear, Ted closed his throat and summoned the will to dive again.

Theron   please   ANSWER ME

Seven feet, ten feet down, to the limits of the light: and Ted could see nothing, no sign of either Marjory or Duane. How long had she been down? Confused and sick, he kicked out in the direction of a looming stalagmite, a twisted pillar of rock he hadn't noticed before.

He should be diving deeper, but what good would it do? Nothing was coming up from the black depths, not so much as a trace of bubbles. If Duane was far below, drowning, wouldn't there be bubbles? Ted came up too fast on the stalagmite and almost ran into it, slanted off to his right where the light still glimmered, a faint afterglow like that of a match in a dark arena, and collided gently with a dangling bare foot.

Ted looked up and saw two figures on the rugged side of the stalagmite. Inching upward slowly. Topmost was Duane, with Marjory by the hair. Exhausted, about to drown, not able to lift her another foot toward the vaguely glowing surface. About to lose his grip on the stalagmite and on Marjory as well. Ted thrust himself powerfully upward, hooked Marjory under a limp arm and kicked, wrenching her from Duane, gesturing with his free hand: *I've got her, go on.* He had a glimpse of Marjory's closed and silent face. Dead? He battled her weight, clawing at the water, and was amazed when she showed a little buoyancy. Unconscious when she went down, her mouth was closed if she hadn't taken on too much water, and if another cold plunge wasn't enough to shut down the brain, then there was a chance.

Above him, alongside the stalagmite that topped out a few inches below the surface, Duane emerged, choking but not drowning. When he could breathe and dive again he returned to help Ted. Finally they pushed her head up out of the water. Marjory's short blond hair was plastered around her face; by mothlight she was green as a mermaid.

"On her back," Ted gasped. "The ledge. Go."

He took one of Marjory's arms, Duane the other. They synchronized strokes and towed her doggedly, freezing and numb, and it seemed to be a very long swim until they reached the edge of the cavern where the flare burned at the heart of pink halos, a spot of welcome heat in the frigid cavern air. They were both trembling violently as they bumped and shoved and

dragged Marjory up to the ledge; there they laid her
out, funereally, on her back. Nothing flickered in her
dismally pale face. The pupil of a blue eye was rigidly
fixed. They gave her CPR, Ted massaging the heart,
Duane breathing for her. Ted counting, soon losing
track of how long they'd been at it. At least ten precious
minutes. In the intervals when Duane was back on his
heels, not breathing for Marjory, he stared dully at Ted,
his teeth chattering.

*Marjory? I'm sorry. Sorry we aren't together. It's very
dark down here. Different, though. Darkness, but not
the vile, disgusting darkness of the strangler fig. I don't
know how deep I am . . . but it's very deep, and I am
far from you. I can't move. Can't lift a finger. Oh my
soul, how long? Will it be this way, for Eternity? I'm
afraid of Eternity, without Theron. But I can't find him.
What did they do to Theron? I know you are still there.
Faintly, but there. I feel your spirit, Marjory. As long
as the spirit is alive, then it isn't too late, you can live,
too. So try, Marjory. And remember me. Always remember your loving Birka.*

Duane was about to fasten his mouth to Marjory's
again when something leaped in her, she twitched the
length of her body. Ted backed off, gasping, astonished. A hand flew up and then she raised her head hard
enough to split Duane's lip. Her face convulsed and he
heard a sound, almost like a toilet backing up; then she
heaved and vomited a gout of brackish water all over
Ted. He had to hold her tight to keep her from falling
off the ledge, propelled by the force of the spasms that
followed.

"Huh. Uh. Uhh!"

"God . . . Marjory . . . !"

"She's breathing!"

"God . . . don't believe . . . I didn't think . . ."

Ted wrapped his arms around her. She tried to talk,
but was incoherent. He was ecstatic, and frightened,

thinking of brain damage. But her lungs were working, her heart was going as she retched. Not over yet, Ted thought. Get her to a hospital. How long would it take Vedders to get back to them? If he'd made it out of the caves at all . . .

Marjory slumped, eyes half closed. She grimaced, turning her head, looking across the pool where the moths had scattered, wheeled big as gulls over the gently undulating surface.

"Birr—ka."

"It's okay, Marj. Honey. You don't have to talk. Help's coming soon, we'll get you out of here."

"Ted," Duane said, in a higher tone of voice than normal, and Ted twisted, arms still around Marjory, looked back and then down at Theron, climbing slowly out of the water toward them.

Marjory, eyes like fogged steel from shock, turned her head and saw him too, over Ted's shoulder. Her mouth opened wide but she shrieked no louder than a mouse.

Theron paused, one white hand on their ledge, all of his wide bony hairless head showing, his nearly lidless eyes deep in marble sockets. Three spread fingers on the ledge, and a gleaming black thorn.

Ted, shuddering, Marjory stiff in his arms, making her mouse-sound.

Theron! Where are you? Help me! Help me!

No. This is your fault, Birka. Stay there until I'm ready to forgive you.

Ted let an arm slip from around Marjory; he groped with his free hand for the holstered revolver he was half sitting on.

Theron reached up with his other hand, gripping rock, and lifted himself slowly, eyes on Ted, then on the nickeled revolver that Ted drew and cocked. He raised the hand with the thorn, palm out, a slow gesture of power and contempt.

"Humans," he said. "But I'm afraid I'm going to need you, for a little while."

"Need us . . . for what?" Already exhausted, he found it hard to speak, let alone deal with a monster.

"Ted," Duane said, his own voice low and tired, "there's . . . a lot of them. Like mummies in a cave. I saw them. Some kind of vine around . . . their necks. They need us to—untie them."

"Who—I mean, *what* are you?"

"We've had many names, in many places. *Huldufólk,* for one. *Huldufólk* will do. A bullet or two might disfigure me, for a while, but it's not harmful, not even painful."

"Where're you from, all of you . . . *huldufólk*?"

"From Paradise, actually."

"Long way . . . from Paradise. You know I'm not believing any of this. Or what . . . a bullet will or won't do when I pull the trigger."

"That's a yokel for you. Can't you think any better than that? Your young friend—Duane, is that correct?— is so much more intelligent. Let me try again, yokel. My name is Theron, eldest of the Four. Leader of all the . . . *huldufólk*. I'm not at my best right now, as you can see, but still I'm immortal, and on my worst day I have the strength to crush every bone in your body with three or four blows from my hand. Not my closed fist. Only my *hand*. Should I want to go to the trouble. *(Birka, be still!)* If I don't, then I have the power to make you crawl up the face of this rock and hang by one finger until you drop and kill yourself. You're very tired, yokel. At the very limits of your endurance already. I doubt that you have the strength to pull the trigger of your . . . what do you call it? Oh, it's a 're-volver.' So. Try it. Try what is left of your strength against mine . . ." *(Birka, I warn you! You don't know me as well as you think. I can be very harsh. There are*

*worse punishments than to spend a century or two in
those depths—Birka, no! You* BITCH!)

Marjory's head jerked, she gazed bleary-eyed at the
pool again, lips apart, listening intently.

"Ted," she said, clearly but in a voice that didn't
sound like Marjory at all, "aim for the thorn on his
hand."

Theron rose up in front of them, a fiend of wrath,
right hand swiping at her face.

Ted's gun bucked. His first shot hit Theron dead center in the palm of the right hand, diverting the blow that
would have broken half of the bones in Marjory's face.

He fired again, the light tricky, the fiend growing still
taller, looming over them. The force of the bullet took
out Theron's right eye and rocked his head back, rocked
him on the narrow ledge. His hands flailed the air as
he tried to balance himself.

Ted stood up suddenly, leaned over Marjory, stuck
the short muzzle of his Smith against Theron's right
hand and shot him again, mowing all three fingers mid-
way between the second and third knuckles and disin-
tegrating the wicked thorn.

For a couple of moments Theron was frozen on the
ledge, apelike toes gripping the rock as he stared with
his remaining eye at the devastation. Something welled
up out of the cavity where the thorn had been attached
to his hand; something that wasn't blood, liquid or partially frozen. It was darker, as slick and dark as oil
pouring from a rent in the earth, from a sunless, pri-
meval depth, and it smelled worse than decay. It welled
and then spouted furiously from the cavity as Ted
ducked, instinctively covering Marjory with his arms,
choking on the stenchy spray, the corrupt essence of
the eternally damned pouring from Theron's stark and
collapsing body. Theron, rooted to the rock, turned and
twisted in an agony of depletion, his bones snapping
and cracking like echoes of the gun. They all cowered

in the face of this furious, writhing transformation. His form, his link to humanness, was vanishing.

The pink light of the flare was diminished by another, kindlier light, from a canopy of moths congregating above their heads. All green, as growing things, with the eyespots of many animals in thick greenery watching, attending yet another banishment. The odor of corruption thinned as Theron writhed down on glowing rock, his once massive and hairless head shrunken, flattening, assuming a spadelike shape, darting in the air, bewildered and bereaved.

In the end there was nothing but the albino serpent, limp and motionless on the rock beside them until Ted rose shakily and kicked it sidelong into the pool. The water fluoresced hotly and bubbled for a time as the spent serpent drifted slowly downward, drifted out of sight.

The three of them were huddled together on the ledge when a shaft of light brilliant as the sun shone down from the jagged hole in the quartz above their heads, skimmed and sizzled on the quiet surface of the pool. Ted noticed that the moths were gone. He heard voices: rescuers, he presumed. He gave Marjory a reassuring hug; she stirred on his shoulder, sighed but didn't speak.

As for Duane, his eyes were on the pool; he continued to stare at the place where the serpent's remains had disappeared. He stared as if mesmerized by a magician's well-staged trick, trying to understand the slick deception, believing in his heart that it could not end so simply.

Somewhere, in some form, Theron survived. And they would all live to regret it.

OCTOBER, 1970:

Alastor and Enid

October 15, 1970

Hi, Duane, it's me again.

Can you believe it? First Jimi Hendrix, and now
Janis. When I heard about it I drove over to Rita
Sue's and borrowed my Joplin albums back. Natu-
rally they were scratched. Rita Sue said they were
scratched when she got them. I never will learn not
to loan her stuff, I guess. I was going to sit up all
night listening to Janis, and burn some incense, you
know?
   I wanted it to be a spiritual experience, not a
wake, a night I would remember for the rest of my
life. But I couldn't even make it through "Summer-
time." I don't mean I fell asleep, although I
was tired like I've been lately, worse than tired.
It's just that, aside from sorry, the same as I'd be
sorry if the mailman's wife died, I didn't feel anything really powerful. I don't know if it was Janis's
fault, for dying without having anything true or important to die for, or my fault because there's
something wrong with my character. Since I was a
little girl I've had this strong feeling that there are
an awful lot of people in the world whom I will
never meet, probably, but who are closer to me
than even my own sister, close spiritually, I mean.
Soul mates. I've had goosebumps sometimes, hearing a voice, seeing a face, maybe somebody famous
like Janis but not always. (Might even be somebody
not so famous with the initials D.E., who knows?)
The first time I heard Janis, I thought, wow, she's
exactly like me! Sort of on the homely side, mad
and fed up with all the dirty treacherous things going on in this world that she can't do much about,
but trying anyhow, letting it all hang out, making
them pay attention— That's me, Marjory Waller,
that's what I feel, what I'm all about, that's how I

*would do it if I could sing! I wrote her a couple of
letters once but you know how that is, all you get
back is a photo where it looks as if she halfway
tried to comb her hair, a photo somebody else
probably signed. But I didn't care. It was the spiritual aspect, the giving of love and knowing some
tiny part of that gift might get through to her even if
she never consciously realized it, that mattered.
Whatever I gave to Janis, whatever tiny cosmic
thing we shared, I guess it wasn't enough. That's
what got me so down, finally. That feeling of helplessness. Do I really count? Can I change anything? What difference does it make, if I love
somebody?*

*Well, Duane, I didn't intend to say all that,
didn't even know I was thinking it. Didn't intend to
write you another letter, for that matter. But it's
two letters you haven't answered and three phone
calls you haven't returned. Maybe I'm too stubborn
for my own good, or maybe all that went on between us, before Dante's Mill, didn't mean that
much to you, that it's a flaw you have I was never
aware of (because I had scales on my eyes, like
daddy used to say), a big flaw lots of boys have in
common, as I am learning to my sorrow. Anyway, in
baseball you get three strikes and this is it, Duane,
your third strike!!! After tonight I give up. I know
what Janis would do, I mean would've done, load
up on Southern Comfort and hotfoot it down there
to Franklin and do something smelly on your doorstep like you deserve. But she was from Texas and
I guess Texans are more crude than us Tennessee
Waller girls, who have a certain amount of dignity
to their names.*

*Okay, I read over what I just wrote, and I'll
leave it in, about your being flawed; I guess none
of us are very perfect, are we? I realize it might be
something else: maybe you're as scared as I am.*

Or worse scared, because so much happened you couldn't tell anybody about. If that's the story, morning glory, okay, I understand. I don't blame you for not wanting to see me again, particularly if there's a curse on our heads (I mean on Enid's and Marjory Waller's heads), which, not only because of the stuff that was in the papers and the dreams I've been having, but because of other

I don't know how to say it so anything makes sense. God, this letter is getting to be such a mess! It would be so much easier to talk to you.

Try again. Maybe I'll do better if I just go back to the beginning, put it all down, what I actually remember, what's just a lot of spooky shadows. Bear with me? That is, if I'm not already in the wastebasket after that remark about your doorstep.

Hospitals. They give me the creeps, even nice modern ones like Wingo County Memorial. Which, of course, is where I woke up almost exactly seventy-two hours after we left my house for a Saturday picnic. Lucky to wake up at all, I guess, and not be a vegetable. I thought we'd all been in a car wreck or something. I might've freaked out, except for all that medication dripping into my veins: hypothermia, then high fevers, a convulsion or two, cardiac arrest, but you know what I'm talking about: I know you weren't in much better shape except I don't think your heart stopped until you got home and decided to stay away from Marjory Waller forever—there I go again. Maybe my brain is part freeze-dried turnip after all.

Still paying attention? Okay, once they allowed I was well enough to sit up in bed and shuffle nine steps to the pottie by myself, and Ted and Enid and a couple of doctors answered my questions, like, where's Duane (parents had him transferred to that private hospital in Nashville because of all the satan-cult stuff in the papers) and Rita Sue (nothing bad ever happens to Rita Sue; I've always thought that hysterics were good for her complexion), and Boyce—I'll get back to Boyce—then they figured I was strong enough to answer some questions myself. The TBI guys came around (one of them was kind of cute, like Paul Newman with blackheads, but I digress), and I told them at least twenty times what I knew: that I got lost in a cave after looking for you and Puff, who were looking for Arne Horsfall, the Grundig radio thief. You found me, but we took a bath by accident in some very cold water, and both of us had to be rescued. Three dumb kids getting lost in a cave, and unlucky Puff is still lost, which I know is not your fault. And that's it.

Except for getting scared purple-pissless that night at Wingo Memorial when those TV maniacs got into my room somehow and woke me up shining bright lights in my eyes and this woman with a microphone and porcelain teeth was smiling at me and asking me what I knew about the mass execution of the old-time folk of Dante's Mill and satan cults and ritual mutilation of animals like the one Boyce finished off with a golf club on the porch of the park lodge. How would I know anything about that? But it may have something to do with the case of the spooks I'm having lately, and Rita Sue and Boyce splitting up and the funk he's been in (he was intercepted five times the other night at Waynesboro, and they beat us 19–zip).

Maybe I should digress again. They say now (they being adults with all kinds of impressive initials before and after their names, signifying how much more qualified they are to be idiots than the rest of us common people) that it was some kind of poor mutant albino bear cub that got into the lodge looking for food after its mother abandoned it. Good thinking on the part of the mother, I'd say, but you know something? It's bs. Nobody really

*knows what it was, and thanks to the incompetence
of some other expert who took the thing away in a
plastic tarp afterward and then "misplaced" it,
we'll never know for sure, will we? Rita Sue says I
ought to be glad I was somewhere else drowning in
the dark at the time, and didn't see it.*

*But I've got news for Rita Sue: I've seen worse
since. And you're the first one I've told. Because
somehow I have enough confidence left in you to
hope you won't think I'm crazy.*

*You know about Arne Horsfall and how Enid met
him. How upset she was when he disappeared, like
it was all her fault. What happened to him in the
woods at Dante's Mill was horrible; I don't know
how anybody, even devil worshipers, or ordinary
homicidal freaks stoned out of their skulls like the
Manson gang, could have done what they did to
Mr. Horsfall and that other guy, the hippie from
Florida who was traveling with Puff. But Enid's de-
termined to feel guilty about that too, maybe for the
rest of her life. She held a memorial service for Mr.
Horsfall at Cumberland State, then went into a
funk that makes Boyce Bledsoe seem positively
giddy. I have to make her talk to me at the supper
table, force her to eat a few bites. She doesn't feel
like going to work. From what shows up in the
laundry basket, she's not changing her unmentionables very often. That is not like Enid!!! She sleeps,
this is no lie, fifteen or sixteen hours a day. When
she's not sleeping, she stays in her room with the
door shut, drawing. She's had me bring her a couple dozen charcoal pencils and five bottles of white
shoe polish from K-Mart—but I'll get to that, what
she's been doing with all the shoe polish. Poor Ted,
he's tried and tried to snap Enid out of it, but he's
been at his wit's end all week. Yesterday he gave
up and said he was going on a hunting trip, good-
bye! I thought deer season started in November. But*

*I don't blame Ted. He can't stand seeing her like
this, either. The last few years us Wallers have
been poor as churchmice, but if I hadn't lucked
into that job at the Toddler Shop, we wouldn't have
a dime in the house. Or electricity. Does Enid
care? I know I must be boring you with all this.
The point is, I'm worried sick she's had a nervous
breakdown. It's getting chilly now with fall around
the corner, but she sleeps on top of the covers in a
flimsy nightgown, if she bothers with a nightgown at
all, and with the windows wide open. I tiptoe in
and shut them, an hour later they're all open
again. Her complexion's bad and her hair's starting
to fall out—found a hunk of it under the washbasin
today. Until a month ago, my sister was Miss
America material! And it's not just her looks. Two
nights ago I woke up (not that I've been doing much
sleeping myself) and checked on Enid, which I do
three or four times a night. She wasn't in her room.
You probably noticed there was a full moon yesterday. So it was as bright as twilight on the lawn at
one in the morning. And there she was, not a stitch
on, ribs sticking out, hair like a mare's nest, just
wandering around with the cats and looking up at
the sky like she'd totally flipped! Maybe I'm not doing the right thing, waiting and hoping she'll come
out of it by herself. Oh, God. Maybe what she
needs is a stay at Cumberland State. Maybe you'll
think we both do, when I tell you what happened,
what I saw, last night.*

*I don't think I ever showed you a portrait that
Arne Horsfall did for one of Enid's art classes at
the funny farm. "Portrait" is probably not the
word. It's a woman, I assume, but she has no
hair—no eyebrows, either. Her face is white, like
liquid shoe polish, which is what he used for paint,
and her eyes are pale blue, the only spots of color
in the picture. She's holding her head with both*

hands, and screaming, I guess—it looks like she's
totally wigged out. That's all. No, I forgot one de-
tail. The little finger on one hand is black and
pointed, like a thorn. I hate that picture. The first
time I ever saw it, I told Enid she better had throw
it away. But it's still in her room, and Enid's
painted maybe sixteen more that are like it, only
better than Mr. Horsfall could hope to do: naked,
hairless shoe-polish people, surrounded by (I hope
you're ready for this) hundreds of luna moths!! Remember that night we prowled around the yard
looking for cocoons? I guess I shouldn't be surprised that we've got lunas again, if only for deco-
ration, or whatever reason Enid had for drawing
them.

What I have is bad dreams: of caves, and shoe-
polish people who glow in the dark, and other shoe-
polish people, lying on the floor in one of those
caves with a lot of holes in the walls. Only this
time they're black instead of white, blacker than
any negro I've ever seen! Black, I guess, because
they've been burned to death, like mama and
Daddy Lee in the train accident. I wake up shaking, Duane, and I swear I can't calm down for at
least an hour after one of those. I've probably had
the cave dreams six times in the past two weeks,
and I had them when I was in the hospital, too.

Last night I dreamed something else, for a
change. It's embarrassing, but I need to tell you.

When I finally doze off after feeling so awful
about Janis, I'm dreaming about being naked too,
and flying in some strange place where there are
volcanoes and glaciers but no trees, flying with a
bunch of shoe-polish people who are friends of
mine. The white ones. Not such a bad dream, at
first: flying's a lot of fun. The trouble is, God
doesn't like us. I don't know why. But he's angry,
and the weather gets rough. There's lightning all

around the sky, and suddenly I'm up there alone, my flying friends are gone. Then I simply forget how to fly. Falling is not fun!!! The volcanoes are gone, nothing but trees below, and I crash through one of them to the ground. I don't die. You can't die in dreams, can you? But it's real hairy anyway. Knocks the breath out of me. The next thing I know, there you are! Good old Duane. It's kind of a tropical place, palm trees and Africa critters. Giraffes. Spotted cats hiding in the long grass. The sun's very bright; I don't know why, but I'm afraid of the sun. Afraid of being burned. But I'm in the shade, lying flat on my back. I can see perfectly well, I just can't move. I'm frozen. My toes, fingers, bubbies, everything. Frozen solid, can't draw a breath. There's something around my neck too, choking me, but you untie it and pull it off. It's a big green vine, Duane, which you put in your pants pocket just as it's turning into a snake. You don't want me to see that, but I do see it—

And then I woke up in a corner of my bed against the wall . . . and I was . . . I just decided not to tell you the most embarrassing part.

This was last night, or today I guess. About three in the morning. When I say I woke up, it wasn't all the way awake. I was really groggy, out of it. I went to the bathroom to get a drink of water. Then I heard Enid. Talking in her room. Or someone else talking: kind of a childish voice. I walked down the hall and the closer I came to Enid's room, the colder I was. I could see my breath. When I opened the door I swear it must have been below freezing inside. Sort of foggy, like the inside of a big meat locker. The windows were wide open, as usual. Enid was on the bed and she looked unconscious, not asleep. I saw something move; it leaped off the floor on the other side of Enid's bed, tangled in a sheet, and hopped twice. God, it scared me! It

*jumped on a windowsill, leaving the sheet be-
hind. I saw it hanging from the sill for a couple of
seconds with both hands, or paws—I couldn't tell
which. It looked a little like one of Enid's portraits
she has all over her walls, but much smaller. Then
it jumped into the tree in front; it was just a quick
white blur in the dark. Another albino mutant bear
cub? Or something that might be even worse? I
know I was wide awake by then, but Lord, I sure
hope I was hallucinating!!! I'm so used to looking
at those creepy people Enid draws, seeing them
again in my dreams, it's probably affected my
mind. I just can't be sure what I saw was real. I
know I had a heck of a time waking Enid up. She's
. . . it's as if she's slipping away from us, a little
more every day. Duane, what's happening to us is
so awful! We don't deserve this. Beginning tonight,
I'm going to take my sleeping bag to Enid's room,
and stay with her. I'll make sure the windows stay
closed. When Ted gets back from his hunting trip, if
she isn't better, then we'll drive her straight to
Cumberland State Hospital. There must be a doctor
smart enough to figure out what's happening to her,
who can make her well.*

*This letter is getting too long. My hand's
cramped from writing. I need to get some home-
work done. Almost seven o'clock, and nearly dark
out already. I'd better try to get Enid to eat something. Don't have any appetite myself. Duane, I
wish*

Oh, never mind.

Your friend,

1

Three days after Marjory mailed her last letter to Duane, he found it, by accident, and read it.

He was baby-sitting, on a Friday night, for his four-year-old half sister Raybeth and another little girl from next door, Emmy McClure. Duane's stepmother, Nannie Dell, a civic-minded woman, had gone to a Williamson County Planning Board hearing that had to do with traffic on their street and the need for four-way stop signs. The two girls were at that age where they could be a real handful. Now that it was getting dark and also pretty cold by seven in the evening, Duane couldn't keep them outdoors on the swings and in the sandbox, and there was nothing on TV that interested them. So they chased around the house and he tried to keep track of them while reading a couple of chapters of *Moby-Dick,* a novel he found nearly impenetrable but had to do a lengthy report on over the weekend.

After a prolonged silence that made him uneasy, Duane called from the living room, "Raybeth, where are you?"

"Inna kitchen."

"What're you doing in the kitchen?"

"Cookies."

Emmy giggled. Raybeth whispered something. Duane put the novel down on the living room couch and strolled to the kitchen. The girls had opened a box of cinnamon graham crackers and poured glasses of milk for themselves, but somebody's hand wasn't too steady; milk was dripping off the dinette table to the floor. They were trying to clean up the puddles with dish towels.

"Was a accident," Raybeth said. She had a way of looking at him with her lower lip stuck out that made him want to laugh, but Raybeth had no sense of humor and if he laughed or even smiled at her when she had the guilts, she would kick him in the shins. Then he would hang her upside down by the ankles and threaten to shake her until her blue eyes dropped out of her head like marbles. When Duane did that, it always got back to Nannie Dell, who would then give him a well-reasoned, patient lecture on all the damage that might result from blood rushing to Raybeth's teeny brain. He didn't enjoy the lectures, but there was no arguing with Nannie Dell. There was no arguing with Patience and Virtue. Besides, she always defended him in conflicts with his father, when John Wesley Eggleston was in one of his prickly, hypercritical moods.

"I'll do that," Duane said. "Eat your cookies."

He wrung out both towels in the sink, rinsed them, and finished wiping the table. They'd emptied the half-gallon milk carton, so he carried it to the flip-top garbage can by the back door. The garbage can was lined with a brown paper sack from Kroger's, and it was full. Might as well carry the sack outside to the galvanized garbage cans by the garage. When he picked it up the bottom of the paper sack, which was soggy, opened, and three days' worth of garbage dumped on the floor.

The girls shrieked with laughter.

"Duane made a mess!"

The back of Duane's neck got red, but he didn't say anything. Eggshells, coffee grounds, sparerib bones, grease, *shit*. A fat white envelope, sealed with Scotch tape, that looked as if it hadn't been opened. Curious, he picked it up, pulled off a teabag that was sticking to the flap, and turned it over. The letter, dated the fifteenth, was from Marjory. Duane was jolted. What was *his* letter doing in the garbage? Had Nannie Dell thrown it out accidentally? No way, she paid the household bills and kept meticulous files. She never threw away any legitimate piece of correspondence. If the letter was in the garbage, it was there on purpose.

He put the letter on the sink counter and got out the dust pan, loaded a fresh paper bag with the garbage and carried it outside, frowning, pulse tingling in his wrist.

"Read us a *story*!" Raybeth demanded when he returned. Four was a very demanding age.

"When I get ready, badbreath," Duane said sulkily.

"Mommy said don't *ever* call me that!"

"Put a lid on it, Raybeth. Go up to your room and pick out a storybook and I'll be there in a minute."

When the girls were out of the kitchen Duane slit the envelope and read the letter standing up against the sink. He was incredulous at first, then angry. Then so frightened he couldn't breathe right.

"Duane! You said!"

"Raybeth, I'm coming. Just wait a minute! Play with your Play-Doh or something."

There was a telephone in the kitchen. Duane looked in his wallet for Marjory's phone number. His hands were trembling, he had to dial twice.

It rang nineteen times before he gave up. Duane chewed his lip. His face was hot. He picked up the receiver again, glancing at the wall clock. It was a quarter to nine. He was supposed to have put the girls down for the night at eight-thirty. He dialed information for Sublimity, Tennessee, and eventually was connected to the sheriff's department.

"I need to get hold of one of your deputies, Ted Lufford."

"Deputy Lufford is off this week."

"Can I call him at home? What's the number?"

"Son, we don't give out that information."

"Well, could *you* call him for me, and ask him to get back to me? My name's Duane Eggleston, and I live in Franklin, Tennessee. Look, this is very, *very* important.''

While he waited to hear from Ted, Duane went upstairs, still tingling from apprehension.

''We want to take a bath.''

''All right, I'll run your bathwater.''

The phone rang while the girls were splashing in the tub with thirty-nine plastic toys. Duane ran down the hall to his parents' room and took the call there.

''Mr. Eggleston? This is Deputy Purloe of the Caskey County Sheriff's Department. You asked me to relay a message that you wanted to get in touch with Deputy Lufford? I'm sorry, but we're told he's out of town and won't be back until Sunday night.''

''Thank you,'' Duane said, swallowing hard. He hung up and thought, *Boyce.*

''Duane, we're ready to get out of the tub now!''

''Yeh, hold on, I'm coming.''

It was nine-thirty by the time he had them in bed in Raybeth's room. She held him to his promise to read a storybook.

''You're reading too *fast*.''

Duane took a breath and read more slowly, fussed with their blankets, left a night-light on, and said as he closed the door, ''No talking.'' He ran back down the hall to the telephone.

'' 'Lo?''

''Hey, Boyce, this's Duane!''

''This isn't Boyce, it's Lamar.''

''Oh, yeh, hey, how're you doing, Lamar? Your voice change since I saw you last? Is he home, I really need to talk to—''

''Naw, the football team's in Lebanon, they won't none of 'em be back until after midnight.''

''Oh, football game, must be where everybody is tonight, I couldn't get hold of—''

''I'd be there too, but I'm grounded.''

"Yeh, well, good talking to you, Lamar, have Boyce call me. I don't care what time he gets in."

Duane hung up. The furnace was on but he felt chilly, a little nauseated. He tried Marjory's house again, with no results.

That didn't leave many options, Duane thought. Call the Caskey County Sheriff's Department one more time, have them go by the house.

What's it about, sir?

Well, I think—I mean it could be—it has to do with—just go look, goddammit, they could be dead! Or—worse.

Duane heard Nannie Dell on the front porch, saying good night to the neighbor who had given her a lift to the Planning Board meeting. His father was out of town on business. The family car, a Buick Riviera, was in the garage, but Nannie Dell couldn't drive. Duane's father wouldn't teach her. He liked having her as close to the house as possible at all times.

Their bedroom was strictly off-limits to Duane, although not to Raybeth. He was not allowed in there for any reason.

He heard Nannie Dell call cheerfully, "Duane!" as she came in the front door. He sat rigidly on the side of the high bed with the hand-pieced Appalachian star-pattern quilt and didn't answer.

Nannie Dell walked up the stairs and turned down the hall to Raybeth's room. All was peaceful there. She walked back to her own room, opened the door, and stopped short.

"Why, Duane."

He just stared at her. She was wearing a gray skirt and burnt-orange sweater, and, as usual, thickly braided pigtails that came down over her shoulders and hung, perfectly straight and glossy, below her breasts. She had a clasp envelope in one hand. She was unaccustomed to Duane staring at her; open hostility on his part was unheard of. Nannie Dell moistened her full unpainted lips and decided to smile, a trifle sternly.

"I believe you know you're not supposed to be in here. What—is something wrong?"

"Yes."

"Well—whatever it is, you look terribly upset. Why don't you give me a few minutes, and then we'll have a talk about—"

Duane pulled Marjory's letter from inside his denim jacket and just held it, not taking his eyes off Nannie Dell. She batted her thick lashes a few times, and pursed her lips.

"This is a letter from Marjory Waller," Duane said in a low voice, gravelly from anger. "She's written me three letters in the past couple of months. She's called, too. What happened to those letters? Why didn't you tell me Marjory called?"

Nannie Dell took a deep, thoughtful breath, summoning Patience, alerting Virtue. She put her envelope aside and joined her hands, not quite prayerfully, in front of her.

"Well, Duane—" she began.

Duane sprang off the bed, thrusting the letter at Nannie Dell, who swayed back, mouth ajar.

"I want to know where you get the nerve to throw a letter addressed to me in the *fucking garbage*!"

"Duh . . . waaaayne!"

He began to sob. "I put up with everything else . . . around here, all of *his* shit, but not you . . . I really liked you! Don't you know what you've *done*, Nannie Dell?"

"Duane, you'll wake the children."

"I don't care! You can't treat me this way! I can't get hold of Marjory! I know she's in terrible trouble, but what am I supposed to *do*?"

"Duane, John Wesley and I . . . all those awful things happened, and it was on *television*, and they made it seem like—you were some sort of delinquent, and after what happened with that car—don't you see, for your own good he just didn't want you *involved* in anything else, *involved* with that girl we know nothing about! I'm sure when you think about it, you'll appreciate that he was only protecting—''

Duane turned away from Nannie Dell, face contorted, sobbing, humiliated and powerless. ''That son of a bitch. Son of a bitch, I fucking *hate* him, you hear me?''

''Duane, you may not ever, *ever* speak about John Wesley again in that—''

''That's fine! I won't! I won't talk about him, or to him! I've *had* it!''

Tears flowed down Nannie Dell's flawless cheeks. ''Duane, you don't mean it. I'm sorry . . . I knew it was wrong, but it's what John Wesley wanted me to do. I'm a Christian woman. I can't defy my husband. Duane, I'm sure if we approach this problem in a prayerful manner, everything will be—''

''No it won't.'' He stared at her, blinking away tears. ''If you ever saw what I saw when I was in that cave, your tongue would stick to the roof of your mouth. You'd never pray again, Nannie Dell, because you'd know it wouldn't be any damn use.''

Duane sagged. He sniffed a couple of times, and then a fresh spate of crying drove him out of her room and to his own room, where he had the presence of mind to lock the door behind him before he fell on his bed with his face deep in a pillow, so deep he couldn't hear Nannie Dell pleading with him outside in the hall, and she couldn't hear his sobs.

2

About ten-thirty they saw the lights of the pickup truck coming along the winding track in the Evernola National Forest, and the two cavers who had been hunkered down beside a campfire got up to stretch and throw away what cold coffee was left in their tin mugs. The driver of the pickup flashed his spotlight on the campsite and they signaled back with their hands in the glare.

There were three men crowded into the front seat of the pickup, which belonged to Wingo County Deputy Sheriff Wayne Buck Vedders. The other men were Ted Lufford and his first cousin, an explosives expert named Bill Whipkey, Jr. Ted introduced them to the cavers, two men in their thirties who preferred not to give their last names. The cavers were both undersized men, dirty, smelly, and bearded. They wore orange coveralls and pockmarked metal helmets with carbide lamps. They'd been underground for the better part of five days.

The caver who called himself Rex unrolled a hand-drawn map and said to them, "Maybe found what you're looking for. It's a big room, about three thousand feet from where we're standing right now. Honeycomb walls, some kind of hairy stuff all over the floor." Ted nodded. "Boogers, too. How many boogers you reckon, Alvy?"

"I must've counted two dozen boogers. Scariest sight I ever seen in my life."

"Naw, the scary part was when that radio cut loose. All them voices screaming." Rex laughed uneasily. "I thought sure the boogers was after us. I don't have much hair on my head, but I know all the hair around my peter done turned white. Hell, it shrunk up so bad I can't even *find* my peter no more.''

Vedders said, ''You need to see one flitting around, that'll set you up for a coronary anytime.''

Rex said, ''What the hell they be?''

''All we're sure about,'' Ted explained, ''is that they are something purely unnatural we don't want running around aboveground. And the first of next week the state proposes to start pulling the boogers out of that cave and giving them what they call a proper burial.''

''Seen 'em yourself, Deputy?''

''No, but they were well described to me.''

The caver named Alvy watched Whipkey unload his gear from the back of the pickup. ''Shit. If he's got nitroglycerin, then you can count me out of this party.''

''It's all plastic,'' Ted assured him. ''Billy's just back from two years of blowing gook tunnels in Veet Nam.''

''That's good. 'Cause it's three or four vertical drops and a couple of muddy squeezes afore we get to where you want to go.''

''What's a squeeze?'' Vedders asked.

Alvy grinned. The front of his mouth was all but toothless. ''A squeeze is a hole in the rock that's about twice as tight as your Aunt Minnie's asshole. Can't get through on your hands and knees; got to wriggle. The ceiling drips like a pisser most everywhere, and the humidity's a hundred percent. That's the bad news. The good news is we didn't see no transparent alligators. Them kind can be a bother.''

Bill Whipkey came over to the group around the campfire carrying his backpack by the straps, and an unwrapped loaf of plastic explosive in the other hand.

''I ain't much for crawling on my belly. I travel first class when I go, and this stuff's my ticket.''

Rex, looking at the plastic, shook his head woefully. ''Ever make any mistakes?''

"Still waiting on my first."

"How's your peter hanging now?" Ted asked Rex.

"It's hangin' out the back," Rex said.

3

By eleven o'clock Nannie Dell, an early-to-bed person and a sound sleeper even without her husband there, was no longer a problem to Duane.

In the kitchen he made another try at getting Marjory on the phone, although instinctively he was sure it would be no use. Hearing the phone ring and ring in their house in Sublimity just gave impetus to his panic. He hung up and went outside to his workroom in the detached garage.

Here he kept everything Nannie Dell wouldn't let into the house: live scorpions in their own terrarium, two tarantulas, more than two hundred specimens of butterflies and moths mounted on dark blue velvet in glass-topped cases he had made himself, various husks and cocoons and dried salamanders and rodent skulls, and an open-top box with smoked-glass panels that contained beetles. He was currently rejiggering the diurnal cycles of a few of the beetles. Over the two plywood-and-sawhorse tables which contained his collections several sunlamps were mounted on a grid. At one end of a table books were piled in two untidy stacks.

He rummaged under the table in a cardboard carton that contained several types of nets, killing jars, and a half-gallon can of carbon tetrachloride. In another area of the garage he located an old-fashioned plunger-action squirt gun for killing garden pests. This he filled with the carbon tet.

He paused for a few moments, suddenly blank and remote, gazing at the leafy spread wings of two luna moths pinned side by side in one of his cases. Ruddy eyespots glowed in the light of a sunlamp overhead. Duane began to shudder, as if the temperature in the garage just out of the sunlamp's range had fallen precipitously.

Marjory hadn't said anything about the presence of real moths in her letter, so maybe he shouldn't—

Bullshit. Pain smote him in the pit of his stomach; his mouth twisted from remorse and dismay. He didn't want, was mortally afraid to go, to expose himself again to the dreadful white floating creatures with pale, grim eyes, their stares that blighted the soul as frostbite withered skin. This time—

No. *This time he was prepared for them.* Marjory, whom he had told nothing, left defenseless, had no hope at all without him. Assuming he wasn't too late already.

Duane knew where the keys to the Buick Riviera would be: in the top drawer of his father's dresser. And he knew, without going near her door, that Nannie Dell had locked it tonight. He had scared her with his anger, and the other threat that had always been there, unacknowledged, his sexual desire for Nannie Dell. Waiting for her on her own bed, then shouting at her, profanely, it was a form of rape, although no more than Nannie Dell deserved and she had known it. He had read her guilt and shame in her eyes and weak gestures, read into abject helplessness that she cared more for him than his father, but this, instead of mollifying him, had made Duane feel all the more aggressive toward her— brutally, dangerously, aroused. A revelation more potent than Christ in both their lives.

He didn't need any goddamn keys! Taking his father's car without them, in effect stealing it, would be a final act of defiance, of resignation from the family. His father would kick him out of the house anyway once he got home and heard what Nannie Dell had to say. So he would travel to Sublimity, and by morning, if he lived to see another sunrise, he would be well on his way beyond Tennessee. Grief bulked in Duane's throat, but he couldn't shed any more tears.

It took him about ninety seconds to strip the ignition wires and start the Buick. At five after eleven he was traveling north on 31 toward Brentwood and Nashville, staying off the Interstate because he urgently wanted to push it, knowing that the last thing he needed tonight was to be pulled over and hauled off to jail again.

4

The cavers had distributed kneepads to Ted Lufford and his party. They had marked the passages below, knew where they were going, and had brought equipment appropriate to the rugged underground terrain, including rope ladders, which made their descent into the byways of the Dante's Mill cavern easier for the novices.

Pausing to rest and grab a smoke on a ledge partway down a 110-foot cliff, Bill Whipkey looked around a stark cave which Rex had already named the Dragon's Mouth on his map. Every time one of them changed his position on the ledge or turned his head, their far-flung shadows leaped or receded on the gnarled walls and curiously slanted stalactites, like jagged teeth, that had earned the cave its name.

"Never saw anything like this in Nam. Heard there

was some such caves up around the boundary with Laos. Haunted, they said.''

"You looking for haunts, you ain't gonna be disappointed," Alvy informed him.

"Just what do these boogers resemble? Bats?"

"Mummies," Ted replied. "Nigger mummies."

"Oh. Well, that ain't nothing. Maybe that particular cave's just where a Indian tribe did their burying a long time ago."

"You won't think it's nothing when they get up and walk at you," Wayne Buck Vedders said, his perfectly round eyes giving him a look of intense credulity. "Except they don't walk. They creep along upside down on the ceiling."

Rex laughed and then had a coughing fit. "You seen that, did you?"

"Damn right we did, me and Lufford. It was like a five- or six-year-old kid. He was just full of sass, too."

"Oh, he talked to you?" Alvy said. "Did you paddle his britches for him, Deputy?"

"No, I shot him in the head. It didn't even slow him down."

Nobody said anything for several seconds.

Rex stubbed his cigarette out, and put the butt into a pocket of his vest. "Where did he go then?"

"Can't say for certain. I allow he's still around."

"Wonder why I never heard none of this before me and Alvy volunteered to come down here?"

Alvy snorted and said to Vedders, "Reckon you got a right to jerk off all you want to, don't make me no neverminds. Just don't splash none of it on me when you're fixin' to come."

Vedders smiled and opened his jacket and drew an enormous revolver from a shoulder holster. "This here's all I jerk off with."

"Lordy, Lordy," Rex said in a jesting tone, "we're all friends here."

"Shoot that thing off inside, hoss, and we'll all be deaf," Alvy said.

"Naw, I learned my lesson last time. Pulled some of the powder, and changed the cartridges. These here are full mercury loads."

"What does that do?"

"I tried them loads on a couple of four-pound rabbits at thirty yards, and there wasn't nothing left of either of 'em but paws and the tips of their ears."

Rex yawned and got up from his crouch. "Gen'mens, it's been purely delightful. But we got us a ways to go yet."

5

Duane couldn't remember the way to Marjory's house and had to ask directions at a Gulf station when he reached Sublimity.

It was seven minutes to twelve when he drove slowly down Old Forge Road and turned into the long gravel drive. A porch light was burning, which made him feel a little better, and Marjory's old car, the rustbucket '62 Plymouth, was parked at the end of the drive near the back porch. He didn't see Enid's car.

He stopped at the edge of the front porch and got out, looking at the house. Except for the porch light, the house was dark in front. They had to be asleep. One of the cats, he didn't know which, looked at him with liquid blazing eyes and slipped under the railing as he approached the steps. Ears of dried corn and a crepe-paper Halloween black cat decorated the front door. He opened the screen and twisted the handle of the manual bell, hearing it ring inside. The porch light glazed the floor of the foyer and showed him the first couple of steps, but the rest of the staircase was dark. He was jittery and had a headache from driving at night; his glasses needed changing again. He needed to go to the bathroom. Should have used the men's room at the Gulf station. *Hi, Marjory, how've you been, I really need to take a piss.*

Hoping for a light to go on in the upstairs hall, Marjory or Enid calling down, everything okay then, he'd stay a few minutes, hit the road, come *on,* Marj. He twisted the bell-pull again, his breath fogging the outside of the glass. The house so still. Cold. Cold seemed to radiate from within, penetrating his buttoned-up denim jacket. Duane shuddered. His hand dropped from the bell-pull to the doorknob, jerked away. *Very cold.* He tried again. The door was locked.

He walked along the porch, cupping his hands, peering in at the windows. Saw only the shapes of furniture in the parlor and dining room, the low gloss on polished wood from the porch light. Silence. Duane retreated, slowly, back down the steps. The corner room on the right, upstairs, was Enid's room. Marjory's bedroom was on the back, overlooking the gazebo and pond.

Duane, gritting his teeth against the midnight shudders and the urgent warnings from his bladder, walked around the house toward the back porch, paused where he couldn't be seen from the road (but no one had come by in the last five minutes, and only the roof of Crudup's barn was visible against the radiant sky from where he stood). He gushed on flowers already frost-killed, wondering what he was going to do next, as if he had a choice: his criminal career would be well advanced before the night was over.

Marjory could be anywhere: spending the night with Rita Sue, for instance. Or she could be sound asleep upstairs and oblivious of the bell. But why was the house so cold? He sensed it was below freezing in there, while the temperature outside was only about 45 degrees.

Duane zipped up and started toward the back porch, remembered something and returned to his father's Buick. He had left the engine running. As he opened a back door a shadow swooped behind him and was repeated on the flash of moving glass in the window. Duane ducked, throwing up an arm.

It grazed the back of his hand, a cold burning sensation, and winged gracefully away, pale green in the moonlight, the eyespots aglow. Luna moth. There seemed to be more of them, flaky silhouettes in the moonlight above the woods on one side of the property, where the weedy show-horse ring and unused stables were located.

Duane reached into the backseat and snatched up the spray gun that reeked of carbon tetrachloride. He didn't take his eyes off the sky, expecting more, perhaps the largest nightflyers of them all with their mock-wings made from human skin. His throat had dried up, his heart was a stone, his fingers, his face, felt numbed and bloodless.

He had forgotten about breaking into the house; he was certain now that it was empty. His eyes were on the graceful moths, the frost-white roof of the stable by the shining pond. He walked slowly toward the low building. Halfway there his feet began to crunch in frozen grass, to leave sharply etched prints. His breath condensed hugely in the windless air, surrounding him, accompanying him like ghosts.

Suddenly there were other footprints in the grass, converging from a dirt path that led to the house, going toward the stables. Duane paused. He could distinguish at least two sets of prints, one of them made by a child. The other foot was small too, more like a woman's. Neither of them wore shoes.

And in the midst of the welter of footprints there was a swath, as if something heavy had been dragged from the house to the stables by the barefoot woman and the child.

His shuddering was like spasms, like a seizure; cold as he was, Duane still felt a sharp tingling shock at the top of his spine. There was a soft sifting noise in the windless night, the wings of many moths fluttering. From far off he heard the mournful horn of a diesel engine. He heard the soft slap of a screen door fifty yards behind him. He whirled.

She was standing there on the lower steps of the back porch, staring at him. Wearing dark clothing, a jacket with a hood pulled up. He couldn't see her eyes or face in the dark, but he thought he knew her anyway.

"Enid!"

His voice, carrying a long way on this still night, prompted a dog to bark across the pond. Duane started toward the house but stumbled, his toes numbed in the moccasins he wore. He went down on one knee, a sudden jabbing pain, and got up awkwardly, hobbled, looking for Enid again.

He saw her running, not to him but to the Buick he'd left in the driveway with the engine running. It looked to Duane as if her feet were bare, but he couldn't be sure.

"Enid, wait! Where's—"

She got into the Buick as he began to run, too. She didn't hesitate. The headlights came on, the car began backing, tentatively at first, veering toward the front porch as if she didn't know how to drive, or because without shoes she couldn't control the car very well. Duane, ignoring the pain in his knee, raced after her.

For a few moments the Buick paused, as if she'd stalled it, back end off the drive and in a bed of yellow chrysanthemums, headlights full in his face. He couldn't see her behind the wheel until he reached the edge of the gravel. Her eyes were large and somber and blackened, as if by an excess of mascara. Her face, what he could see of it within the loose-fitting hood of the jacket, was barely recognizable, looking pale and artificial, as fragile and white as eggshell, as if she'd made herself up for an early Halloween party. Or something more sinister than partying.

"Hey, no!" Duane shouted witlessly. "That's my dad's car, I stole it!"

Enid stepped on the gas. The back wheels spun, the car rocked back and nudged against the foundation of the house, then shot forward, straight at him.

Duane threw himself out of the way and rolled as the Buick skidded by him, made a wide turn, missed a fig tree by inches and roared on down the drive, slewing from one side to the other until it reached Old Forge Road. By the time he was on his feet, still clutching the spray gun in one hand, all he could see of his father's car were the taillights. She was going west.

Duane limped to the house and inside by way of the back porch, shouting for Marjory, looking for a light switch that didn't work when he tried it. The house was freezing cold, illuminated only by the moon.

"Marrrrjorrrryyyy!"

Even in his frenzy something made him stop, reconsider. Instead of roving through the dismal house he retreated, hurried down the back steps and headed for the walking-horse stables again until he picked up the dragged path through frosted grass, the footprints.

They led him straight to a wide stable door that seemed stuck or locked when he pulled on the handle. Touching it was as painful as putting his hand in a fire. He was able to open the door an inch. Duane stuffed the bulky spray gun inside his denim jacket. Whining in fright and frustration, he dug in his heels and seized the edge of the door, yanking furiously, dragging it across the frozen ground.

The door yawned open, rusted old hinges screeching.

Inside it was like Christmas, as Christmas might be celebrated in hell. Moonlight shone through a construct of spun silk as finely wrought as frozen breath in which trapped luna moths fluttered and glowed, bleeding their soft pastel colors down the delicate strands. All the myriad strands seemed to converge, like the cables of a fabulous suspension bridge, on a lumpy object near the center of the stable floor between the dark and long-deserted stalls. It took Duane a couple of moments to realize he was looking at a flayed human body: red shinbones and feet sticking out of the faery maze, skinned hillock of rib cage as if gnawed over by rats. But it was too cold for rats in this hideaway of fiends, almost too cold for Duane to think and move; unfortunately he could still feel and be shattered.

"God . . . *Marjory*."

Alastor looked up, the bloody juices of the skin he was rapidly chewing dripping from his chin, running down his skinny white torso. Apparently he'd been chewing up luna moths too, blending them with the opaque human skin that already had an iridescent sheen. He was half crouched, half sitting on the unseen head. His eyes blazed with the same obscene lividity as the flesh of—

"You little . . . s-ssson of a bitch."

Alastor chortled.

"Birka said I could! Said I was old enough to make my own wings. She'll help me when she gets here. They're all coming tonight, she said!"

"You s-sssson of a *bitch*!" Duane almost lost sight of him through the cloud of expelled breath that instantly froze in front of his face. "She's not coming. S-s-she drowned. I s-sssaw her drown."

"Ho-ho," said the pint-sized monster, "that's what you think! *Huldufólk* cain't drown. She just crawled and crawled on the bottom of the pool till she could crawl up the side and get out. See? You cain't never hurt none of us!" Alastor stirred, lowering the piece of macerated skin he was working on, licking his lips. He began to rise on bowed legs, grinning at Duane. Every tooth in his head glowed like radium. "But we can hurt *you*."

"N-no you w-won't," Duane said thickly, knowing he had to run and aware that he couldn't, he no longer could feel his feet in the flimsy moccasins he'd been dumb enough to wear without socks. His face was so stiff it felt crystallized. Only his hands, thrust inside his denim jacket, had much feeling. He stared at the remains on the floor, the pale blur of the soles of Marjory's feet, untouched in the skinning. Alastor continued to rise, setting aside his handiwork on a skein of silk mobbed with little jewels of frost.

"I need you," he said. "Need you before you get too cold and I can't flay you. I need your sssskin!"

"D-don't t-t-touch me. I'm w-w-warning—"

Alastor sprang up from the stable floor, into the midst of the spun cocoon, and traveled through it like a spider responding to a signal from the edge of its web. He was so skittishly quick that all Duane glimpsed of him were the glittery little eyes and the gap-toothed radiant smile, the needle-tipped curve of Alastor's fledgling thorn. He heard Alastor's high-pitched excited laughter.

Duane took a bumbling step backward and was hung up in clinging, stubborn silk. He sagged close to the floor, knees not quite touching, and opened his jacket. He did't need to raise his head to know that Alastor was almost on top of him. His nose was stopped up with crystals of ice. He breathed through his mouth, searing the back of his throat.

"What's *that*?" Alastor growled as Duane brought both hands up, holding the spray gun. They were less than two feet apart, Alastor reaching out with his thorny hand.

Duane shoved the handle of the gun home, and showered Alastor with carbon tetrachloride.

The little fiend reacted like a normal child thrown into a scalding bath, except he couldn't scream: there was no air in his lungs to scream with. But he writhed, vomiting, in the strands of the cocoon, his dead white flesh toning to an almost-human pink, then shading again, swiftly, giving off a noxious vapor worse than the chemical smell of carbon tet, turning several shades darker, to the greenish-black of tainted meat, the purple of deep bruises. He tried to reach Duane again with the deadly point of his little finger but stabbed ineffectually. The horrible retching continued. There was nothing in Alastor's stomach; he was vomiting up the stomach itself, the esophagus, then the unused lungs in liquefying handfuls. As he flung himself about the steel-strong cocoon his body seemed to be collapsing on its skeleton, the babyish sticking-out bones.

Duane held his breath and sprayed Alastor again, full in the face, and saw the eyes melt in their sockets, his little radium teeth fall like the dimming sprinkle of suffocated moths throughout the stable. Then he had to turn away to vomit himself while the strands of the cocoon vibrated in concert with Alastor's violent throes. Kicking, flailing, Alastor unjointed himself and literally came apart, nearly all melted down to gleaming bones, the emerging skull with its skull-like grin. Duane couldn't look away, he saw it all, but he didn't see—

The hollow black thorn. Where was the thorn?

All chilling silence inside the stable now, except for Duane's ragged breathing. The dangerous inhalation of carbon tetrachloride was making him woozy.

The thorn, the thorn! Find the thorn . . .

But he was fainting from lack of air, he couldn't remain in the stable any longer.

Duane was almost out the door, staggering, gulping a clean lungful of air, when he heard, from somewhere inside the stable, a muffled cry for help.

6

Enid Waller drove the Buick Riviera past the main campground at Dante's Mill State Park, going toward the millpond and the restored town. According to the clock on the dashboard, it was ten minutes to one in the morning, but she hadn't looked at the clock during her forty-five-minute drive from Sublimity. "Time" was an abstract concept in which Enid no longer took an interest.

Halfway to the town of Dante's Mill an impulse made her slow down from an already sedate twenty miles an hour and look for a turnoff, a nature trail not ordinarily accessible to automobiles. When she found the trail she drove a couple of hundred yards into the woods, scraping the Buick through shrubbery and low-hanging branches.

When it seemed she must be in the right place she stopped. There was no ignition key, so Enid left the motor idling and got out. She stood by a front fender of the Buick, staring at a full display of stars, listening to owls in the woods, the occasional rustle of small animals in the understory. Her right hand was in the pocket of her lightweight parka, gripping a pair of pinking shears. She waited patiently, eyes on the sky. The temperature was near forty degrees and dropping. She didn't feel the cold.

At first it looked like a slightly-larger-than-average star, faintly colored and slowly adrift above the tree line; then, as Enid concentrated on this oddity, it grew in size and took on a definite shape, complete with wings, like the wings of a butterfly or moth, but infinitely more beautiful. It was coming toward her now, through a gap in the tree line, and Enid's lips parted in wonder. She saw a wrapped, oval face, like that of a nun, a piercing blue eye. The gently undulating wings were like a veil across her field of vision; then Birka alighted a yard or two in front of her. She was firmly nude, with a figure no better than Enid's; but so beautifully white. Enid wanted to touch her, as if she were a piece of sculpture. But she kept a hand in her pocket, and the other politely by her side.

I'm so glad you came, Enid.

Enid licked her pale lips with a nearly bloodless tongue and looked puzzled.

"That's good. You perceive, but don't quite receive me. I was afraid you'd turned completely already, even though I was very specific to Alastor."

"Turned?"

"Become one of us. He's overeager, like any child. Pricking here, pricking there. That can have no effect, or some effect, or catastrophic effect. A terrible muddled thing neither human nor *huldufólk*. Never mind." Birka stepped toward Enid, who didn't move as Birka lowered the hood of her parka. Enid's hair had become very thin on one side. Birka covered her head again, tenderly. "You'll be *huldufólk* soon enough. But first we need your help. *Will* you help us, Enid?" It was a kind of false pleading; her smile was sly. But Enid was too stunned by the changes that had come over her during the past few weeks to make fine emotional distinctions.

Enid licked her lips again. She pulled out the heavy pinking shears and showed them to Birka.

"Is this what you wanted me to bring?"

Birka's eyes glinted. "Yes, darling. Those should do nicely. Now we'd better be going. I'm afraid to let the others lie there even for another hour. The sanctuary was violated, and I'm concerned that it might be again.'' Birka was folding her wings as she spoke, compactly, so that she could carry them like a small cushion in one hand. "By the way, how is your lovely little sister?"

"Marjory?" Enid frowned, as if it were difficult to remember anyone by that name. "Oh. I think she died. He wanted me to help him drag her to the stables. So I helped him. Then I came here."

"Well, I certainly hate to lose Marjory, but I had to give the boy *something*, you understand. To keep him from getting rambunctious and possibly giving us all away. Why don't you just follow me? It will be rather difficult going for a while, but you're up to it, aren't you?"

"Yes."

" 'Yes, Birka,' darling. Hm?"

"Yes, Birka," Enid said, eager to please.

7

Duane did not want to go back inside the stables, even though the air seemed to be warming slowly inside, as if with the dissolution of Alastor there was no longer a source for the intense, life-threatening cold.

He heard the dog again, breaking into howls on the farm across the pond. And the muffled groaning inside, as if the poor mutilated girl on the floor still lived.

Oh, God, what could he do? But he knew he must do something, and quickly.

Duane put his shoulder to the stable door and pushed

it as wide as he could, to allow a little more of the moonlight to penetrate the foggy silken interior: to let the cold and the nauseating fumes out. Moonlight glinted on the haphazard arrangement of bones and parched skin that had been Alastor. Harmless now, chemically rendered into a death more final than the Black Sleep, but still Duane was afraid, at the point of full-blown terror. Beyond the bones, the motionless flayed body, big feet foremost: seeing Marjory like that would be in his dreams forever.

But her feet, seen more clearly in a better light, without freezing clouds of his own breath to obscure his view, were almost too big to be Marjory's. Too ugly.

Duane crept back into the stable, crunching old frozen straw, skirting the menacing bones blackly freckled by carbon tetrachloride, his eyes on the frozen heap of body.

It wasn't a woman after all. It was a man: skinny, flaccid, gray-bearded. Missing teeth in the open mouth. Dark eyes open too, pierced, frozen solid, his dying fear frozen into them for eternity. *Who?* A relative of Marjory's? Duane had never seen him before. It was obvious he had been dead for hours. He could not have moved since Duane—

There was a rustling in a stall behind him as he bent closer to look at the face of Alastor's victim. Duane wheeled in horror, throwing himself off balance; he windmilled and pitched into a rusty chain across the entrance to the stall, came down hard on his knees. One knee was already sore from his earlier fall, and he cried out in pain.

The zipped-up sleeping bag thrown into a corner of the stall wriggled, and he heard her moaning, the sound so low it was as if she could barely breathe.

Duane scrambled into the musty stall, uncovering a stiffened rat in old straw, and pounced on the sleeping bag.

"Marjory! Marjory?"

She moved inside the sleeping bag; joyously he felt her, an elbow here, a knee there, the shape of her head. He fumbled for the zipper, breaking off a fingernail, and yanked. The zipper didn't work very well. It yielded a balky inch at a time.

Her skin was white too, beneath the pale blond hair; her eyes were closed. For a few moments fright stopped him. What if—? He touched her; she was cold, that was obvious, but he couldn't tell how cold. There was, however, a welcome, human stink of urine from deep in the bag. He fought the zipper again. Marjory moaned softly. She had been stuffed naked into the bag.

"Eennidddd," Marjory said, through clenched teeth.

"Marjory, it's Duane!" He had the zipper open halfway, and began to pull her out of the sleeping bag. "Come on, come on, let's get out of here!" An arm and hand were free, but the hand flopped uselessly. He grasped the bottom of the sleeping bag and tugged hard; Marjory fell out in a heap, and immediately curled herself into a quaking ball.

"No, Marj, get up!"

He stood her on her feet, which crossed, the ankles wobbly. She looked all right, just confused, disoriented, half-smothered. Brain damage? Worse? He had to know, he had to see. Holding her with one arm at the waist, he explored the back of Marjory's neck with his fingertips. No indication of a puncture.

"Marjory? Talk to me. It's Duane!"

"Dway—"

She was beginning to take in great lungfuls of oxygen. "Say *Duane*," he demanded, leaning her against him, awkwardly walking them both out of the stall.

A smile flitted. Her eyes opened halfway for a moment. "Tha you, Dway?"

"Yes! You're gonna be all right!"

"I know. You here. Tha's good, Dway."

"*Walk*, Marjory, goddamn it, I can't drag—"

"Where go, Dway?"

"House. Bath. Clothes."

"Don' have . . . clothes on, Dway. See me . . . na-ked."

He lost control of her as they emerged from the stall. Marjory took two puny swaying steps and went down hard, right in the face of the corpse on the floor. She opened her eyes and stared solemnly at Alastor's victim. Duane got his hands under her arms again. Marjory looked around at him.

"Happened to Mr. Crudup?"

"He's dead, Marjory."

The word released something previously jammed tight in Marjory's mind. Her face, which had been slackly expressionless, began to twitch in alarm. She gasped, rapidly, shallow explosive sounds.

"Nooo . . . ooooo . . . get *him* . . . 'way from meeeee!"

She was trembling so hard he found it difficult to get a grip on her. "Marjory, who's in the house?"

"*Him!*" Marjory said, wildly, then her teeth began clacking.

"No. Not him. I got him. Look, Marjory. On the floor. That's all that's left, he won't hurt you."

He was rough with her, turning her head, forcing her to see the little skull. Marjory made meaningless sounds. "Stop. Hurting me!"

"Are there any more of them in the house?"

"No. No more. He . . . G-G-God! . . . was in Enid's room. Came in window. Something wrong . . . with Enid. Where is—"

"She's gone, Marjory. Stole my father's car. That makes two of us tonight. Come on."

The struggle went out of Marjory. Her knees lost what little strength they'd had to this point. He had to half carry her to the stable door.

A few feet from the opening something stabbed through the sole of a moccasin, penetrating the arch of his right foot. Duane hobbled and almost fell with Marjory, but kept his eyes on the house fifty yards away. Marjory would take one step and sag, two steps and sag. By the time they got to the porch steps she was steadier, except for the violent trembling. He knew she was at least as cold as the night in the cavern when he had pulled her from the pool. Almost lost her then. Hypothermia. He knew what to do now. The hell with Enid, with everything else, he was going to take care of Marjory.

He pulled her up the stairs to the bathroom, and put her into the tub. Still no electricity. The house was not as cold as he had assumed it would be, but he was shaking too, and his pierced foot throbbed. The gas was on, there would be hot water. He filled the tub rapidly. He held Marjory upright in the tub, but he was beginning to dim out himself. Dark in the house, a grayness inside his skull, he almost nodded off. Could it be happening to him, hypothermia? Duane slowly dragged his own clothes off, and crawled into the tub with Marjory, the water level rising almost to the brim. Marjory put her arms around him. Two ice floes, chattering in each other's faces. He began to rub around her heart as briskly as he could manage.

"Duane?"

He was pleased that she wasn't chattering any more. His own tremors had lessened, but the heart of him felt like a cold chunk of iron. Marjory seemed deathly tired, unable to keep her eyes open.

"Duane?"

"Uh-huh."

"This doesn't mean . . . we're married."

That tickled him, but he couldn't laugh.

"I can't get married, Marjory. I have to go to reform school first."

"Oh," she said, in a tone that indicated she hadn't understood him.

"Maybe my dad will let me"—he sighed, and all the

sorrow in his heart broke loose—"join the Army, to get me out of the house."

After a few moments, Duane began to sob. Slippery, exhausted but surviving, as primitive and essentially innocent as First Children, they held each other in the overflowing tub.

8

Going down into the caverns again was a brutal experience for Ted Lufford. The trouble he might possibly get into with various state or Federal authorities didn't weigh on him; but the sensation of being swallowed up in an evil place had his heart pounding before they'd finished the first descent.

They weren't talking much, communicating mostly in monosyllables, trying not to waste energy. Rex and Alvy led the way into the new entry they'd discovered after days of meticulous prospecting. It made good sense for Ted and Wayne Buck Vedders to duplicate their motions in order to avoid trouble. The immediate area was a rocky pitch, nearly thirty degrees, widening in a funnel from a rabbit-hole far above their heads. The worst thing about it was, bats used the funnel, too.

"Yeh," Rex said, when they took a break, "there's a bat cave somewheres nearby, but we didn't track it down."

"Bats," Vedders said grimly.

"They're out for the night, reckon. But we don't want to be coming out when they're a-coming home. Wasn't for the bats, though, we wouldn't of found this hidey-hole. Well, let's move. Bear left here, gen'muns."

"I hear water," Ted panted a few minutes later.

"Oh, yeh. Be right slippery the other side that passage."

"*What* passage?" They had come within ten feet of an apparently blank wall.

Alvy grinned. "He's talking about Aunt Minnie's asshole. You'll just about notice it when you get right on top of it, if you got sharp eyes."

Bill Whipkey put his pack down. "Time for this old boy to get to work."

Alvy looked doubtful. "Well, I don't know. You could close Aunt Minnie's for good with them 'splosives."

"Hoss, I do this for a living! Give me fifteen minutes to wire it up. Yeh, I could wire up the ground you stand on and set it off, and guarantee you wouldn't get a speck of dirt on you. Might make you a little deaf for a couple days."

"Might blow my pecker off, too."

Ted looked at his watch. It was a few minutes after one A.M. "Let's get this done," he said. "I've got a bad feeling."

9

Birka was aware of the first explosion, sensing it through vibrations. She didn't think it was a natural rockfall.

Enid sat hollow-eyed, pains in her chest. Her bare feet were cut and bleeding. She looked up when Birka touched her shoulder.

"We must hurry."

Enid got slowly to her feet, wincing.

You feel no pain. It won't be necessary to stop again.

Enid nodded.

Humanness is such a wretched condition.

Enid looked at the swirl of luna moths above their heads. It was as if her face had been touched by the supernatural light of a vision.

Birka smiled, but she was anxious. She put a gentle hand on Enid again, guiding her, hurrying her along.

10

Three hours; they had covered two thirds of a mile underground. Nothing looked familiar to Ted. He said, for the tenth time in ten minutes, "Are you boys sure—"

"That's our mark on the wall, ain't it?" Rex replied, turning his helmeted head to shine the carbide lamp on the chalked insignia. They were sideways in a passage with little headroom. Rex sounded surly. One of his eyes was redly swollen and smarting from grit lodged under the lid.

"Well, how far do you think—"

Neither Rex nor Alvy bothered to answer him. Ted looked back at Wayne Buck Vedders, whose face was a mask of mud, except for the whites of his round eyes. Buried in mud, his expression was still miserable. He breathed harshly through his mouth. Bill Whipkey, bringing up the rear, whistled a monotonous tune. Tight spaces didn't bother him. For a few yards they were almost ankle-deep in bitingly cold water. Then the wa-

ter drained away mysteriously, the passage angled upward for thirty yards, gradually widening so that they
were no longer on top of one another. Alvy, the lead
dog, hiked ahead confidently, then stopped, the beam
of his headlamp fading into a vast chambered darkness
sprinkled here and there with the mild pastel glow of
luna wings. The smallest noise now raised a sharp echo.
Ted felt a welcome draft of chilled air on his humid
face.

Alvy switched on the electric lantern fastened to a
steel ring on his coveralls.

"There they be," he said, looking down. His tone
was pensive. His breath plumed. "We are in Booger-
land, girls."

They took turns filing up to the jagged hole in the
wall of the cavern where, standing next to Alvy, they
could look down and see by the focused light of his
lantern the shimmering cocoon that filled the floor
space, drifting in places, like a primordial, pristine
snowfall, to a depth of five or six feet.

"Resembles a spiderweb, sure 'nuff," Bill Whipkey
said.

"Well, I ain't going down there," Vedders said vehemently. "Only one thing spiderweb means to me,
and that's spiders. Goddamn, but it's cold!"

"You notice that?" Alvy said. "Maybe twenty degrees colder in here than anywhere else. Damn near
freezing."

"This here what you saw?" Rex asked Ted.

"No, I never did see it for myself. But Duane was
here, and this is exactly how he described it to me.
What do you think, Billy?"

Whipkey flashed his own brilliant torch light around
the walls and fanged ceiling of the cavern, peering into
stalactite crannies and passages opposite them. Here and
there luna moths were glowingly fixed to the walls.

"It's a bitch," he said finally. "Piece of Swiss
cheese. No way I'd get that ceiling to fall right, even if

I could get up there with the plastic I have. It'll take me a long time to rig charges just to plug up all the holes in the walls. Six, eight hours maybe."

Ted rubbed his grimy forehead. His eyes hurt from straining to see in dark places. He had a sinus headache. He still had a bad feeling. They were there, and now he wanted to go home. "How much plastic you toting?"

"Twenty pounds."

"Let's go down there, pile it all in the middle of the floor, and touch it off."

"Hoss, depending on what's underneath, that floor might drop to the center of the earth."

"Good."

"We want to be well away from here when that much banger goes off. All the way outside, would be my recommendation."

"How do we do it?"

"No problem. I brought three timers along. Just set 'em for three in the morning and make tracks. You know, I don't see none of the boogers you gen'muns advertised. So far it ain't been worth missing the opening of deer season for."

"They're in there, all right," Rex told him. "You can't hardly walk without steppin' on some."

"Let's sling some ladders and get started," Ted advised.

They anchored two rope ladders with pitons hammered into the floor of the passage. Rex and Alvy went down first, their combined breaths rising in clouds like live steam from a pit. Ted followed. Bill Whipkey stayed behind with Vedders to prepare the explosive charges: three packages of plastic, each with a timer. Whipkey whistled through his teeth while he worked. Vedders fidgeted, getting up from time to time to cast his light around the cavern.

"Looking for bats? No batshit, no bats."

"I don't know what I'm looking for."

On the floor of the cavern Alvy was looking through the maze of silk, parting it with gloved hands. A remote dark face, slick as pitch with closed lids like patent leather, came into view. And another. Ted felt a stricture around the heart.

"That's something I didn't notice before," Rex said quietly. "Look there, around the neck. Like they been strangled with that vine. The both of 'em."

"They were strangled, all right."

Alvy continued to prowl as if taking inventory. "Little one over here," he announced. "Man, what preserved them this a way?" Vedders's light cut across his back and wavered against a wall. "Hmm." Alvy reached deeper into the cocoon, groped for a few moments. He straightened. "Looky here at this," he said, turning. He held up a piece of dried strangler fig. It had been cut. "You can see here where one of 'em was lying. This silk stuff's all tacky with something, some kind of fluid." He turned his head again, looking for Ted, carbide lamp flashing redly.

"Better move on back toward the ladder," Ted told him in a choked voice. "Bill! How long?"

"Got a jammed mechanism here. Couple minutes more."

Vedders's light swept back across Alvy's face, and Alvy put up his other hand. The light moved on a few feet, then jumped behind Alvy and stayed there.

"Jesus Christ!" Vedders called hysterically. "Get out of there! Run! Get out!"

There was movement in the cocoon behind Alvy, a glossy undulation. He turned haplessly as something surfaced just behind him: a domed, hairless head white as shaped marble, the vaguely human face finely drawn. It had a kind of dolorous, primitive beauty, and was fantastically endowed with living, blazing blue eyes: light and furious, accusatory and deadly. She rose from the cocoon with a long slashing motion, flicking a hand at Alvy just below the chin. He gave a little start, and

stiffened, his helmet slightly askew on his head, the
light of the carbide lamp picking up little blips of fresh
blood, dotting her face where once she had brows. Then
the blood jetted from his opened throat and Alvy sagged
down into the agitated silk, helplessly clutching himself
while his life pumped away.

"Lord a' mercy," Rex said, "what kind of booger
be *that*?"

As he spoke Ted reached out and snatched an arm,
hauled Rex through the obstructive silk toward a ladder.
Rex didn't need to be told to climb for his life.

Birka was coming, gliding toward Ted. He looked
her in the eyes.

"I had a feeling," he said dismally. He didn't try to
run, or even back off a little. And his seeming lack of
fear gave Birka pause. She smiled, reluctantly.

"You again?" Birka said.

"Hard to kill, ain't you?"

"We don't die."

"Well, whatever you call it—" He had one hand in
a pocket of his deer-hunter's vest. With the other he
gestured. Stalling a little, giving Rex time to grunt and
bang his way up the wildly swinging ladder. Vedders
still held his flashlight beam on Birka, isolating her like
an apparition in the midst of the cocoon. *How many
more?* Ted thought. *How many of them on the loose?*
She read him perfectly. But her own expression was not
difficult for him to read. Birka scowled, and he knew.
Just her, so far. It gave him heart to face the next few
moments, which he knew would be the most difficult
of his life. The thorn! God, she was so quick with that
thing! "Whatever you call it, like them asleep in here,
reckon if it ain't death, it'll do."

"In just a little while there will be no more sleepers."

"Yeh, well I reckon"—Ted paused to breathe, to
steady himself, and gleaned another truth in the darkness beneath his feet, from the Dark Ones themselves—

"reckon if you could do something about the state they're in, you would've done it already."

Her smile was slight, and rueful. She said nothing, but started for him again, right hand at the level of her breast, slightly clawed, the three inches of black thorn standing out from the marbled fingers. Ted felt a flurrying panic.

"You need help, don't you? Can't touch them yourself, once they're . . . asleep like that."

"Ted!" Vedders said in a strangled voice. "Get the hell out of the way, let me get a bead on her!"

"No, don't shoot! Won't do no good. Let me handle her. We're . . . like old friends, kind of." He spoke to Birka. "What's your name, anyway? Folks have names where you come from?"

Stay away from me, bitch.

You are cunning, aren't you? Perhaps we should keep you. Now I wonder . . . what treachery you have in mind?

"I'm Birka."

"Ted."

"Yes, I know. I know everything about you. Enid told me."

Enid!

Everything you suspect . . . Ted, and more. Well. Why don't we just distract you for an instant, and let me get this over with?

Beams of light crisscrossed the cavern and Vedders screamed, "There's another one coming up!"

Ted turned, plenty distracted, all right, and saw Enid's pallid face inside the hood of her parka. Blinded by the bright lights, she cowered, her hands in front of her face. In one hand was a sturdy pair of scissors.

"Birka!" she called, shrilly. And Birka, instead of

falling on Ted with her slashing thorn, delayed momentarily to savor this moment.

No no you don't have her you don't you fucking

"Bitch!" Ted screamed, yanking his hand from the cargo pocket of his vest, uncoiling a whiplike strand of recently cut, green strangler fig, weighted at the tip with several ounces of lead fishing sinkers. The lead gave direction and impetus to the improvised lash, which Birka barely saw coming and could not avoid as it flicked around and around the slender column of her throat. Her mouth was frozen in a silent shriek, her pale eyes flashed on him. She touched the encircling vine with both hands and the tips of her fingers blackened instantly, dark as the thorn on her right hand.

Still she made an incredible effort, leaping, trying to destroy him with a single jab that Ted avoided, pivoting awkwardly in the clinging silk, yanking on the anchored, three-foot length of vine. He sent Birka crashing off balance almost to the floor. She kicked and struggled but could not reach him. Her eyes fumed, a burning deep in their desolate blueness. Her neck had turned the glossy black of congealing tar. All the unused veins and arteries of her body revealed themselves in almost limitless tracery, like the silhouette of a leafless tree against a mild twilight sky. She sank deeper into the shining cocoon, hands now clawed and lifeless. The Black Sleep overtaking her, rising to the level of her frantic eyes.

No! I will give you the world—you will be a king like no other! I, I can do this! Release me! Oh, Ted . . . please don't do this to me!

"Goddamn, I had a feeling," Ted said, holding on grimly, watching the immobile lips seal, her eyelids fall and darken until there was only a distant gleam of blueness, and they sealed too; and everywhere, from toes to the shapely dome of her head, Birka was in the deepest night the temper of God had ever willed.

"Enid?"

She was standing where she had risen, shocked, blinded; he made his knots secure around Birka's shrunken neck and plunged through the cocoon toward Enid.

"Bill! Got those charges ready?"

Enid swung around at his approach, gasping; he touched a cold cheek and she hacked ineffectually at him with the scissors, fending him off. He'd been prepared for that, knowing she couldn't be in her right mind, just hoping . . . He took the scissors and pocketed them, and Enid was a mumbling heap in his arms.

"Somebody give me a hand down here! Boogers ain't gonna bite! Boogers is done for! Get Enid out of here, and Alvy, what's left of him!" He sounded hysterical to his own ears, and didn't care. "I want to blow it! Blow it now! Send them all to kingdom come! Now, now, give me all that shit, Bill, we're blowing it *now*!"

11

Duane heard the telephone ringing and rose through depths of sleep, only gradually becoming aware that he wasn't at home, in his own bed.

Marjory's arms were around him, but she was sound asleep, breathing against his neck. She hadn't heard the phone. Duane began to shiver as he woke up. They had piled all the quilts and comforters they could find on her bed, but he was still cold.

He disentangled himself and Marjory rolled over

complainingly, took up a pillow in her arms instead. He
caressed her bare bottom, teeth chattering, and slipped
out of the bed, plucked a quilt from the layer of bed-
clothes and wrapped himself in it.

Pain in his right foot when he put his weight on it. He
hobbled in the direction the telephone was ringing, for
a good three minutes since it had awakened him, and
found the phone in Enid's room. A window was open;
cold air poured in. It was dark outside, except for a
distant streetlight. He thought of teeth that glowed like
radium, bones in the stable, a corpse. His stomach con-
tracted painfully. His foot was sore and throbbing.

"Hello?"

"Who's that?" Ted's voice.

Duane felt a rush of relief. "Ted. This's Duane."

"Duane? You need to speak louder, I'm partial deaf
from—what're you doing there? Is Marjory—"

"She's all right! I think! Sleeping! Tonight we— Listen.
He was here! Alastor, I mean. I told you about him."

"Yeh, yeh, I know, Big 'un. *What happened?*"

"I got him. Carbon tetrachloride, I used carbon tet.
Sprayed him like a moth. Awful. But he's—" Duane
coughed, and it turned into retching. "I don't want to
think about it. He killed somebody. Marjory's neighbor. Mr. Crudup. Body's in the stable. Alastor skinned
him before I—you better get over here."

"Can't right now. I've been sure enough busy myself. I'll tell you later."

"Ted! Enid stole my—my dad's car. Something
wrong with her, you've got to find—"

"I've got her, Duane. Enid's with me. She's all right.
I'll bring her home in the morning. You stay there until
I come, hear?"

"Yeh. Wait! Ted, what if there's more of them
around?"

"There won't be. I took care of it tonight. They're
all buried, Duane, under fifty-sixty feet of rock."

"How—?"

"Can't talk about it now. I'll see you."

"Got to get my dad's car back."

"Don't worry, Duane. You will. Take care of Marjory."

When Duane got off the bed after hanging up, the pain in his foot was intense; he saw stars and thought, *The thorn*.

A cold clutching in his stomach. He couldn't breathe properly. A good lungful of air was a precious thing. His fear was more intense than the pain in his throbbing foot.

The thorn.

In the bathroom he went through the contents of the medicine chest and found a pair of cuticle scissors, a straight pin with a little green knob on it. He ran hot water in the basin, soaped the scissors and washed them off, then sat trembling on the edge of the tub where earlier he had tried to soak the cold from their bones. He cocked his right leg across his other knee and touched the spot on the arch of his foot, swollen the size of a pigeon's egg. Not soft, like a bulging blister. It was a hard white cyst, enclosing something uniquely poisonous, life-threatening. Duane gasped when he touched it. Then he ground his teeth and with his left hand stabbed the center of the cyst with a blade of the scissors, and screamed.

Marjory found him sitting naked on the bathroom floor, holding his bloodied foot and sobbing. She didn't speak but kneeled slowly beside him, took his fist in her hands, opened it. Blood in the palm, and the ragged black remnant of a wicked thorn.

She took it from him, and flushed it down the toilet.

"Did you get all of it?"

"I don't know."

Marjory sat next to him, and tenderly lifted his bloodied foot. She bent her head and put her mouth to the wound. Sucked gently. He put an arm around her, and his head on her shoulder. Marjory sucked harder, spat onto the tiles, sucked again. After a minute or so she rose and went to the washbasin, rinsed her mouth. She came back and settled down between his knees with her back to him and bent to the wounded foot again, licking gently, saying nothing. When all the tremors in his body ceased she straightened, turned slowly so as not to disturb him. Knees on either side of his thighs, she leaned to kiss him. The taste of his own blood on her lips completed his arousal. He put his hands on her waist.

Marjory brushed his lips again with her own, back and forth a few times, lastly with the tip of her tongue.

"Oh, Marjory! I'm still so cold."

"Come on, Duane. I want to go back to bed."

Her body, her embrace, her continuing slow kisses proved to be more of a sedative than an aphrodisiac. A creeping warmth; he dreamed, although he was not asleep. Rocked on her breast, lulled by the animal heartbeat, the surging pulse in her throat, he dreamed of wild places, a hot noon sea. The throbbing pain in his foot had diminished to a dull ache. In napping green, within a shaded thorny place, she sighed beneath him, thrillingly; there was a stillness of depletion.

At dawn he was awake, sitting beside her sleeping form, looking at the frost-rimmed windows, dappled gold by the rising sun, magical as first fruit.

He touched Marjory's shoulder, he touched a peeping nipple, she stirred and smiled without awakening. He wanted, not to be happy, that was asking too much, but to comfort and be comforted. *The thorn,* Duane thought.

the thorn the thorn

the

thorn

This day there were two less children in Eden.